The Woman
Who Lost China

Rhiannon Jenkins Tsang

Published by Open Books 2013

Cover image "the last empress" Copyright © Melissa Haggit

Learn more about the artist at
www.cornerstonemultimediagroup.com

ISBN: 0615810446

ISBN-13: 978-0615810447

For William

NANJING 1949

Rhiannon Jenkins Tsang

1

*T*hree gunshots pierced the silence of the night. Manying jerked out of her slumber. Again they were shooting Communist Fifth Columnists in the coal yard. She groped for the matches and oil lamp. There had been no power since lunchtime and it was past nine in the evening. The cloth wick was too long. The flame writhed and smoked, filling the room with confused shadows. She wound the wick down and replaced the glass chimney, taming the flame. Tiptoeing across the room she checked her four-month-old son, asleep in his cradle in the corner. His breathing was heavy and slow, that of an old man. How could she possibly divine the weave of the threads of his fate? Returning to her chair, she sat in the grimy, orange light and waited.

Should she stay in Nanjing or should she leave? Communists were massing north of the Yangtze River, or so they said. Surely the capital city could not fall to those bandits? But bandits had ended dynasties before and even the most patriotic of her friends appeared to have decided the game was up and had left for Shanghai at the beginning of that year, 1949. Her best friend, Mei Ren, had tried to persuade her to leave with her family, but the regiment of Manying's husband was reported lost at the Battle of Huai Hai. She had not seen him since the previous spring when he had left on an anti-communist campaign, and there had been no news since before the birth of their son. She would not leave without her husband. All through the winter and now the spring as the shuffling exodus from Nanjing continued, she did as she had done all her married life; wait.

Once again the flame in the oil lamp began to flicker in distress, and the coterie of ghosts returned to mock her from the top of the cupboard, and the nook by the door. She picked up the lamp, weighing it in her hand. As she suspected, not enough oil. Damn the maid. Was there anyone left she could trust?

Taking a key from her pocket, she opened a wooden chest where she kept emergency supplies out of reach of the servants. By the light of a weak electric torch she emptied the last of the oil into the lamp. It was heaven-knows-what kind of vegetable oil, and it filled the room with an acrid smoke before eventually settling into a yellow flame. It was enough to banish the lonely ghosts of doubt, at least for a while.

Suddenly she heard the sound of a car coming down the lane; the secretive, grinding nighttime purr that had become all too familiar in recent months. It was wise not to ask questions. Blowing out the lamp, she tiptoed to the window and opened the creaking shutter only an inch.

The shadow of an American jeep rested on the corner, its nearside wheels up on the pavement. A man jumped out and walked towards her along the farside of the street. The jeep bumped backwards out of the lane and drove off down the main road.

The man moved slowly in and out of the shadows, stopping for a time every few paces. As he got closer Manying saw that he was wearing an officer's hat. Suddenly he was coming straight towards her, out of the blackness, crossing the street. She lost sight of him for a few seconds. He was standing directly beneath her window. He took a step backwards and flashed a torch light up to her window—he must have seen her. In that instant he removed his hat and turned the torch light on himself just long enough for her to identify him, then turned it off and disappeared into the shadows.

Him! Not her husband, but him!

She felt as if the blood were draining out of her legs. Was it really seven years since that night in the restaurant when he had said those things? She hated him. She could not bear to think of his home life—the sweat, the smell of faeces, blood and cooking oil. Angry words, his index finger held in the chubby fist of a smiling baby, tired exchanges, grunts, coughs and above all the warmth of the other who was always there. It was irrational, she knew, for she had married first. But she could not help herself.

Her heart thumping, she grabbed the electric torch from the table and went downstairs. Afraid the servants might hear she slipped off her slippers, abandoning them as untidy footprints. Her breath came short and fast, her legs trembled as she tiptoed into the hallway.

There was no window in the door. She put her head flat against the hard, cracked wood and whispered his name.

"It's me. Quick! Let me in!" came the reply.

He was through the door. She was leading him towards the staircase, her finger over his lips. But he stopped and put down the black cardboard suitcase he carried. Like a well brought up child he sat on the bottom of the stairs, untied his white leather spats and removed his boots.

They stood on the far side of the living room in front of the shuttered windows so as not to wake the baby. By torchlight, she scanned his face, reading the lines, filling in the blanks, and making sense of the lost years. His cheeks had shrunk inwards, making him look thinner than he really was. His once fine fingers were knobbled with the soft, red stumps of old calluses, and there were long white scars on the back of his hands. His hair, still black, was receding in gentle arcs from the corners of his forehead. The boyish enthusiasm was gone, replaced by the stiff authority of a much older man. He did not take his eyes from her, and she knew from the morning mirror that she too had changed. Her face was rounder, with the beginnings of sagging around the jaw line. Her once smiling lips now pursed determinedly downwards, and her svelte figure had swollen gently with the curves of motherhood. But it did not matter. In him, she saw all that was lost and gone in herself; great spaces of things unknown that needed no words, knew nothing, yet everything.

"Manying, you must leave Nanjing before morning. There's a train leaving at three a.m. I can get you and the baby on it."

"Why did you come?" Manying was bewildered.

"Mei Ren." He was still slightly out of breath. "Your friend Mei Ren asked me—if things looked bad... Before she left, she was worried about you." He half cocked an eyebrow.

"I might have known!"

"Manying, you must pack. The jeep will come back and pick us up in a couple of hours. You cannot stay in Nanjing."

"I can't leave without my husband."

"For God's sake!" He grabbed her by the shoulders and she was shocked by his familiarity and the ferocity of his grip. "Acting President Li had meetings with senior generals today. We can't hold the city. The communists are crossing the Yangtze now, right now!" She stared at him in disbelief. "China is lost. We Nationalists no longer deserve the Mandate of Heaven. You have to get out, now! Tonight, or it will be too late."

"I can't go without my husband," she repeated.

Realising that he was not getting through to her, he loosened his grip.

"Little Lamb, Little Lamb! Always so good and kind. But you can't stay. The Communist bandits are going to win. Don't you see? Already they're prosecuting men from the rank of General upwards as war criminals. They will shoot your husband and God knows what will happen to you and the boy."

There was a long silence. She plumbed the depths of his eyes for the truth.

"Before he left, my husband told me that if worst came to the worst, I should go to his brother in Hong Kong. He has an optician's shop there. I have never met him, but I have an address." She spoke slowly, as if awakening from a long sleep. He nodded.

"Then that is what you must do. Your husband will know where to find you."

A lone tear escaped from the corner of Manying's right eye, rolling down her cheek. Instinctively he reached out and caught it with his finger. With this tiny gesture, the frayed ropes of restraint that had been holding them apart all these years were broken. His mouth was on hers. Gasping, sucking, he fought past her tongue. Her teeth cut his lips in reply. His fingers scratched hopelessly at the buttons of her blouse in their tight cotton loops. Impatient, he cupped her breasts in his hands, biting at them through the material. Burying herself in his warm, pulsing neck she pulled at the buttons of his jacket. It slipped onto the floor and she felt him guiding her hand back to the stubborn buttons of her own blouse. He raised his head to watch as slowly, deliberately, the white cotton fell away, revealing one small pert brown nipple. Groaning, he put his mouth to it, and she cradled him to her.

When he picked her up and carried her to the bedroom, she did not resist. The threads of their fate had always been thus entwined.

They lay in the dark, a limp tangle of legs and arms, he

on top of her. Her hand pressed him down into her on the small of his back. She did not want him to withdraw, for when he did she knew that it would be the end and that she would have forever lost part of herself.

"I never meant it to be like this, "he whispered. "I always meant to do my duty to your brother and look after you. Now I have betrayed you both." He felt her tears on his cheek.

"Hush," she said stroking his hair with her hand. "I know. I know everything."

"I will think of you always, living in a big white house in Hong Kong with children playing in the garden; a wonderful place with long, green lawns, peacocks and a fountain filled with jumping goldfish."

The needles on the little bedside clock crept towards eleven o'clock. They lay side by side, the tears like hundreds of tiny mirrors reflecting the other. She traced the fine lines in the crevices between his eyes and the bridge of his nose. They were a whole world that needed to be mapped in her mind before it was too late

"What will you do, you and your wife and son?" She swallowed hard to stop herself from choking on the bitter words of reality.

"There are planes leaving for Hangzhou tomorrow morning. Maybe we will go or maybe we will stay. I am just a lieutenant colonel. No one will bother with me." He tapped his smooth bare shoulders where his pips would have been.

"Know why I never got promoted beyond this rank?" She shook her head. "Because I worked with the Americans; with General Stilwell and General Dorn. You know Dorn went up to Yenan to meet Mao." He sniggered. "So, you see, even to my own side, I am tainted by association! Of course my superiors use my English skills and exploit my contacts and experience when it suits them. But they don't really trust me. It's the fate of Chinese who have been educated by foreigners! So what have I got to lose? Let's face it; the Communist bandits can't do any worse than we have. Bastards might even do better!" He began to laugh. But once he had started, he could not stop. His head thrown back on the pillow, he howled to the heavens like a wolf.

The baby began to cry. Hearing the wet nurse's footsteps on the stairs Manying went into the sitting room, leaving the man to dress. She was past caring what the servants thought. This was the final act of this crazy civil war. Soon it would all be over and there would be nothing left.

"Get dressed, Manying! We should be leaving soon."

The wet nurse gasped, putting her hand over her mouth at the sight of a half dressed officer striding out of her mistress's bedroom.

"Bring only essentials. I have already packed you a bag." He pointed to the suitcase he had brought with him.

He had lit the oil lamp in the bedroom and Manying dressed in an old cotton trouser suit and took a peasant-style padded jacket from the wardrobe. She knew from experience that when travelling it was best not to draw attention to oneself. What else should she take? For a few seconds she stood marooned, at the end of the dishevelled bed, spinning round on her heels. The wardrobe full of her precious collection of cheongsam dresses? The chest of drawers with the bed linen? Where to start? Sitting at her dressing table, she took a photograph of her mother in a white shirt and little black cap, and one of her father in a long gown on his wedding day. She pulled out a little drawer to the left of her dresser and lifted out a brown envelope containing some letters, a few American dollars and her jewellery; the gold wedding bangles and a gold necklace her husband had bought her belatedly in India, and which he had given her at the end of the war in 1945. She stuffed everything into a small cloth bag in which she kept her identity papers. Tipping her head forward, she put the bag around her neck and hid it underneath her clothes.

It felt as if a giant eagle had suddenly landed on the back of her neck, gripping it in its claws.

In the living room, the wet nurse and the cook stared sullenly at the strange army officer. What were they going to do if Madame left? What about outstanding wages and references? Idly stroking the back of the mahogany chair in front of him, the officer cast his eyes slowly and deliberately over Manying's possessions, but said nothing. Realisation dawned. The cook rushed off to find some provisions for Madame to take on her journey while the wet nurse began to change the baby. But there was no time. The jeep had already returned and he was putting the baby in the cloth papoose usually worn by the wet nurse, and fastening it around Manying's shoulder. Then they were clattering down the wooden stairs and out into the night.

At the train station, power had been restored, but in the main departure hall only a few lights bulbs remained. In the gloom soldiers and civilians pushed and shoved, their shouts, screams and outstretched hands reaching up to the roof like the pleas of souls abandoned in purgatory.

"Hold onto me!" he ordered. "Don't let go!" Manying grabbed the arm that held the suitcase. Setting his shoulder into the crowd he pushed his way forward. A red, pock-marked face, a gaping toothless mouth, an elbow ramming repeatedly into her side, a stinking bedroll patterned with yellow daisies; each minuscule experience made up a few dislocated seconds of the frenzy.

With gritted teeth, he fought his way forward and Manying understood how it was that men survived in battle. They reached the curtained, glass door of the first class departure lounge, ringed by five heavily armed guards. One of them appeared to have been expecting them and snapped miraculously to attention. Shouldering his weapon he pushed the door open as if he were a doorman at a luxurious hotel.

The bamboo chairs in the waiting room had been

pushed back to the sides and the room was full of wounded foreigners on stretchers. Despite this, it preserved the hushed air of exclusivity, which already belonged to a previous era. A fan whirred in the far corner and a waiter in a white jacket was collecting empty tea glasses and arranging them carefully on a red lacquer tray balanced on the palm of his hand. The wounded were being tended by two foreign devil nurses.

He shook the hand of a wide-eyed, young foreigner in a suit. The man had not shaved for several days and his face was drawn with fatigue.

"Hurry! For God's sake, hurry! There won't be another train after this one...Good luck!" The foreigner pointed towards a pair of double doors at the far end of the room, propped open so that stretchers could be easily carried out. Again the two men shook hands, and then her lover led Manying onto the platform

More heavily armed guards held the shouting mêlée at bay to create a passage for the stretchers. They followed. As soon as they boarded the train, the sound from the outside ceased as if a radio or gramophone had been turned off. Gruff orders were given in English. The wounded swore, coughed and moaned. Manying moved towards the carriage but he put his arm around her, pushing her roughly across the junction plate between the two carriages and opening the door to a toilet compartment.

"In here. Stay inside, and whatever happens, don't come out until you get to Hong Kong. Don't even get out at Shanghai. They are wild dogs out there. You'll never get back on again. Do you hear me?"

Manying nodded but could not speak. Their eyes locked and his lips were on hers, gentle and soft. Drawing the last precious breath from her, he closed his eyes to savour her taste, and pulled back. She reached out and laid the palm of her hand on his cheek. He shuddered at her touch. Slowly, slowly she drew her hand away, clenching her fist to capture his warmth in the tips of her fingers.

"Zheng," she whispered his name, as if to engrave him on her soul.

"Get in and lock the door from the inside!" he ordered, nodding his head in a curt military way and trying to smile. "If you have any trouble, open the top compartment of the suitcase. Your answer is in there." Manying knew that she would never see him again.

He kissed the baby on the head, thrust a torch into her right hand and the suitcase into her left, pushed her roughly inside the toilet compartment, and then closed the door. She drew the bolt from the inside as he had ordered, heard him briefly scrabbling about outside the door and then the clanking of his boots on the metal junction plates as he walked away.

The stench of urine and faeces hit her. Groaning, she wretched through the toilet hole in the floor onto the track. "God forgive us! What have we done?"

It was then she remembered the prophecy:

Whirling girl, dancing girl,
changed the axis of the earth
and the stays of the heavens.
For fifty years there will be no order.
Whirling girl, dancing girl; whirling girl, dancing girl

2

*M*anying sat huddled on the suitcase, her back against the door of the toilet compartment. For the moment no one disturbed her. The rushing blackness, metal cold, clanked and roared through the toilet hole in the floor. She felt as if she and her child might fall in at any moment.

Snuggling around the warmth of the baby on her chest, she slept fitfully. Her mind would not be still, running on and on through the rushing darkness.

And the eyes of both of them were opened and they knew they were naked.

Soft, caressing, liquid nakedness.

And the Lord said unto the woman, What is this that thou hast done? And the woman said, the Serpent beguiled me and I did eat.

"Wife of mine, where are you?" The ghost of her husband flitted briefly above her and disappeared.

"Xiong! Bear!" she called her husband's name. "I'm coming!" She was climbing over the rocks by the sea as a child, her little dress hitched up into her pants so that she could run fast.

"Manying! Manying!" A different voice was calling from a small straw hut.

"I'm coming!" She ran even faster, scrabbling on her hands and knees up to the door. In the darkness, a man cowered face down in the straw. Over and over he muttered something, but she could not understand what he said. She went inside. He rolled over. He had been beaten, his face purple and blue with bruises and swollen almost beyond recognition. He stank like an animal. Covering her mouth and nose with her hand, Manying saw that he was lying in a pool of glistening faeces. Still mumbling, the man reached up to her, trying to open his eyes, which were caked with blood.

Upon thy belly shalt thou go, and dust shalt thou eat all the days of thy life.

Shy whisps of dawn mist began creeping through the hole in the floor and the baby stirred on Manying's chest. Her shoulders and back ached from the cold and unaccustomed weight. Stiffly, she lifted the child out of the papoose. Rubbing his eyes with his fists he smiled up at her. Realising that the child would soon be crying for food, Manying felt the eagle's claw tighten on the back of her neck.

Squatting down with the baby on her hip, she opened the bottom compartment of the suitcase. Underneath some old towels someone had packed a thermos flask, an old army water bottle, a lunch box, chopsticks, an enamel mug, a paper bag containing peanuts in their shells, a baby's feeding bottle with a yellowing teat, and an orange. Manying stared at the plump, opulent flesh of the fruit. It seemed like an illicit jewel.

The thermos contained hot water, the metal box a small mountain of rice, some pork, a hundred-year-old egg, and pickled cabbage. Most likely it had been Zheng's own lunch for the previous day. In amazement, she fingered the contents of the suitcase. It was obvious what was intended: the old towels were meant as nappies. She remembered with a pang that Zheng was a father. In all likelihood the feeding bottle had belonged to his son.

The handle of her door turned, turned again and spun back home. Someone was trying to get in. The person on the outside cursed and rattled the door violently with his body. Manying remembered Zheng's words.

"If you run into trouble your answer is in the top of the suitcase." But she could not move.

"Hey Mate! Out of order!" A soldier with a thick Sichuan accent shouted. "Daft bastard! Can't you read?"

She heard the soldiers' tired, gruff laughter and the chorus of coughing and spitting as they greeted the day. Canteen lids clattered open, followed by a concentrated silence.

Manying returned her attention to the suitcase, tears of frustration welling up at the sight of the baby's bottle. Such kind foresight was all very well, but there was no milk. A wet nurse had fed her son since the day he was born. Roughly, she massaged her own small, barren breasts until they ached.

I will greatly multiply thy sorrow and thy conception; in thy sorrow thou shalt bring forth children.

It seemed hopeless. Soon the baby would start to cry and they would be discovered.

The train rattled into the new dawn. The first rays of sunshine climbed over the wooden window frame. Taking the top off the thermos flask Manying poured an inch or so of steaming water into the cup. She waited for it to cool down before dropping some of the rice into the water. With her index finger she worked it into a paste, bit by bit, adding more water and rice until she had a warm porridge. It was not milk, but it was the best she could do.

At first she tried to scoop the food directly from the cup into her son's mouth. But the precious mixture dribbled down his face and was wasted, so she decanted it into the bottle and added more water. Tipping her son back on her lap, she put the teat to his mouth. Surprised by the artificial teat, he looked at her with big puzzled eyes and tried to push the rice water back out of his mouth with his tongue. But soon he was soothed by the warm, easy flow and, closing his eyes, sucked vigorously on the worn teat. When he had finished Manying replaced his nappy with one of the old towels, throwing the dirty one through the hole in the floor. She would not allow herself to waste precious water on washing her hands, merely wiping them as best she could on an old handkerchief she found in the pocket of her padded jacket. Sitting the baby on the top of the suitcase she ate three pieces of pork and some cabbage and allowed herself three gulps of cold water from the army canteen. She thought of Zheng during the war against the Japanese, sitting in the sunshine on a snow capped mountain peak, drinking from the same battered canteen.

Invigorated by the food, the child lay on the top of the suitcase playing with his toes and smiling at his mother.

Cursed is the ground for thy sake; in sorrow thou shalt eat of it all the days of thy life...thorns and thistles...thorns and thistles.

Choking, Manying tried to smile back at her child. She had betrayed Bear. What was done was done. Yet, if she were to re-live the last twenty-four hours, she knew that it would be no different. And now Zheng was dead to her forever. She must expunge the memory of him from her mind.

It seemed an eternity before the miraculous red and gold of the setting sun began to filter through the grubby window to Manying's cell. Again she fed the child and laid him down to sleep on the suitcase. Hunger gnawed at her own stomach, but, calculating that they would have at least another day and a half of journey after Shanghai, she only allowed herself a few peanuts and enough water from the canteen to stop her tongue from sticking to the roof of her mouth. Sitting with her back against the door she prayed for sleep's embrace.

Therefore the Lord God sent him forth from the Garden of Eden to till the ground from whence he was taken. So He drove out the man.

Manying was in a great temple, burning incense in front of a giant cast iron burner with swirling dragons on it, as she had done once secretly with her mother. On the steps leading up to an altar, from which radiated a blinding golden light, stood the American Pastor from her childhood. Arms outstretched, he was preaching. His voice, high pitched and clipped like that of the Generalissimo, echoed from loud speakers fixed to the blue and yellow eves of the temple.

"And God looked upon the earth, and, behold, it was corrupt; for all flesh had corrupted his way upon the earth...the end of all flesh is come before me; for the earth is filled with violence through them; and, behold, I will destroy them with the earth."

His words rose to a screeching crescendo as bombs began to fall.

Amidst the falling rubble and dust, Manying was bowing in prayer, still holding her incense sticks. One of the glowing tips caught on the ends of her hair setting it alight. Desperately, with her bare hands, she tried to put out the flames, but the more she struggled the stronger the flames became. Screaming, she tried to run out of the temple. But it was too late. Darkness caved in around her.

She awoke crying in the toilet compartment, her fists clenched in anger. How could God allow such suffering and destruction? Was He not supposed to love all his children? Yet in the end no one had been able to escape. The war had corrupted them all.

The train arrived at Shanghai in the early hours of the following morning. Manying was tempted to try to find somewhere to fill the thermos and buy more food. Peering out of the lower window, she realised the wisdom of Zheng's warning about leaving the train. The platform, floodlit like a stage, was heaving with soldiers and refugees. A fleet of foreign devil women pushed officiously down the platform. They were led by a large middle-aged woman in a bright blue dress and a white cloche hat, who viciously wielded a black man's umbrella against anyone who got in her way. They were looking for someone or something.

Seeing a foreign devil soldier on crutches with a bandage around his head climb down from the train, the woman in the blue dress shouted something in English and raised her gloved hand to encourage her followers. They had, it seemed, come to help the foreign wounded. One by one, injured foreign men climbed out of the train. The men on stretchers were unloaded by porters and shepherded by one of the foreign women into the first class waiting room with a curtained glass door at the end of the platform. Once more the door was propped open to facilitate the movement of stretchers. Inside were yet more foreign women, in an assortment of hats, handing out sandwiches and large white mugs of tea. All the while the woman in the blue dress superintended the operation with her umbrella, her voice cawing above everything like that of a great rook.

Why were there foreigners wounded, Manying wondered? It was a Chinese civil war. It did not involve foreigners.

After the foreigners had finished unloading their wounded, a bespectacled young man with hair slicked back and a woman in a fur coat arrived with a barefoot porter. The man and the porter started to load their mountain of luggage onto the train. A group of Chinese soldiers climbed into the carriage and threw the couple's bags back onto the platform.

"No room on this train. Priority for military personnel."

"Nonsense!" The young man picked up a soft leather bag that had been thrown off the train and attempted to get back on. There was a scuffle as the soldiers removed him.

"But we have valid tickets!" his companion tried to

reason with a tall lieutenant in the faultless Mandarin of a
school mistress.

"Dog's fart! Black market tickets!" he sneered in
Shanghainese, tearing them up and throwing the pieces
into the air to fall like confetti.

"What is your name and rank? I will report you to your
commanding officer. Have you any idea who we are? "

But the lieutenant grinned with tobacco black teeth and
grabbed her around the waist.

"Let's dance little lady! I am going to claim you as lost
property and take you to Hong Kong to warm my bed.
One, two, three!" He yanked her around in an ugly waltz
circle, pulled her head back by her hair and forced his
open mouth onto hers. The woman kicked him and
scratched his face.

"Leave her go!" The soldiers jostled the man, tearing
his glasses from his nose and throwing them between
them, over his head.

"Ever fucked a lady in a fur coat before? Nice and
warm. Nice!"

Clanking and swearing, another group of soldiers took
up the space between the carriages outside Manying's door.
They spoke Mandarin with a heavy accent that she could
not place, but she could just about get the gist of their
tired talk.

"Those foreign devils must be the wounded from that
English ship the communist bandits hit in the Yangtze."

"Nothing to save Nanjing now! They say our great
Generalissimo's already retreated to Taiwan. How heroic!"

"Fucking fiasco! When I get to Hong Kong I'm going
to get me a nice round Cantonese wife, with a soft warm
pussy and live like an Emperor."

"When I get to Hong Kong I'm going to the Beautiful
Country: to America! America! America!" The speaker
chewed over the English word for the Beautiful Country.
No one interrupted, for in the noise and dust of chaos, the
utterance of this simple foreign word was exotic poetry.

Just after dawn the train left the station and the men were soon cursing the draughts from gaps between the carriages. Manying was glad to hear them stacking their guns and bedrolls against her door then moving back towards the carriage door to sit.

His pathetic face smeared with dirt, the baby began to whimper. Manying knew that his nappy was full, but she only had two more clean towels and decided not to change him until the evening. She took the cork stopper off the thermos and peered into the shiny silver inside. Shaking it gently from side to side, she judged it to be half full.

The train powered purposefully onward. It seemed to Manying that her own heart had stopped beating and it was only the pumping of the engine that was keeping her alive. Many times that day soldiers clanked across the metal junction plates towards her toilet door. Sometimes they were stopped by the weary voices of defeated soldiers who just did not want to be disturbed anymore.

"It's busted. Best just piss out of the door." But other times someone would reach the toilet unchallenged and rattle the handle and push on the door.

Another day turned into night. Manying would not have noticed the day's passing had it not been for the routines of the baby. He had played fitfully that day, sucking his index finger, and looking at her with wistful, sad eyes. She mashed up half the orange into some rice water to feed him. Afterwards she removed his nappy and, holding him over the hole in the floor, whistled to him softly to encourage him to pass water. He slept briefly on her breast but soon awoke crying, his screams amplified by the metal walls of their tiny cell.

He would not be placated. Manying tried to give him some more rice porridge but he turned his head away. In desperation she opened her shirt and put him to her breast. But his little fists beat the air, and he turned red with rage. Rocking him to her she put her hand over his mouth to muffle the sound. How could the soldiers not have heard? But the baby wailed and wailed. Manying's hand pressed harder and harder. The child turned blue. Manying never knew how long it was before she removed her hand. She held the child upright. Between screams he gulped great gasps of air, his little face contorted with the effort.

Manying was resigned to her fate, but strangely no one came. The night wore on and the baby was eventually exhausted and fell asleep in her arms. Her arms ached and her clothes were damp with his urine, but she could not bear to put her son down.

At last the train stopped. People shouted in Cantonese, her husband Bear's native dialect, and she felt the relief of homecoming. It turned out to be a small country station and the soldiers got out to stretch their legs. She could see the light of their cigarette ends outside the window, and hear them peeing against the carriage. After a while the train started. Calculating that it was probably only half a day to the Hong Kong border, Manying fed the child the last of the orange and rice. Her own mouth was so dry that she could hardly chew the peanuts, but again she allowed herself just one mouthful of water.

As the day wore on the southern sunshine warmed the cold carriage. The train arrived at the Hong Kong border in mid-afternoon of the 23rd of April 1949. They had been in their tiny compartment for nearly three days.

"All change!" A man's voice ordered from the platform. The soldiers cheered.

The crunch of boots and the excited voices of the passengers faded into the distance. In the drowsy stillness of the afternoon, listening to the humming of the crickets, Manying waited. At last she judged it to be safe and emerged from her cell. The baby was limp and heavy in her arms; her own legs trembled with fatigue. Closing the door she saw that Zheng had written a notice and stuck it on the outside of the door. She recognised his clear, elegant characters she had known since childhood.

Out of order
Please use alternative facilities

Standing on the platform, blinking in the spring sunshine, she smiled at the bizarre nature of a war, where a tiny notice could afford such protection against the violence and chaos around her.

The passengers stampeded across the small bridge that crossed the border to the British Colony of Hong Kong. A tiny figure lost in the valley between the plump green mountains, Manying followed slowly in their wake. Crossing the bridge, she looked down at the cracks in the boards beneath her feet. Far below the cool clear water of the small river gurgled happily on its way.

At the little station on the Hong Kong side of the border, passengers pushed and shoved to reach the one little window that was selling tickets for the final leg of the journey to the city of Hong Kong itself. Fists flew, chickens in wicker baskets squawked and a live pig trussed on a pole between two men squealed appeals for mercy.

How would she ever get a ticket? Looking around she saw that not everyone was rushing to buy tickets. Some soldiers had stripped off their shirts and were washing at one of the trackside water taps. Laughing, they splashed each other and scrubbed away until their skin was red raw. Leaving their damp towels around the backs of their necks, those that still wore uniforms ripped the badges and stripes off their hats and coats.

Manying waited until a group of soldiers was moved off by a border guard and took her place with two other women at a tap. She filled her metal cup with water. It glistened like liquid diamond in the sunshine. Greedily she gulped it down. Washing her face and hands, again and again she scooped up the water, letting it run over her head and down her neck. When the other women had finished, Manying undressed her baby and bathed him under the tap. At first he cried from the coldness of the water, then he started to kick his legs sending water splashing everywhere. The British officer in his green beret, overseeing the arrival of the refugees from the corner of a Customs shed, laughed. He watched Manying hold her baby up to the golden sunshine, the water dripping off him like long strings of pearls.

When the local train from Hong Kong arrived, those passengers who wanted to disembark were met by the tide of refugees rushing to board. In the crush, Manying and the other women at the pump took their opportunity to get to the window and purchase tickets.

The journey through the New Territories to the city of Hong Kong lasted about two hours. There was no room to sit and Manying was crushed up against the door of a carriage. She looked down at the little black head of her son peeping out of the papoose. He did not move. She tried to adjust her position and raise the child up onto her shoulder but it was impossible, and if she lifted the child too high she was afraid he would fall out of the open window.

At Hong Kong station, Manying struggled to remain upright as the carriage door was opened and the press of people inside pushed her out onto the platform.

Outside the station, hundreds of wide-eyed faces pressed up against the railings, to see if by chance they could find one of their loved ones. There were many tearful reunions but, as she left the station, Manying saw that most people were leaving in disappointment.

Half an hour later she sat on her heels by the harbour next to the white Star Ferry terminal with its little clock tower. Giddily she looked over to Hong Kong Island, its white, colonial buildings and mountain peaks shrouded in mist. In the exhaustion induced by lack of sleep and lack of food she almost believed it could be the Penglai Islands of the Immortals.

The Star Ferry left the far side of the harbour, weaving its way across the busy waterway. There was a large party of foreigners on the top deck, the men in white jackets and the women in brightly coloured dresses and big hats. The ship appeared to be decorated with gay bunting. The ferry bounced against the rubber fenders on the dockside. There was a series of thuds as gangplanks fell, and passengers disgorged onto the quay. The foreigners' laughter was like the chatter of roosting birds in the late afternoon.

The ferry was immediately ready for its return journey and Manying boarded the crowded lower deck. She stood by the rail at the back of the ship, and when the coolies next to her moved away, she remembered that her trousers were damp with the baby's urine.

She was an outcast: her belongings all were gone, and she did not know if her husband and the father of her son were dead or alive. She readjusted the heavy load of the child in his papoose and raised her face to the sun and the wind.

3

*W*hen Manying arrived, the people of Hong Kong were enjoying the first glorious hour of freedom that greets the end of the office day. A shabby, exhausted woman with a battered suitcase and a baby in a papoose, she was, to the smart office workers and sassy shop girls, indistinguishable from the thousands of refugees who had been arriving in recent weeks.

Swept along by the crowds Manying found herself in a broad street running parallel to the coast that was lined with little stalls and shops with large Chinese signs. Everywhere goods were stacked high; fruit, clothes, cosmetics, all overflowing onto the pavement. Busy, prosperous people hurried about as if the war years of suffering and deprivation under the Japanese had never happened. Bewildered, Manying took refuge in the corner of the door to a department store and looked for someone to ask for directions. The passers-by studiously avoided her eye. Seeing the sign for a Chinese medicine shop she pushed her way along the pavement to the doors.

The shop smelt of stale incense. Its dim walls were lined with wooden drawers and a red light shone from the little altar at the back. Three impassive, grey-bearded Gods stared coldly at Manying from their cosy Heaven. As she approached the counter the young miss in a blue cheongsam looked her up and down. Manying drew herself up to her full height.

"Excuse me, Miss, I am looking for Wong the Optician. He lives..."

The girl pretended not to understand and flapped the backs of her hands at Manying as if swatting a fly. An old man in a traditional black gown and skullcap behind the opposite counter called out to Manying.

"Who did you say?"

Manying enunciated the address carefully in Cantonese and went over to show him the back of the old envelope with the address her husband had given her the summer before he had left on the anti-communist campaign. The old man peered at her, squinted at the paper, took out a scrap from his receipt book, licked the tip of his pencil and briefly sketched a map.

"Mr Xiong, the Optician. I know him. It's up the hill," he said. "Not far, but quite a climb. Sure you can manage?" Too exhausted to speak, Manying nodded quickly and clasped her hands in thanks.

As the city slipped into darkness, Manying turned off Queensway and began to climb the steps and narrow alleys, following the old man's instructions. Her son lay heavy and still in the papoose, his eyes closed and his cheeks pale and pinched. He had not moved since they had got off the train. The papoose cut into her shoulder and the little suitcase now felt as if it were full of lead. One by one, lights came on, garlanding the velvet hillside with strings of diamonds interspersed with rubies and emeralds. Imperative, guttural Cantonese flew in great streams from open windows high above, woks clattered, fat sizzled and the smell of meaty juices leaked cruelly into the night air making Manying gasp.

It was the domesticity that made her hesitate: she no

longer deserved the hospitality of a good family. Turning heavily, she shuffled back down the steps. She had not gone far when she heard men shouting. Rounding a corner, she saw a gaggle of half a dozen northerners, probably soldiers who had discarded their uniforms in favour of working men's clothes. They were haggling with local men about accommodation. The Hong Kong men were trying to persuade them to come into their guesthouse for an exorbitant fee. Tempers flared and a scuffle ensued. There was no way through. What else could she do? Turning again, Manying went back up the steps. Her son was not well and he soon would die if not given proper care. She could at least see if her husband's brother's family were good people and leave the baby with them. If she disappeared forever in a few days, who would care?

The sign for Pacific Fortune Spectacles and Optical Equipment was illuminated by the white light from the windows of the flat above. The black characters jumped fuzzily before Manying's eyes. The wooden shop front was all closed up. Mustering all her strength she banged heavily on the door, shaking the rusty padlock and chain. Even when she heard shouting from above, she did not stop.

"Who's there? What's all the fuss?" a man's voice bellowed down.

"It's Little Bear's wife; your brother's wife. Please, let me in. Please!" Manying burst into tears.

*I*n the tiny living room above the shop two little boys in well-pressed shorts and white shirts were playing with tin soldiers on the floor. Two opposing armies were laid out in precise formations.

"Boom! Boom!" cried the elder child, pulling the tiny cannon back in recoil as it fired.

"Boom! Boom!" The second child, halfway between baby and toddler, scattered the half of the army on his side with a sweep of his hand. They laughed and looked up to see their father with his arm around a filthy, stinking, peasant woman whom he introduced as their aunt.

In his vest and slippers, Bear the Elder, known to everyone as Big Bear, was a gentler, fatter version of his younger brother. His wife, Ling Ling, was a myopic skinny woman with a pointed face. Their kindness was overwhelming. They asked no questions, expected no answers.

Ling Ling fed the baby from her own breast whilst Manying washed and then ate. Manying knew that she was gulping and slurping her food like a dog, but could not help herself. When the baby had been fed and changed Big Bear took his nephew in his arms and examined the child, stretching out the tiny fingers in his and playing with his toes like little pearls.

"His hands are just like my father's." Gently he touched the pudgy nose and lower lip that was so much thicker than the upper one and so characteristic of his brother. "Well, there is no doubt that you are a Bear cub. We will just have to take care of you and your mummy."

Manying remembered the old white suitcase Zheng had given her. It sat on the floor by the door, already a souvenir from another world. Head spinning, she crossed the room and knelt to open it and see if there were anything left she could offer Ling Ling as a token gesture of thanks. She unhooked the top section of the suitcase. A revolver slipped out of a folded pillow cover onto the wooden floor. No one said anything. Manying remembered Zheng's stubbly chin scratching her ear, his hot, urgent breath. "If you run into trouble, your answer is in the suitcase." She stared at the gun, its polished, wooden handle and shiny black muzzle. The gentle fingers that had cleaned it, the youthful eyes that had admired it, and the broad breasts that had born it, all were gone; her brother's gun, her lover's gun, a weapon of honour and betrayal.

"Give it to me, now! Get to bed all of you! It's late." Manying laid the gun in Big Bear's outstretched palm. It was fully loaded. Slowly, the optician meticulously removed the shiny bullets from the chamber. One by one he lined them up next to each other upon the table, as if he were putting his lenses back in their case after an examination.

*I*n the middle of the night Manying awoke with a start, remembering the notices that she had seen at the Lo Wu border post the previous afternoon.

Crown Territory of Hong Kong
Possession of firearms is a capital offence
No firearms beyond this point.

In panic, she hurried into the living room. Big Bear sat smoking in his vest and shorts, his legs up in a wicker chair.

"The gun? The gun?" She tried to keep her voice low.

Slowly Big Bear looked up, grinning like a naughty boy. For an instant she almost mistook him for her own husband before the Burma campaign.

"It's all sorted." He puffed smoke up toward the ceiling. "Your brave brother-in-law has survived the blackest and wettest of nights and dropped the gun to the very bottom of the harbour! Plop!" He sniggered and wiped one hand against the other. "Got quite used to running the curfew under the Little Devil Japanese. It's good to keep in practice! Nothing to worry about! Get to bed! We can talk in the morning. By the way, Manying, just exactly which way did you intend to point that gun of yours?"

4

*T*hree days after her arrival in Hong Kong Manying awoke with that damp sticky feeling between her legs. Her periods had not re-established themselves since the birth of her son and she was taken by surprise. Not having the necessary articles with her, she whispered red-faced to Ling Ling who was frying eggs for breakfast. Leaving the fractious baby to cry, she fumbled in the shadows by her bed with the pins and pads. Later, when her brother in law had gone to the shop, she hastily washed the blood from her pyjamas in a bucket in the tiny bathroom area at the back the flat. The pyjamas were a brand new pair that Ling Ling had lent her. She said she had bought them last Chinese New Year but never worn them. Terrified that there would be a stain Manying scrubbed the pink cotton between the legs until it began to fade. Even once the fabric was clean she continued to scrub. At last, she rinsed and wrung them out. They were suddenly heavy in her hands. She wrestled to put them onto a wire coat hanger and lift it with a bamboo pole to hang on the line running along the back window. And when the job was done, she slumped down, exhausted, on the tiled floor. Ling Ling found her there an hour later, sitting with her head on her chest.

Despite her fragile frame, Ling Ling was an organiser in the manner of a gentle tyrant. Ling Ling put it all down to a lack of proper care during the first month of traditional confinement after childbirth.

"You're too yin! That's the problem. No family to look after you. Terrible times!" She insisted that Manying stay in the house and rest, and set about making up the nutritional deficit, buying huge bags of red dates and cooking sesame chicken in rice wine and other assorted women's delicacies.

By day Manying was carried along by the minutiae of domestic routine. With two small children and a baby in the house, it was an endless cycle of washing, ironing and cooking. Her life seemed like a film where the glorious music had been turned off, leaving her only with senseless, disconnected sounds to punctuate the day; the chop-chopping of a knife on a wooden board, the shrieks of the children in the street at lunch time on their way home from school, and the whirr of the fan in the corner of the room; and always the well meant fussing of her brother-in-law and his wife, who steadfastly avoided the issue of whether they would ever see Bear again.

At night, sleeping on a camp bed behind a makeshift curtain in the tiny living room, Manying was unable to hold back the tides of despair.

Whirling girl, dancing girl, changed the axis of the earth and stars of the heavens. For fifty years there will be no order. Whirling girl, dancing girl, rainbow skirts swinging in the noose!

It was Aunt Grace's prophesy about the infamous Prized Consort Yang Gueifei who had so infatuated the Tang Dynasty Emperor Xuanzong with her dancing, that he no longer cared for official business and allowed General Anlushan to lead a rebellion that ultimately brought down the dynasty. In her mind's eye Manying saw the Imperial guards dragging the Prized Consort away from the Tang Dynasty Emperor Xuanzong who, knowing what needed to be done, raised his silk sleeve to cover his face. Yang Gueifei screamed and kicked and scratched and bit as they fastened the noose around her neck. And when it was done there was no one to take down her body, and it was left hanging in the wind. But the precious sacrifice was to no avail for the Dynasty was already lost and everyone knew that what had been done could not be undone.

Manying sought solace in the warmth of her son sleeping at her side, the fluttering beat of his heart, the snuffling and sucking sounds as he rooted for an imaginary feed she could no longer offer. Gradually the shadowy greys of dawn revealed his face, the countenance of God as she might have once known Him, as had been described to her and the other children in the little church school by the American Pastor. She remembered how, when the Pastor talked, his face illuminated with joy and the lines of age were as if smoothed away... Jesus, Lamb of God who taketh away the sins of the world. Jesus who dwelt at the right hand of God the Father with angels and archangels and all the company of heaven... She screwed up her eyes with the effort to see it; the golden vision of forgiveness and compassion that had compelled Pastor Wesley to live in a foreign land, and in which he had never doubted...but she saw nothing.

Every night, she packed her things and resolved to leave. By the time morning finally came, sparkling and new, such was her anger that she wanted to tear down the fat clouds from above and rip to shreds the audacious blue sky.

It was difficult to leave with her bag without Ling Ling noticing. Instead she waited until the baby was sleeping, kissed him, each time for the last time, on the forehead and sneaked out empty handed to wander all over Hong Kong and Kowloon. Down on the docks she saw scrawny painted girls draped around huge American sailors who were all dressed in white, like toy men. In the markets she watched beggars picking maggots out of rotting mangoes. She had no plan and did not go to the same places every day. Sometimes she would go to the station where it was her turn to press her face against the railings and sift through the day's offering of bedraggled refugees. Some of the soldiers were still in uniform, but without their equipment and pride; even the older men were like exhausted, bemused children.

Towards the end of summer she started going to the streets around the Tung Wah Hospital. Some Nationalist soldiers and their families had set up cardboard and zinc homes on the pavements surrounding the hospital, and they were dependent on its charity. A lost bee seeking nectar from barren flowers at the end of summer, Manying flitted around the stinking, humid streets. She wanted to find just one familiar face, someone who might know what had happened to her husband.

"The Fifth Army? Anyone with the Fifth?"

Once she went into the hospital to ask the wounded for news.

"My husband, General Xiong, is with the Fifth Army. Any news? Anyone, any news?" But seeing the pretty young face with hope still in her eyes, the men just shook their heads or looked straight through her.

Throughout September she went almost every day either to the station or to the hospital. She saw hundreds and hundreds of tired and lost faces. Sometimes she asked a soldier about his plans, and often he said that he wanted to go to Taiwan to join the Generalissimo and the Nationalist army. What if her husband had already gone on to Taiwan?

One day, outside the Tung Wah Hospital, she was aware of a middle-aged soldier watching her as she came along the street. He got up off his heels where he had been crouching under the cardboard roofing of his shanty home. Shading his eyes from the sun with one hand, he called out to her. "Lady," he said in heavily accented

Mandarin, "I've seen you here before." Manying looked at him without recognition. Unusually, he still wore his sergeant's stripes stitched boldly onto his shirtsleeves. Inside his cardboard dwelling on the edge of the pavement his bedroll was neatly folded and bound with cooking utensils stacked on top. "I was with the Fifth Army. We went to relieve the One Hundred and Eighteenth in December. But we never got there. They got it bad, Lady. They say that the One Hundred and Eighteenth Division was all but wiped out in Datudui. Even General Huang commanding the Twelfth was captured."

Manying nodded. The sergeant's story tallied with the news of Nationalist defeats at Huai Hai that they had been getting in Nanjing in the early months of the year.

"Lady, I've seen you coming and asking around every day. I thought that you ought to know the truth." Manying nodded again. Then, in a totally matter of fact way and with no trace of embarrassment, "Lady what will you do? I've seen you sometimes with a baby going around. My wife and daughter were killed by the Japanese six years ago. I'm going to Taiwan. I can work hard and buy land. I'm a good man. Do you want to come with me?" It was on the tip of Manying's tongue to say yes. What had she to lose?

"I'll think about it," she heard herself say.

The next day she returned to thank him for his kindness and explained that she had family in Hong Kong. Still the sergeant looked concerned.

"Are you sure you'll be all right, Miss? Hong Kong is no place for a lady on her own. Anyway, if you change your mind, come and find me. You know where I am. Sergeant Wu, that's me. I'll be here for a while yet, I guess. Don't forget now!"

*T*he months wore on and there was still no news. Every time she left the flat it was her intention never to return. Sometimes as darkness fell she would sit by the harbour on the Hong Kong side, an old lady already amongst the whispering young lovers. Mesmerised by the reflected lights from the buildings, the red and green of the Star Ferry as it bobbed its way towards her, the gentle slapping of the waves against the wooden pillars of the harbour wall, the tempting, silky black water. How easy it would have been to jump.

But in the emptiness there was something that drew her back; thoughts of the gurgling, trusting face of her son looking up at her, of Zheng who had risked himself to save her, and her husband who depended on the idea of her continued existence to stay alive. She knew that if she left now, her husband would not survive, and that she must keep faith with him until she knew he was safe.

On the little red kitchen altar at the back of the tiny living room, Ling Ling kept incense burning. The bitter sweet smell mingled with the smell of cooking, permeating Manying's clothes and hair, like the sweat of her soul. The lines of smoke from the incense sticks wending upwards to the fat-stained ceiling became the only link to her husband. She began to get up in the night to make sure that the incense was kept burning, and the chain was not broken.

But Manying's absences were not unnoticed, and Ling Ling thought it best to find her a job. It was not easy. She tried to get her a position teaching in a local primary school, but the Headmaster said that her Cantonese was not good enough and that there was no demand for Mandarin in the Crown Colony of Hong Kong. In the end a friend found her a job as a piece-rate seamstress working for a department store in Central. The pay was poor. Ling Ling had hoped for better. But she could work from home using Ling Ling's sewing machine, and it would keep her mind off things, or so Ling Ling told Big Bear. And there were perks; the first in the form of off cuts of material that could be used to make children's clothes, and the secondly, the amusement gained from the odd proportions required for foreigner's suits.

Ling Ling and Manying began to settle into a steady domestic routine. Manying welcomed the opportunity to be busy, so much so that Ling Ling now worried she was driving herself too hard. Forehead furrowed, lips pursed in concentration or perhaps pain, Manying hunched over the sewing machine into the early hours, endlessly turning the hand driven wheel: whirr-whirr-whirr, another seam, another knot, cut and fasten, finished, done, and gone. But routine brought acceptance of her fate. She was a vagabond, a wanderer. She had lost her father, her mother, her brother, and her husband. She had lost China. Her family had lost China. It had been so, ever since the night over half a century ago when her father, still a boy, had gone with his brother to the Temple of Ten Thousand Years.

GUANGZHOU 1894

5

Arriving in the southern Chinese city of Guangzhou on the morning of the first day of the seventh month in the Jia Wu year, in the reign of Emperor Guangxu, the two sons of Wen En, former Chief Justice for the Province of Sichuan, had no idea of the bloody sacrifice that would change their lives and those of their descendants for ever.

The wooden masts and rigging of the passenger junk groaned and screeched with the effort of holding the great sails against the river wind. The younger brother, Huaming, pulled his pigtail over his left shoulder to stop it whipping across his face and stood on tip toe to look over the prow. He had travelled much within the Empire of All Under Heaven during his short life, but never had seen a sight to equal this one.

The broad Pearl River teamed with morning industry. Before and aft, all along the middle of the river were junks, their sails like dark brown butterflies. Hundreds of sampans belonging to the river people carelessly criss-crossed each other's paths plying their trades: a green grocer hawking piles of peaches and watermelons glistening like luscious jewels, a shabby boat with no awnings, its higgledy-piggledy load of fire wood causing it to list precariously to starboard, and a much smaller boat where a man sat on a stool having a shave. Through it all came a deep vibrating boom. Ahead in the distance was the huge white ocean steamer from Hong Kong, its funnels cutting black silhouettes out of the blue sky. Huaming jumped up and down.

"Wah, Big Brother, look!" Again and again the ship boomed its arrival, the sound echoing around and around the delta.

But his elder brother paid no attention. His gaze was fixed on the walls and towers of the provincial capital, the city of Guangzhou. He looked but did not see, as if his sights were set on something far beyond. It was just over three weeks since they had left their hometown of Chaozhou in the northwest of the Province, and Big Brother had told him time was short. Here in the great city of Guangzhou the fate of their father, and with him the whole family, would finally be decided.

"Big Brother, look!" Huaming pointed at the great, white, square buildings with long lines of gaping windows and doors that were the warehouses belonging to the foreigners on Shamian Island. He noticed the fluttering flags and huge black lettering in the language of the foreign devils on the top of one building. He could not read it and knew everyone hated the foreigners, but that recently Big Brother had even talked about learning the language of the devils.

"Our world is changing. We must adapt or perish."

Frowning, Big Brother turned abruptly away from the ship's rail, cleared his throat and spat a mouthful of bitter yellow phlegm onto the deck. Huaming thought that perhaps he was cross. Big Brother's dream had been to go to the provincial capital to take the crucial Provincial Level Examination, which he had hoped would lead to a career in the Chinese Imperial Service like their father. But with things as they were, Big Brother had been unable to concentrate on his studies and so far had only completed the first part of the preliminary tripos examination.

"Now where is that lazy servant of ours?" Big Brother turned and went down to the hold.

It was not long before the boat dropped anchor and was surrounded by a crowd of smaller boats waiting to take the passengers to shore. They bumped up against each other and the boat people screamed their prices up to the passengers on the junk. All of a sudden it was crammed with impatient passengers, jostling coolies, luggage and the bare legged boat women who squawked and shrieked, the Water Hens who had boarded the junk to tout for fares. Pressed against the rail by two coolies carrying a large crate, Huaming looked round for his Big Brother. He saw him across the deck, a tall, slim figure maintaining the impassive cultured manner of his father, as their servant, Young Chen, haggled with two Water Hens. Ducking down, Huaming squeezed under the coolie's box. They cursed him in Hakka, a dialect that he did not understand. But recently he had become accustomed to abuse from unexpected quarters and ignored them pushing past a bamboo cage of squawking chickens towards his brother.

As he reached him, one of the Water Hens grabbed Big Brother by the arm. Not to be outdone, the other woman grabbed him too, putting her neat shiny black bun decorated with ribbons onto his shoulder. A gentle tussle ensued.

"Young master, I beseech you! So handsome! Come with me!" Young Chen pulled the women away as Big Brother laughed. His eyes danced from one woman to the other with the practice of a privileged young gentleman of the world and Huaming was reminded of the way Big Brother had looked on his wedding day, when guests had conspired to tease the bride and groom, and he felt again the tight, breathless pain in his chest that came whenever he remembered how things used to be and what had happened to them all.

By the time the brothers and their luggage were finally off the junk, and Young Chen, following Big Brother's strict instructions, had ruthlessly haggled down the price of two sedan chairs, agreeing the weight and price for carriage of their luggage to their lodgings, the hour for lunch had come and gone, and the crippling white heat of the day was upon them. Slouching in his sedan chair while waiting for the coolies to shoulder their last box, Huaming pulled the sleeves of his gown above his elbows to cool himself, puffed out his cheeks and slowly and noisily blew out the air. Why was Big Brother always so stiff- necked over just a little cash? And why couldn't they take one of the new-style rickshaws with wheels from Japan instead of these smelly old chairs? And why was that fortune teller with one arm, squatting by the wall with an old crow on a string, staring at him?

It was then that he first heard the shouts coming from the far end of the waterfront.

"War! War! Emperor declares war!"

Peering through the glassless window of the chair, Huaming saw a black-turbaned man hawking the local gazette. A small shoal of grabbing, pushing people followed, among them Young Chen, whom Big Brother had no doubt dispatched to buy a copy. Young Chen's height and girth gave him an advantage and he soon returned with his prize. Shading his eyes, Big Brother quickly scanned the flapping sheet.

"Big Brother, what's the war?"

Seeing Huaming sticking out the chair window, Big Brother snapped, "Don't hang there like a stupid monkey. People are watching! Here, look for yourself." He shoved the Gazette into the boy's hand and climbed into his own chair.

Huaming read the heavy words of the Emperor's Edict.

Hence we command "our general" to give strict orders to our various armies to hasten with all speed to root the Woren out of their lairs. He is to send successive armies to Korea in order to save the Koreans from the dust of bondage. He understood that Woren was the derogatory word for the Japanese and that in recent months people had been agitated by the presence of Japanese troops in Korea and by the appointment of a "Regent" loyal to Japan. But for now it was hot, he was hungry and the characters on the sheet were complicated, so he did not read the Edict to the end.

*T*he two coolies that were to carry him that day grunted in unison and lifted his chair onto their shoulders. Instinctively Huaming sat up straight, fixed his eyes forward, put his legs apart and placed one hand on each knee. This was the way a young gentleman should appear in public. However it was not long before the gentle humph-humph of the coolies lulled him to sleep, his head lolling to the right.

In truth, the city was of little interest to him. The narrow streets of Guangzhou with two and three-story buildings tilting so close that they often touched at the top, were not that different from those in other cities he had visited, except perhaps that they were longer and the shop keepers more noisy. The coolies turned into a street of hosiers' shops with rows and rows of signs carved in the shape of stockings. Next the milliners' street with dangling, black top hats and red and gold lettering, then the butchers' street adorned all the way up with wooden pink pigs and yellow chickens, wafting gently in the breeze.

So used to travelling by chair was Huaming that when his chair met another coming the other way and the coolies began their ritual shouting duel to persuade the other party to give way, he barely stirred from his slumber. In this case the coolies of the opposition were quicker off the mark, crying out that the passenger in their chair was a doctor on the way to treat an urgent case. Huaming's coolies shuffled his chair to the side like a huge crab, but the man at the front caught his foot on an uneven paving stone causing the boy's chair to lurch violently to the right under the eaves of a butcher's shop, along which the owner has strung out the best of his wares. Huaming woke with a start to find himself staring right into the bloated face of an inverted pig, its trotters resting ridiculously on the window frame of the chair. He tried to push the heavy head away but the harder he pushed the more momentum the bloody, gaping mouth of the pig had to swing back at him through the chair window

He cried out for Big Brother but his chair was much further up the street. Feeling the chair swaying precariously above them the coolies cursed. Fearing damage to goods and property the shopkeeper emerged from behind the counter waving his chopping knife. It was several minutes before the situation resolved itself and Huaming's chair could continue up the street. But by then everything seemed to be moving twice as fast. The coolies struggled to regain their accustomed rhythm. Huaming hung on for dear life to the sides of the chair. On his left and on his right, the rows and rows of hanging animals appealed to him with dead eyes. He passed a stork in a cage. It was still alive, its eyes sown up with red thread so that it could not see to bite. All around him people shouted at him in a guttural Cantonese dialect that he did not understand. The long streets were never ending and Big Brother's chair was nowhere to be seen.

A chorus of barking of dogs heralded the arrival of the sedan chairs in the courtyard, and the Secretary of the Chaozhou Merchants' Guild did as he always did with new guests, and peeped through the corner of the lattice window from his study. His assistant and a young man greeted each other with hands clasped and bows. A dishevelled looking boy of nine or ten, his face as white as that of any powdered singing girl, climbed out of the second chair. Barely aware of what he was doing, the Secretary counted the number of servants, pieces of baggage and assessed the quality of the young men's gowns. They were well-mannered, educated, but not well to do. It was only when he looked again at the open, oval faces of the boys, the elder one with fashionably plucked eyebrows, that he saw a likeness of the father in the sons.

He was taken aback. He himself remembered His Great Excellency Wen En arriving back in their hometown of Chaozhou after his retirement with honours from the Imperial Service. The procession on that occasion was made up of at least thirty chairs carrying members of the family followed by more than a hundred family retainers, including Buddhist and Taoist monks. Now here were the sons of Wen En travelling in tired, silk gowns with just one servant. Tucking his hands into the sleeves of his gown the Secretary hurriedly removed himself from the window. He had hoped that this day would never come. It was too embarrassing.

Last week in a private meeting with the Chairman of the Guild and a white suited merchant and former Comprador for a foreign trading house who had just happened to be in town, the situation had become clear to him. Whilst the members of the Guild felt they could not refuse hospitality to the sons of such an eminent official and local philanthropist as Wen En from their home region, the Guild could not afford to be seen as officially lobbying in support of the case. Moreover, should the sons do anything that might be deemed to bring the Guild and its members into disrepute, their hospitality would be withdrawn immediately.

The Secretary removed his skullcap, put it back on, and removed it again. Unlike many men who discarded their caps in the hot summer weather, the Secretary was never seen without his. His wife believed it was because he was a hypochondriac, terrified of catching a chill, whilst his assistant and servants at the Guild commented snidely that it was because the cap denoted his official rank of Graduate of the Provincial Examinations, which he had finally achieved at age forty-nine on the seventh attempt.

Hearing his assistant's footsteps on the veranda, he hurriedly popped his cap back on and withdrew through the door at the back of the room to the toilet where he went to play a game of mah-jong with three elderly members in a secluded spot in the corner of the garden. From here he was able to plead ignorance of the arrival of the young guests. Furthermore, it gradually became too late for him to be expected either to offer or to accept a dinner invitation.

Sure enough, when he finally returned to his study in the early evening his assistant presented him with a red calling card in the name of the elder son, Wen Huaguang, and a large box of tea from the province of Fujian.

"Your Excellency, Wen Huaguang requests the honour of a meeting with you at your pleasure."

The Secretary opened the box of tea, bent down to smell it, idly picked up a few twisted green leaves and put them into his mouth to chew on the flavour. He spat them out into his empty teacup. "Riches never last more than three generations!"

6

The wife of the British Consul in Guangzhou, Mary Adams, had heard it all before. There was not a viewpoint about China that had not been expressed around her dining table over the years. There were the take-a-horse to water, buccaneering types who insisted that Asiatics could only be made to see what was right through the use of force, countered at the other end of the spectrum by the "idealists" who loved the yellow race more than their own and indeed in some cases even advocated the superiority of Chinese civilisation. As the conversations ran a predictable course, the appearance, age and vocation of the guests was not necessarily an accurate indication of the likely turn of opinion. Mary knew many priests and missionaries who, embittered after fruitless years in China, punctuated by brutal incidents with the natives, were the first to call for gunboats when the going got tough, even as an oafish Scottish trader could display the utmost compassion and understanding for those he described as heathen.

This evening she let the conversation of her dinner guests wash over her and cast her eye around her dining room. The house on Shamian Island in Guangzhou was in the Italian style, typical of the foreign treaty ports. She was particularly proud of the dining room, with its three huge windows as high as the ceiling leading onto a small walkway lined with banyan trees, next to the river wall. A practical type, Mary had long since minimised the amount of soft furnishings in her house because of the impossibility of preserving them in the southern humidity and chosen instead to furnish her room with a collection of Chinese porcelain displayed in glass fronted cabinets. The pots, as her husband called them, had been bought in Shanghai from the Chinese widow of a British tea trader who had died under mysterious circumstances while in Fujian province chasing the blasted weed. As she told her mother in a letter home at the time, the brisk turnover of lives, as well as property among foreigners in the treaty ports in China, was something one just had to get used to. It was a matter of survival and one really could not afford to observe all the proprieties. Mary returned her attention to the faces illuminated by the sepia lamplight. They were the usual group of assorted diplomats, adventurers, dreamers and misfits: including the American Consul, his wife and her friend Celia, and Celia's nephew, a missionary newly arrived from Hong Kong. Year after year these people came to China, as surely as moths fly into a naked flame.

"It is my opinion that Confucian values err in their reliance on the strength of the self. There is no doubt that our Chinese Confucian gentleman wishes to make his thoughts sincere. To this end he will happily spend all day contemplating a bare wall, but he is bound to fail. Why? Because he does not understand the power of the Holy Trinity to make man anew. That, Sir, is the crux of the Chinese problem." The young American missionary, Wesley Hutton, was very sure of himself. "Only the Holy Spirit has the power to transform the world."

It was late, and replete with food and drink, the other

guests did not relish the challenge of a philosophical conversation with a keen young missionary and graduate of Harvard.

"So why did you decide to become a missionary?" As usual, the portly trader had drunk too much, but he was aware that he had asked the same question earlier in the evening. The young American was, however, nothing if not patient.

"My work with the Indians convinced me of the need of unfortunate peoples who had never had the opportunity to choose the religion which promises salvation."

"But why China, if there are still those in need of salvation at home?"

"You have been in China many years, Sir; is it not true that the foreign need is the greater?"

"In your two years with the Church in Hong Kong, exactly how many converts have you made?" The Scottish doctor, working in the Guangzhou Ophthalmic Hospital, was only thirty, but overwork backed up by fear of failure made him look a gaunt fifty.

Opening his palms upwards on either side of his plate, Wesley sighed. "It's difficult to say exactly. The problem, you see, is the quality of the converts."

"Hah! That's because you are putting the cart before the horse!" The doctor now had the admission that he wanted and was delighted by an easy victory.

"The Chinese I see in the hospital are ignorant of the simplest laws of natural philosophy, chemistry and astronomy. They are enslaved by medieval superstitions and beliefs. Under such circumstances, how can you expect to make meaningful conversions? Read the Bible to them as long as you like, but if you are really serious about planting the Church of God on Chinese soil, then you need to offer them proof in the form of science, and new modes of government, and law. It is the spirit of universal enquiry that will change the aspect of China, not the Bible alone!"

Wesley rose to the challenge embracing all the tempered charm of a New England drawing room on a Sunday afternoon.

"Education is important. I myself will be supervising the mission school when I take up my new post in Shantou. But with regard to the cart before the horse, I am afraid, Sir, that I beg to differ. In order to make use of a new government, of science and technology, China must first confront her spiritual needs. One would hardly argue that the United States of America has been uplifted by steam and electricity! What China needs is righteousness. And in order for her to attain it, she needs knowledge of God the Father and our Saviour the Lord Jesus Christ. Our primary task is to reach to the heart of the heathen and thus transform Chinese society."

The trader stubbed out his cigar in the creamy residue at the centre of his dessert plate.

"Humbug! I have been in China thirty years, and I can assure you that Asiatics have an inborn inability to comprehend the most basic meaning of the gospel."

Mary was relieved to see her Head Boy come into the dining room and surmised that the boat that was to take the American party back to the Guangzhou side had arrived. She scratched her left ear in a pre-arranged signal to her husband.

"Sorry to break up the party. Best not keep these boatmen waiting. They can be so fickle, especially in times of war." There was a scraping of chairs and a flurry of napkins as the guests seized the opportunity to make for the French windows and the refreshing night air of the Bund.

Later, Mary lay in bed watching her husband as he stood by the open window. The black treacle night dragged on the body and mind. He sipped from a glass of whisky and looked across the river at the lights of Guangzhou. This was to be his last posting before retirement, and Mary knew that her husband was brooding on that crucial promotion that had gone to someone else nearly ten years ago. She tried to distract him.

"That young American was a bright boy. At least he has a sound grasp of theology and I can definitely say that he is not a homosexual! All of which makes a pleasant change!"

The Consul snorted. "Yanks! With their precious Republic and pious preaching!" He drained the whisky, drew the curtains and took a deep breath. Mary knew that her tactic was working.

"Do they think they are somehow better than the rest of us out here? It is a far greater undertaking than we can imagine, displacing the religions and traditions that have been embedded over thousands of years."

The Consul lumbered across the room and climbed into bed. The smell of crisp, clean sheets made him sigh and he reached his arm out for his wife to come and lay her head on his shoulder, as she had first done on their honeymoon in Simla all those years ago. For a while he listened to the splash of oars and shouts of people on the Pearl River that never slept.

"At the very least our young American ought to keep the Consuls in Shantou on their toes, sorting out all the troubles he creates with the natives." He chuckled and rolled toward Mary. "I know that type. He'll never be satisfied with saving the souls that present themselves to him in port: although heaven knows there are enough of them in that God forsaken place. No! His ambition is far greater than that. He wants to change the world!"

7

*W*aking to servant's voices speaking in his native dialect in the courtyard, Huaming thought he was at home in Chaozhou. Smiling to himself he snuggled into his summer quilt, savouring the morning smell of fried eggs and hot sweet soya bean milk. Then he remembered: he had climbed the previous night into the far corner of the huge wooden bed that he was sharing with Big Brother in their room in the Merchants' Guild.

Opening his eyes he saw Big Brother Huaguang sitting tall and straight, writing at a round wooden table near the open door. He wanted to call out to him but the morning sunshine illuminated a look of such smooth calm on his brother's face that he almost did not recognise him. His writing brush whispered quickly across the page, his body seeming to pulse with his breath. Every so often a breeze wafted small pieces of torn scroll that had been abandoned to the floor. They were practice pieces, and Huaming knew that Big Brother had most likely been thus engaged since dawn. He made a series of short decisive strokes, his signature. Slowly he laid his brush on its rest and surveyed the finished work that was held down by four shiny black stones, one in each corner. Stretching his hands above his head, he pushed back the chair. Huaming took this as his signal and sat up in bed.

"What are you doing?"

"Writing a letter requesting an audience with the Literary Chancellor." Big Brother turned round and came to sit on the bed next to him, his face suddenly grey and with effort.

"Will he be able to help?"

"He is a member of the Hanlin Academy, an old friend of Father's. As Provincial graduates they studied in the light of the same window. I am sure that he will speak to the Chief Justice on our behalf."

Big Brother sighed and the boy knew that he was thinking, if only...if only he had made it to Provincial Graduate before all the trouble had started, he would have had status of his own and it would have been much quicker and easier to get audiences with officials. Big Brother smiled and reached out to smooth down the tuft of hair that was not yet long enough to be plaited into the boy's queue, and which when the wind blew, or after sleep, had the habit of standing on end like a peacock. Huaming pulled a face and pushed his Brother's hand away. Adults were always doing that to him.

"What are we going to do today?"

"First, send Young Chen to deliver the letter to the Literary Chancellor. Second, get some breakfast, and third, chew a little bit of cud. I let you off your lessons too lightly while we were travelling."

Huaming groaned and rolled back onto the bed, shaking his head in protest. Soon the two brothers were exchanging playful punches.

*T*he Secretary of the Chaozhou Merchants' Guild scanned the tables on the third story of the Lucky and Bright Teahouse. Business was brisk and there were not many vacant tables. He indicated to the bowing waiter with a waft of the back of his hand that he preferred a table away from the noisy group of men in grubby cotton gowns who were bent so low over the their food that they looked like pigs round a trough. Instead he found himself sitting next to a young, foreign man in a black Chinese gown who was reading a book in Chinese as he ate. Staring at him, the Secretary thought he looked like a monkey dressed as a man. Despite himself, he was intrigued and was just about to ask the monkey what he was reading when he saw the Chairman of the Guild puffing his way across the room. He was sweating heavily and plumped down in the chair, pulling his gown out over his chest and undoing the top buttons of his collar. Greetings were exchanged with speedy familiarity, both men clasping their hands together and bowing slightly.

"Pu er and chrysanthemum tea. Pork dumplings. Sticky rice and chicken's feet... Okay, okay..." They grunted their culinary preferences in a similarly efficient manner. The tea and the chicken's feet arrived first and the round-faced Chairman sighed with the satisfaction of a child being served his favoured treat, and raised his chopsticks. But the Secretary had come to know that the Chairman's country bumpkin face and scatter-brained manners were deceptive. He had a very successful business with the Antipodes and spoke many dialects and languages. But he had come up the irregular route to officialdom, purchasing his rank, a luxury that unfortunately had not been available to him.

"Heard the news from Korea?" The Chairman crunched on a chicken's foot. "The Japanese devils have torpedoed the *Kowshing*. The audacity! The ship was under a British flag." He spat out the bones onto the table. "Then the bastards machine-gunned our Chinese troops in the water."

"Terrible times indeed..." The Secretary popped a pork dumpling into his mouth. "Have no fear, Sir. With our modern navy and weapons, vengeance will surely be ours."

"You mark my words, the Woren will not stop at Korea. We will see much worse before the year is out."

The Secretary blinked and choked on his dumpling. Defeat was unthinkable.

It was not until the meal was nearly over that the two men addressed the business in hand.

"How did the meeting go with the Wen boy?"

"He's a fool." The Secretary sneered over the rim of his teacup. "Spends the mornings teaching his scrawny little brother and writing letters in his best calligraphy to officials he thinks might help his case."

"Which officials?" The Chairman spoke with his mouth full.

The Secretary blinked quickly. "He always sends the letters with his own man."

"Well, have him followed." The Chairman popped the last mouthful of pork into his mouth, and for the first time during their meeting looked directly at the Secretary.

"Don't worry, Sir. He's just another little master trying to be a big man." The Secretary reaffirmed his view and quickly excused himself for a pee.

*I*dly the Chairman picked over the last pieces of cha sui pork sticking to their lotus leaf covering, comparing in his mind this information with other intelligence from different sources. He envisaged a very different scenario for the meeting between the Secretary and the son of Wen En. He saw a shrunken, myopic scholar whose humble background and lack of means had not helped his career, confronted by a vigorous, young man with all the natural grace and bearing that came from growing up in association with educated men of power and influence.

The food gone, he too pretended not to stare at the skinny Foreign Devil at the next table, who in turn pretended not to stare back over the top of his book. Finishing his tea with a decisive swig and calling loudly for the bill the Chairman ended their tacit duel.

The Literary Chancellor in charge of Provincial examinations and provincial graduate students always worked at his summerhouse in the cool of the late afternoon. Taking his favourite large calligraphy brush from its stand, he dipped the tip into the ink on the stone, letting it draw up just the right amount before applying it to the paper. The series of long, thick movements took only seconds, and the work was complete: a glistening, black Chinese character a foot and a half high at the centre of a long piece of scroll.

For forty years the Literary Chancellor had been trying to paint the character of *ren*, the virtue of humanity and benevolence that was the goal of all Confucian gentlemen, and although his calligraphy was greatly admired, never once had he been satisfied with his work. This time was no different and he dropped the brush into a water jar to wash it. He knew he would try again the following day, and the day after that, and ever after until the day he died. The discipline helped to keep the temptations and regrets at bay, for there were many students who aspired to the rank and privilege of Imperial Service and his post was known to be lucrative. He tried to live up to the ideal of strong and effective government through securing the service of the honest and true and hoped that, in this way, one day good governance of All Under Heaven would somehow put an end to the rule of the foreign Manchus. The Literary Chancellor was certainly less corrupt than many, but his family was large and his sons had many wives and children.

Sitting down, he took a scroll from a number standing in a porcelain jar on the floor. He had received the letter the previous week and the case had so disconcerted him that he had agreed to see the petitioner. Of course he had taken notice of the gossip about the case of his fellow member of the élite Hanlin Academy, Wen En. It was almost unheard of for such a Senior Official and protégé the now deceased great scholar official Zeng Guofan to be sentenced to death for murder. He had not seen his friend for nearly thirty years, but remembered him to be a mild-tempered young man who liked to philosophise, a man of vision particularly dedicated to work with refugees and the poor. Something must have gone very wrong for his friend. Critically, he surveyed the son's letter. The sincerity of the young man's hand was evident from the strong clear brush strokes.

Hearing voices in the garden, the Literary Chancellor looked up. His servant conducted a young man, a boy and their servant across the grey stone bridge toward him— Wen En's sons. He hurried to wipe the ink from his hands and straighten his gown.

No sooner had the two boys entered the summerhouse than they fell on their knees to kowtow.

"Great Excellency, we are honoured to be received." The deep voice of the young man and the high-pitched voice of the child drowned out the gentle buzz of insects. The boys sat back, tense on their heels. The dappled light from the tiny pieces of the blue inlayed glass window fell around them like bits of ice. Without expression the Literary Chancellor looked into the faces of first one boy and then the other, until he was at last satisfied.

"Welcome, welcome, the sons of Wen En. Sit down! Make yourselves comfortable! Fresh tea!" he told his servant.

The boys gave the Literary Chancellor a small pendulum clock made in Paris that had been a present to their father from a French priest in Sichuan Province. The Literary Chancellor protested that such gifts were not necessary between old friends. Young Chen placed the clock on the table and retired to the servant's quarters. Opening the little glass door with its rose pattern, Huaguang picked up the little key and explained about the winding and maintenance. The Literary Chancellor experimented with the key himself then gently closed the glass door as if afraid of interrupting the process he had set in motion. The great official and two boys stood in front of the machine, mesmerised by its uneven ticking and the swinging pendulum.

At length, the Literary Chancellor indicated to Huaguang that he should take the place of the senior guest on the chair to his left. For his part, the younger brother dithered in front of the row of three chairs along the sidewall before sitting on the second of them. He could not sit back in the chair and bend his knees, so he perched on the edge, his legs dangling

"How is my old friend, Wen En?"

"My father is not well, Your Great Excellency. He was in prison for some time, and his health has been damaged. Thankfully, we have had permission for him to live at home...at least until..." Huaguang seemed ill at ease with the informality of his reception and made a stab at a formal speech about the great injustice that had been done to his father, but was quickly derailed by the Literary Chancellor's detailed and insistent questions about the alleged circumstances of the murder for which his father had been sentenced to death. The Literary Chancellor had deemed it best to meet here in the summerhouse, away from public gaze.

Quickly the Literary Chancellor reviewed the facts of the case in his mind with the practice of a man who had spent his life in the civil service, receiving petitions and making decisions. The so-called facts of the case were simple. It was common knowledge that Wen En had fallen out with his good friend Li Shaoming over a girl in whom both had an interest. The girl, who had already acquired a reputation for grace and beauty despite the fact that she had barely reached puberty, was the daughter of a cousin of Wen En's senior wife. The two men had quarrelled very publicly over the matter at a meal following a meeting of a local gentry's Friendly Society to which both of them belonged. A few days later Li had taken the girl into his house as a concubine, despite his friend's objections. Fuming with rage, Wen En had tabled a motion to get his old friend thrown out of the Friendly Society. The other members of the Society saw the case as a matter of sour grapes rather than of family and morality and voted in Li Shaoming's favour. Not long afterwards Li failed to return home after a night in town. His body was found with a pistol shot to the chest in a ditch on Wen En's land about a month later. If that were not enough, the girl, however, was beside herself with grief and had gone to live at Wen En's family courtyard at the insistence and under the protection of Wen En's senior wife, who considered it an act of charity to take in a vulnerable member of her family. People said that Wen En had taken her to his bed, when in fact she had been put to work in the house, given responsibility for feeding the chickens and collecting eggs and slept with the other unmarried female servants on the floor in the kitchen. The final blow was, however, the emergence of credible witnesses to say that they had seen a drunken Li Shaoming being bundled into a sedan chair by Wen En's men as he left the tavern on that fateful night.

"Do you like to tickle carp?" The Literary Chancellor noticed the boy was fidgeting in his seat and pointed to the pond with its stone bridge in the middle of the garden. Huaming looked first to his elder brother for approval, then nodded. The Literary Chancellor signalled for his servant.

"Ah Fong, take the boy to see the fish. Better still, take him to the women's quarters and see if you can find my grandson. They are about the same age."

The old man and the young man watched the boy go down the steps holding the servant's hand. The Literary Chancellor folded the sleeves of his gown above his elbows and poured more hot water into the little terracotta teapot, the excess water splashing onto the wooden latticed tray below.

"You should have come to me earlier..." He calculated that there were only two months left before the annual time for executions in the autumn.

"I never thought it would come to this..." Huaguang did not need to be told what the Literary Chancellor was thinking. "Anyone who knows my father knows that he is not capable of such a deed. The whole thing is so clearly a fabrication. The trouble is that I don't know who is behind it, and I can't get any sense out of my father. The whole thing has been such a shock to him; it is as if he has retreated to the safety of his own childhood. Sometimes he does not even recognise us—his own flesh and blood!"

The Literary Chancellor tutted.

"Your father is a man of principle, and such men have many enemies. How much money do you have left?"

Huaguang's jaw dropped. "Is it that obvious, Your Great Excellency?"

"The case has been running for how long? About two years, and you have managed to get your father bailed out of prison. I would calculate that it has all been very expensive."

"My father's health was so poor that I mortgaged what was left of our land to bring him home and fund this trip." Huaguang dropped his head.

"Wen Huaguang, your father is blessed with such a dutiful son. It is a great injustice for a man such as your father to be treated in this way, and it reflects badly on us all. I will speak to the Chief Justice and see what we can do. But I must warn you; I cannot promise success. The warrant has been signed by the Emperor himself, and it will not be easy to reverse."

The lazy breeze brought the men snippets of shouting and laughter from the garden. The Literary Chancellor rose and went to lean on the balustrade. He wanted to help, he really did. But the Festival of the Ghosts was nearly upon them when the gates of hell were thrown open and the spirits were free to wander at will. Even the most enlightened people were cautious about receiving visits, and he himself did not like to go out too much during such a period. Best if he just wrote a note to the Chief Justice instead. He flapped his sleeves down to cover his hands, a gesture which indicated to Huaguang that the discussion was over.

The day was drawing to its close and members of the family were starting to come out to enjoy the comfort of the golden hour before darkness. A deep green carpet underlayed a bed of white lilies with yellow centres in the pond, as if someone had cracked fresh eggs upon the water. Huaming crouched with another boy and a maid, barely more than a child herself, all three of them with their arms in the pond trying to stroke the gold and silver carp as they passed. An old lady of the house sat on a seat in the shade, being fanned by another maid.

"Ssssh! Not so much noise! You'll frighten the fish!"

A third maid carried a young woman with bound feet, in a pink embroidered gown, on her back from the house towards the bridge.

"Come meet my wife and daughter-in-law." Taking his stick the Literary Chancellor led the way down the stone steps into the garden.

But as they approached the pond a disaster was in the making. Challenging each other, the little boys reached further and further, and deeper and deeper into the pond.

"Little Brother! Watch out!" The maid grabbed both boys by the back of the gown, just in time, hauling them back. Splashing, shouting, water dripping from their queues and sleeves, the boys showed their indignation at having their play interrupted. But the daughter-in-law, now standing on the crest of the bridge, threw back her head and laughed. She laughed with none of the coy affectation of many ladies of her rank, ladies who covered their mouths with a hand. One by one the others started to laugh, even Huaguang, who laughed just a little too long and a little too loudly.

8

*T*he blond American with his books had become such a common sight on the third floor of the Lucky Bright Tea House that regulars had long since ceased to pay him much attention. Such tea houses, with their wooden panels and paintings, were all over the city, but this one was far and away Wesley Hutton's favourite. It was particularly clean and well run, and the windows on the third floor were always left open to allow what little cool air there was to circulate. But the main reason he liked it was because it was frequented by people from the Chaozhou, Shantou region speaking the dialect that he had been so painstakingly learning over the last year. The tearoom was the first place outside the protected environment of the Church in Hong Kong where he could test his new skill.

It excited him to escape the fussy care of Aunt Celia at the American Consulate, put on his Chinese gown, tie back his fast growing hair into a Chinese- style pony tail, and wander freely around the city. His biggest thrill still came from the assumption made by the Chinese that he could not understand them, which meant that he could listen to the most intimate of conversations, unsuspected.

On this day he had managed to get his favourite table in the corner opposite a painting of bamboo covered in a thick blanket of snow. He really liked the picture, although he never knew quite why, but concluded that it was probably the thought of snow and ice in the summer heat. The busy lunch hour was virtually over and Wesley and a few tardy customers were the only ones left. As always in idle moments he took out the photograph of his fiancée from the place he had kept it since he had left Boston nearly three years ago: in his Bible between the end of Old Testament and the beginning of the New.

Emily Jones...they had met when she was just seventeen and he was in his final year at Harvard. She was the daughter of a local surgeon, and when he completed his degree he had asked her father for her hand in marriage. Her father had opposed the match on the grounds that Emily was too young and because a life as the wife of a minister of religion would not suit his daughter. The couple nevertheless became secretly engaged and planned that as soon as Emily was twenty-one, she would sail to China to join him and they would be married. In the early days of their separation when Wesley first arrived in Hong Kong the mere sight of her picture had instantly evoked the smell of her lavender perfume, the warmth of her hand in his and the touch of her soft lips. Recently, although he could not admit it to himself, his memories had become less distinct. Today, as he picked up his pen to write to her, he saw a pleasant looking girl with a slightly plump face, wearing a high-necked white blouse and black skirt, standing next to a photographer's potted palm.

My Dearest Emily,

You would be proud of me! At last I am making progress with the people here. The long hours of pouring over Chinese texts with smelly old Teacher Wong in Hong Kong are beginning to pay off. When I tell you that several weeks ago I was fortunate to enough to encounter a young Chinese of the gentry class and his little brother, and am now their teacher and friend, I am sure you will understand why I have not written since my arrival in Guangzhou. Dear girl, can you forgive me?

I had noticed the brothers on several occasions in the teahouse before we actually met: the two of them distinguished by clean gowns, good manners and the utter concentration in their faces as they conversed. (Just as I come to the teahouse to read, so the Chinese boys come to do their lessons: Chinese classics, of course.) Whenever the little boy gets something right, the Elder Brother smiles and nods his head approvingly, and the little boy chooses a piece of dried fruit from the lacquered tray in the centre of the table, common to all these establishments. Despite the stories of infanticide and the like that one hears so often back home, the Chinese are in fact a family—loving people, and the relationship between these two brothers is clearly based on affection.

One lucky day they came to sit at the table next to mine. They had of course noticed my red-haired foreign devil appearance on previous occasions, but this time their proximity meant that even the Elder Brother could not refrain from some surreptitious staring. (To give him his due, after a while he did admonish his sibling with the ubiquitous "Don't stare at the Big Nose!")

By this time, I had worked out that they were natives of the city of Chaozhou, so I buried my head in my book in order to listen more discreetly. Seeing me reading Chinese, the Elder Brother could not contain his curiosity for long and addressed me in Mandarin, which is, as you know, the educated language of scholars and officials here. I understood enough to know that he was making an inquiry as to my reading matter. My Dear Girl, you should have seen his jaw drop when I replied in his own native dialect that I was in fact reading poetry by the famous Chinese poet Du Fu! Thus my first effective contact with educated Chinese inside China was made!

The Elder Brother asked where I had learned Chinese and if I had read the Chinese Classics, and we had a long discussion about the writings of Mencius, who was a disciple of Confucius and most famous for arguing that human nature is innately good. We met on subsequent days, and you will not be surprised to know that we had our differences, the Eldest Brother dismissing Christianity as just another subversive superstition. In response to this I opened my Bible at One Timothy, Chapter Two, Verses One and Two, which as you surely remember, reads, "Exhort therefore, that, first of all, supplications, prayers, intercessions, and giving of thanks, be made for all men. For Kings and for all that are in authority; that we may lead a quiet and peaceable life in godliness and honesty." He seemed quite impressed, nodding his head reflectively and pouring me more tea.

By the occasion of our third meeting Huaguang (the elder brother's name means China Shines) clearly had an agenda. He shifted in his seat and rambled on at length about what he called the Restoration (of China of course!) which he believes will come about through a combination of a return to the true Confucian Way and an adoption of Western inventions such as science, steamships and railways. (Incidentally these three words were the only words of English he knew when we first met—how great is our task here!) He was quite passionate about it all, and I couldn't help liking him for that, although he would not go as far as to say explicitly to this foreign devil that he wanted an end to Manchu rule. It is very difficult for the gentry here, knowing that their Emperor is a foreigner. A few eccentrics do still choose not to serve in the Imperial Service, but since it is the way to power and influence here, most make the compromise.

Alas, whenever I tried to talk to Huaguang of the power of the Holy Spirit to give new life to all men, his face clouded over with impatient suspicion, and I fear I must bide my time or lose his friendship. Eventually, however, he came to the point, and asked if I would teach him and his Little Brother English! Forgive me if I say again, I cannot tell you what a joy it has been to finally have some meaningful contact with educated natives here.

So, my Dear Girl, you must not worry about me. The last few weeks have passed with the usual round of American Consular social life and the Chinese boy's daily lessons, the latter being certainly the more interesting part of the day! Both my pupils are bright and keen and you will like them: for I am sure you will meet them when you come. They soon had the ABC all fine and dandy, and are now starting to make passable conversation. The supreme tragedy of their situation is of course that they still see Chinese Classical learning and passing Imperial Examinations as the way to success. Poor things! They cannot see how the daily rote learning of such classics in fact acts to stunt their intellectual growth and hampers the progress of the whole nation.

Despite all this, I regret that over the last week or so I must report that I have noticed a worrying change in my senior pupil, Huaguang. He is distracted, and increasingly only the younger brother, Huaming, turns up for lessons, in the company of an oafish young servant with teeth stained red with betel nut which working men chew here. Huaming is a good boy and tries very hard and indeed helps me greatly with my Chinese, patiently correcting me with a disparaging raised eyebrow when I make a mistake! But when I ask him about Huaguang his eyelids droop and his response is always the same.

"My Big Brother has big busy business in Guangzhou."

Yesterday Huaguang came for the first time this week. At the end of the lesson he sent the little boy off to pay for the tea and, looking me straight in the eye, said, "Teacher is very good. China have very many bad things. Fight Japanese. Fight French. My little brother, his teaching is very important. Very important now. You are a good man. Thank you." He is clearly much troubled by the state of his benighted land. How I hope that one day he will come to know the Love of our Lord Jesus Christ.

So, My Dear Girl! At last you will be twenty-one at the end of September! Let me know as soon as you have booked your passage. Aunt Celia will adore you for sure. The mission is expecting me in the port of Shantou at the beginning of September, so I will leave Guangzhou at the end of August when the weather starts to turn cooler. The position promises a nice house, and I promise to have it all ship shape before your arrival.

Your loving fiancé, Wesley.

Guangzhou 18th August 1894

The summer worked slowly toward its climax; the ghosts

were duly placated, people jostled past the trestle tables set out in the narrow streets by the shopkeepers to offer the spirits fruit and delicacies, and the white smoke from the burning of fake money and incense irritated the eyes of the passer-by. The Japanese army consolidated its position in Korea; Chinese navy ships were routed by the French navy in Fuzhou harbour and little Huaming feared the changes he saw in his elder brother's behaviour.

Early mornings were replaced by late nights. Accompanied by Young Chen, who carried some of the gifts of tea and silk they had brought with them from Chaozhou, Huaguang took to going out in the early evening to dine with an assortment of officials and provincial graduates: increasingly, anyone who might be persuaded to lobby in their father's favour. More often than not, he returned supported by Young Chen, who helped him to bed. Huaming pretended to be asleep but he witnessed it all: the vomiting into the chamber pot, the clumsy movements as Huaming counted their remaining cash and dwindling stock of presents by the light of a single candle, and in the early hours the agitation under the bed sheet which ended with his Elder Brother's anguished moaning of his wife's name.

Once more the brothers put on their best gowns and went to see the Literary Chancellor. They arrived early, but already the clerk told them the Literary Chancellor was too busy to see them until late morning. To pass the time the brothers went under the high stone gates and into the examination halls. They wandered up and down the long rows of hundreds of tiny cells, open at the front, where candidates would sit for days and write their papers. Huaming remembered Big Brother shimmying up the mango tree in the family courtyard.

"Little Brother can't catch me! I shall be Zhuang Yuan! First of the Firsts in all examinations in All Under Heaven!"

But that day Big Brother walked heavily, the front sole

of his left shoe flapping loose. Idly Huaming kicked stones, raising clouds of dust. He anticipated an admonition from Big Brother.

"Stop it! You will ruin your shoes. Do you think money falls down from heaven?" But Big Brother did not seem to notice.

He tried to cheer Big Brother by counting the examination cells and peeping out of each one while making a monkey face. "Five hundred and sixty-nine. Five hundred and seventy. Whew, what a stink! There is a dead bird in here"

"Hurry up! It's time to go!" Big Brother shaded his eyes to look one last time up and down the rows of empty cells, abandoned to weeds and lizards until the next examination.

It was late afternoon before the Literary Chancellor received them, this time in the outer hall of his Yamen. They were not invited to sit down. The old man muttered something about patience being a virtue, and about dutiful sons. The muscles of his face moved just enough behind his thin white beard and wispy moustache for Huaming to see that he was missing his front teeth. Was he wearing a mask? Huaming was not entirely sure that he was the same man as the kind old grandfather who had previously invited him to play in his garden. A flap of the Literary Chancellor's right sleeve indicated that the audience was over. A secretary appeared out of the shadows and made to wheel Big Brother by the elbow to a side door, but Big Brother pushed the flat of his hand towards him to hold him off.

"I thank your Great Excellency for the honour of the audience. I wish Your Excellency long life." He patted Huaming on the back of the head to indicate that it was time for them to kowtow, then took him by the hand and led him at a measured pace to the big doors at the rear of the hall.

Amidst all the uncertainty Huaming actually looked

forward to his lessons. Even if Big Brother was increasingly bad tempered when he made mistakes in recitation, at least he was predictable. Sometimes Huaming was tempted to tell the kind English teacher who spoke such funny Chinese about his family's problems; but even he was wise enough to know that there were certain things that were not discussed with foreign devils.

On the occasion of the Festival of the Emperor's Birthday, Huaming was relieved to see a lightening of Big Brother's mood. Big Brother suggested that they attend the Festival itself in the Temple of Ten Thousand Years and indeed he spent the whole of the afternoon prior to the night of the Festival calmly engaged in calligraphy: something he had not done for some time.

The festival took place in the early hours and they had to get up at two o'clock in the morning in order to be at the Temple in good time. Remembering all the preparation —best gowns, hats and sedan chairs—that the family used to make when his father attended the same ceremony as Chief Justice in Sichuan Province, Huaming could not sleep. Lying in the bed he looked through the open doors into the courtyard. Four men were playing mah-jong around a single lamp in a room on the far side. Laughter and jokes had long since left the click-clicking tiles to do the talking. Crickets whirred and Big Brother sat in the shadows of the veranda in his undershirt, his feet up on the wall. The bittersweet smoke from his cigarette crept like snakes through the lattice door. Huaming thought of his father sitting out on the veranda at home during summer nights. Unexpected tears rolled down his cheeks and would not stop. There was no one left to comfort him. His mother had taken to her bed after her father's arrest. His nanny was gone, and Big Brother would just say, "Don't start! Do you want me to beat you? Stop being a sissy." So he stuffed his face into the quilt to suffocate the sobs.

"Is it time yet?

"Not yet. Go back to sleep."

Wiping his nose with the back of his hand, he tried to cheer himself by making rabbit ear shadows on the wall with his fingers until at last he heard Young Chen's footsteps crossing the courtyard. It was time to go.

"Wait for me!"

Huaming ran to keep up with Big Brother as he strode through the empty streets of the outer city to the temple. Ahead of them, leading the way, Young Chen's lantern coaxed deformed ghosts out of the shadows, leering and bulbous, skeletal and spider-spiky with reaching tentacles: they were everywhere.

Huaming was relieved when they rounded a corner and saw the Temple of Ten Thousand Years. Its roof tiled in imperial yellow shone like the sun in the reflected light of the hundreds of tiny candles that had been lit in the central courtyard. They arrived just as the chairs and rickshaws of junior officials were arriving and being carried through the massive granite archway into the first courtyard. These were followed by servants, trunks slung between them on bamboo poles, containing their master's court robes. With all the comings and goings, no one seemed to notice as they made their way into the third inner courtyard and took up a position at the entrance to a corridor between two robing rooms in the surrounding cloister.

"Magnificent!" Big Brother inhaled the incense and looked across the courtyard to the Nine Dragon Steps leading to the great shrine containing the red Emperor's Tablet.

"May the Emperor reign ten thousand years. Ten thousand years times ten thousand years!" Big Brother's lips hardly moved. The candlelight cast a golden halo around his face, smoothing the brow lines that had been chiselled over recent weeks. His smile was so beatific that Huaming thought of a statue of the Buddha in the temple in Chaozhou, and for the first time in many months he thought briefly that perhaps everything would be all right. Looking away from his brother he turned his attention to the huge gilt throne in the centre of the Emperor's shrine, which, he had been taught, was the same as the Emperor's real throne in Beijing, and the centre of the ordered world of All Under Heaven. Soon the familiar ceremony would begin. Everything was just as it should be. Perhaps adults were not as incompetent as they had appeared over recent months. But, he wondered, if it was forbidden to enter the Emperor's shrine, then how could the throne have got there in the first place? Who cleaned it and dusted it? For it shone blinding white like the noonday sun in the light of hundreds of candles.

The senior Mandarins began to arrive one after another in order of rank and proceeded to their robing rooms, where their juniors advanced in silent rows to the door to greet them. Once dressed in their blue and gold court gowns and pointed hats with pearl shaped buttons of their respective ranks, they sat around and talked, smoked or drank tea. In the corner of one robing room Huaming noticed the Literary Chancellor fanning his nether regions with his gown.

At last, to a fanfare of trumpets and beating of drums, the viceroy himself arrived and processed towards the two most senior men already present: the governor and the Manchu general. He moved with much grand deliberation, lifting each knee to a right angle before placing a big, black, silk boot on the next paving stone. Huaming hoped that he would grow up to be such a great man as this. After greeting each other the three senior men placed themselves side by side in front of three kneeling mats in the centre of the courtyard facing the shrine. All the other Mandarins arranged themselves in order of rank behind them. A great shout rang out.

"Advance, kneel, kowtow." First with the left foot and then the right, the army of Mandarins advanced to kneel and knock their heads three times on the ground. They rose with a great rustling of gowns, then thick silence.

"Advance, kneel, kowtow. Advance, kneel, kowtow." The whole ritual was solemnly repeated three times. Chandeliers were lit around the shrine and the folding doors at the centre painted with branches and fruit of pomegranate trees, birds and imperial dragons, were thrown wide open. The Emperor's Tablet was illuminated in a blaze of light.

The main ceremony over, the Mandarins retired to their robing rooms, removed their formal robes and hats, drank yet more tea and chatted. It was at this point that Big Brother became agitated, dragging him roughly from one door to another looking for someone. Huaming was glad when Young Chen found them and suggested that he take him to watch a play that was being put on in one of the Temple's side courtyards. Holding the servant's hand, the last image Huaming saw of Big Brother that night was of him calling out to a Yamen official in a pointed red-fringed hat. The man's bare feet were huge and were spread like a duck's.

9

Out of the darkness Huaguang felt something soft stroking his face. Feather-like, it caressed his right cheek, traced the line of his mouth, and tickled up the left cheek, gently exploring one eye, then the other. Far, far away he heard women's voices.

"Leave him, Madam. He's nothing to do with us."

"But he's hurt. What if he dies here on our doorstep? It's bad luck."

Huaguang struggled to lift himself out of the blackness, but it was too heavy, pressing him down like a huge weight. There were hands on his shoulders, arms around his waist; he was being lifted up, his feet dragging and bumping over a threshold; the stifling smell of stale cooking oil and dank poverty reached his nostrils.

"I can't see! I can't see!" But no one seemed to hear him. He fought against the restraining hands and at last was free. In panic he swung dizzily round and round, his hands over his eyes.

"I can't see! I can't see!" The hands were grabbing his arms, pulling him down.

"Hush, hush. It's the blood from your wound." Again something touched his face and he recognised it as the warm, reassuring touch of the palm of a hand on his cheek. With it came a voice that was as calm as the dawn. "Hush, hush. You're safe now."

Huaguang allowed himself to be led to a bed. Lying down, he was overcome with waves of nausea. The woman with the calm voice supported his head and held a cup of cold tea to his mouth. His lips cracked apart like a shrunken walnut, the water stung viciously and tasted of blood. Gently the woman washed his face and eyes, and he grimaced with pain. It throbbed in his head and blistered all over his shoulders and back.

"That's better. Now try to open your eyes."

Instinctively he turned his head back to the wall, away from the early morning sunlight that was creeping through the shutters. The woman cupped her hand across the side of his head to shade his eyes. Looking up at her, he thought that she was the Guan Shi Yin Buddha herself. But even dilute sunlight was still too painful on his wounded eyes and he could not keep them open.

"What happened?" she asked. But he could not remember. One hand still touching his cheek, she opened the fastenings at the side of his gown and eased his arms out of it. Her hands felt methodically across his collarbones and up and down his rib cage. He winced.

"Good, good. At least nothing's broken. Just badly cut and bruised."

"Really given you good beating!" Huaguang forced himself to open his eyes and saw the owner of the other voice, an older woman in a white blouse: a maid.

"And whips too. Not your ordinary thugs, that's for sure." She pursed her lips disapprovingly. "One, two, three."

In an instant the two women had raised Huaguang to a sitting position and removed his cotton undershirt. He whelped with ripping pain. As they lowered him back onto the bed, he saw great bloody weals across his shoulders, arms and chest. It was then that it began to come back to him.

*H*e had been asking a Yamen official to tell him where he

might find the Chief Justice. The official had said that the Chief Justice's procession was due to leave from a side courtyard. Passing the stage where Huaming and Young Chen were watching the play, he had arrived just as the gongs signalled that the Chief Justice's procession was about to move off. Pushing through the onlookers, he'd obtained a good position on a step near the arch under which the procession would have to pass. First came the lantern bearers, followed by a host of pageboys carrying the banners and insignia of the Justice's rank, next the equerries on scrawny white ponies and finally the Justice's golden sedan chair. The curtains were open and Huaguang could clearly see the man's face. It was not what he had expected. He hesitated. The Chief Justice was surprisingly young and handsome for such a senior official: his expression almost benevolent.

Already the chair was nearly past him and the first lantern bearers were going under the arch. At the last second Huaguang pulled a scroll from the sleeve of his gown and threw himself on his hands and knees at the side of the chair, offering the scroll upwards above his head with two hands.

"Your Great Excellency, please receive my humble petition."

The Chief Justice had never received the petition. It was snatched away from Huaguang by the same Yamen Official who had earlier directed him to the procession. Four or five Yamen Officials in red pointed hats then appeared from nowhere and man-handled Huaguang into a side room off the first courtyard. It was filled with junk: sedan chair poles, an old wooden table, and the broken frame of a decrepit gilt throne.

The first Yamen Official took off his hat, arranged the red fringe to fall symmetrically all the way round and laid it carefully on top of the table. Squaring his shoulders, he swaggered towards Huaguang.

"You've been causing a lot of trouble lately, Mister," he

hissed. His companions chuckled ominously. Holding the petition scroll up with one hand he let it slowly unravel. "But you've gone too far now, Mister." Before Huaguang could reply he ripped the scroll from top to bottom. Huaguang could not believe what was happening to him. A gentleman, no one other than his old school teacher, had ever laid a hand on him. When the first blow landed on his face, he did not lift a finger to defend himself. The men came on thick and fast. At first they used the whips, taunting him like a dog in a ring. But once he was down, they beat him with the wooden handles of the whips and rammed their heels mercilessly into his stomach. Huaguang fought to stand up but it was not long before his strength was gone. He curled into a ball with his hands over his head to protect himself.

"Let this be a lesson once and for all." It was the voice of the first Yamen official—a great thump on the side of his head, and then nothing.

Lying on the bed, Huaguang heard the two women arguing. He opened his eyes. They had their backs turned towards him on the far side of the room, in front of the shuttered windows.

"We have to get rid of him quickly. Heaven knows, he could be a thief, a murderer, a rapist!"

"Don't be such a silly goose. He's a gentleman."

"How can you be so certain?"

"I just know." The younger woman waved her hands in a graceful, dismissive arc.

"I am not a murderer, and I will leave now. I have already caused you too much trouble." Huaguang sat up, but the thumping in his head was too much and he was overcome with dizziness. Groaning, he leaned back against the wall. The younger woman came back to him, feeling her way to him on the bed with her hands, and easing him back into a lying position. He realised with a shock that she was blind.

"You are not in a fit state to go anywhere right now. Besides, I need to clean your cuts, otherwise they'll go bad." Her eyelids dropped like heavy veils over her roaming eyeballs; it was this that had given him the impression of Guan Shi Yin Buddha. He reached out and touched her cheek, just as she had done to him.

"You can't see?"

"I am Blind Singing Girl. I work in the Song Houses. It was done when I was a child —for the sake of my trade. Blind people, it is said, make better musicians." Huaguang winced as she applied rice wine to the cuts on his back. "No matter. Important things can be seen without eyes; and I have Amah to look after me."

By the time she finished treating his wounds Huaguang was sweating with shock and exhaustion. Singing Girl drew a curtain to separate the bed from the rest of the room and once again held a cup to his lips. This time the liquid was hot and the steam carried the bitter smell of medicine. He pulled back suspiciously.

"Don't be afraid. There is no opium, just herbs to help your wounds heal. The effect will be slow and gentle, I promise." Her voice whispered like an evening breeze at the end of a summer's day and Huaguang realised that he no longer cared. All that mattered now was to escape from the horror of all that had happened. He sipped the black medicine, sighing as its soothing warmth made its way from his stomach into his veins. Great pent up tears began to pour down his cheeks. He tried to choke them back, but when Singing Girl reached out to him he allowed her to cradle him in her arms. She rocked him back and forth like a child, her breasts soft and warm under his cheek

"Aigu Guai Tsai Tsai Guai. Hush-a-bye baby." He could feel the soft breath of her words on the top of his head.

He told her everything: how he had let everyone down, how his father would be executed and the family ruined. What would become of his mother, his little brother, his wife Feng? They had trusted him and he had failed

She stroked his cheek.

"The Chief Justice, you say? He is a regular at a house where I sing. I know him. He is not a bad man: easily led maybe, but I can't believe he would knowingly let this happen. If you could just see him in person, then I am sure he would make it right. Perhaps I can arrange it?"

Huaguang nodded. Sleep was upon him and he only half understood what she was saying. He felt her lay him down, then felt and the warmth of her body as she stretched out next to him.

10

*B*y late afternoon the following day, Huaguang was well enough to return to the guild. Having received a scrappy note from Huaguang delivered by Singing Girl's maid earlier in the day, Huaming, Young Chen and Wesley Hutton anxiously awaited his return. Seeing the purple bruises all over his face they fussed with suggestions and questions until Young Chen put his foot down, shepherding them, arms open wide, onto the veranda.

Relieved to escape their questioning Huaguang eased himself into a chair next to the table.

"If there is anything I can do to help...anything at all. The Lord is always with us." He heard the missionary whispering confidentially to Young Chen. He looked around the big room with its heavy, mahogany furniture. On the table his ink stone and brushes were meticulously laid out, just as he had left them the previous afternoon. How could they be so unaffected by what had happened? His hand fell on a sealed letter. The three characters of his name ran vertically down the centre. The letter crackled authoritatively as he opened it.

Mr Wen Huaguang is respectfully requested to visit the office before noon.

It was signed by the clerk to the Secretary of the Guild and it was already too late.

Even before he had lifted a foot over the threshold of the Secretary's dingy office, Huaguang knew what was coming. Seeing him enter, the clerk quickly lowered his head. The Secretary of the Guild sat, shoulders hunched, fanning himself to the right of his desk. He had been looking forward to the visit all morning, but pretended to finish reading some papers in order to make Huaguang wait. He cleared his throat and spat noisily into a spittoon by his feet.

"Mr Wen, thank you so much for coming to see me. I am sure you will agree that the Chaozhou Merchants' Guild has been more than generous with its hospitality." The speech had been well rehearsed and the Secretary savoured the delivery. "However, there appears to have been a change in circumstances and the members regret to inform you that your room is required by another guest."

"I will settle the outstanding bill now, Sir, if I may." Huaguang was surprised to recognise in himself the same tone of calm authority that he had heard his father use in difficult situations throughout his illustrious career. Money exchanged hands. The long grubby fingernails of the Secretary tapped on the desk as he counted the coins. He left ten in the centre of the table and deftly flicked the rest into a drawer.

"The end of the week will be early enough. You are, Sir, I think, not well." He was now confident enough to look Huaguang in the eye. "My assistant will give you a receipt."

Huaguang crossed the room and the clerk fumbled with his receipt book.

"Your seal please, Mr Wen." Huaguang dipped his seal in the red ink pad on the desk and the clerk followed with the seal of the Guild to verify the document. Fumbling, the clerk dropped the seal onto the floor. It rolled under the table. Huaguang bent down stiffly, picked it up and handed it back.

"Sorry, Mr Wen. So sorry, thank you, thank you." The clerk blushed from his neck to the tips of his ears. Huaguang smiled, took the receipt, folded it and turned to leave the room. As he reached the door the Secretary could not resist a parting shot, his voice squeaky with excitement.

"Such a shame that a great man like your father has been reduced to this by the rash actions of a son." Huaguang did not turn around.

Young Chen sat on his haunches outside their room waiting for his Master. As Huaguang approached, he stood up, dropping his head quizzically to the left. "Shall I start packing, Master?" Nodding, Huaguang lifted his gown to cross the threshold into his room, but Young Chen would not be so easily dismissed.

"They say a young gentleman handed in a petition at the Temple of Ten Thousand years the other night." Huaguang knew that he could hide nothing from his childhood playmate, the elder boy who had played hide and seek with him in the garden and taught him to catch fish. He hoped that his expression had not given too much away. The responsibility was his and his alone. Young Chen shifted from one foot to the other.

"Well done, Master!"

Huaguang nodded stiffly and stepped quickly inside.

He slept the rest of that day and by the morning of the following day the thumping in his head had almost disappeared. He was able to teach Huaming his lessons and in the afternoon when Wesley Hutton came to the Guild for the boy's English lesson, he spent the time calmly writing letters in his room. That night, however, he slept fitfully.

Singing Girl was surely right. The Chief Justice could not be a bad man: if he could just get to see him and convince him of the merits of his case. But what if she let him down and never arranged the meeting? His strategy now depended on the whims of a blind singing girl. How could he have sunk so low?

In the late evening of the third night after the beating, Singing Girl's maid did indeed come to the guild with a message. Without question Huaguang followed as she scuttled like a mole along the dark streets to a song house not far from the Temple of Ten Thousand Years. Suddenly she stopped in the shadows, bowed and pointed to a staircase lit by two red paper lanterns.

Upstairs one large room was surrounded by lots of smaller rooms that were curtained off. The chairs and tables, made out of a variety of rare of knobbly wood, were occupied by men and young woman eating, drinking or playing mah-jong. There was one exception in the crowd: a heavily rouged, pointed-faced old lady with the tiniest of bound feet, resting on a little stool. She sat alone in a corner smoking a cigarette in a long ebony holder. Seeing Huaguang, she waved him to a table in the centre of the room with a well-practiced, still elegant waft of her hand. No sooner had he taken his seat than a thin young woman appeared at his side. Like all the other women her eyebrows were shaved and painted into high black arches. She too was heavily powdered and rouged, but all this could not disguise the grubby tinge of the spots beneath. Her hair was decorated with such a variety of red, green and gold hairpins, it was comical. She was in fact simply wearing all her assets all at once. Huaguang smiled and complemented her on her unusual coiffure. The girl giggled with genuine pleasure and shyness.

"I always do my hair myself." She went off to bring some wine, nuts and dried fruit. Huaguang looked around the house but could not see the Chief Justice, or the Blind Singing Girl.

Before long, warm with food, rice wine and flattery, Huaguang was on the point of forgetting the purpose of his visit to the Song House. Blind Singing Girl, however, had arrived, and standing at the front of the room, she began a lament for a lover lost forever on the Western frontiers. Concentrating on the exquisite tension in the changes of the pitch of her voice, Huaguang's eyes began to close. But a sudden movement to his left attracted his attention as the curtains to one of the side rooms were pulled noisily apart. It was then that he saw them: playing mah-jong with two women, the Chief Justice and another man: a Chinese man in a white Western suit, a man who stood on the docks in Shantou personally supervising the loading of the dregs of humanity that were his cargo, a man who was feared in every one of the Chaozhou counties and far beyond. Huaguang stared. The Chief Justice wore a plain black gown instead of his ceremonial robes, and his face was red and distended with drink, but it was he and no mistake. The man in the white suit played his hand and looked across the room at Huaguang as if he were expecting him. Very slowly, almost imperceptibly, the corner of his mouth leered upwards as he nodded his head. Yes, yes! So now you know. You fool!

At once the pieces of the puzzle fell into place. Huaguang remembered how, since his retirement, his father had been leading some members of the local Chaozhou gentry in a campaign against a spate of press ganging for coolie labour abroad. At the time Huaguang had been so busy with all his young man's distractions that he had never paid the campaign much attention—at least it served to keep his old man busy. Money had been given to improve the local militia and organise meetings in villages. Posters had gone up all over the county: pictures of skeletons working on top of skeletons in burning mines of hell entitled, "A better life?" So his father had been set up, and they were all in on it; the man in the white suit, the Chief Justice, and yes, even the Literary Chancellor.

A wave of blackness came over Huaguang's eyes; like a huge ink blot silently spreading across a piece of paper, it obliterated all that had gone before. Out of the darkness came a shadow: his father walking to the scaffold, his sick body weighed down by the wooden collar around his neck. He saw him struggling to prostrate himself with dignity and watched the executioner's blade as it rose and then fell. He knew now that their cause was hopeless. There was no way out. Nothing would ever be the same again.

*I*n those few seconds Huaguang saw it all: great bolts of fire raining down on all under Heaven, whole streets, whole cities consumed by the unstoppable inferno. The heat seared the flesh from his arms; his eyes bled with smoke, but he needed to know what was going to happen. Insatiable flames leapt across the yellow roof tiles of the Temple of Ten Thousand Years. Down in the courtyards, long, twisted tongues of fire roared up the Dragon Stairs to the Emperor's shrine and the golden throne was devoured in a blaze of red and black madness. Above him the great wooden roof beams seemed to be resisting the spitting flames. But in the end they fell: first one supporting beam, then the next, until it seemed the sky itself had collapsed around him. Then Huaguang saw them: emaciated, festering in rotten rags, shuffling through great wastes of smoking ashes. People: the sightless white-eyed agony of hundreds and thousands, millions of lost souls reaching out of the whiteness towards him.

Huaguang did not know how he paid his bill and got out of the Song House. He felt the warm night air on his face and found himself walking down the lantern-lit streets. On and on he wandered, stopping only once, bending double and vomiting painfully into the gutter. Hearing the hollow, echoing voices and sounds of the river, he followed the direction of their call.

He found a piece of broken wall in front of a warehouse and sat down. For a long time there was only the blackness of the night. Gradually his eyes focused on a light left burning in a window of one of the foreigner's houses on the opposite bank, and on the tiny moving lantern lights on the back of boats. He became conscious of a deep, regular booming, louder and louder, until in the distance he saw a large boat, followed by several other smaller boats, strung with hundreds of coloured lights reflecting on the water: a funeral procession. Buddhist monks chanted in time to the beating of a large gong in the lead boat. Huaguang was entranced. The boats floated toward him—nearer and nearer. The monks threw burning paper money and paper clothes into the river as an offering to the spirits, and all around, and in the wake of the boat, candles floated in earthenware vessels to light the way for spirits to the offerings. Slowly the ghostly procession passed by, gliding downstream, fainter and fainter, until he was left with the steady beat of his own heart. He knew now what he had to do to save his father, to save China and return her to the true way, and he knew that when the time came he would not be afraid.

11

The afternoon of the 31st August 1894 was to be a day that Wesley Hutton would never forget. The vicious white heat of the summer was on the wane, replaced by the gentler, gold tinged sunshine of early autumn. Despite the change in weather, Wesley Hutton was not in a mood to teach.

A letter had come from Emily that morning telling him that she was engaged to be married: to a lawyer from Boston apparently. Of all things, he had never imagined this. If only he had written more regularly. Curse his selfishness! It was of course an impossible letter for her to write, and even Wesley had to admit that she had done a good job of it.

The fault was hers, she wrote. She had been too young to understand the commitment. She was weak and unsuited for the trials of missionary life. God would find someone better than her to be his companion in his great enterprise. She would forever carry the memory of their friendship in her heart.

Wesley read the letter twice, tore it up and put a match to the pieces. Whenever he had pictured life as a missionary, it had always been with her at his side. Emily: an angel in white lace, reading to heathen children crouched around her in the dust. Emily, in her big straw hat with pink ribbons, handing out hymn books at the church door. God help him, for he did not know if he had the strength to do God's work alone.

Arriving at the guild, Wesley found that he was not the only one out of sorts. His little pupil was listless and distracted. He thought that maybe it was because the war news was bad: the Japanese were now on Chinese soil and had attacked Port Arthur. Together teacher and pupil made a stab at the story of Moses and the burning bush, but they ended up releasing Huaming's prize cricket from its cage. Chins resting in their hands, they watched it steadily mountaineer along the spine of the up-turned Bible. Suddenly they heard footsteps in the courtyard. Two women rushed into the room, a maid leading a tall blind girl.

"Mr. Wen Huaguang? Where is he? I must find him," the blind girl panted, the whites of her eyes rolling toward the heavens. But even as she spoke her face turned ashen. "Oh heaven, he has already left. We must stop him, before it is too late."

His pupil was already out of his chair, following the blind girl as she dragged her maid out of the room.

The street market in front of the Judicial Yamen was in full swing, the cooler weather encouraging the stall holders to shout their prices with renewed vigour. The blind girl pushed her way through the crowds, the maid and Huaming in her wake. Wesley Hutton hurried after them. Strange, she seemed to know where she was going even though she could not see. She was making for the Yamen gate, with its parade of emaciated, rotting prisoners with wooden collars around their necks, displayed as a warning to others. Attracted by the foreign face, beggars pressed around Wesley: a ragged child with a hunched old man who was agile enough to keep pace with Wesley despite his stick, and a lumbering, hulk of a man with square folds of drooping deformed flesh for a face. Repeatedly they pushed opened palms into Wesley's side.

"Help a poor man, one piece of cash."

He saw the blind girl reach the edge of the empty piece of land in front of the Yamen gate. The maid shouted and tried to pull her back, but the blind girl pulled herself free, running now with Huaming at her side. Wesley too began to run, although he did not know why. The beggars, realising that he was crossing towards the Yamen Gate, suddenly drew back, as if they had reached the very gates of hell. Wesley remembered Aunt Celia had once told him that Chinese would never willingly enter the gate of the Judicial Yamen.

He had come too far to stop now. The blind girl and Huaming passed into the shadows under the great gate. He took a deep breath and hurried after them.

The grey paving stones of the Yamen courtyard lay as silent as tombstones. Wesley stopped in his tracks: in front of him in the centre of the courtyard stood the blind girl and Huaming; Huaguang stood upon a raised dais, his old grey gown glistening silver in the sunlight. Lifting his gown Huaguang knelt down, fumbled with his neck and placed some scrolls on the floor to his side. Slowly, deliberately, he bent forward to a right angle. Helplessly, Wesley watched as Huaguang's right hand reached up and pulled a rope.

It was all over before he could comprehend what was happening. A flash of light, a noise like a flight of swifts passing over head, and the blade fell from the guillotine. A thump and Big Brother's severed head rolled down a shute, hitting the Gong of Justice with a mighty thump.

Time stood still.

At last the deep reverberations were no more. Instead, the blind girl was screaming over and over again, her hands over her eyes.

"Brother, Brother!" Huaming ran stumbling across the square, scrambling up the steps to the dais. The slumped body of his brother was still moving: the legs going up and down as if he were climbing stairs. Eyes to heaven, the head rested against the still, golden gong. Like a puppet jerking on tangled strings Huaming dithered between the head and the body. Finally he picked up the head. It was heavy and he needed both hands to carry it, staggering with the weight. The blood poured from it, like wine out of a jug. Returning to the body the little boy sat cross legged, the head in his lap, trying to fit it back onto the twitching body.

And then they came; the Chief Justice running for the first time in his adult life with his gown hitched up over his white knobbly knees, his hands stained black with ink for he had knocked over the pot in shock. Next the people, in dribs and drabs and then hundreds of them filling the courtyard of the Yamen; shopkeepers with red strings of cash dangling from the their hands, rickshaw chair pullers wringing their sweat soaked turbans in their hands, the man with the deformed face and his half naked beggar friends, and lastly the women in black, leaning on sticks, hobbling on bound feet or being carried like sacks of rice on children's backs. Some of them still in nightclothes looked as if they had not seen the light of day for decades. They stood and gaped at the boy on the scaffold and the ridiculously blue sky. None of them had ever heard the ancient gong before. No one could even remember the last time it had been used. But they knew what it meant: the most terrible of gongs, which sounded its appeal for justice with a sacrificial head.

It was many hours before Wesley and the Chief Justice were able to persuade Huaming to leave his brother's body. As he stood up to leave he carefully undid his brother's pigtail which had been wrapped around the front of his head, in the practical way of a workman, so as not to obstruct the falling blade. With blood encrusted hands, he gently stroked it back into place then picked up the wooden placard that had fallen from his brother's neck.

My hands are tied. I can only die a dutiful son.

SHANTOU

12

An old foreigner in a frayed, grey cotton suit waited on the quay at the port of Shantou. Like faithful old hounds, his suitcase and battered briefcase sat at his heel. The newspaper, carefully stowed under arm, remained unopened. At a glance, other foreigners would have quickly categorised him as a teacher, a missionary who had stayed too long and gone native; an oddball, who in truth belonged to neither camp, an embarrassment on the few occasions he was crass enough to accept an invitation to the Club.

The years had indeed not been kind to Pastor Wesley Hutton. Age, disappointment and a Chinese diet had eaten away at the firm muscle tone of his easy New England youth. He dangled like a wooden puppet, all legs and arms, his shoulders stooping slightly forward as if a couple of strings were loose. He retained the curious bouncing walk that, as a young man, had counted as enthusiasm but was now a hallmark of eccentricity.

In the blue distance of the bay, Wesley watched one of the port's pilots make a precarious leap from his motor launch onto the rope ladder dangling over the side of a departing steamship. The man climbed to the lower deck, welcomed by the outstretched arms of crew members strategically placed to catch him if he should fall. The upper deck was spotted with the black heads of the passengers, above them sea gulls swirled like confetti. Some of the passengers still waved hands and hats in the direction of the quay, but if there had been any one there to see them off, they had long since departed. The tugs hooted as they released their charges and Wesley had a clear view over the bay to the garden island of Gok Sek that had become his home.

Eagerly his eyes wandered along the dark, winding line of fluffy green trees that marked the well-worn path up the hill to the church and the surrounding village. The lazy sea breeze barely disturbed the waves, but carried to him the rustling of trees, Sunday morning hymns, and the tired voices and shuffling feet of children returning home from school. Wesley had arrived back from Guangzhou by boat that afternoon, from a meeting with visiting representatives of the American Association of Baptist Churches. The summer heat was on the wane earlier in Shantou than Guangzhou and he removed his Panama hat, unconsciously holding it on his chest, as if paying his last respects at a graveside.

In the distance a small white motorboat charged its smoky way towards him; the raucous, rattling of the old engine pierced the golden day like bullets from a Gatling gun. The closer it came the quicker it seemed to move, until suddenly, the motor slowed to a series of short splutters, gave a final thump and then stopped. The little boat was left bobbing helplessly on the water some five or six feet away from the quay. There were about half a dozen passengers, all of whom were foreigners. In the incestuous treaty port community, Wesley knew them all. Among them was the portly wife of a former American marine, now Chief Pilot at the port and known in treaty ports from Hong Kong to Qingdao as Shantou JD, because of his penchant for a certain brand of liquor. There was also a young enthusiastic California doctor who specialised in skin diseases, as well as the new and very young French priest, who on the one occasion he and Wesley had met socially, insisted on speaking French, even though Wesley could not understand a word of the language. Shantou JD's wife waved and Wesley put his hat back on his head, touching it to acknowledge her. She and her husband had been in Shantou nearly as long as Wesley himself. A rope was thrown to a barebacked coolie on the quay, who hauled the little boat to the steps. The task appeared to require as little effort as lifting a cup of water to his lips.

"Not today, thanks." Wesley waved down to the grinning driver of the boat. He did not like motorboats; everyone knew it. Modern contraptions, they shook up his stomach and confused his thoughts. Last year, and much against his better judgement, he had taken a motorboat and as a result was unable to preach the following Sunday. He had pleaded illness and asked Huaming, now a so-called native Pastor, to fill in for him. Huaming's young son might tease him, calling him an Ancient Piece of Wood, but Wesley preferred to make the crossing between Shantou and Gok Sek as he had always done, by rowing boat. It took well over an hour, compared to half an hour by motorboat, but he had long since ceased to respond to the youthful dictates of clockwork time.

Wesley was the only passenger in the little rowing boat and he revelled in the quiet. Leaning back against his suitcase in the prow, he loosened his shoelaces, stretched out his legs and closed his eyes. The late afternoon sunshine teased out the tired wrinkles around his eyes and almost eased his tight jaw into a smile. Yet however benevolent the late summer sunshine, he never really enjoyed it. He had bought a newspaper this morning but had not opened it. He knew the date: the 31st of August 1921. Could it really be over a quarter of a century since Huaguang's suicide?

Every year, as people sighed with relief at the cooling of the weather, the trauma of that awful event came back to haunt him. He could have, should have, done something. At its worst the unwanted memories took the form of an insatiable plague of night time ants crawling over him, eating away at his eyes, his nose, his testicles, the pain burning and festering for days.

After the suicide, Wesley had felt it was his duty to go with his little pupil Huaming, the servant Young Chen, and the body back to the family home in Chaozhou, before going on to take up his post in Shantou. The great courtyard house where the Wen family had lived ever since anyone could remember lay in ruins and reeked of night soil that had not been removed. The surrounding land had been sold off and there were squatters in the outer courtyard. Of the members of the family that had made up the thirty chairs in Wen En's triumphant homecoming procession, there was little trace. Only Huaguang's widow Feng remained to look after the old people.

They arrived too late to save the boys' mother. On hearing of her son's great sacrifice she had somehow hobbled on her bound feet a mile or so from the house to a shady corner of an abandoned field and swallowed a piece of raw opium, dying in the end not from the poison but from choking on her own vomit. She was never to know that her elder son was to become a folk hero. The case was reopened and this time justice was swift. Her husband was exonerated, and the white-suited former Comprador for Coopers & Co. who had been responsible for the original murder, forced labour, and other smuggling and opium related crimes in the region, executed along with other members of his gang, for their wrongdoing.

Wesley heard all the details of the execution from Aunt Celia who had witnessed the event with her friend Mary Adams in Guangzhou and written to him about it.

Would you believe it! When the miserable wretches arrived at the Horse's Head execution ground the leader of the brigands turned out to be one of those too weak to walk. Our man pointed him out to us. He was carried in a wicker basket, a placard announcing the crime of murder around his neck. When it came to his turn however, he mustered the strength to climb the scaffold unaided. Hair matted with filth, gaunt and twisted with pain, it was hard to believe that he had once been the leader of such a notorious gang. At the last minute, before they put the noose around his neck, he raised his fist into the air.

"Down with the Manchus!"

The executioner quickly silenced his subversive cries and hit the poor unfortunate (for by this time it was impossible not to feel pity for him, despite his heinous crimes) on the back of the head with a baton and he fell to his knees. The crowd howled with delight and a great wailing arose from the female relatives, who threw themselves repeatedly to the ground in the manner of a bizarre Buddhist prayer ritual. Our man, who as usual had all the local gossip, told us that the brigand was the head of a large family, hence the crowd of relatives, even children, assembled for the occasion. These people! That they should let the innocents witness such a sight!

The whole affair was miserable beyond measure and even now, three days later as I write to you, I feel sick to the pit of my stomach. But my dear Wesley, for what it is worth, I can confirm to you and the poor Wen family that justice was done. I pray that Wen Huaguang will at last rest in peace.

After the execution the Emperor had given Huaguang

the posthumous title of Yin Jian, for martyrs in public service. On hearing this news his father Wen En, a shrivelled, shrunken skeleton in a stinking, torn gown, miraculously regained his clarity of mind. In his last days he questioned Wesley vigorously about Jesus Christ, the Trinity, the United States of America and the Republic. Wesley understood that he was a man of great intellectual ability and integrity. But when in the darkness of his final hours Wen En eventually declared himself for a Christian God, Wesley experienced none of the triumph he had so long anticipated, just a drowning despair at the enormity of the task that lay ahead

The pastor yawned, stretched and opened his eyes towards the island before him. They were near enough to see the beautiful houses with white verandas and well kept gardens built by the foreigners along the coast. In the early days of the treaty port, Chinese hostility had forced the small foreign community to seek refuge on the island. Now that most of the business and trade was carried out on the Shantou port side, the island had become a different kind of haven: a place for residential and holiday homes, for prayer, learning and healing. People came from hundreds of miles to attend the hospitals and schools set up by missionaries of different religious denominations.

The boatman gave one last pull on his oars, tucking them up in a trail of crystal drops, and the little boat thumped gently against the landing stage. The jetty was quiet, just a couple of dozy boat men and rickshaw drivers waiting for fares, and a one armed old fortune teller with a black turban and an old crow on a string. A small boy of about six or seven years old in shorts and a white shirt squinted up at Wesley and addressed his pastor in the Chinese way.

"Hello, Master Shepherd. Dad sent me."

"Good man!" Wesley smiled and handed the boy his briefcase, keeping the heavier suitcase to carry himself. In his early years in China Wesley had surprised himself with his ability to keep up appearances, even during the darkest moments of doubt. But he had become so practised at merging the private and the public that he was no longer aware he was making the distinction. The boy and Wesley set off up the hill to the church.

Despite the recent tempering of the heat, the moist cool of the narrow tree-shaded track was a welcome relief after the open sky. The crickets buzzed, and Wesley's leather soles crunched on the nutty, sandy ground. The boy's cloth shoes made no sound. Panting softly they climbed higher and higher. The sea disappeared from view, leaving the sunlight mottled ground and tunnel of trees before them. The quiet magic of Gok Sek was upon them and they did not speak. The path took a turn to the left; on the corner stood an ancient tree laden with fat green gourds. Wesley and his dishevelled flock had passed this way when they had first arrived on the island from Chaozhou all those years ago. Then he had welcomed the ripe gourds as a sign of plenty and knelt on the ground to give thanks to the Lord for their safe arrival.

At the time of his conversion to Christianity, old Wen En had ordered what remained of the family to sell up and go with Wesley.

"There is nothing left for us here. The end is nigh for me, and for my China, Confucian China. Christianity is the word of God, the way of the future. Go with the Pastor. Respect and honour him as your own father. Go and learn anew from him," he had told his only surviving son. In one tearful session Wesley had used a wooden bathtub to baptise Wen En, Huaming, the servant Young Chen and Huaguang's widow, Feng. And like Moses and the Israelites arriving in the Promised Land, they had all come to Gok Sek in time for Christmas.

A crow, startled by the passing of the Missionary and the boy, cawed into the sky. The spell was broken.

"Did you eat dog meat in Guangzhou? My friend says

that in Guangzhou dogs are the sweetest." The boy's eyes twinkled. It was an old joke between them.

Wesley laughed. "Foreign devils don't eat dog—you know that!"

"Did you see the French Cathedral then?"

Wesley nodded. "A magnificent building with great spires." He raised his left hand into the air to indicate the height. "But I prefer our little church here." The boy looked up at him, wide eyed.

"Why? We don't have a spire."

Wesley hesitated. "Because it is ours; the house we have built for God. It belongs to us all." How could he explain to the child that the church at Shantou was all he had left. With Huaming as Assistant, the local Baptist Community had grown from a handful to well over a thousand throughout the region and into the next province.

Wesley watched the boy struggling now with the weight of the briefcase, but never complaining, merely transferring it back and forth between hands. His name was Zheng, meaning upright, honest, and he was the youngest son of the servant Young Chen and Huaguang's widow, Feng. Wesley himself had married them thirteen years ago—no one could say that the couple had not been patient. Zheng was a beautiful child; high cheek-boned, pale skinned, his face was flawless. It was the face of an intelligent, cheeky boy, yet between the grins and bouts of tomfoolery, there was the unmistakable shadow of wisdom beyond his age. Such was the spirit of David waiting to fight Goliath, thought Wesley. Zheng was a child who had been born to make a difference. He deserved to inherit the earth.

At the top of the path they saw the square white pillars and great iron gates to the church, the red bougainvillea trailing like a royal cape over the walls of the compound. Wesley asked Zheng to come into the house for supper, but at that moment Huaming came along the road from the village and disappeared through the side gate into the compound. Zheng shook his head—his mother was expecting him.

"Next time, hey?" Wesley patted the boy on the head and gave him something for his trouble.

The sins of the fathers....he sighed as the boy hurried away into the village. His former pupil Huaming had great strengths, and deep down Wesley knew that he could not have achieved all that he had in Shantou without his help; indeed he was the closest thing he had to a son. But Huaming had not spoken to Young Chen since the day he had married his elder brother's widow and did his best to avoid the fruit of the union, including their youngest child, Zheng. A marriage between a lady and a former servant was beyond the pale. Wesley had long since given up trying to reconcile the two men, who were becoming increasingly stubborn with age.

The huge irongate creaked on its hinges as Wesley pushed it open. There was his funny little church in all its glory! It had the base of a Methodist chapel, a Greco-Roman portico and the blue and gold-tiered roof of a Chinese temple. When it had first been completed it had been an object of ridicule for some members of the foreign community: a bastard church for the Baptists. But Wesley did not care. It was his church, and he was proud of it.

"Master Shepherd! You're home!" Old Amah, pruning the roses in the garden, put down her scissors. Wesley put his finger to his lips to signal quiet. In the kitchen his wife was singing a song from a Chaozhou opera, the mysterious, undulating melody wafting towards him like incense. He remembered the first time he had heard her sing her native songs. The hidden sensations and joys in the mysterious quartertones—he had never heard anything like it. She was the exotic Princess of the Arabian Nights. Even after all these years his wife's simple melodies still captivated him. He stood for a few moments, his head on one side, his eyes half closed.

Then there she was—Grace: with her peculiar way of sensing things she always knew when he was home. She stood on the doorstep, grey haired, slightly plump in an old purple cotton trouser suit, smiling her crooked smile. He gave her a big American-style hug, but she pushed him away.

"Don't be so childish!"

Wesley washed, changed into an old Chinese gown that smelled of mothballs, and ate supper. Comfortable at last, he sat to down at his desk to catch up on church business. Old Amah clinked the crockery in the enamel bowl in the kitchen, dogs barked in the village below, and Grace sat knitting, rocking peacefully back and forth in the creaky old chair that Young Chen had made them for a wedding present. Wesley looked through the service and events list for the following week prepared by Huaming. Everything was in order and he turned to his real passion, his translation work. Ever since Wesley had arrived in Hong Kong as a young man to learn Chinese, he had had quite a reputation as a scholar. Apart from translations of Old Testament stories for use in missionary primary schools, over the last twenty-five years he had, with Huaming and other Chinese assistants, also produced an updated dictionary of the Chaozhou vernacular, a translation of the New Testament, and he was currently working on a translation of the work of his favourite Tang dynasty poet into English.

He took out some translations of Du Fu's earlier work to review.

> *Fallen boulders slant upon mountain trees*
> *and clear ripples trail sheets of algae.*
> *Towards evening I look for the road I must take,*
> *with tattered clouds flying past horse's flank.*

"What time is it?" Wesley was surprised. Although his wife was blind and could not see the face of the great grandfather clock in the corner of the room, whose hourly chime had long since given up the ghost, she never asked the time.

"Almost nine."

"Time for bed." She wound the spare wool back onto the ball, stuck the needles into it and, feeling for the little drawstring bag hanging from the arm of her chair, plunged the knitting into it.

Wesley listened to the slightly hesitant yet never-changing rhythm of her steps as she groped her way up the wooden staircase, and then the soft creaking of the floorboards above him. He sat for a long time before opening his briefcase and taking out a letter that had been given to him by a member of the church delegation in Guangzhou. Laying it on the table he smoothed over the velvety, white watermarked paper with the tips of his fingers. Thick and luxurious, it was so...civilised...so tempting. Carefully, he took it out of the envelope. He knew what it said, for he had opened it almost as soon as he had received it.

He looked again at the university crest, the firm confident black letters that bit into the paper. It was a letter from the President of the University of Berkeley, California no less, inviting him to apply for a Chair in Oriental Languages and Literature. What an honour! He knew that he ought to jump at the chance. It was high time the Baptist Association lived up to its rhetoric on the autonomy of native churches and left the Chinese to run their own affairs. If the foreigners did not retreat voluntarily, the Chinese nationalist movement would eventually force them out. The writing had long been on the wall, and when the time came, even their little paradise island would not escape the turmoil. The world had changed. The revolution of 1911 had been as old Wen En predicted, finished All Under Heaven with the emperor at the apex of an ordered world. China was now a republic with a new flag, modern schools, education for some girls and an end to both foot binding for women and the symbol of Manchu oppression for men, the wearing of the pigtail. But ripples from the Great War in Europe were already lapping on China's shores. The outrage caused all over China by the post war Versailles Treaty, which gave Germany's concessions in Shangdong Province to Japan instead of returning them to China, had led to disillusionment with the duplicity and moral leadership of the West. It was becoming ever more uncomfortable to be Chinese and Christian. All this Wesley knew, but he could not go to Berkeley, for he could not take Grace.

Grace, Blind Singing Girl from Guangzhou, had become his wife. US Immigration law did not permit the naturalisation of the Chinese wives of American citizens. Even if exceptions could be made—Wesley tried to imagine Grace and her Old Amah in their Chinese-style pyjama suits going around the streets of Berkeley, or Grace's voice sounding harsh and metallic as she tried so hard to make the unfamiliar English words, or the fear and confusion on Amah's face, and of course the fox-furred ladies sniggering behind white gloved hands. He felt dizzy and sick, symptoms he recognised as homesickness. America—the other world—the place he had left over thirty years ago. All of a sudden thoughts of home flooded his senses. All the things he had long since ceased to miss or crave. Cheese: mature cheese, creamy white. Tomatoes: from his mother's greenhouse served with fresh bread and butter for Sunday lunch. When he had first come to China certain tastes and habits had revolted him, the worst being the sight of people eating garlic fishheads, gleefully sucking out the brains and savouring the eyes. It was, however, as they said in the clubs and salons of the treaty ports, amazing what one got used to, and fishheads without the garlic in addition to chicken's bottom had become a part of his household menu. Both delicacies were said to keep women young; Amah said they were good for his wife's health.

Over the years Wesley had carefully blocked off thoughts of home behind a great dam at the back of his mind, classifying them as indulgences, weakness of spirit, lack of fortitude. He knew many who sought the cure for this foreigners' malady in drink or sex; many good men and women and regular churchgoers too. In the early days of his marriage he had tried various tactics himself, and even taught Grace, and by extension Amah, to make beef stew and dumplings seasoned with salt and pepper, like his mother used to make. But the smell of the cooking had contorted his guts with a bizarre pain, and as the pepper was used up the recipe had mutated under the guidance of Amah into pork stew with soy sauce and Chinese mushrooms, and he had not protested. He sighed. The dam must hold. To give in now would to be to lose his life's work, and with it himself. He laughed: a great chortle bubbling up from his belly.

Dear Grace! How wise she was. She herself often made the joke that Old Father in Heaven must have been having an off day the time he entwined the red ribbon of fate around their fingers as babies. Grace! She had simply turned up out of the blue, one Sunday morning after church, not long after his arrival in Gok Sek. Her Amah had brought her into the compound, begging Wesley to help them. Through the tears and grabbing, imploring hands, Wesley understood that after Huaguang's suicide Grace had lost her mysterious "gift", and with it the ability to sing, and thus her livelihood. At first Amah had thought that her voice would eventually return, but after four months it had not, and they were wasting away

Wesley found Grace and her Amah a place in the village and they stayed. At first Wesley was too busy with his new job to take much interest in the odd pair. But as Grace's condition improved she became a regular member of the congregation. The first time Wesley remembered taking notice of her was when he saw her standing at the church door one Sunday handing out hymnbooks. She was statuesque by Chinese standards, as tall as the biggest of Northern Chinese men. Unlike the time he had seen her in Guangzhou, she wore no make up, her square face defiant and pure.

The following day he went to visit her in her lodgings on some pretext about the church choir. When he asked her if she would be interested in joining, she merely shook her head. With the help of the Amah, he had eventually persuaded her to come and listen, and a few months later the miracle happened; her voice returned. Everyone said she was blessed with the gift of angels and it was not long before Wesley handed over the running of the choir entirely to her. She proved an energetic enthusiastic member of the church. She did not expect much, yet nothing was too much trouble. She was physically strong and not afraid of hard work. She had even been known to carry some of the ladies with bound feet up from the village or hospital to the church on her own back, as if she were a maid, for her feet had never been bound. Just like his former American fiancée, Grace had a way with people that Wesley knew he lacked. She always knew what to say, how to comfort people, how to make them smile. Furthermore, once Grace and her Amah came into his life the whole host of mundane irritations and misunderstandings between himself, members of the congregation, shopkeepers, printers and the like simply disappeared into thin air.

They married just after Chinese New Year in 1899. Wesley's good friend, an Irishman and the Catholic Bishop of the Diocese, had foreseen with great accuracy the present dilemma and privately advised Wesley against the match.

"A good white girl will come along, if you just hold your horses. Keep her as a mistress if you must man—she probably wouldn't expect much better—but for God's sake don't marry her!" Wesley did not heed the Irishman's advice. Her past did not matter and he knew the

105

distinction between a singing girl and a prostitute even if others did not. He was, however, still a young man full of ideals and passion. She would make a perfect partner for his part in God's great enterprise in China. He could not be persuaded against the marriage.

Wesley moved his neck from side to side to ease the tension. Sometimes he had wondered if the marriage was indeed cursed. They were happy enough, but there had been no children. After years of trying, Grace's only pregnancy had ended with a stillborn child. His friend Sandy Macleod, who had died five years ago and was distinguished as being one of the first American doctors in Shantou, had put it down to some of the concoctions she had been given as a child to make her blind. "...and most probably made her sterile, too." He had patted Wesley on the shoulder in the manner of a teammate at the end of a prestigious ball game which they had unexpectedly lost, floundered briefly around the back of his desk, since he knew Wesley did not drink, and hauled a gin bottle from the bottom drawer. Pouring the liquor into two grubby mugs, he shoved one into his friend's hand.

"Medicinal purposes?"

Grace had not sung for over a year after that, and although she and Wesley still slept together under the big red and white North American patchwork quilt that his mother and sister had sent for their wedding present, Wesley never tried to make love to her again, and she never asked him to.

He got up and went to stand at the open window overlooking the village cradled between the hills. The evening cooking fires had been extinguished hours ago. In the moonlight, the grey tiles of the houses seemed to be covered in a supernatural Christmas snow. Now and again a shout or a tired wisp of conversation drifted upwards through the silence: *the day Thou gavest is ended.*

For better or worse Gok Sek was Wesley's home. He was the Shepherd; these people his flock. He had crafted this community of God out of a raggle-taggle band of outcasts, cripples, opportunists and malcontents. He had broken the ground for the new church with his bare hands, sweating with the labourers to lay the bricks. These people depended on him to lead the way. He could not abandon them now. There was so much work still to be done, still so many that had not heard the word of the Lord.

Closing the window, Wesley went back to his table, folded the letter and put it back in its envelope. Lifting the glass cover off the oil lamp, he dipped the corner of the letter into the flame. With a gentle roar, it greedily devoured the thick paper. Wesley held onto the top of the letter for as long as possible, turning it this way and that, encouraging the flame. At last he dropped it into his teacup. The keen flame spluttered in the residual liquid, leaving a smoking, black mush of tealeaves and ash.

13

The old, one-armed fortune teller squatted against a shady wall on the docks in Shantou. With his scrawny black crow, little wooden table and tiles with pictures on them, he was at least as well known as any other major landmark in Shantou, except that he was not always to be found in the same place. With the crow perched on his shoulder, he went wherever business took him, sometimes sitting outside shops, sometimes getting the boat over to Gok Sek to wait for the foreigners to take their evening promenade by the sea. Today, a passenger ship was leaving for Singapore, and as usual he was doing a good business amongst the migrants waiting for departure.

They always wanted to know the same thing—holding their breaths in reverend anticipation as the crow disdainfully picked its way among the little tiles of fate laid out on the rickety wooden table—would they get rich?

Some said the fortune teller was a wise man who had seen many things; that he had been a Minister to the Emperor or a Taoist monk in his past lives, and in this life had been press ganged into coolie service as a boy, surviving the choking guano pits of Peru, where he had lost his right ear and his right forearm as punishment for trying to escape. Others said he was a thief and a crook who had worked as an overseer in sugar plantations in Jamaica and had been injured in a fight with his boss over the man's wife. But whatever people said, everyone knew that nothing happened in Shantou without him knowing about it.

With the string round its leg, the crow scratched its way across the table, taking its time to turn over the tiles with its beak: an axe, a bride, and a coffin. The old woman having her fortune told gasped in horror, covering her toothless mouth with her hand. The fortune teller rarely said much, preferring that the customers furnished their own interpretations. In this instance the old woman never even solicited his wisdom. Rising quickly she hobbled on her bound feet back across the quay to the passengers, corralled and waiting for departure. Shouting the nickname of a relative she poked her stick at intervals into the line as if looking for a lost dog in a field of maize. But her voice was lost on the wind.

Expectantly, the fortune teller looked up and down the quay at the familiar scene: the ever-present lines of bare-backed coolies with pieces of old sacking in their hands, lining up to walk the gangplank and pick up their loads from a ship. When their time came, they swung the pieces of sacking over their heads to protect the back of the neck and shoulders, and braced themselves to receive the load from their two colleagues on deck. Trembling under the weight they placed one flat foot directly in front of the other with the precision of dancing girls, and made their precarious way back down another gangplank. The thump of sacks being dropped, a warning shout, the creaking of the planks, the tinkling of an old bell on a distant buoy, the surging shoving protests of the crowd, all ebbed and flowed on the tidal breeze.

In the distance, sauntering slowly towards him, the fortune teller saw a gentleman in a black cotton gown and trilby hat, carrying a rolled black umbrella: the Chinese Pastor from the Gok Sek Church, Wen Huaming. The fortune teller grunted. Unlike other priests at other churches in Shantou, on the few occasions he had gone up to the Gok Sek church to enjoy the fresh air, Pastor Wen had always moved him on. Once he had been outside the foreign bank in Shantou when the Pastor had gone in through the shiny wood and glass swing doors. And what do you know? The bank's flunkies came out and moved him. The fortune teller cleared his throat noisily and spat on the ground to his left. Christian pigs; always stirring up trouble with their churches that disturbed the feng shui, and barbarian practices of drinking blood and drowning orphan babies at birth. But something was afoot that day for he had never seen Pastor Wen down on the docks before. Oh no! The only surviving son of the illustrious Wen family would never sink so low! Look at him now marching along with his head high, eyes fixed ahead as if he were a great official like his father. Did he not realise what people really thought of him? Slave of the crystal-eyed foreign devils!

Anticipating trouble, the fortune teller began to clear away the tiles on his table, throwing them in handfuls into a little black bag hanging at his waist. Suddenly an angry roar came from the lines of passengers. Impatient with the formalities people at the back were pushing and shoving. With a bombardment of curses and truncheons, members of the ship's crew waded into the mêlée and a sullen order was quickly restored. The fortune teller's leathered face remained impassive beneath his grubby white turban. Some things were as inevitable as a whore getting the pox. The British had their procedures for ships bound for Singapore. Prior to boarding, tickets had to be checked, all passengers had to be cleared by a doctor, and at the very last moment, a Customs official would board the ship to confirm the head count, which he would wire ahead to the authorities in Singapore.

The fortune teller scanned the lines of the passengers. Sitting on their bedding rolls, the women with babies swaddled to their backs stared blankly forward, defeated, even before they had begun their journey to a new life. Here and there he was able to pick out a familiar face. At the front of the queue he spotted a large group, the dregs of another family whose reputation preceded them. Again the fortune teller cleared his throat and spat. The thick green spittle gleaned pristine in the gutter. Irritated by it and by uncomfortable associations, he scuffed it into oblivion with the toe of his soleless shoe.

The foreign doctor and his assistants in white coats checked the passenger's one by one, pushing and pulling them like horses; mouths, eyes, hair, skin, chests. A young man, a woman then a little girl of three or four years old: their daughter. The assistant called to the doctor. The little girl stood as ordered, her thin bare arms outstretched, palms turned upwards. Like an abandoned angel she stared at her feet. The doctor came over and raised the front of her shirt to look at her stomach. Stepping forward, but keeping a dubious distance, he pulled the front of the child's pants, peering briefly down them. Retreating quickly he shook his head and held out his own hands to an assistant who sprayed him with disinfectant.

The child tried to follow her mother and father but they were already hurrying to the gangplank; a burly sailor with a stick blocked her way.

"Mama!" the child screamed. Her mother looked back only once then turned her back on the child, deliberately hiding herself amongst the crowd of passengers climbing the gangplank.

"Mama!" The child tried to push past the sailor but he grabbed her by the scruff of the neck. "Mama!" Again and again the pitiful cries rang along the quay as the child strained at her leash.

The fortune teller was not surprised to see Pastor Wen pushing his way through the crowd to talk to the doctor—

here the Christian pig goes again, meddling in the business of others. The doctor listened then nodded, and Pastor Wen went over to the child. Meticulously lifting his gown above his knees so it would not drag on the floor, he bent down to speak to her. She nodded. He hoisted her onto his shoulders and began to walk up and down the quay next to the ship. Desperately the child looked up at the lines of faces peering down from the deck.

"Mama! Mama!"

But the fortune teller saw the parents and the rest of the family scuttling down into the hold of the ship. They were not going to risk forfeiting their precious tickets for the sake of a diseased daughter.

"Mama, Mama!" Long after the ship had departed the fortune teller sat cloaked in thickening shadows. The child's cries mingled with those of the circling seagulls, as Pastor Wen put her in the rowing boat with him to take her back across the bay.

*T*hings did not work out as Pastor Huaming had hoped with the little girl, who said that her name was Lai Di, or "Next a Brother", and that she had no other name. That night he took her straight to the Mission Hospital. As always the young California doctor was working late. Putting on a pair of gloves, he asked Lai Di in perfect local dialect, if it was all right if he had a look at her tummy. Seeing his wild blond hair and white coat, the child backed into the far corner of the room.

"Answer the doctor!" Huaming snapped.

"Have you been itchy?" The doctor said softly, bending down so that he was her height and moved slowly towards her. The child looked into his blue fisheyes and nodded.

"Can you show me where?" She stuck out her left arm and with her right pulled down the side of her trousers. The skin around the side of her legs and genitals was raw and bloodied with constant scratching. The doctor sucked air in between his teeth and raised the child's shirt to look under her armpits. Her skinny body started to shiver and tears rolled down her face.

"Curse these goddamn people. It's scabies! That's all! I can cure her completely in three weeks."

*H*uaming had been confident that a member of her family would appear to claim the girl, or that someone from the community would offer to have her—as a maid perhaps. But three weeks passed and no one came. Furthermore word got around that the child was diseased. When he asked amongst the congregation if they knew anyone who might take her in, they prevaricated: maybe a wife's cousin, or the friend of a husband's brother. But no one ever got back to him.

When Lai Di first came to live with Huaming and his family it was supposed to be a temporary arrangement. "It's our duty to provide a moral example to the community and show some charity to the orphan," Huaming told his wife, Jade.

"So many orphans in Shantou. Why this particular child?" Jade carried on slowly turning the handle of her sewing machine and did not look up from the shorts she was making for her son. Surprised by her unusually forthright expression of opinion, Huaming could not think of a satisfactory answer. In the end he resorted to the old staples.

"As Christians we cannot be seen to pass by on the other side. The doctor assures me she is no longer infectious, but she will sleep in the kitchen, away from the other children. It won't be forever..."

14

Pastor Wen Huaming's little daughter Manying always remembered the day Lai Di arrived at their home on the island of Gok Sek. She was brought one spring day in 1922 by a fat, smiling American nurse from the hospital, who gushed an enthusiastic attempt at some kind of Chinese. Not understanding a word, her mother gave the foreigner the benefit of the doubt and offered tea. Clutching her meagre belongings knotted up in an old piece of sheet, Lai Di perched like a bony imp at her side on the big wood and rattan armchair in the sitting room,

"Like your dress. Pretty." Manying pointed at Lai Di's pink and white, western-style dress. The nurse and her mother laughed awkwardly, and Manying was sure that the tiny earthenware teacup would to be crushed between the thick thumb and fingers of the nurse's hand.

"How old are you?" Manying's mother asked Lai Di. The child did not respond.

"Doesn't talk much." This time the nurse's words were just about comprehensible.

"One step at a time," her mother responded with the universal platitude for such situations.

"I'm a tiger and Manying's a sheep. What are you?" Manying's six-year-old brother Manye asked referring to the year of their births. For fear of missing anything important he was playing half in and half out of the house.

Lai Di hesitated then whispered, "A snake."

Expecting a reaction Manying looked at her mother and saw her take a sharp breath.

*T*he arguments started after Lai Di moved in.

"Why can't she eat in the kitchen with the maid? I won't have that piece of flotsam at our supper table. She is just not family." Manying's mother clattered the teacups on their bamboo drainer and slopped tea into her father's teacup.

"She can sleep in the kitchen but she should eat with us and go to school with the children." Manying's father ignored the tea, rose from his chair and went over to his desk.

"Of all the street children in China, why that raggle-taggle orphan? Why us?"

"She needs to learn to read and write so she will not be a burden to us in the future."

"Future? You said it would just be temporary! I won't have it, I tell you. She was born in the year of the snake. Slimy, devious and not to be trusted." Manying's mother would have stomped out of the room if her bound feet had allowed it. Instead she made fists to beat the arms of her chair and glared. Manying's father took his hat from the stand.

"I am going to the church. Don't wait up."

*I*t soon became apparent that Lai Di was far and away the brightest of the children. When she first arrived she could not even hold a writing brush, but once in school she quickly made up the lost time. Soon she could read more characters than the other children and her calligraphy was light and clear, unlike Manye's impatient scribble and Manying's shaky strokes and messy inkblots. While Lai Di did sums in her head, casting her eyes briefly up at the ceiling as if party to some divine vision, the other children tortuously lined up ebony beads on the abacus in order to produce the correct answer—clack, clack, clack. The only subject where anyone could give her a run for her money was English. The same teacher taught them Mandarin as well as English. She was a benevolent dragon of an American spinster who had in fact been born in Shandong province to missionary parents and had spent only a few years at college in her own native land, yet oddly she had acquired a pucker English accent. She maintained it was Young Chen's son, Zheng, who far and away had the best command of the language. Nevertheless, Lai Di usually got the top marks because Zheng, a boy, was just too lazy to apply himself to the discipline of classroom tests.

*D*espite her double burden of domestic chores and homework, Lai Di always managed to finish both jobs without fault and in record time, so that Manying's mother had no choice but to let her go and play with the other children on the hills surrounding the village.

Lai Di had not been living with them long when she suggested Manying might help her comb and braid her hair. Manying was over the moon to help the elder child. She skipped over the living room, standing on her tiptoes to reach the red lacquer box in which the elastic bands and ribbons were kept. Fifty gentle strokes until Lai Di's course black hair gleamed with a sheen like feathers. With deep breaths and great precision Manying would make the parting dead centre, just as Lai Di liked it.

"Ouch, you're pulling to hard!" Lai Di gave her a sharp pinch on the arm, and a subtle but practised elbow right in the pit of Manying's stomach.

Always careful to be demure and undemanding in the house and in the presence of adults, Lai Di dutifully went about her tasks. But her pointed face, which one day would be considered beautiful, would soon twist with spite if the play did not go her way. Stocky, rather than tall, she was the strongest of all the children. Her little legs and arms had grown like small tree trunks; no doubt, it was said, from the toil necessitated by the hardship of her early life. Even as a small child Lai Di was streetwise. It was always she who had all the ruses and invented the new games. The boys, Zheng and Manye, never resented this prowess, simply co-opting her as an honorary boy in their play.

Manying never really knew what to make of her "big sister." Indeed, it was Manying who first affectionately started calling Lai Di by this title for she always wanted to be her friend, yet she soon learned to be wary of her vicious moods. Sometimes Manying resented Lai Di's intrusion into their lives, and above all her friendship with her brother. The two of them were as thick as thieves. But on the other hand she looked up to the feisty girl who, for better or worse, was leaving such mark on their lives. At times even her own father was heard to chide his lazy son, "If only you were as clever as Lai Di."

One day the children sat at the table in the living room doing their homework. The door and windows had been left open to coax a breeze from the mire of summer heat. Dipping her brush in the ink on the ink stone, Manying carefully copied the character for horse onto her paper; three short horizontal strokes for the mane, one, two, three, a vertical one through them slightly to the right for the neck, a long curve around to make the body and then her favourite part, four slanted dots for the feet, one, two, three, four. It did indeed look like a horse. That was the joy of Chinese characters. They were pictures. Even the more complicated ones that she could already recognise but not write, were pictures within pictures, each with its own story to tell. English letters, she thought, were far inferior, merely crude symbols for harsh sounds.

Manying's work was punctuated by great sighs and the

thumping of feet from Manye, whose gaze, more often than not, was drawn to the temptations of the garden beyond the open door. He hated studying, preferring to climb trees or play in rock pools. Manying ignored him.

"I can't stand this!" Manye thumped his pencil down in frustration. "Ping, ping, ping, ping. Characters that are pronounced the same are so stupid anyway."

"Let me see!" Lai Di, sitting next to him, pulled his book towards her. Manying raised a disparaging eyebrow. Lai Di always knew the answers to everything. "Ping for apple, ping for flat, level, ping for comment, criticise."

Manye's face was screwed up with the effort of concentration.

"And this one?"

"Ping for rely on. Shall I write it for you?"

Manying heard her mother calling her from the bedroom upstairs and felt a wave of nausea rising in her throat; the task she dreaded all week. There was no escape from it. It was time to help her mother wash her feet, which had been bound in the traditional way when she was a child. Swallowing hard, she put down her brush and wiped her hands again and again on her apron.

"Don't go without me!" she warned the others, but the authority intended was lost in a shiver of fear. She knew full well that as soon as they had finished their lessons, they would go out to play, forgetting all about her.

Manying entered the bedroom as the maid was leaving. Immediately the heat soaked away her strength, and the stench of stale flesh from her mother's bound feet made her guts churn. There was only one window in the room, which her mother kept closed for fear of flies and mosquitoes. Manying steadied herself on the doorframe, wondering if it might be possible that she could hold her breath for the entire fifteen minutes necessary to complete the dreaded task.

Her mother sat like a shrivelled witch on a three-legged wooden stool leaning against the bed. Her still bright eyes were shrunk back in her skull, which seemed too heavy for her body. Her near side was in shadow, her right side illuminated by the light from the window, as if caught in the still of a black and white photograph. The pink roses on the large chipped enamel bowl at her feet, and her red silk wedding slippers that she kept on the dresser, were the only spots of colour in the room. Steam rose like prayers from the water in the bowl, and her little bandaged feet stuck out of the bottom of her black trousers, withered as dead twigs drooping in winter snow. Steeling herself, Manying went to the dresser and carefully moving the tiny wedding slippers to one side, opened a draw and took out clean bindings and a pot of salt.

"Here you are! Do I have to wait all day? Is your father home yet?" Her mother's voice was high-pitched and brittle, always sounding harsher than she intended. Manying shook her head. He had gone to Shantou that morning on the boat. Kneeling, Manying measured out the salt into the hot water just as the American doctor had shown her.

"Ahhh. How I eat bitterness!" But Manying was immune to the repetition of her mother's complaints and stories. Steadily she stirred the water with the single wooden chopstick reserved for the purpose.

"Still too hot!" Her next line was right on cue.

Moving the bowl, Manying took her mother's feet onto her knees. They were hard and cold, like stones in her hands. One by one she massaged them gently in the palm of her hands to stimulate the circulation.

"Ahhhh, Manying. You're a good girl. What would I do without you? I am old. I have always been old. Ever since the day they came to bind my feet...."

Manying could recite by heart what was coming next. Taking a deep breath she concentrated on unwinding the layers of white bindings around her mother's feet, trying to block out her mother's litany of woes. She worked quickly, and soon two yellow, scaly, shrunken stumps rested in the palms of her hands. Her mother winced and looked away.

"See how I suffer... But at least you can run free upon the hills. My generation eats bitterness so that yours will not. Look at me, cooped up in the house all day with nothing to think about except whether the maid is buying cabbages with maggots inside them again and pocketing the difference, or what happened to that Italian nun from the Catholic church who ran off with a Taoist priest."

"Ah Ma! You know what happened!" Manying interrupted impatiently. "Dad says they founded the Temple of the Hundred Virgins in the French concession in Shanghai where men and women together received absolution for their sins." She picked up a metal nail file and lifted up the left foot to find the toe nails; black and horny, bent back underneath and difficult to get to. She felt a wave of sickness rising to her mouth and tried to distract herself.

"You'll never guess! The other day Young Uncle Chen told me that the French authorities have shut the temple down and the nun and monk have gone off to Sichuan Province where they achieved nirvana by jumping hand-in-hand off the top of Emei Mountain!"

Mother flinched as Manying eased a crushed toe away from the foot in order to reach the nail. She was dizzy with relief when the filing was over and her mother closed her eyes and lowered her feet into the salt water out of sight.

"Ahhh! Your father used to love my feet! I will never forget... on our wedding night he held them in his hands in their little red slippers..." 'Like baby robins,' he said, nestling them and stroking them. Then, gently, very gently with his forefinger, like this," Mother stroked the back of her hand, "he parted the embroidered petals of the trim and touched the white inner sock... More hot water! Did that girl leave any in the jug?"

Sloshing the water into the enamel bowl, Manying wished that her mother would let the maid or Lai Di wash and bind her feet. But she understood that her mother was ashamed; such was the intimacy of the grime and suffering that no one other than she and the American doctor had ever seen her mother's feet without their bandages.

After the 1911 revolution Zheng's mother, Aunt Feng, had been the first among the local women to unbind her feet, an act Manying knew her father much admired. Over the years, with each new anti-foot binding initiative, her mother had tried to follow suit. At first she had prayed to her new Christian God to help her endure the painful process, but she whispered to Manying that she found it difficult to believe in a God who did not have a face, and whose church, with whitewashed walls and a coarse wooden cross, was so plain. The fact that the Christians did not make offerings to God also troubled her. One Good Friday a few years ago she had plucked up the courage to suggest to father that regular gifts of fruit and money might make the God more amenable. Her father had choked on his soup and wiped his mouth with the back of his hand.

"What kind of chicken shit is this, old wife? Do you set out to make me lose face? It is just such primitive superstition that keeps China poor and backward. If I ever hear you say such a thing again, I shall beat you myself with a slipper."

Manying knew all too well her mother's desperation. Last Chinese New Year, when her mother made her annual visit to her maternal home, she had taken Manying and secretly gone to the temple. Manying had never been in a temple before. At the gate they bought incense sticks and paper money from a crippled boy whose legs were folded, wasted and useless beneath him, sitting on wooden board with wheels. Unsure what to do, she tagged along at her mother's side.

"Just copy me, Manying."

Jostling with the crowds they lit their incense sticks from the huge cast iron burncr, bowing several times to the gold statue of the Buddha before placing them in the sand in the burner. Manying watched as the charcoal line of smoke from her stick mingled with the sweet smoke of hundreds of sticks rising to heaven. Moving on, they tossed chunks of paper money into the great furnace to the right of the shrine where the Buddha, so calm and compassionate, looked down at her with half-closed eyes, like a sleeping baby, around him the host of Buddishavas with all-knowing, ruby jewelled eyes. In front of the altar they kowtowed to the Buddha three times, but when mother prostrated herself, Manying started to cry and an old monk took her to one side.

"Be still! Let your mother pray awhile."

Watching her mother struggling to stand, her hands in prayer and then repeatedly lay herself down on the stone flags, mouthing prayers, Manying did not understand, and she was afraid. Who was this woman she called Mother?

At last they made offerings to Buddha, leaving them on the wooden table in front of the shrine, a plump mango, bananas and shiny apples with not even a tiny bruise.

But even with prayers to two gods, the foot unbinding process had proved too long and painful and eventually her mother had given up trying.

So there she was, sitting on her stool soaking up what little pleasure she could once a week from a bowl of luke warm water; and young as she was, Manying understood that her mother was out of place, someone people would rather forget about, left over from the time of the Emperors of China, and something of which her father had become deeply ashamed.

At last it was done, and the feet were rebound. As usual, when Manying got back downstairs, Manye and Lai Di were nowhere to be seen, their own books and papers piled neatly in the corner of the table. Through the open door a precious breath of late afternoon breeze flapped at the pages of Manye's copybook. Stomping to the kitchen, Manying shouted to the maid to collect the dirty water from the bedroom and made her escape into the sunshine.

Anticipating that her brother would have gone to call for his best friend, Zheng, she ran down the narrow sandy lane to the bottom of the village and into a winding alleyway between the houses. She stopped once to wretch the lumpy yellow and green contents of her stomach into the bushes.

Outside Zheng's house his father, Young Uncle Chen, was sawing wood for furniture and his mother, Aunt Feng, sat on a stool at the door watching him.

"Manying! You've just missed them." Aunt Feng raised her arm gracefully to the hill behind and smiled. She had the most beautiful smile Manying had ever seen: her whole face merry and light, her eyes so gentle, so kind. Manying loved her. At Christmas time in church when they read the Christmas story and sang Christmas carols, it was Aunt Feng's serene face that Manying saw as the Virgin Mary. Why couldn't her father make up with Young Uncle Chen? It was all very silly and confusing. Her mother had told her that Aunt Feng had once been a very grand lady in a big house and that was the trouble, but seeing her there, dressed like a maid in her old white blouse and black trousers with her bare feet cocked indecently on a stool in the soothing sunshine, Manying found it difficult to believe.

"Have some crispy rice? A nice bit left over from the bottom of the pot?" Aunt Feng picked up her shoes to put them on, but Manying was already on her way, kicking up a trail of dust in her wake.

"No thanks!" She waved.

Young Uncle Chen downed his saw and, shading his eyes against the sun, shouted after her. "Make sure you're all back before dark. There's trouble brewing in Shantou."

Arms out like an airplane, Manying flew out of the village and up the narrow track between the trees. The raw heat of the day had long since expired and everything was light and easy. Higher and higher she climbed, exchanging the stale domesticity of the village for the crystal sea air and a chorus of crickets. The path petered out. There were no more trees, only spiky bushes and bare rock.

"Battle of the Red Cliffs!" Manye appeared from the top of a rock, a piece of cloth that Manying recognised as the greying remnants of an old towel he had cajoled off the maid last summer tied around his head like a bandit. On the opposite side of the path Lai Di and Zheng slowly drew their arms as if shooting arrows high into the air.

"It's the evil Cao Cao, caught in our trap!"

"Burn!" Another volley of imaginary burning arrows was fired down onto Manying. Fearless Manye jumped down from his rock leading the charge towards her.

"Kill! Kill!"

Manying's heart sank. Whenever they played stories from the novel *The Romance of the Three Kingdoms*, they made her the baddy, Cao Cao. It wasn't fair.

She knew it was useless to run away, for they were all much faster than she, so when the inevitable happened she prepared to defend herself with words. Lai Di pushed her to her knees, but she did not struggle.

"I am the Great Liu Bei," announced Manye in front of her with his arms folded across his chest. "This is my blood brother Guan Yu," he pointed to Zheng.

"And I am the Mightly Wizard Zhu Geliang, and you are our prisoner!" Lai Di finished triumphantly.

"Rubbish! Guan Yu wasn't at the Battle of the Red Cliffs!" quipped Manying raising her head.

"Silence slave! If you wish to be freed, you must do what we say," Manye dithered searching his mind for an impossible task.

"Climb to the top of the Dragon's Head!" Lai Di pointed to the top of a flat- topped pinnacle of rock at the edge of the cliff.

It was hopeless. There was no way out. Manye led the way up the path and Lai Di and Zheng, each holding an arm, marched Manying behind. Reaching the place from where the ascent of the rock began they released her, standing back in a guard formation.

"The Little Lamb is scared!" Lai Di scrabbled up onto a rock, disappeared round the back of another to reappear a moment later. "Little Lamb can only make daisy chains! Little Lamb can only make daisy chains!" Her voice echoed throughout the valley.

Biting deep into her bottom lip Manying began to climb. She was much smaller than all the others and the rocks were big and cruel on her knees. Nearing the top she saw once more the terrifying final step that needed to be made in order to stand on the piece of flat rock at the top. All the others had climbed up many times before, Manye daring them to stand on one leg once they got there. But below her was the long drop to the blinding blue sea. She could not do it. But Zheng came up behind her.

"I'll hold you. Go on!" he whispered. His thin, warm hand grasped around her ankle and at last she was able to take that final step.

"Now stand on one foot," Manye hollered from below.

"Leave me alone! Hah Hah Hah!" To her surprise Manying found she was laughing and imagined that even the sailors on ships on the distant horizon would hear her and laugh too.

15

*T*he night was unusually dark. There was something not quite right about it. The children kept quiet and close together as they made their way home up the village street. For once, even Manye was afraid and he did not tell any of his favourite stories of red and green ghosts that devoured little girls. The trees swayed ominously in the breeze, calling to each other with shushing secret whispers. There were not many fireflies and those that there were kept to their ditches. Manying was afraid of them. Her teacher had taught her that they were insects, their light a special kind of electricity. But Big Brother had told her that they were lost souls of the dead. She was glad when they rounded the final bend and she saw the light from the windows of their house just below the crest of the hill.

Suddenly the children stopped dead in their tracks, grasping one another tightly. Heavy, uneven footsteps were coming towards them.

"Ghosts!" breathed Lai Di.

"A ghost with leather shoes," Zheng retorted.

Over the crest of the hill a figure appeared out of the

shadows, lurching towards them. Illuminated from the side by the light from the house, he was indeed a ghost in white.

"Dad?" Manye was first to recognise his father and ran towards him, arms outstretched. "Dad, what's the matter?"

Inside the house, seeing her father's torn gown, Manying thought that he too must have been climbing rocks. Shame-faced she looked down at her own bloodied knees. But hearing her mother's horrified scream, she knew it could not be. Father was without his hat and umbrella; he never went anywhere without them. Then she saw that his face was covered in dried blood and he held his folded handkerchief to a wound above his left ear. He limped over to the nearest chair, groaning, as he sat down.

"For God's sake, what happened?" Her mother was at his side. It was surprising just how fast she really could move on her bound feet.

"They called me a traitor. They called all Christians traitors. The fools!" Her father panted.

"Who did?"

"The bastard British shot into a crowd of Chinese students protesting against warlords and imperialists on Nanjing Road in Shanghai yesterday... eleven dead, twenty-one wounded. People were on the streets in Shantou today. Big banners: *Support the May Thirtieth Martyrs! Kill the Foreign Devils!* I went over to see what was happening and someone shouted, 'Here is a snake! It's the pig preacher who works for the foreign devils.' And then they turned on me."

Manying had never seen her father like this before, his face pale with fear and fatigue.

"Afterwards they left me lying in the gutter. No one would help me. Shopkeepers I have known for years turned their backs. In the end they let me shelter in the bank. The British had it all boarded up with armed guards outside."

"But you are not responsible for the actions of the

British." Her mother sounded so calm, so reasonable.

"When has that ever mattered? I tell you, it'll be the bloody Boxer Rebellion all over again and we Chinese Christians will be in for it as well. Bloody foreigners! The sooner the foreign bastards leave China to the Chinese the better. My son, run up to Pastor Wesley's and tell him to put a watch on the church! Then go to Young Uncle Chen's and tell him to look out for the school and hospital." Manye hesitated. Father never mentioned Young Uncle Chen.

"Well, go on boy! Don't pretend I don't know that you and his boy are as thick as thieves. Jump to it! The boatmen are organising a strike in protest of the massacre. With any luck we will be spared the worst of it. Madness, such madness!" He cradled his head in his hands. Manying was not sure if he was crying.

*M*anying always looked forward to Sundays. She enjoyed the cool, ordered calm of the church, the purposeful whispering people, and the women in their best cheongsam dresses. This particular Sunday, the first after all the trouble, she was particularly relieved to find everything going on as usual. The deep, slow sounds of the harmonium reverberated through her feet as she went in through the main door. There was Aunt Grace, handing out hymnals.

"Hello, Manying!" How come Aunt Grace always knew who people were even though she could not see them? She reached out her two hands to pull Manying's hands towards her and plonked a worn red hymnbook into her palm. Manying helped her mother to their pew on the right of the church, next to the side door. Opening her hymnal, she breathed with reverence the musty smell of beautiful foreign worlds and ages gone by. Referring to the wooden hymn board, she set about finding the hymns for the service. When she had finished she sat back and looked at the great crystal windows to her right that reached almost from floor to ceiling, and the small moon-shaped stained glass window, one of only two in the church, that was above the side door. It was a very simple window, but the sunlight streaming through it cast dazzling pools of purple and gold onto the stone floor and illuminated the backs and sides of the faces of the people in front as if they were like angels.

Pastor Wesley gave the opening address. Manying was fascinated by his shiny baldpate and the few remaining grey curls that flourished around his ears like blown cabbages. Aunt Grace led the choir and congregation in the first hymn: "All things Bright and Beautiful". She sang the first verse as a solo, her soaring voice making the back of Manying's neck tingle. After the lesson and another hymn Manying's father stood up to give the address. How she loved his stories and sermons! She scrunched her eyes tightly in anticipation of the pictures of mystical deeds and exotic lands that would soon appear in her head.

Almost as soon as her father had opened his mouth Manying knew that this was going to be no ordinary sermon. Instead of the honeyed melody of his usual delivery, the words were harsh and clipped.

"This week has been a difficult one for all Chinese Christians. Some of you, like me, have been abused by the mob for our so-called foreign faith. As Christians, we have learned to live with oppression, as indeed our own dear Saviour the Lord Jesus Christ was in his turn oppressed. But in this difficult time, let us never forget that our suffering is nothing compared to those who have given their lives for our nation. Thank the Lord: our church, our schools, our hospitals have, for the most part, survived unscathed." An expectant rustle of clothes and hymnbooks around the congregation, her father took a deep breath and folded up his script before continuing.

"The foreigners blame the May 30th protests on Bolsheviks, students and militarists and say that such is the chaos that occurs when we Chinese are left to our own devices. But I say that disturbance is no bad thing...."

Jaws dropped in the heavy silence.

"But no, I hear you say! This is not the way of the Christian. But you are wrong." He thumped his fist on the pulpit. "I tell you all, Jesus the Prince of Peace is the world's greatest disturber! For centuries his gospel has been troubling the world and this is exactly what it should be doing. Jesus himself said, 'Think not that I came to bring peace. I came not to bring peace, but a sword.' I say to you, the time has come for all true Chinese Christians to stand with our fellow compatriots, for only then will our nation be free of all foreign oppression." There was a long pause then a whispered murmur of assent followed by another and another and an unholy stamping of feet.

"Long live the Republic of China! Long live the Republic of China!"

Heads bowed, shoulders hunched, the various foreign members of the congregation hastily ushered their children out the side door. People averted their eyes. A little girl's straw hat, still with pink and yellow Easter ribbons, lay abandoned in an aisle, and no one came back for it. Pastor Wesley charged up onto the platform and squared up to face his flock. This time all he could do was open and close his mouth a few times like a fish, then flee in the wake of the other foreign devils. When wide-eyed with excitement Manye and Zheng climbed up on to the pews, nobody, for once, stopped them. At last fighting, patriotic talk they could understand!

"Down with the Imperialists! Long live the Republic of China!"

*L*ater that day Manying was finishing bandaging her mother's feet in the bedroom when Pastor Wesley stormed into the house.

"Wen Huaguang. Where the devil are you?"

"Quick! Go see what's the matter! They must have the church." Manying's mother grabbed the end of the white bindings. Manying hurried down the wooden stairs.

"Just what the hell do you think you are playing at?" Pastor Wesley, hands on hips in the middle of the living room, glowered at her father, who sat legs crossed revealing his cotton under-trousers, arms resting languidly on the sides of his chair. Pastor Wesley was so tall that every time he visited Manying thought he was sure to hit his head on the ceiling. This time, however, it was his face that caught her attention. It was red and seemed to swell before her eyes.

"Jesus the Grand Disturber? Free the nation of all foreign oppression! Dog's fart! Don't kid yourself! Without us foreigners you Chinese would still be living in the middle ages!" Spittle flew from Pastor Wesley's mouth, some of it catching on the corner of his chin and hanging there for a few seconds like an elongating icicle. Confused, Manying backed away into the shadows at the bottom of the stairs.

"Pastor Wen, did you deliberately set about to make my position untenable in this church?"

There was a long silence. The two men, once pupil and teacher, eyed each other, like dogs circling for a fight.

"Maybe it is time for you to retire, Master Shepherd." Her father's voice, once again soft and measured, broke the silence. "The Church is always talking about the need for more native control." He sneered the word "native" in English. "No one asked you to come here. How would you like it if we went to America and told you how to run things? Now it is time for you foreigners to live up to your promises."

Clenching and unclenching his fist, Pastor Wesley wiped his chin with the back of his hand.

"Think you are ready to do the job? Think one year's theological training in Guangzhou is enough qualification? Go on then! Go ahead! We'll see how well you do!" He made a terrifying, high-pitched gulping sound and it was a few seconds before Manying realised that he was actually laughing. "I made you! Without me and the church, you and your descendants would be begging on the streets." His entire body shook with the effort of his words.

"I made you?" Now it was her father's turn to laugh. "It was me who made you! Without my help where would all your illustrious translations be? You used me: me and the other native pastors, to further your own ambitions."

"Huaming, you are like a son to me. China is my life. How can you do this?" Choking, Pastor Wesley put his hand to his chest and, gasping for air, reeled backwards. He would have collapsed on the floor if Manying's father had not rushed to catch him as he fell.

*E*veryone said that Pastor Wesley made a remarkable recovery from his stroke. He was hospitalised for several months but in the end never regained the use of his right arm and the muscles on the right side of his face. That was not so much the problem. Rather it was the severity of his speech impediment and the all-pervading viciousness of mood that made it obvious to all who knew him that he could never work as pastor again. Just before he was discharged from hospital Aunt Grace and her Amah vacated the big house in the church compound, moving to a smaller one in the village, and Manying's father, Wen Huaming, became the Senior Pastor of the Shantou Baptist Church. It was, it was said, such a shame, but in the end quite the best solution all round.

16

Chinese New Year 1937, the year of the ox: a time for feasting and family gatherings, children thickly padded in new clothes, hopping from one foot to the other in anticipation of crisp new bank notes in lucky red envelopes, their chubby hands outstretched to laughing fathers, teasing uncles and indulgent aunts, a time to settle debts, put aside the old, and hope for better things to come.

But time was short for the young people. Like each new generation they believed they could change the world and were filled with the zeal to make a difference. Clothed this time in the mantle of the Nationalist Party and the Republic, another batch of young men went out to live life to the full and save the nation from the Imperialists, whilst the girls nourished by cinema, magazines and cheap novels dreamt of love, choosing their own husband, chubby children and a house with running water and electricity.

Hunched over her mother's old sewing machine, Manying hurried to finish her new cheongsam dress in time for the festival. According to tradition, new clothes must be worn on the first day of the New Year to bring good luck. The Mission Primary School where Manying taught had only just closed for the holidays and with the following day already New Year's Eve, there was still much to be done. Coming to an end of a seam she expertly trimmed and tied the threads and looked over to the side of the room, where Lai Di was cautiously cutting out yet more cloth, this time for a new trouser suit for Manying's mother.

"Make sure you leave plenty in the seam. She hates things too tight."

Manying and Lai Di got on much better as adults than they ever had as children. Seeing them arm in arm laughing as they went to the cinema in Shantou, people forgot that they were not blood sisters. But Manying had not seen Lai Di since Christmas and was glad to have her home for the New Year holiday. When Lai Di had completed her training and got a job as a secretary in the British bank in Shantou, Manying had been the first to congratulate her.

"You were always so good at English!" It was not really practical for Lai Di to continue living in the church compound, so she had taken lodgings with a Christian family on the Shantou side. Manying missed her and looked forward to their meetings, when Lai Di, hair permed in what she assured Manying was the most up-to-the-minute Shanghai style, would be full of the Shantou gossip.

Manying fingered the soft blue velvet she was sewing. It was Lai Di who had bought her the cloth for Christmas, along with a pile of old magazines with pictures of western and Chinese fashions from which Manying had copied the lace trim at the neck for her new chongsam dress.

"Manying! Come see if this is straight." Hearing her mother calling, Manying raised a conspiratorial eyebrow towards Lai Di. Mother had been like an ant on a hot pan all day anticipating the return of Manye from Guangzhou.

Outside the front door Manying found her mother leaning on her stick, armed against the chill in an old red padded jacket and black woollen cap. Manying looked at the grey overcast sky and shivered. Standing on a three-legged stool the maid was holding up the first of the red New Year couplets, which were to be pasted on either side of the door to bring good luck. *May the Ten Thousand Things be as you Desire*, her father's ornate black characters confidently announced.

"Down a bit!" a voice called from behind them. A man in uniform was framed by the drooping foliage around the side gate.

"Brother!" Manying ran towards him and he reached down, picking her up and swinging her round. He was a big man, and she was like a child in his embrace.

"Put me down! Put me down!" At last she felt her feet back on solid ground and looked up at the grinning face under the army captain's hat. Like his hero the Generalissimo, he had grown a short moustache. She hugged him to her, the wool of his uniform rough on her hands, her cheek resting just for an instant on the leather buckle of his gun strap. His smell was strange. Was it boot polish or cologne?

"Where shall I put it, Sir?" A bow-legged coolie, who Manying knew had difficulty getting work due to his age, appeared at the gate with Manye's leather suitcase.

"Leave it here. I'll take it in myself." Manye reached into his pocket to pay the man, who, receiving more money than he had expected, bowed repeatedly as low as his arthritis would allow, his hands cupped in gratitude.

"Thank you Sir! Thank you. Happy New Year."

"Happy New Year!" Manye replied and started to turn away. But the old man dithered, looking at his tatty cloth shoes.

"They say that soon the Generalissimo is going to show the Japanese what's what, Sir?"

"That's right boss! You just wait and see what the

Chinese army can do!"

Hearing the quiet authority in her brother's voice, Manying understood for the first time something of what her brother had learned at the Military Academy in Guangzhou, and just what it meant to be an officer and leader of men.

Manye could not stop grinning as his mother, with repeated pawing of his shoulders and cheeks, ushered him to the house.

"Have you eaten? You must be hungry? We waited for you at lunch, but there is plenty left over." And to the maid, "Quick! Quick! Hot water! Heat up the noodles and pork and how about an egg omelette, Chaoshan style? So delicious!" She nipped her son on the cheek as if he were a baby. "You look thin. Don't they feed the heroes of our nation? Hot water for tea! Quick, quick!"

"Ah Ma! I ate in town. Don't treat me like a guest!" Manye raised his left hand, holding the top of his hat like a shield to fend off his mother's attentions.

Manying looked round for Lai Di. Her sewing was still on the table but there was no sign of her. She had been anticipating Manye's return just as much as the rest of them.

"Have some fruit then? Here!" His mother picked up a pear from the bowl on the little table between the chairs. Her head cocked coaxingly to one side, she thrust the fruit in her son's direction. It seemed impossible that all the vigour and perfection of this youth could have issued out of a shrunken old lady whose happy smile revealed gaping holes where teeth had once been. Yet taking the face of the young man as a template, it was still possible to make out the same square jaw and small, lively eyes among the sagging wrinkles and age spots of the old lady.

"OK, OK! A pear!" Realising that he would not be left in peace until he had eaten something, Manye raised both hands in a gesture of surrender and sat down in one of the wooden armchairs arranged along the walls of the room.

"Lai Di! There you are!" their mother exclaimed as Lai Di appeared at the bottom of the stairs. Lai Di had changed, Manying noticed, into a tight black short- sleeved cheongsam and she was wearing lipstick. She was beautiful.

"Woo hoo, Lai Di! Isn't that cheongsam a bit small?" Manye surveyed and swallowed back a grin of mock surprise.

"Don't be so cheeky. It's fashion!" Lai Di retorted unabashed, her long white arms outstretched, twirling to better display herself.

"Aiya! So vain!" their mother scolded as she peeled the pear for her son.

"Where's Dad?" Keeping his eyes on Lai Di, Manye took a cigarette case out of his top pocket but did not open it. There was an awkward silence. In going to the Whampoa Military Academy from the Gok Sek Boys' School, Manye had been much admired as a trailblazer. Subsequently, he had been followed by at least half a dozen patriotically inclined boys including Zheng, who had joined the class of '34 the following year. But in following the military path, Manye had defied his father's long cherished wish that he train for the priesthood in America. But so great was the nationalist tide that his father had been unable to stop him, and in the end had been reduced to feeble pleading.

"Your mother wants to know who is going to look after her in her old age."

In fact, her mother had told Manying that in her opinion the military was a far better bet than the priesthood, but Confucius had said, "a wife's words should not go outside her own apartment," and she was content to be proud of her hero son in silence. In retrospect everyone could see that the Whampoa Academy had been the making of the unruly brother who had always preferred sport to books and had always struggled to live up to his father's expectations. But even though father and son were once again on speaking terms, it was never easy when both of them were under the same roof.

Manying poured more hot water into the tiny earthenware teapot and, collecting the empty cups scattered round the table, lined them up on the bamboo lattice drainer. The so-called Patience Tea was so beloved of the Chaoshan people that outsiders often said it was not blood that flowed in their veins, rather the pungent amber liquid. The repeated brewing and refilling of pots and cups was the key ritual at the heart of the family. Finger on top of the teapot, Manying poured out the nectar, the little cups steaming oases of warmth in the winter air. So habitual were her actions, she was barely aware of what she was doing and never took her eyes off Manye as he talked about his battalion, his friends and the bright lights of Guangzhou. The sight of him in uniform still surprised her. It transformed him: the stiff, almost too stiff way he walked, or rather marched, how he sat, bolt upright, his knees apart and smoking his *Capstan* cigarettes, the way he looked straight into a person's eyes when speaking to him, as if he were the only person that mattered in the world. He was relating the hilarious story of some of his fellow officers, who, wishing to make the strength of their disapproval clear to a certain lieutenant general, whom it was suspected had supported the kidnapping of the Generalissimo at Xian, had climbed into his compound one night and peed on his favourite rose bushes. The roses, it was reliably reported, were dead by morning. As Manye talked, the layers of modern military stiffness gradually peeled away, to be replaced by the sharp gawky gestures of an excited, happy little boy.

The highlight of the New Year was Lai Di's unexpected invitation to a party. A good friend from work, she told them rather enigmatically, had invited her, and the invitation had been extended to them all. Manye and Zheng needed no persuading. Neither man could remain in a chair for more than five minutes. They were constantly rushing around, shaking hands, drinking, eating and seeing old friends that were home for the holiday. Manying thought they must surely find the pace of homelife rather tedious after life in the big city.

*T*he party was held on the second day of the New Year in a foreigner's big house on the waterfront on Gok Sek. In high spirits the young people set off at the ridiculous hour of eight-thirty to make the twenty-minute walk down the hill.

"An hour when all righteous people should be going to bed," their mother admonished, but with a smile, as the young people were leaving. "Look after each other! Take care!"

The bang of the iron side gate behind them was an affront to the silent magnificence of the night. On the hilltops the full moon glided coldly in and out of the mists, and the silver river of stars proffered infinity.

Manying was so excited. The whole day had been spent in anticipation of the party: washing and curling her hair, ironing her new dress, polishing her best high- heeled leather shoes. As a child Manying had often gone with her father into the homes of foreign missionaries and doctors, and of course there were Pastor Wesley and Aunt Grace who, since the death of their old Amah, Manying visited regularly to help Aunt Grace keep a check on the performance of the new maid. Aunt Grace was always pleased to see her, even if Pastor Wesley ignored her. But Manying had never been invited to a party in one of the foreigner's houses on the waterfront.

At the bottom of the hill the gentle waves sighed onto the narrow beach. The shadows of the big houses loomed along the waterfront, electric light flooding out of the windows onto the lawns and rose gardens. Ribbons of dance music fluttered towards them on the gentle sea breeze.

"So who is this mysterious friend of yours?" Zheng

quizzed Lai Di, not for the first time that day.

"If you must know, he is an American businessman; his name is Teddy."

Manying began to feel uneasy. She would have to speak English.

The music led them through an open gate and into the compound of a red- bricked house with colonial style verandas. The heels of Manying's shoes slipped on the deep gravel of the path as she walked on tiptoe up to the house. The large wooden door with its brass knocker seemed to open of its own accord.

Stepping into the hall of the house her first impression was that she must have been living her whole life as a rat in darkness. The blinding power of electricity assaulted them from all sides: dazzling out from beneath cream coloured lamp shades, reflecting from the white panelled walls and bouncing in white balls off a gilt framed mirror opposite the door. Ahead of her, double doors were thrown open to a long sitting room: an ethereal world of glittering people, tongues, noses, necklaces, rings and raucous laughter. A hand raised itself above the heads of the people. A big foreigner in a white tuxedo pushed his way, with his glass in his hand, through the crowd.

"Deborah! At last!"

Lai Di smiled and kissed him on either cheek in the foreign fashion. Manying was shocked.

"Teddy, this is my sister Manying, my brother Manye, and my cousin Zheng." The long, light English words tripped off her tongue with no trace of hesitation.

Manying thought she had misunderstood when Lai Di described Zheng as a relative, but her English was always better than she liked to admit and she'd heard correctly.

"At last I get to meet Deborah's family! She has told me so much about you!" Teddy offered a fat hand in her direction. Manying hesitated, blushing, for although she considered herself a modern young woman she was not used to Western manners. His grip was enthusiastic and sweaty. He seemed to hold on for such a long time. She had to stop herself from pulling her hand away and putting it behind her back with the other one to bow to him as she taught the children in the school to bow to the teachers.

"You two don't look like sisters!"

"Manying is much more beautiful than I am." Lai Di, or rather Deborah, for that, she remembered, was the name she had adopted since working with foreigners at the bank, touched Teddy's elbow, her shiny lipstick-covered mouth tilting at him with the softest of smiles.

"Captain Wen, we are honoured, and Lieutenant?" Teddy turned to the men.

"Lieutenant Chen, at your service." Zheng made a short crisp bow as he shook Teddy's hand.

"Gentlemen, I am afraid your reputation precedes you. Deborah tells me you are the football champions of Gok Sek."

Manye laughed with delight at the memory.

"Certainly we played on the school team that won the national championships a couple of years ago."

"My friend here is too modest. He was captain and I had the honour to play with him," Zheng interjected. "Alas, it seems such a long time ago. We are getting old!"

"Perhaps you would enjoy the opportunity to relive your youth later this evening. We have a game planned!"

Manying was wondering how on earth one could play football in the dark when a blond foreign woman in a cream satin dress sailed toward her on a wave of sickly scent.

"Deborah! Teddy has been like a bear with a sore head waiting for you! Oh, the heroes of the Chinese army! What an honour! Jane Winston...my brother and sister-in-law are our hosts tonight. I'll introduce you." She turned to the gently undulating group of people in the other room. "Heaven knows where they are! Where on earth is that maid? Leaving you all standing in your coats like this!" A tiny girl with a huge red birthmark blighting the left side of her face shuffled out of a side door. Manying recognised her as one of the church orphans called "Twenty Three" because that was the year she was found abandoned at the church gate. People always said she was stupid and was an ideal maid, but Manying thought she was simply wise enough not to question fate, which had indeed already been kinder to her than to many. She gave Manying a shy smile, bobbed half a foreign curtsey, half a schoolgirl bow.

"Teacher, good evening," she whispered as the guests piled their coats into her outstretched arms, almost burying her alive.

"Do you live in Shantou, Miss Winston? I haven't seen you before." Where Manye's accent let him down, his charm made up the deficit. Clicking his heels and bowing crisply he offered the woman his hand. His eyes danced lightly over her body; the luminous skin of her neck and shoulders and soft white mounds of copious breast hidden among artfully draped folds of satin.

It had never occurred to Manying before that her brother could be so 'salty and wet!'

"Heavens no! I live in London! Just visiting until the end of the summer season. I suppose you could say I am a tourist!"

"Jane, before you start your life story, shouldn't we get these poor folks some drinks?" Leading the party toward the drinks table on the far wall of the sitting room, Teddy's hand roamed over the small of Lai Di's back. Manying began to wish she had stayed at home.

Champagne was bitterer than she had expected. Cautiously, she sipped again, hoping it might taste better the second time. Hovering, almost hiding at Zheng's side, she surveyed the scene through the clouds of cigarette smoke. There were not many Chinese, but there were familiar faces among the foreigners, mostly doctors and their wives from the hospital. Like the hall, the wall panels of the main room were painted white. At one end a wood fire blazed in a huge fireplace, above it a western-style landscape of the greenest river she had ever seen, and behind it a field of yellow flowers and black and white cows. The furniture was simple by Western standards; two settees upholstered in brown were arranged on either side of the fireplace with a shiny mahogany coffee table between, and some rattan chairs that Manying supposed had been brought in to provide extra seating for the occasion. At the far end of the room, all the furniture except a large gramophone cabinet had been cleared to provide space for dancing.

"So, you do not believe that the Anti-Comintern pact between Japan and Germany will mean China becomes more pro-Japanese?" Teddy tried to sound casual.

Zheng laughed.

"Ridiculous! I really do not understand why you foreigners get so worked up about this issue."

"The Chinese army has many German military advisers. These people are bound to have influence over the Generalissimo..." A short, fat, red-haired Englishman, Philip, persisted with a string of political questions, not all of which Manying understood. Zheng was irritated.

"It is true that over recent years we have been working with the Germans to modernise our army. Some of my own teachers at the Whampoa Military Academy were German, and good ones too. But if you will forgive me for being so frank, they are merely paid employees of the Chinese State. We Chinese are masters in our own house and will not tolerate any further Japanese military expansion, or any expansion by any other power for that matter. Of that, I can assure you." With a tight smile, he raised his glass. "Gentleman, your very good health."

Manying watched Lai Di, tall and elegant, lean gracefully towards Teddy. Her pink fingernails hung like fuchsias around her champagne glass, her black cheongsam perfectly cut to flatter her generous breasts, the slit at the side, just a little bit higher than the norm, but not too high. Where had she acquired such taste and poise? It certainly was not from anyone Manying knew. Further down the room Manye leaned forward to light a cigarette for the woman in cream satin, their black and blond heads touching for a few seconds too long. Making pretence of straightening her skirt, Manying twisted awkwardly in her homemade dress. The lace around the collar suddenly seemed like a childish indulgence in contrast to the simple elegance of the other women.

"Would you like to dance?" It was a few seconds before Manying realised that the red-haired Englishman was talking to her.

Against the background of the foot-tapping clarinet music, she had difficulty understanding what he said. He spoke quickly out of the corner of his mouth, more in a series of gruff grunts than words. She understood when he asked if she worked, and when she replied that she was a primary school teacher he nodded and said that it was a good thing that modern women were independent and able to do what they wanted. But in the end it proved easier just to let the conversation lapse. As the dance progressed, he tried to pull her closer. His fat stomach pressed against her and she stiffened her arms and back to resist.

"Don't you like Benny Goodman?" He breathed the smell of alcohol and ash into her neck. Manying had never been so close to a man before and this foreigner was disgusting. She felt sick and turned her face away from him. His eyes were so pale, like a dead fish. Why on earth was the record going on so long? At last, the final fanfare. Forcing a smile she made her excuses, but he continued to hold her arm.

"I think the next one is mine!" It was Zheng. He grabbed Manying roughly around the waist, almost dragging her across the dance floor. She was saved!

Like students in a dance class, they held each other at a distance as they waited for the record to be changed. There was a scratching sound as the needle furrowed to the start of the track. Still, Zheng said nothing. The music was a slower, quieter tune that Manying was not familiar with. His grip was gentle, yet at the same time firm with a clear lead.

He was her brother's best friend, and a childhood playmate, but it was as if Manying were meeting him for the first time. His face was remarkable for a Chinese. Under his thick black eyebrows he had double-lidded eyelids, like a foreigner. His eyes were not brown but black, and when he looked at her she felt as if she were falling into them. Yet his eyes were never still for long: quietly suspicious, watching, checking, assessing people, constantly calculating and reviewing the situation. But now and again, just for a moment, it was as if a thick frost had settled over them. Manying had only seen him like that once before, when he was talking politics earlier that evening.

Moonlight in your eyes, Moonlight in your eyes, crooned the woman on the gramophone, and Zheng smiled at Manying. Her hand in his; his hand, so warm and strong. This time Manying wanted to be held close, but he did not do so.

Moonlight in your eyes. Moonlight in your eyes. The words spun round and round in her head. She wished to stay like that forever.

Barely had the record ended when Deborah and Manye were upon them.

"Come on! Time for the game."

Despite the winter night, the crazy foreign devils had moved the party outside! The ladies were artfully draping themselves in fur wraps and lining up along the back veranda. Teddy was superintending the choosing of teams.

"I'll take the Chinese army!" he hollered when he saw Manye and Zheng.

"No! That's not fair!" the Englishman, Philip, protested.

"You'll have to split them up. Captain Wen on the

American team. Lieutenant Chen on the British team." There was Deborah, or was it Lai Di, in the midst of all the men organising and directing, so brazen. And so it was agreed, and the game commenced with the diminutive, grey-haired French priest in shiny leather patent shoes as the referee to ensure fair play.

It was not a game Manying was familiar with. They called it "touch rugby" and it involved throwing rather than kicking the ball. A swirling, grey mist had now rolled over the mountains and the end of the long lawn was invisible. The game seemed to progress with a series of shouts, thumps and curses in a multitude of tongues. The score mounted first in favour of the Americans, and then the British. They changed ends, and before long time was running out and things got serious. Manying started to shiver in the night air.

"*Allez*, Go on. *Guolai. Kuai*!" Urgent shouts came from the gloom at the far end of the garden.

"Whaaa!" A great thump as Teddy ran into an older British man with a moustache.

"Foul! Advantage les Anglais!" the referee shouted, slipping and sliding out of the shadows. The Americans booed. Picking up the ball, the man with moustache began to charge down the lawn in the direction of a house, and the others following like thumping, steaming horses. Again Teddy made for the man with the moustache. At the last minute the man lifted his left hand and sent the ball soaring across the lawn. It was Manye on the right who leapt like a ghost in a white shirt, out of the mist to make the catch. Everyone held their breath. For a moment it seemed that the ball would slip out of his hands. But he was blessed that night, and reaching just a little bit higher, controlled the ball with the tips of his fingers.

"Go on man! Go!" Bending down, the man with the moustache put his hands on his knees to catch his breath. Ball under his arm, teeth bared like a wild dog, Manye sprinted toward the imaginary try-line on the veranda.

"Come on! Come on!" The woman Jane, in cream satin, screamed, but he was so fast no one could catch him.

Teasingly, he tipped the ball out of his hand onto the middle of the top veranda step. It made a dull thump on the wooden boards and rolled towards the open door, the white light streaming from the house, forever illuminating his face with the immortal triumph of youth.

It was just after midnight when Manying left the party. She had gone to the toilet and when she returned Manye, Lai Di, Teddy and the woman in cream had all disappeared. Most of the lights had been put out and there was a lot of canoodling going on in the living room. Seized by a strange panic that she could not understand, she hurried into the hall and called for the maid. It was there that Zheng found her. Together they fetched their own coats, for the maid, too, had disappeared.

Outside the stars and the moon were no more. The thick mist again enfolded them both in its heavy silence. Manying was sure Zheng would hear the chattering of her teeth and the thumping of her heart.

"This way, silly melon!" she whispered, grabbing his arm as he missed the turn to the track leading up the hill to the church.

"Ai ya! I have been away too long! Become a city boy!"

"Lai Di looked so beautiful tonight, didn't you think so? Like the film star, Butterfly. I felt like such a country bumpkin." Manying tried to sound normal.

"Some might find her attractive, with all her cute dimples and sweet smiles. Sure she is pretty, but not really beautiful. I prefer a woman with an intelligent face."

"But Lai Di is very clever," Manying protested. "Everyone says so."

"Clever maybe, but not very wise. If she thinks that her American businessman will marry her, she's a fool." He spat out the words, and deep down Manying knew that he was right. Foreign men were notorious. Every respectable Chinese girl knew that. But the way he said it sounded so callous. There was an awkward silence.

"You're cold. Take my coat." Zheng tried to make amends. Manying protested. He insisted. The army great coat smelled musty, as if it had been soaked by rain and left out to dry once too often. It was actually too heavy for the southern climates, but Manying welcomed the warmth from his body seeping into her bones. They did not speak further until they reached the gate of the church compound. Removing his coat, Manying reached up behind him to help him put it on. He turned to her.

"Manying, I need to ask you something, something very important."

Manying could barely breathe.

"My parents, you must promise to look after them for me while I am away. I am afraid I won't be a very good son to them."

It was then that Manying realised why the men were different that New Year's holiday.

"You and my brother will be fighting the Japanese this year, won't you?"

"War is coming, Manying." He hesitated. Then, as if it were the most natural thing in the world, he bowed, took her hand in his and kissed it.

"Manying, you're very special. Don't...well... anyway, you'll find someone better than me. I can't...well...very pretty anyway." Turning smartly on his heel, he walked away and was swallowed up by the mist.

"Take care of yourself." Manying wanted to kick herself. She sounded just like her mother. She stood in the cold and dark until the regular crunch, crunch of his footsteps had faded to nothing, and then wept.

17

Aunt Grace's body was found in the early morning of the 7th of August; the day the Japanese army made its official entry into the northern city of Beiping. Out walking her dog, the wife of Chief Port Pilot Shantou JD found her, washed up by the morning tide, floating peacefully face upwards, arms outstretched in a quiet corner of a rock pool. Aunt Grace was dressed in her best cheongsam with the gold cross that Pastor Wesley had given her as a wedding present around her neck. The investigation was swift, the cause of death recorded as misadventure.

But Manying knew that Aunt Grace had not been herself for some time. All of a sudden her body had seemed to whither and shrink. When she walked, she buckled forward as if toiling with a horrendous burden, but refused to use a stick. She stopped going to church and the young maid said she just sat in the chair muttering the same old gobbledegook.

Whirling girl, dancing girl, changed the axis of the earth and stays of the heavens. For fifty years there will be no order. Whirling girl, dancing girl, whirling girl, dancing girl!

When Manying asked Aunt Grace what was the matter

she became even more agitated, her sightless bloodshot eyes rolling around in their sockets as she scratched the bald patch on her crown, rearranging the remaining long wisps of hair to cover it.

Manying had seen her for the last time three days before she died, the slow regular creaking of her rocking chair the only sound of life in the dead heat of the afternoon. Suddenly, Aunt Grace looked Manying straight in the eye, as if she could see her.

"When I was young, I could see things other people couldn't. Once I saw something awful happening, but when I got there it was too late to stop it." Aunt Grace lowered her head. "After that, I lost my sight. But recently it has come back."

"And what do you see?" Manying asked gently.

Aunt Grace cupped her hands over her eyes in despair "For God's sake Manying, don't ask. You do not want to know."

August progressed and the mangoes ripened on the tree in the Wen's garden. With her brother away, Manying asked two of the bigger boys from her class at school to climb the tree and pick them for her. Their labour over, she sat with them, all elbows and knees as they gorged themselves on mountains of oozing orange flesh, and she dreamt of the day when she might be blessed with sons of her own. But the summer heat was becoming unbearable. Between the hours of eleven and five nothing moved. On Gok Sek, people sat indoors, lulled by the buzz of crickets, and waited. In Shantou, fans whirred, office workers slept with their heads on their desks, shop assistants stretched out on top of their counters, and rickshaw pullers rioted because a mobile urn ran out of tea. On the 13th of August fighting between the Japanese and Chinese broke out in Shanghai.

Then the planes came.

*M*anying was in a shady spot on the hill above the village, making daisy chains with children from the school.

"Look! Planes!" One of the big boys jumped up, shading his eyes with his hand and pointing. "Whaaah! So many!" All the children climbed a rock to get a better view. The planes were beautiful, a shoal of silver fish in the deep blue sky. They flew in from the east along the bay, the black lines of bombs falling on Shantou. It seemed an age before the sound reached them; boom, boom, boom until it was just a continuous roar of thunder. One by one the faces of the younger children cracked into tears.

"Quickly! Quickly!"

Manying ushered them down from the rock to take them back to the village to safety. But the leading plane was banking to the west and heading towards them.

There was nowhere to hide except under a scraggy thorn tree. The plane screeched out of the blue; the children huddled around Manying, unfinished daisy chains around their necks and crowning their shiny black heads. Bombs fell. The children screamed. Great plumes of smoke rose from the direction of the houses on the Gok Sek waterfront. With a roar, the plane flew out of the blinding sun, over the crest of the hill and directly above them. It was so low that it ruffled their hair and Manying could see the young Japanese pilot in his flying hat looking down at them—somebody's brother, husband, and son—strange that he should be wearing such a thick hat in the middle of summer.

At last the planes were gone, leaving the children whimpering, the unfinished daisy chains already crushed in their hands.

The wounded began to arrive on Gok Sek in the early afternoon, brought in motor boats: a man with both his legs blown off, his long gown hanging in tatters where his knees once were, a rouged woman with her left cheek in shreds, hundreds of nameless faces, black and bloody with disbelief. It was then that Manying heard that the house where the party had been held had taken a direct hit. All the inhabitants, except the husband who was at work, were dead. She thought of the blond English woman in cream-coloured satin, her arms and legs twisted like a discarded doll, lying underneath all the rubble.

The Japanese planes came again in the middle of the afternoon, bombing the docks, and again the following morning and afternoon, and again the day after that and the day after that. Every day Manying went to help in the hospital. She was not a qualified nurse, and not permitted to change dressings, but she made beds, emptied bedpans and comforted the wounded and their families—as if hard work and a ready smile could somehow change reality.

Over the next few weeks the city remained under heavy bombardment. In comparison with the city and the port, Gok Sek got off relatively lightly, although several of the waterfront houses were left in smoking ruins, and most of them had been damaged in one way or another, even if it was just that their windows had been blown out. The foreigners began to leave and there was talk that the British would close their consulate. One morning early in September, Manying was pushing a linen basket to the hospital laundry when one of the young American doctors came running towards her, his left hand holding his stethoscope to stop it from slipping from his neck.

"They've hit the church. You'd better go. I'll take the basket. Hurry!"

Manying ran up the hill to the village. The sun was eclipsed by the black cloud of smoke.

"Oh God, not my father. Please, God. No."

In the church compound people ran around, squawking, flapping like geese with a fox in their midst. Through the billowing smoke, Manying saw her father, at the edge of a huge crater, a cloth tied around his mouth, throwing water from buckets into a gaping hole in the side of the church. He was coughing, his head twisted away from the smoke and flames.

Young Uncle Chen stood at the head of a chain of people with a crazy assortment of buckets and washbowls, passing water from the kitchen pump. Another chain of people stretched out of the side gate, bringing water from the house across the road. The entire village was there: children, old men, and even her mother with her bound feet. Manying joined the line.

"Thank God it wasn't Sunday." Aunt Feng passed her the washbowl with flowers on it that her mother used to wash her feet.

Like the old man who moved the mountain, they worked. Manying's arms ached; her hands were sore from the bucket handles, her face and eyes burned with the heat and smoke. Pausing to wipe the sweat and tears from her smarting eyes she saw Pastor Wesley coming through the main gate and calmly closing it behind him. Unaware of the bedlam around, he sauntered towards the Church—as if it were a normal day. As he began to climb the steps to the portico, Manying realised what was happening.

"Stop him! He's going into the Church."

She began to run. Removing his hat, Pastor Wesley opened the front door. Before she could reach him he had gone inside.

Young Uncle Chen and another man pulled her back. Her chest burned and she gasped for air. She saw her father and Young Uncle Chen, wet towels around their heads, disappear into the black clouds of smoke coming out of the door.

Huaming carried Pastor Wesley out, the big American slung over his slim shoulders. He was alive and sat on the ground next to his rescuers, all three of them rasping and gulping water from bowls. It could have been funny; with their blackened faces they looked like the unreliable, comic mud Buddhas from the opera stage.

It was a long day. But as darkness fell, the exhausted David with his puny buckets overcame the rage of the mighty Goliath. The fire was quenched and the church, though badly damaged, was pronounced saved—a miracle indeed!

They took Pastor Wesley into the house, but he no longer recognised anyone. He sat in the sitting room, twisting his beard and shaking his bowed head. "What have we done? What have we done? God forgive us. God forgive us."

When Huaming brought a bowl and towel to wash his face, he acquiesced like a small child, poking out his chin and screwing up his eyes tightly against the soap and water. But when Huaming had finished, Pastor Wesley refused food, and once more began to shake his head, back and forth, back and forth, reciting over and over lines from a poem they all recognised—a poem by Du Fu.

> *A kingdom smashed, its hills and rivers still here,*
> *spring in the city, plants and trees grow wild*
> *I run my fingers through my white hair until it thins*
> *My cap pin will no longer stay in place.*

Huaming took his old friend and mentor in his arms, rocking him like a child, and Manying saw that her father was crying, the tears running in rivers down his smoke blackened face.

The Japanese bombardment continued throughout the month of September and the port of Shantou was at a virtual stand still. For fear of their lives, farmers stopped bringing food into the city, and shops and business closed as people fled to safety. In the third week the news came that the British were indeed evacuating their consulate and Huaming decided that enough was enough and it was time for Manying and Lai Di to leave too. A party of about twenty people from the church, led by a keen young lay preacher and protégé of his, were planning to take refuge with the community of one of their family of churches up river near the ancient walled city of Chaozhou. The girls should join them. They would have to go by boat. With her bound feet, the journey would be too much for his wife; Manying and Lai Di would have to go on their own and chaperone one another.

The decision taken, her father dispatched Manying to Shantou to fetch Lai Di. It was widely held that midday was the best time to travel, for the Japanese needed to eat and never bombed at lunchtime. Even so, Manying was the only passenger in the rowing boat. It was a beautiful early autumn day, the wind teased her umbrella parasol only lightly, and the waves slopped playfully against the side of the boat. For a few minutes she could almost believe that the world was at peace. But she knew it would not be easy to persuade Lai Di to come to Chaozhou. Despite her father's repeated requests, throughout the course of the bombing she had consistently refused even to return to the relative safety of the Island of Gok Sek. Manying could see her now, wafting her manicured hand.

"Chaozhou? What on earth would we do in that God forsaken little town?"

Manying had not been to Shantou since the bombing. After the ravaging heat of August, the day was so benign that it was hard to believe that anything would have changed. As the boat approached the steps of the jetty, Manying surveyed the scene. In the distance, long black clouds of dust and ash scythed ominously across the blue sky. On the dockside, a half a dozen rickshaw men scratched around futilely, like scrawny birds that for one reason or another had not migrated with the flock. They demanded quadruple the normal fare to the bank in the city centre and would not compromise, so Manying decided to walk.

In the silent streets, the acrid cocktail of explosion, fire and sewage pricked her nostrils. She held her handkerchief over her mouth and nose. Here and there a shop was open, the owners hiding like frightened animals, deep in the shadowy recesses. But mostly the folding wooden doors of the rows of shops were locked and barred. In the distance she heard a gentle rumbling...coming closer. Turning a corner, a Chinese-style wheelbarrow with wooden wheels thundered along the metalled road. Pushed by the father, it was loaded with the entire possessions of the family: bedding, cooking pots, boxes and stools. A dirty, tired child sat on each of the platforms on either side of the wheel. The mother shuffled behind, her face pinched with exhaustion and fear, two long white sacks filled with rice bound across her chest. A warning peep came from an approaching car. The father and mother did not look up. In the car were two Western women wearing white straw hats and pearls.

Nearing the centre of town, Manying saw damaged and burnt out buildings: the lifeless shell of an office block, black holes where windows and doors had been, like sightless eyes. The debris had been cleared onto the pavement; piles of bricks, bits of tables, a heat-twisted filing cabinet, a woman's white leather shoe, and a Chinese gentleman's black silk cap. Now and again people scuttled in and out of the shadows like rats.

Turning into the main street, she was relieved to see the bank. Its windows were crossed with brown tape; sand bags and barbed wire defiantly defended the building. In spite of them, the fortune teller sat with his little table and crow next to a pillar to the left of the portico. The mangy bird fluttered impatiently on its string as Manying pushed through the swinging doors.

The vast lobby was cool and silent. Sunlight streamed through the glass dome, falling in gold patches on the white marble floor. Eyes peeped suspiciously through the holes in two counter grills. There was a short queue of Chinese men at one of the mahogany counters; the whispers of teller and customer, and the slow rustle of paper, the only sounds in the emptiness. To the left and right of the hall were two staircases with flanking black marble pillars. When Manying was a little girl and first heard the story of Samson destroying the pillars of the temple, she had imagined him chained up here, inside the bank. Climbing the red carpeted stairs to Lai Di's office she still thought of the story, and it was not until she got upstairs that she realised no one had asked her business.

She turned left down a dingy corridor lined with partitioned offices. There was none of the usual click-clack of typewriters, or the ringing of telephones, or gentle conversation. Even before she entered Lai Di's office, she saw through the glass door that Lai Di was not there: her desk with its typewriter, a neat stack of letters in the wire in-tray, abandoned. Manying crossed the room and timidly knocked on the door to the boss's office. There was no reply. She turned the handle.

The room smelled stale, like rotting oranges, but was deserted, the wooden desk efficiently cleared. Closing the glass office door softly behind her, Manying heard voices coming from the far end of the corridor. In another stuffy room, identical in layout to Lai Di's office, Manying found two foreign devils and a Chinese clerk. The men were going through piles of brown files strewn all over the floor and desks. Shirts open at the neck, sleeves rolled up, their faces grey with stubble, the men worked quickly, grunting to each other like coolies. For a moment Manying wondered if she had stumbled upon a robbery.

"Excuse me, I am looking for my sister, Deborah. She works here," she said in English

"Who?" The taller of the foreign devils, a sandwich in one hand, a file in the other, did not look up. "Hasn't been in for two days now. And I thought I could count on her." The Chinese man replied in Chaozhou dialect, looking Manying up and down as if she were the one at fault.

"Do you know where she is? Her wages will be docked."

Manying felt a vibration welling up inside like that caused by the noise of the bombers. She clamped her teeth and bit her tongue to control the shaking. "How should I know?"

The Chinese man shrugged his shoulders and, feeding paper into a shredder, began to turn the handle.

Manying stood under the shady portico of the bank, grateful for the fresh air after the stuffy offices. How could she feel so cold, yet still sweat? She wiped her brow with her handkerchief. Where was Lai Di? Lying buried in the ruins of a house, or sick, or... She knew she should go to her lodgings, but she did not know where they were. Last time she had seen Lai Di at Easter, she had told her that she had moved lodgings to somewhere nearer the office.

"You're looking for your sister, Miss?" The fortune teller gawped up at Manying, his mouth half-empty with filthy, red betel nut teeth. She nodded. "I'll take you." With one practised movement, he folded the legs of his little table, and stood up to put it into a cotton sling over his back. The crow cawed in anticipation of action.

"You know where she is?" Manying was taken aback. The fortune teller barely nodded and strode off down the steps into the street, saluting jauntily to the soldiers in passing.

Manying had only seen him sitting hunched up over his little table. She was surprised how tall and bulky he was. Despite his age he walked quickly with the long, bouncing strides of a young peasant. Manying had difficulty keeping up with him, her high heels scraping on the pavement.

How ridiculous to follow this vagabond! Yet people said he knew many things. If anyone would know, he would. Ahead of her, he turned left into yet another street.

"How far?" she called out in doubt again, but he did not reply. They were in a tree-lined residential street with brick Western-style houses. Opposite her a house with an iron fence and big garden had had its facade blown off, a mountain of rubble left where the front rooms had been. But the back half of the house was still standing, displayed to the street in all its intimacy: a bedroom with flowered wall paper, a double bed with a pink satin cover, a western toilet and a bath, white towels hanging over a wooden stand. Something was moving up there...a Chinese man in a short gown and turban with a basket on his back clawed his way up to the bedroom. The rubble slipped, sending bricks bouncing into the courtyard below. The man hung on like a spider on a wall, waiting for the dust to settle before continuing his ascent.

The fortune teller crossed the road diagonally and stopped in front of a house that opened directly onto the street. It was a grand western townhouse: not the sort of place Lai Di could afford to live. Manying's heart sank. The pavement in front of the house was littered with tiny pieces of coloured glass, diamonds, rubies and emeralds glittering in the sun, that crunched to dust under foot—all the windows of the house, including the stained glass windows of the front door, had been blown out. The fortune teller loitered just past the front door and gestured with his head for Manying to enter. She hesitated. She had never been in such a grand house in Shantou.

"Go on! Upstairs." Incredulous, Manying took hold of the big brass door handle and, turning it, found to her surprise that the door opened.

Beneath her feet a mosaic of red, green, black and white triangles stretched out in the shape of a star; to her left and right, doors: 1a and 1b. Some plaster had fallen from the ceiling over the door to number 1a and been swept into a neat pile in the corner of the hall. In the centre of the hall was a lift with an iron grill door. Manying took the stairs. On the second floor flats, 2a and 2b.

"Lai Di? Deborah?" She dared only to whisper. The place was as lifeless as a grave. On the third floor the door to 3a was ajar. Taking a deep breath, Manying pushed inside. She was in a narrow lobby; this time tiled with many small red and white stars; in front of her a wooden coat stand with a mirror and a black gentleman's umbrella.

"Deborah...Sister?"

Walking to the end of the passage she found herself in

a large sitting room with white shutters that reached from the floor almost to the ceiling. All were closed, except the central pair. Lai Di stood with her back to Manying, smoking and looking out into the garden at the back.

"Oh Sister! I've been looking all over for you."

Lai Di said nothing for a long time, flicking the ash out the window. Birds tweeted happily to each other like peasant women in the cool of the afternoon, and a deep green ocean of trees swayed in the soft breeze. The room was sparsely furnished with two leather armchairs, a coffee table and a mahogany sideboard, above which hung a mirror on a chain and a calendar of Western film stars. It was still on the page for July. On the floor was a suitcase. Lounging over the back of one of the chairs Lai Di's black fox fur stared at Manying with glassy eyes.

"He left without me." Lai Di turned to face Manying. She was not made up; her eyes and skin were red and blotchy from crying.

"Who did? Teddy?"

Lai Di nodded and turned back to the garden.

"He said that it wouldn't be easy, but that he would arrange for me to leave for Shanghai on the ship with him and other foreigners. He told me to pack my bag, that he would come for me from the bank. I waited all morning...but he didn't come. I called his office and called his flat, but no one answered. In the end I went down to the docks myself. When I found the berth they told me that the ship with the foreigners had left at six this morning." Lai Di's voice cracked. She swallowed hard. "I told them that there must be some mistake. But they said not. I waited until dark and came back here. The spare key was in the usual place. But all his things were gone." Again she tried to swallow, but the sobs would not be controlled. She sank to her knees. Manying tried to take her in her arms, but she pushed her away. "Except that..." Lai Di pointed to a white envelope on the coffee table. "Money, he left me money. Enough for three months rent and an envelope with *Good luck always* and my name written on it. Money!" She spat out the word, before her voice disintegrated with grief. With great effort she struggled on, gasping between sobs. "I loved him... He talked to me about having children together...he wanted four...we would have a car and a big house in Boston with swings and slides in the garden for the little ones.

"Hush, hush."

Manying rocked her sister, curled like an injured child, in her arms. Lai Di's body shook and she shoved her fists into her mouth to smother the great choking cries that welled up from inside.

*M*anying and Lai Di set out after dark to return to Gok Sek. It was after nine by the time they got home. Entering the compound they saw that the light in the main sitting room was still on: odd as their father usually worked in the office in the evenings, and their mother would normally be in bed by now. Manying supposed they were waiting up for them.

As soon as she entered the sitting room she knew that something was wrong. The port pilot Shantou JD was there. With his drinking and gruff manners, her father did not like him. Thankfully, the two of them usually had nothing to do with each other. On this night instead of grubby khaki shorts and a sweaty short-sleeved shirt that displayed his forearms with bulbous tattoos of dragons and mermaids, Shantou JD wore a crisp white shirt with gold epaulets, freshly ironed and starched shorts, white knee-length socks, black garters, and shiny leather shoes. Resting like a wreath on his knees was his cap with the badge gleaming in the lamplight. A man dressed as a boy! Foreign men in summer attire with their ridiculous fat hairy legs usually made Manying and her friends snigger with embarrassment, but not on this occasion. Her mother sat with her head bowed opposite Shantou JD. The little teacups clustered unused around the terracotta teapot on the table. Her father cradled a small piece of printed paper.

She knew without being told, perhaps she had always known. Gently she took the paper from her father. A fleeting look of puzzled disorientation on his face, he released it without a word

> *To: Arthur Jones, Shantou Port Authority. Urgent. Please convey Pastor Wen Huaming Pastor Shantou Baptist Church. Regret inform Captain Wen Manye Eighty-Eighth Division Seventy-Seventh Corps killed in action Shanghai afternoon nineteenth September. He died that China might live. Chen Zheng 24th September 1937*

"Zheng sent the telegram from Shanghai via British Customs. Mr Jones has been kind enough to come all the way here to deliver it to us in person." Her father's voice was business-like, as if he were giving out church notices. It was strange to hear Shantou JD addressed by his proper name, instead of the usual "that drunken foreign devil."

"I'm so sorry," Shantou JD said in perfect Chaozhou dialect. "I think Zheng wanted you to know as soon as possible. I'm sure he did the right thing."

Her father nodded

"I should be leaving you now. If there is anything..."

"No, thank you. You have already been very kind."

Shantou JD got up and hesitated, ringing his hands with their chunky gold rings, like a nervous woman. "My wife and I, we too will soon be leaving Shantou. I am getting old. It's time to retire back to America." He tried to make light of it. "Do you think Pastor Wesley should come with us?"

"That's very kind of you. But Pastor Wesley's sister died five years ago. He has no one else in America. We are his only family now. It is best if he stays here, where people who know him and love him can care for him." Manying's father stood up. "On second thought, there are some papers... I was going to send them to the American Baptist Association, but under the circumstances, it might be better if..."

"Just tell me where to deliver them." Shantou JD nodded and the two men shook hands.

"You and your wife have made a great contribution to our community in Shantou. We will all be the poorer without you. God bless you," Manying heard her father say, and realised that he actually meant it.

18

All over China, out of the fissures in the sun-parched land, they came: the rich, the poor, the young, the old, the lame, the sick, scurrying, limping, crawling; by bus, by train, by boat, on foot; millions of refugees, marching into a new wilderness, fleeing the advancing Japanese.

Bedrolls strapped to their backs, the party from Shantou was like a long line of worker ants toiling up a rocky hill. They had been walking all morning along narrow paths through the thorny scrub. There was no cloud to shield them from the brilliant autumn rays, which reflected off the low yellow hills and were as cruel as those of any summer sun. The jagged stones cut the soles of the girls' leather court shoes, bruising their feet. Their arms ached with the ever-increasing weight of their small suitcases. Lai Di's face was pink with sweat, but still she wore her fox fur tied round her neck.

"Look! We're nearly at the top!" One of the young boys in the party, his school satchel slung across his chest, danced around on top of a rock as if he had been born in the wilderness, and pointed to the place above them where the path disappeared round the crest of the hill. But

Manying felt no excitement. What looked like the top was not always the top, and she was not so quick to rejoice, ploughing on at a steady pace as the others hurried on, eager to complete the climb.

Manying and Lai Di had left Shantou with the party for Chaozhou two days after the telegram from Shanghai. Huaming was not going to lose more children to the Japanese. The parting had been easier than Manying had anticipated. Just as when Manye had first gone to Military School and Lai Di had moved to Shantou, their mother distracted them all by fussing about what food and clothing they should take. As fast as she gave them things—dried beef, soy sauce, nuts, dried noodles, a padded jacket she had never worn—their father took the things back.

"For heaven's sake, old wife! They won't be able to carry it all."

When the actual time to leave came, no one cried.

Her mother's last words: "Look after each other! Take it steady!" Her father's: "Never forget God is always with you. Write!" As Manying turned at the gate to wave goodbye a mango fell from the tree to lie with the others rotting on the ground.

The journey had not gone as planned. Such was the exodus from Shantou in the wake of the bombing, that on the first morning when they reached the little river port there had been no boats left for hire.

"It's just not good enough." A young man with a pock-marked face and tiny eyes demanded aggressively of the lay Pastor in charge. A shipping clerk in Shantou, he was dressed in a crisp white shirt and tie and carried his jacket slung over his shoulder, as if he were expecting a normal day at the office.

"Tomorrow. There will be boats returning tomorrow."

The sixteen travellers had spent the previous night in the little port town, Manying, Lai Di and the other single women in the party sleeping on the floor in the small

white-washed church. There were eight of them. Lai Di,
Manying and five girls between the ages of thirteen and
twenty, all from Gok Sek families, and the taciturn maid
with the birth mark who had worked for the British family
who had held the party. Manying knew all the girls: some
from school, some from church and one of them, Ping
Ping, had been her classmate and was a fellow teacher at
the Mission Primary School, and her best friend.

Manying had not slept much that night, thinking about
Manye. How could a scrap of telegram paper be a fair
exchange for a life? Perhaps Zheng was mistaken? Perhaps
her brother had survived after all? She imagined Zheng,
bombs falling all around, running cap in hand into the
British Customs House in Shanghai. Panting, he leaned
heavily on the counter, his uniform torn and blood stained.
The sad beautiful eyes that drew you in and never let you
go fixed on an earnest young secretary. The soft palms of
his hands moved in gestures of pleading, as, with gentle
whispers, he induced her to let him send the telegram. No!
Manying knew the truth. Zheng's best friend, her brother,
the family's only son, was dead.

"Lie still. You're keeping us awake." Ping Ping's voice
hissed out of the darkness.

"I can't get comfortable. The floor is so hard," a voice
whined. A ripple of groans, admonitions and complaints
came from the other girls. Only the maid and Lai Di, lying
wrapped in her bedroll at Manying's side, said nothing. Lai
Di had hardly said a word since they returned to Gok Sek,
meekly going along with everything like an obedient child.
But it was because she was past caring—Manying knew
that. Without a word of protest or sign of regret, she had
left behind her most precious cheongsam dresses, to make
way for food. The only item of luxury that she refused to
part with was the fox fur: a gift, Manying suspected, from
Teddy. She rolled over, away from the cold wall. The
important thing now was to look after Lai Di. That is what
Manye would have wanted.

They had been woken just after dawn by explosions and shouting in the streets. "The Devil Japs are coming!"

Rushing outside, the now familiar bitter smell of burning filled the air. Along the river front, red flames clawed up at the soft blue dawn. A single plane casually made its escape up the snaking, silver river. It was the first bomb to hit the town.

"Must have been aiming for Shantou. Devil Jap probably got lost." The shipping clerk pronounced his opinion. Six houses had been destroyed and thirty people killed.

There had been no boats to be had for love or money that morning either, so the local Pastor had suggested that he arrange a guide to take them by foot upstream to another village, where it would be easier to hire boats.

"What! Walk?" The wife of the shipping clerk was the worse for wear for her night in the countryside. Without its usual nightly attention, the carefully arranged curls of the previous day had dissolved into lank locks. "All that way! And who says there will be boats when we get there?"

A prolonged argument ensued, but in the end everyone agreed that since they were still at risk of bombing, it would be better to move on anyway, even if they had to walk.

Manying watched the clerk's boy ahead of her reach the crest of the hill. But when she got there herself there was no end in sight. The path stretched across a barren valley, winding up and around yet another hill. Strange, she thought, for they had long since walked off the edge of the map. Despite the urging of the stocky guide that they must press on if they were to reach their destination before nightfall, the party stopped for lunch. Safely enclosed by the quiet valley with only the humming insects and occasional cawing bird to keep them company, it was hard to believe that there could be such a thing as war. Manying opened her tin lunch box full of cold rice, hoarded from the previous night, and gave it to Lai Di. She shook her head.

"Eat. Keep up your strength," Manying urged her. After a few minutes Lai Di began to pick at the food.

Sitting opposite them the clerk's wife took off her high heeled shoes. Her feet ans toes were covered in blood.

"Ai ya! I can't go on. Husband, didn't I tell I you we should never have left Shantou. But oh no! You knew better. Look at us now, out here in the wilderness like beggars." Mrs Li, an old Hakka lady who had married a Shantou man and lived on Gok Sek as long as Manying could remember, took out a brand new pair of black cloth slippers from her bundle and offered them to the clerk's wife. They were not shoes that any self -respecting modern lady would have worn, but with silent tears the clerk's wife accepted the gift, and protested no more.

As the afternoon wore on, the guide became increasingly impatient.

"Hurry up! Hurry up! Pastor, they must walk faster or we'll never get there before dark."

The Pastor tried to encourage his scattered flock with *Onward Christian Soldiers*. The girls struck up in support, but the rally was short lived; everyone was tired. The clerk's two boys no longer ran ahead like wild goats, but instead shuffled in the dust at their mother's side. For once, she did not even bother to tell them to tuck their shirts into their trousers. There were no more jokes or giggling chatter. They walked in silence.

As night came, the party reached a cluster of three large, white crescent-shaped tombs set back into the hillside, around them poorer tombs, marked by a single stone and in some cases just a mound of earth.

"Certainly a fine resting place!" Surveying the craggy hills softened by fluffy green scrub, the pastor inhaled the cool evening air. But Manying thought it strange that the tombs were so well maintained. According to the guide, there was no village nearby, but the vegetation around the large tombs had recently been cut back and the round stone platform in front looked as if it had been swept only that morning.

"We must spend the night here," the guide announced truculently. "Wasn't expecting to spend two days over this trip. The women and children walk too slowly. The extra night will cost you."

Calmly, the pastor raised the palm of his hand to silence the man.

"Don't worry about that. The extra will be taken care of when we arrive. But let's move on a little further and leave the spirits in peace."

The shadows of night were gathering thick and fast, and by the time they found a sheltered clearing between the rocks, it was already dark. On the other side of the hill, away from the tombs, everyone felt much more at ease. Everyone privately ate what he could from his own stock of food, and lay down to sleep on the hard ground.

Manying looked up at the sky. A few stars braved the silent blackness. On her face, the deceptively feathery touch of mosquitoes. Ignore them...do not think about them! In her mind she drew a large box on a piece of paper and began to draw a series of smaller boxes inside, a game she had played as a child. Smaller and smaller, until the last dot made by the tip of the pencil, and then she tried to imagine smaller than that. Smaller and smaller until she could think no more.

Sometime later, Manying awoke to a smell like rotting cabbages. Something breathing heavily was snuffling around beside her. She opened her eyes: a stooped, hooded figure stood with its back to her; stood in the spot where Lai Di had been lying. Slowly the figure turned round. The face, white against the darkness, was the face of the devil.

Manying screamed repeatedly. Startled, the figure backed away down the hill, wheezing in great gasps. The others were awake now, shouting and screaming: they were surrounded by hundreds of devils with no faces.

"Help, Help!" In the distance it was Lai Dai.

The pastor put on a torch; the clerk lit a candle. The horrendous creatures were revealed, backing slowly out of the clearing and down the hill. Dressed in rags and carrying sticks, they had no hands, no arms, no eyes, and no noses.

"Lepers! Away! Away!" the clerk's wife shouted as if swatting swarming flies, and dispatched the intruders back into the darkness.

But where was Lai Di? Her bedroll lay neatly folded on the ground where she had left it. Frantically, Manying groped around the rocks where they had been sleeping. The clerk came to help her, holding his candle high and nursing the flame with his palm.

"She's here. She's here." A shout came out of the darkness—it was one of the clerk's boys. Two figures emerged into the clearing, Lai Di leaning on the arm of a leper.

Unlike the other lepers, he wore no hood and walked with commanding dignity. The left side of his face, including his eye and most of his cheek, was bound in white bandages. The right side was untouched by the disease, the smooth, tanned skin glistening in the candlelight. He was young, no more than thirty.

"Begging your pardons, Your Excellencies. We startled you. We live in the village below and thought that you might be bandits come to raid us. It has been known." He spoke good Chaoshan dialect, but in the way of an outsider. "I frightened the lady here by accident when I was coming up the hill."

"I couldn't sleep and needed the toilet," Lai Di said sheepishly, still holding onto the young man's arm.

"I shouted for her not to be afraid, but she ran away and fell and hurt her foot. I don't think it is serious. Just a strain. Your Excellencies, I am truly sorry for the trouble. If I might enquire where your Excellencies are going? We don't have such honourable visitors very often."

"That's none of your business," the guide snapped.

"Where are you from, Sir?" The pastor responded in kind to the young leper's politeness.

"From Shanghai, your Excellency. I was training to be an engineer when I got the disease. At first I hoped for a cure, but when all my money was gone I was too ashamed to go back to my family. So I came here to the village to be with my own kind. The government gives us some money and we make and sell ropes to the boat people. It is not a bad life."

"We are going to pick up boats to Chaozhou. We come from Shantou. Things are not good." Satisfied, the pastor replied to the original question.

The young man nodded wisely. "So I have heard. The world is going mad. But if it's the river and boats you're after, then you really have come the long way round. There's a much shorter route. I can take you in the morning. It's not far from here by the back road."

When the party awoke at dawn the leper village was revealed below them in the valley; an orderly collection of straw houses along a single main street. Set against the backdrop of mountains draped in the morning mist, it could have been an idyllic scene from a painting. There was, however, no sign of their guide.

"I never did trust him—the bastard brought us the long way round to get more money out of us." The clerk cleaned his glasses on the end of his tie.

"Bloody war! If we are not careful, it will bring out the devil in all of us," the pastor said quietly, folding his bedroll.

Manying took a fresh look at Lai Di's foot by the light of day. It was not broken, but the muscles on the outside of the foot and around the ankle were turning a light purple colour and it was tender to the touch.

"You must have turned over on it. If I bandage it, do you think you can walk?" Lai Di nodded.

171

The young leper was true to his word. He led them down the hill, along the valley floor, and down to the river, toward his village. He walked slightly ahead of them with Lai Di leaning heavily on his arm. Despite the leper's kindness, she was the only one in the party who was not afraid of infection. It took them under an hour to arrive at their destination. Stopping under some trees at the side of the track on the outskirts of the village, the leper indicated with the stump of his diseased left arm for them to continue alone. The pastor offered money, but he refused.

"Keep it, Your Excellency. You have more need of it than I."

The pastor hesitated. "When the bombing stops, you should try our mission hospital."

The young man nodded. "Maybe. But it is the young ones who should go. The disease is not so advanced in them. They might have a chance."

"I will come back this way and we can talk some more," the pastor said.

"Good, good. We don't get many visitors. But in such times there are others who need your services more than we do. Do not worry about us, Master Shepherd, we have found our peace."

The travellers bade the leper goodbye; all except Lai Di, who waited behind with him in the shade. Turning round to wait for her, Manying saw the leper lift the bandages from his face. His nose and cheeks had been eaten away by the disease. The young man looked at the floor. Slowly, Lai Di reached out her hand; lifting his chin she bent forward and kissed him on the cheek.

*T*he river village without name, not far from the leper colony, consisted entirely of straw houses. As the party walked down what passed for the main street, naked children and barefoot women, aged beyond their years by poverty and toil, stood at the doors of their houses and observed them without expression. Flies hovered in thick clouds over the open drains, and the stink of the morning's faeces made Manying and some of the other women retch into the dust. There were, however, boats for hire, and after a half hour's haggling, a price was agreed.

The problem was that there were sixteen in the party and there were only three boats, the normal capacity of each being four passengers and two crew. The boatmen were reluctant to take on the extra load and consequent risk. Manying, Lai Di and Ping Ping ended up sharing a boat with old Mrs Li and her husband, since they were the only people willing to be near Lai Di after her contact with the leper. That left the pastor, his wife, the maid and two girls in one boat, and the clerk, his family and two girls in the other.

This last boat was the most problematic since it contained six people, and although two of the passengers were boys there was still not enough space for the luggage. The clerk fell into an argument with the tiny, turbaned laoban of the boat.

"Don't you play the grand squire with me, Mister!" The laoban, his arm and leg muscles as thick as trees retorted to the clerk, "I don't come to Shantou to tell you how to run your business. I'll thank you not to tell me how to run mine. Take it or leave it. Four people, same luggage. Six people, half the luggage."

Screeching and flapping like vultures, the village women in big black hats descended on the small wooden jetty, picking over the precious possessions of the clerk's family and the girls. Pink and blue flowered cheongsams, brassieres, pyjamas, shoes, a small wooden train engine, an inlaid picture frame and even books; all were sold off in minutes for fractions of their value.

It was a relief to finally get under way. Manying sat in the prow of the boat. Eyes half closed, she was mesmerised by the regular swaying of the laoban's mate standing on a wooden platform at the bow, pushing the single long wooden oar. To and fro, to and fro, it creaked gently on its metal hinge, the water sloshing lazily off its planed sides. The boat had a mast with a sail folded and tied neatly around it, but since the wind was blowing in the other direction, and they were travelling upstream, it was useless. A black butterfly fluttered across the boat settling on the amber varnished side. Its wings were like velvet. Manying drank in the moist river breeze, letting it soothe her dusty lungs. Every few miles they passed a tall white Buddhist pagoda or a small temple to the Goddess of the River, the red light burning on the altar quite visible inside. Her father had often told her of such sights when he returned from his visits to the country churches.

"The river people are some of the most devout in our land. But there are still so many ignorant of the Love of the Lord Jesus Christ and are led astray by superstition."

Manying slept a while and was awakened by the agitated conversation of the laoban and his mate. The young mate, barely more than a boy, pointed to heavy black clouds, moving quickly in their direction from the coast.

"Typhoon?" His brow crinkled.

Leaning on the oar the laoban shook his head. "Just rain. With any luck we'll track up the white water before it hits us. Anyway, this lot are Christians. Good men are immune to the lightning strikes and thunder! Isn't that right, Sir?" He addressed himself to Mr Li.

"To be sure. Heaven protects the righteous and good!"

"Ah, but there are no good men in China!" The boatman cackled so hard at his own wit that Manying thought he might topple into the water

A group of half a dozen seagulls screeched overhead. The air was damper and the wind was rising. The river narrowed, and as they rounded a bend, Manying saw bare, yellow hills rising out of the water to form a steep gorge. The boat began to bump about in the choppy water. The boatmen headed for one last piece of rocky flat land to their left. To her amazement Manying saw people coming out of caves in the rock. There were also a few straw huts and she realised with horror that people were living there. A gang of men gathered silently at the water's edge waiting for them. They were the thinnest, most motley gang of coolies she had ever seen. Mouths stained black from tobacco, eyes sunken from opium, they were more beast than man. Manying was afraid.

"Trackers," said Mrs Li and pointed to a narrow path cut into the rock face above the gorge. "They will pull the boats up the rapids from the tow path up there."

"All out!" the laoban shouted. "Can't haul you fat city pigs, too." With a sick feeling in her stomach, Manying realised that they too would have to walk along the tow path.

Lai Di got out of the boat without complaint, but she had only taken a few steps when it became evident that she could not make the climb. Her foot had swollen and was now deep purple.

"My sister is hurt. She can't walk," Manying called to the laoban of their boat, who hopping lightly ashore was walking barefoot over the rocky beach. Looking down at Lai Di's petite foot and lily white leg, he shook his head and cursed under his breath.

"All right, all right. But make sure the rest of you take all the luggage, hers too."

Manying's boat was the last of the three to be tracked and she sat on the rocky beach with her companions eating dried fish and some hot rice that they had bought from one of the women in the village: it tasted like the food of the Gods. Above them the passengers from the other boats were already making the slow climb along the tow path ahead of the first team of trackers. Each boat needed five trackers, who harnessed themselves across their chests to long ropes attached via pulleys to the prow of the boats. The laoban stood in the bow of the boat using the oar to steer; he banged on a little drum to give instructions to the trackers. The mate in the prow held a long pole to keep the boat off the rocks.

By the time Manying's boat was ready to leave the sky was black with clouds and the trackers were cursing to get the job done before the weather broke. According to the laoban's instructions, Manying and her school friend Ping Ping settled Lai Di in the centre of the boat and divided the luggage between them. As they left her, Lai Di smiled at them and waved her hand. It was the first smile Manying had seen since Teddy had left.

The rain started as a miserable drizzle just as the boat was pushing off. By the time Manying and her party had climbed the narrow path from the beach up to where the tow path began, it slashed at her face like hundreds of long cold knives.

The towpath was in fact a three-sided passage that had been carved out of the rock face. It was barely two feet wide in places and the height of the roof was irregular. Carrying Lai Di's bedroll as well as her own, Manying had many times to stoop down, nearly onto her knees, to get through.

The roar of the wild, grey water in the chasm was deafening and the narrow gorge magnified the beating of the laoban's drum and the shouts of the trackers. Worst of all the wind blew the rain onto the passage, covering the floor and the walls with treacherous sheets of glistening molten glass. Fearing that she would lose her footing, Manying rested her hand on the slimy black rock wall and looked back at the trackers a hundred yards behind her. The face of the lead man was contorted with effort, as bending double he used his hands to balance himself over a particularly narrow piece of path. Below, the little boat ploughed its miraculous way between the sharp rocks jutting out of the swirling water. Breathing deeply and steadying her gaze on a spot on the floor just in front of her, Manying braced herself to move on.

Suddenly the beating of the laoban's drum became more insistent. The boat was swinging across the current.

Only the laoban with the long oar levered against a rock was stopping it from spinning headlong down the river. For a second or two it seemed as if he would defeat the torrent, then a great judder went through the oar, snapping it in two and flinging him high into the air. In that second the trackers knew they could not hold the boat and released their harnesses to save themselves. In the maelstrom the boat spun round and round. The mate jumped into the water an instant before the boat crashed up against a large rock. Lai Di was flung into the water: a black head, an outstretched arm, and then she was lost to the tumult and spray. The trackers lay crouched on all fours, their heads in their hands, panting heavily.

The travellers waited three days in the next village for news. The laoban had managed to cling onto a rock and was hauled by rope up to the towpath. On the afternoon of the second day the news came that the body of the mate had been found washed upon the shore downstream. By the third day there was still no news of Lai Di, and the pastor reluctantly decided that they had no choice but to continue their journey.

Manying sat under the bamboo awning in the back of the boat. Ahead of her were the ancient grey walls and bridge of Chaozhou. Her world dissolved into mists and tears.

CHONGQING

19

*I*n the sparse living room of a little white house high on the cliffs above the city of Chongqing, Mei Ren, the wife of the secretary to the Minister of Education, was kneeling amongst her meagre collection of a half-dozen carefully-hoarded tin cans and paper packets. Once, when she was a little girl, she had accidentally broken a precious Ming bowl belonging to her father. Seeing the cans and packets scattered around her on the floor, she felt the same confused panic she had experienced all those years ago. These days life seemed to be an endless quest to recreate the lost pattern from the shattered blue and white fragments and glue them back together. The trick was to ignore the crazy lines overflowing with yellow glue that snaked all around the bowl and convince oneself that it was as good as new.

Looking up, Mei Ren saw that an audacious spider had spun a web across a corner of the open window. The web glittered in the spring sunshine. Taking a dusting rag from the wooden table in front of her, Mei Ren got off her knees and went over to the window. She lifted her face to the warmth of the golden spring sunshine. At last, the winter was over. Lost in its creeping mists and slimy darkness, the long cold months had seemed an eternity, the ice so beautifully cruel, daily etching fresh pictures on their window panes; her husband and two young sons in hats and scarves huddled around a single charcoal burner, eating oranges while the armies fell; Hong Kong on Christmas Day 1941, Singapore in February. Now Burma and the South Western provinces of China, Yunnan and even Sichuan where Mei Ren and her family had taken refuge, hung in the balance.

At last the filthy soot and fume-laden winter mists, as thick as clouds of wadding that you could play with in your hands, had evaporated into the spring sunshine. Far, far below Mei Ren watched the paddle ferry ploughing its habitual foaming furrows through the grey waters of the Yangtze River, above it the terrifying blue of the naked sky—for now that the winter mists were over it was the season for Japanese air raids. Mei Ren felt her throat go tight: the wail of the sirens, the rush to the caves, ground-shaking thunder, mothers' breasts bared to their babies to prevent them from crying, and her youngest son, his eyes big like a rat in the dark, shaking uncontrollably on her knee. Mei Ren lifted her duster, and thinking of the Buddha and of her next life, lowered it again. The spider sat contentedly at the centre of his web, catching the last gentle rays of spring before the burning of the summer.

Mei Ren returned to her provisions. That morning, as he was leaving for work, her husband had told her that he had invited two American journalists for dinner for the following evening.

"Seven or eight courses will be about right, hey Old Wife!" He had grinned.

She looked at him in his shabby silk gown that was fraying around the cuffs and wearing through at the elbows. She had urged him to wear cotton over-cuffs to preserve his sleeves at work, but he had refused saying it would make him look like a common clerk. Her face must have fallen, for he went on, "It's important. Times like this—we Chinese must show the outside world that we are surviving with dignity."

Sighing, Mei Ren knelt down; she was so tired. In front of her were the paltry remains of the delicacies they had brought with them from Nanjing in 1937. As the Japanese advanced on the city, Generalissimo Chiang Kai Shek and his government had relocated up the Yangtze River to Chongqing, making Chongqing the wartime capital of what was left of Free China. Taking up her note pad Mei Ren squinted at the list of food items that had long since been crossed off; dried scallops, Oolong tea, tinned beef, dried cherries. Her mouth watered at the thought of tastes long lost. She took a bottle of premium soy sauce from among the offerings. It was so much better than the vinegar and floor sweepings that were sold as soy sauce in Chongqing. Putting the bottle on the chair behind her, she crossed it off the list. Slowly, she picked up a paper packet that had been bound with brown tape. Cradling it with both hands she raised it toward her face so that she could read the characters scrawled in her own script on the front of it, although she need not have bothered for she knew what the precious packet contained: top quality dried mushrooms. She had been saving them for a special occasion. Carefully, she opened a packed and tipped them into a bowl on the table. One, two, three...there were eleven left. She would use three for luck, soak them well to get a good soup, and chop them small.

Turning to the back of the note pad, Mei Ren slowly wrote a list of the things she would need to buy for the dinner; pork, chicken or duck, green vegetables, spring onions, melon, grapes and soya bean curd. She rubbed her forehead with the tips of her fingers, easing out the strings of tension tightening around her head. They could do with some dried shrimps and Shaoxing wine for the repeated toasts her husband would insist on making, even though he knew that foreigners were much more comfortable left to sip their wine in their own time, rather than partake of endless ritual toasts. Unfortunately, they had used the last dried shrimps and Shaoxing wine at Chinese New Year. These things were obtainable but were expensive and needed to be haggled for. When they had first arrived in Chongqing things had been cheap, but the savvy people of Sichuan province had soon realised the business opportunity presented by the influx of what they called "down river people." Now they never missed an opportunity to take advantage. No good sending the maid, Mei Ren thought, I will just have to go myself. She put the stores into the bottom of a wooden cupboard and padlocked the doors. I must not complain, she admonished herself. People are suffering and dying all over China. My family is much better off than most, and certainly the arrival of their lodger had improved their financial situation.

Mei Ren had not been at all pleased when her husband told her that the army had billeted the wife of a major in the New First Army to live with them. Their house had only three rooms plus the tiny kitchen and veranda at the back. It was very cramped compared with their old house in Nanjing.

"Another mouth to feed, and where will we put her? We've got no space."

"According to the army, we have plenty of space—at least by Chongqing standards." Her husband fished the last pieces of white cabbage off the plate in the middle of the table and meticulously used them to sweep up the last grains of rice on the side of his bowl before popping the whole lot into his mouth.

"She'll pay for her board and lodgings from her army allowance. Besides, in my position, I can't say no. I'll lose face. We'll have to move our bed into the living room, like we did last summer. It's much cooler out here anyway. Just make sure you get as much money out of her as you can, that's all. Of course it is our patriotic duty, but no point making a loss out of it!"

"But for all we know, she could be a stinking peasant who pees in the corner of the room and steals things."

"Whoever she is, she is the wife of an officer in General Sun Li Ren's army. Those men are the best we've got. Right now they're fighting for China in Burma. You will treat her with respect and make the best of it. I'll hear no more on the matter."

One morning early in March Mei Ren had been standing at the door watching her sons play when Manying emerged from under the cracked, mist-draped archway that led into their courtyard. A petite woman with a plain blue padded jacket over her cheongsam, she was accompanied by a balding, bandy-legged corporal who carried with ease her two small cardboard suitcases and bedroll.

"Lady Yao..." Manying addressed Mei Ren with the honorific reserved for wives of senior officials and, cupping hands, bowed her head in the traditional greeting. "It is very kind of you to have me."

Mei Ren's heart went out to her. The carefully applied powder and touch of lipstick could not disguise the pinch of fatigue. She was so young: not much more than twenty, barely more than a child.

"Welcome! Welcome! Come in!

Watching Manying drinking tea in their sitting room, the bed with its bright red quilt now in the corner, Mei Ren assessed her lodger. Despite her journey she was clean, tidy and well-mannered. It could not be said that she was beautiful. She was not possessed of the sweet dimples and rosebud mouth so beloved by Chinese men, but she had a long elegant face and her smooth ivory skin stretched dramatically over her high cheekbones and forehead, giving the impression of honesty and intelligence. But what Mei Ren noticed most about her was her easy-going nature. Later, as she came to know Manying better, she saw it as a gift, the ability to ignore the greater questions and thus make light of things in the face of diversity. That was why she would survive.

"I am so happy that you speak Mandarin," Mei Ren giggled despite herself. "I was terrified they would send me someone who spoke Shanghainese or Cantonese, someone that I couldn't even talk to!"

Manying laughed. "That's funny! I too was afraid that you wouldn't speak Mandarin. Then what would we have done?"

The matter of rent was also solved with ease. Anticipating problems, Mei Ren had done her homework, finding out from the ladies with whom she played mah-jong exactly how much Manying's army allowance would be. She was surprised when Manying herself proposed handing over virtually all of her monthly allowance, keeping only a small amount for personal expenses.

"I really think I got a good deal. What's more, she is a good girl: used to be a schoolteacher before her marriage, helps my sons with their homework," Mei Ren announced proudly to her mah-jong companions at the end of Manying's first week.

"More like stupid, if you ask me. The woman billeted with me haggled like a harpie. In the end my husband had to negotiate with her. Mei Ren, don't you dare tell him how much you are getting from your billet—he'll be furious!" The jade bangles around the stubby wrists of Mei Ren's partner clonked on the table as she placed her tiles.

"The only thing wrong with Manying is that she doesn't play mah-jong: says it's against her religion. She's Christian...well, a lapsed one. Actually, she says she hasn't been to church since her brother was killed in '37 in Shanghai." Mei Ren tried to change the subject

"Doesn't play mah-jong?"

"What on earth is she going to do with herself in Chongqing? God knows there are no decent films, and there is certainly nothing worth buying, and all the interesting men are away!"

Looking at her watch, Mei Ren listened to the distant roar of cars and the peeping of horns filtering up from the city below. It was nearly twelve o'clock. Soon her sons would be back from school and Manying from town. Poor Manying! Once a week she went to visit a contact of her husband's in the Ministry of Defence to see if there were a letter or any news about his Division. Mei Ren doubted that she would be so cheerful if her husband were fighting the Japanese in a foreign land. Perhaps Manying would get a letter today. She hoped she would.

The four years since the Japanese invasion had turned Manying, along with millions of others, into vagabonds. She had travelled a lot and seen much: the twisted bodies of communists with bullets in the backs of their heads left lying in the middle of a shady colonial boulevard, a well-known English professor from Beijing dying of malaria in a little wooden hut, a Japanese prisoner weeping into his hands when a Chinese soldier offered him a bowl of rice, a blackbird singing as a woman bled to death in childbirth under the shade of mulberry tree, pot bellied children like swarms of flies pulling at her shirt and clinging to her legs, and countless others who through physical infirmity or simple bad luck never had the slightest chance of survival.

Manying no longer went to church. She had not been since she left Shantou. She did say the Lord's Prayer every night before she went to sleep but did not hope for much. So when her visit to her friend in the Ministry of Defence that day brought no news of her husband and his Division she was inclined to be philosophical. Even the remarks she overheard the young lieutenant making to his sergeant as she left his tiny office did not dent her spirits unduly.

"Rain or shine the 'pretty one' comes once a week to

get news of the Thirty-Eighth. I've told her we have her Chongqing address and will send any mail onward. But new brides, you know! Hadn't been married six months when her husband was deployed. Such a shame! "

Most people in wartime Chongqing were not there by choice. The fortunate ones had enough to eat, a roof over their heads and were perhaps able to take solace in the passing of the seasons over the yellow gorges of the Yangtze River, a plum blossom in a ruined corner of what had once been a scholar's garden, and the amazing ingenuity of a nation in bringing its factories, schools and universities thousands of miles from the Japanese occupied east coast, to rebuild them in the interior. Foreigners complained of the medieval squalor of the narrow stinking alleys, where human beings and vermin lived side by side, and took refuge in the Chongqing Club on the south bank. Emaciated scholars and students working in tiny hovels and straw- roofed country cottages turned their minds to the great post-war Chinese renaissance, which was sure to come. But Manying felt more at home in Chongqing than she had at anytime since leaving Shantou.

Putting all thoughts of her husband out of her mind, she set off up the Street of the Seven Stars. There were hair salons, tailors, wine shops, and restaurants. Many of their crude, hand painted billboards proudly proclaimed *Formerly of Shanghai*. On the wall on the side of a little teashop was a faded poster of the deceased Father of the Nation, Sun Yat-sen. Next to it someone had made a fresh chalk painting. It was a colourful kaleidoscope of the flags of the members of the Alliance. Testing herself as she might, one of her little pupils recognised those of America, Britain, China, and Russia. Manying felt taller at the thought of China now as a nation among equals. Her brother would have been proud, and she felt a stabbing pain in her stomach that always accompanied the thought of him.

A crowd had gathered around a wooden stall at the entrance to an alley.

"Pretty lady! Come see! Lipsticks, powder, hair pins." The wife of the laoban was touting for business. The wares were laid out on a table covered in red paper. When a purchase was made, one of two little girls, their heads and arms just about reaching above the level of the table, carefully wrapped the object in folded pieces of brightly coloured paper. They were doing a swift trade. Manying's eyes fell on some hairpins with small cloth butterflies glued on the end. It was the pure indulgence of colours that attracted her: pink, red, orange, purple and blue. She bought a purple one for herself and a pink one for Mei Ren and had the stall girl wrap them in complementary coloured paper.

That was the end of Manying's money until the next week, but she did not care. She thought of Mei Ren, her dainty face like a dimpled peach: the beautiful elegant wife, the patient, loving mother. When Manying was a little girl she had wanted to grow up into a lady just like Mei Ren. But inflation was eating away at all their incomes and at Chinese New Year Mei Ren's mah-jong debts had outweighed her winnings. Old nail varnish was no longer removed, a fresh coat merely added on top, and the remains of her perm were now sustained by nightly curling with rollers. Mei Ren took pleasure in telling Manying exactly the last time she had had her hair done. It was the wonderful, euphoric day of the Pearl Harbour attack which brought America into the war as China's ally: outside the hairdresser's shop the news had brought dancing in the streets.

Manying puffed her way up the hundreds of steps that led up the hills and through winding alleys to Mei Ren's house. When she had first arrived she had the impression that everyone in hilly Chongqing was constantly climbing steps through clouds, seeking daylight. But today with the warm blue sky above, she could almost believe that she was climbing the stairs to Heaven. She passed under the arch leading to the courtyard in front of Mei Ren's house. It had been damaged by a bomb blast the previous autumn and the Qing dynasty carved dragon on the white marble lintel had cracked in two. The large head with gaping mouth was severed from the ornate, scaly tail and hung slightly lower, supported by a rickety bamboo scaffold. This had been erected by the residents who judged it was too much trouble either to repair the arch or demolish it, when any day another little Jap devil bomb might make the decision for them.

Mei Ren's sons were playing with the neighbour's children around the magnolia tree. The pink tips of its buds were primed to burst into flowers. Brandishing crude wooden swords the children were engaged in a battle, each child with a square of paper pinned on his shirt with identifying characters: *American Plane; Japanese Destroyer; Chinese Tank.*

"Any news?" Mei Ren asked hearing the door open, but one look at Manying's face told her that there was none. "It will come soon; last night I asked the Buddha for it my prayers."

Manying smiled. "Well, I am doubly insured! Thank you!"

Manying gave Mei Ren the present and insisted that she open it. Using the little hair pin to curl back her fringe where it was getting long, Mei Ren looked as if she were going to cry.

"You soldier's wives are very brave. I admire you, Manying. "

"I married a man who is proud to be a soldier. It is my fate to watch and wait."

20

*M*anying avoided looking out of windows from the house during the day when the rocky cliffs falling away to the Yangtze River below were revealed with all the horror of a recurrent nightmare. But at night she was not afraid. She stood in her cotton pyjamas by the open window of her bedroom. Far below, the green lights of the paddle ferry floated slowly towards her. In the darkness the ferry docked and a minute or so later small red flames lit in quick succession, three or four at first and then a whole cluster. At night the disembarking passengers bought plaited bamboo flares from the little boys waiting by the dock to light their way home. Manying watched as the puffs of red smoke floated slowly up the Wong Lung Men steps, dispersing at the top, like nocturnal dandelion puffs, and gradually petering out into the darkness.

Mei Ren's dinner party had gone well that evening; at least the Americans and Mr Yao had drunk copiously and enjoyed themselves. When Mei Ren's sons in blue sailor suits that were too small for them giggled at the foreigners struggling to manipulate chopsticks, the guests entered into the joke. The little boys responded with offerings of schoolboy English: 'Long live The Republic of China' from the elder and 'I like strawberries' from the younger. Thus the evening got off to a good start.

"Mr Yao tells me your husband is an army major." A fatherly American with a sagging white chin and bald head, called Stanley, addressed himself to Manying.

"Yes, with the Thirty-eighth in Burma."

"Burma! Tough posting...jungles...problems with Stilwell and his Chinese generals...British haven't got the will to hold...not going too well." The younger American with wild blond hair was talking enthusiastically with his mouth full and Manying could not understand all he said.

"It is unthinkable that Burma should fall and China be cut off from the outside world," Mr Yao weighed in assertively.

Seeing Manying's face twisting up with concern Stanley said gently, "Yes, yes exactly."

"But what if Burma does fall?" The younger man pressed on fumbling for another piece of chicken. "What then?"

"Then we will fight on alone, as we have being doing for the past four years." Mr Yao was irritated. Quickly changing the subject, Stanley asked Mei Ren the meaning of her name.

"Mei Ren is not my real name! Just a nickname I got it as a schoolgirl because I was always curling my hair and wearing make up!" She laughed.

"It means 'The Beauty!' My wife is so vain she won't even wear spectacles! Maybe you can succeed where I have failed, gentleman! Persuade her of the error of her ways!" Harmony restored, Mr Yao grinned affectionately at his wife and topped up his guests' wine cups.

As the evening wore on, the Americans enthusiastically asked Mr Yao all sorts of questions about the Chinese government. He was glad to oblige, pontificating at length about the necessity of a strong leader, how he admired the Generalissimo above all men, and the need for every citizen to follow the spirit of the New Life Movement and sacrifice himself for the unity of the nation. Sleepy with food and wine and lulled by the sound of the daily litany of propaganda, albeit translated into English for the Americans' benefit, Manying had longed for the guests to depart.

From her bedroom Manying could hear the soft sounds of the Yao's love-making next door: Mei Ren's smothered sighs and Mr Yao's final grunt, followed by the rustle of bedding being rearranged.

"Don't catch cold," Mei Ren whispered

"I want a glass of water," Mr Yao replied. There was a thump and clinking as Mei Ren reached over to the box by the bed and poured water out of the flask she had put there earlier: it was the same every time they made love.

How Manying missed her husband! Going to her bed she took a photograph from under her pillow and returned to the window. A stocky man with a chubby face under a major's hat stood stiffly at attention in her hand. His eyes looked disdainfully past the camera, as if he were concerned with greater matters than being photographed, his upper lip pressed down on the thicker lower one in a defiant frown. In her mind's eye Manying saw him bounding into the room they had shared after their marriage in Guizhou, every sinew, every fibre quivering with excitement at the news of the Burma deployment.

"At last we have the chance to show the world what we can do!"

She had watched him strip at the wash stand, the taut muscles of his back and arms glistening with sweat from the day's training. Lying face down on the bed, he sighed with satisfaction as she massaged the knotted muscles of his shoulders. She smelled the warm, shiny sweetness of his neck, and when he rolled over and pulled her to him she felt the strength of his thick thighs against her.

Manying was surprised to find she was crying and quickly wiped away the tears.

As with most marriages Manying's had come about in a round about way and had not been what she had been expecting. She had met her husband, known universally as Bear after the character Xiong for his surname, in the late summer of 1941 in a small town in Guangzhou province that lay outside Japanese control. After fleeing Shantou, Manying and Ping Ping had arrived there the previous summer and secured jobs at a local primary school. It was Ping Ping who had suggested the introduction, although not in the first instance to Bear. Six months previously Ping Ping had married a local highschool teacher, Mr Wong, whose younger brother was also with the Thirty-eighth. This younger Wong was visiting his family home while on leave, accompanied by his friend, Bear.

"What do you think? Wouldn't it be great if we were sisters in the same family?" With her crooked front teeth Ping Ping's mischievous smile was irresistible. "Our children would be cousins." Leaning back in her chair she patted her ripe belly with satisfaction.

Wearing her best cheongsam, the one with the lace neck she copied from a magazine and had worn that night in Gok Sek, Manying went to dinner at Ping Ping's home. It proved a riotous evening, reminding her with a sharp pang of the happy times together with her own family. The younger Wong was tall, skinny, well mannered and a great talker.

"We Cantonese in the regiment have to stick together. Bear's family is in Hong Kong now, and the poor chap was in dire need of some good Cantonese home cooking. So I said, 'why not take your leave at home with me?'"

"Well! It's unfortunate that I married a Chaozhou girl then!" quipped Wong the elder without looking up from his rice bowl.

"Chaozhou cooking is just as good Cantonese! In fact it is better!" Ping Ping was not going to give up easily.

"I wouldn't go that far," Wong teased. "But you're

making progress, Old Wife!"

It was not, however, the younger Wong who caught Manying's attention, rather the older, thickset Bear, who smiled rarely and said little. Although he was small, his pulsing energy filled the room making him seem bigger than he really was. He looked at her and she blushed.

The following day at lunchtime a heavily pregnant Ping Ping puffed and panted her way to the school.

"I don't know how to explain this, Manying. I am so sorry."

"What's the matter?" Manying thought some terrible disaster had befallen them.

"Young Wong has been seeing another girl in town; apparently it's quite serious. I must have misunderstood. It's so embarrassing. Sorry, sorry." To her relief Manying did not seem too upset. "The thing is, Bear would like to meet you again. That is, if you agree..."

*I*n the cool of the late afternoon Bear was waiting for Manying outside the school with a watermelon in a red string bag. She had only seen him seated and he was even smaller than she expected. He was not particularly handsome, but then neither was he bad looking. He suggested that they find a quiet spot somewhere on the outskirts of town to eat the melon.

He took long, loping strides and had to slow down so that she could keep up in her heels. Half nervous, half flattered, Manying sneaked glances at the face of the stranger who was probably ten years older than she was. She had to concentrate hard to understand what he was saying since he spoke to her in Cantonese and her command of the dialect was still far from fluent.

They sat in the shade of a tumble down bamboo farmer's hut on the banks of a small stream, a gentle breeze rustling the scrawny remains of the straw roof. A peasant woman in black, hidden under a large conical hat, moved slowly through the golden haze, baling rice stalks for fodder. Manying and Bear did not speak, the silence filled by the twittering birds scavenging insects in the wake of the peasant woman. Modestly arranging her cheongsam Manying sat on her hip, her legs to one side. Bear, sitting cross legged a foot or so a way, took out an army knife from the soft leather sheath on his belt and set about the watermelon. He placed the tip of the silver blade in position on the crown of the melon. One short sharp thump of his fist and the blade pierced the thick green flesh with a dull hollow sound, slipping easily inside. Pleased, Bear nodded. "It's a good one!"

Patiently, meticulously, he moved the knife around the circumference of the melon until, soundlessly, it parted in his hands. Ripe, red flesh and shiny, black seeds glistened in the sunshine. The sweet delicate scent of overflowing juices filled the air. Holding the great chunks of melon away from them they ate with their heads thrust forward to avoid the juice staining their clothes: sucking, slurping and smacking their lips. When they had finished Bear gave Manying a neatly folded white handkerchief to wipe away the juice. Dabbing away the stickiness from her chin, she smelled the crisp, clean scent of good, pre-war soap.

After a while, Bear talked slowly and proudly about his regiment and its general, Sun Liren, who trained with the men every morning.

"He's amazing—nearly died of bullet wounds in Shanghai in `37. We're very lucky to have such an enlightened commander who cares about his men. Under his leadership we can do great things for China." Bear's small eyes were so earnest they were almost sad, as if he carried the weight of All Under Heaven on his shoulders. Manying was desperate to make him smile. She told him about a little pupil of hers who had asked that morning why foreigners smelled so awful.

"And what did you say?" He cocked his head impishly to the right.

"I told him that it was because foreigners liked to eat

milk and cheese."

Bear's face broke into a plump, boyish smile. She wanted to hold him to her and make everything right.

Occasionally communication broke down. Laughing at the comic distortions of the other's dialect or pronunciation they resorted to Mandarin, or in the worst case a little brown note pad that Bear carried in his shirt pocket. Exchanging the pencil like shadow boxers, their hands almost touched and Manying trembled within herself. He looked her directly in the eye as he talked now. Embarrassed, she stared down at her hands, or across the fields at the peasant woman who was wending her way home towards a small village in the distance where the smoke from the evening cooking fires was already rising in long twirling wisps.

Bear and Manying met every day for the five days for a walk and a simple supper at a street stall. Manying felt different. Her movements were slow and long and her face soft with smiles. She had not realised how lonely she had become after marriage had taken Ping Ping away from her. Time flew by and soon there were only two days left before Bear was due to return to his regiment. They were enjoying the last rays of the afternoon sunshine in the spot where they had first eaten the watermelon.

"I know people don't have much respect for soldiers, but our regiment is different. We are professionals, a modern army. Our officers are educated, our men volunteers. They have boots and are regularly paid and well fed." Bear paused, searching Manying's face for encouragement. "I am not saying that army life is easy. I would be away a lot, but the army will look after you when I am not there. You would have an allowance and wouldn't have to work." In desperation he took her hand in his. Manying's breath came short and fast as her head spun.

"I'm nothing, just a wanderer. Why do you want me?" Her voice sounded thin, weak; her Chaozhou accent unusually heavy.

"Exactly because you are a wanderer, that's why I want you: wanderers are the survivors. In this war those who stay put and do not adapt will perish. I know that you can look after yourself when I am away."

His pulsing grip tightened around her hand and she was afraid of his strength.

"I did have a wife before; the match was arranged by my parents. I told you that my family has land just outside Guangzhou, which my cousin now manages. My wife was the daughter of a neighbouring family. I was seventeen and she was sixteen. She died a year after our marriage, in childbirth, and the child with her. He would have been my son." He hesitated. Manying was confused.

"She was a country girl, a good woman but illiterate and not very robust. Manying, I want my sons to be educated in science and English. I need a strong, educated, modern wife."

Now that he had said his piece he looked so forlorn. Manying wanted to cover his face in kisses but she just nodded. He put his arm around her and she leaned her head upon his shoulder.

"I wish I could offer you more," he said

"It is already more than enough."

*I*t had not been the kind of wedding that Manying had dreamed about. There was no red bridal dress, no clashing of cymbals and blaring of trumpets, no excited relatives or bolts of silk. But Bear gave her all he had: two small gold bangles that had belonged to his mother, and she was grateful for that.

Two signatures on a register in the Regimental Headquarters in Guizhou and they were married. They had a simple meal in the mess with young Wong and some friends before returning to the small musty room that had been allocated to them. It was furnished with a bed and mosquito net, two chairs, a table, Bear's trunk and Manying's as yet unopened suitcase. Above the bed someone, probably young Wong, had made a paper chain of Double Happiness characters.

Bear had never even kissed Manying, and now that they were alone there was an awkward silence.

"I need to change," Manying whispered.

"I'll have a cigarette outside." He groped for the packet in his breast pocket.

When he returned she was sitting on the edge of the bed wearing an old pair of pink cotton pyjamas and combing her long hair. She smiled at him, and he stared at her as if trying to capture the moment in his mind.

He washed, and starting to undress, said to her, "Don't look. I do not want you to be afraid."

"I'm not." Calm now, her hands resting on her lap, she looked up at him.

When he came to her Manying hardly recognised him. His face was glazed with the shiny yellow light of the oil lamp, his eyes raw, greedy like an animal with its prey in sight. But his touch was gentle, smoothing her hair and slowly undoing the buttons on her shirt. She stroked the back of his head and buried her face in his neck.

"Hey Hey! What's the matter?"

"Nothing. It's just... just..."

He kissed her on the lips and slowly opened her out with his tongue.

There was no pain, just a mild discomfort. She heard a voice cry out and realised it was her own. Above her, Bear's face was that of a stranger, his eyes screwed tightly shut, his forehead creased. In the last moment his mouth contorted in the grimace of a wild dog, and a drop of his spittle fell onto her cheek. She was left with a feeling of overwhelming relief. At last the great shadow that had been living inside her all these years was free. She lay at her husband's side, drugged with deep, warm pleasure. He was already asleep, snoring gently.

In the morning when they got up, she tried to cover the blood on the sheets so he would not see it. Laughing at her protests and restraining her with one arm he pulled back the quilt, triumphantly examining the blots, already dry and brown. When he had departed for the parade ground she looked at herself in his shaving mirror and was surprised to see that her face was just as it had been the day before.

*I*n Chongqing, Manying heard voices outside her bedroom window. Below two flares were moving up the narrow cliff path towards her. An old man with a long beard and a round-faced boy were leading two small Tibetan pack ponies, the red halo of their flares dyeing their faces like autumn berries. The slipping, clip-clop of the ponies' hooves on the rock got louder; the smoky light spread up the side of the hill towards her like a giant spreading stain. It crept up the house wall and over the window ledge, colouring her hands and seeping slowly across the picture of Bear that she held in her hands.

21

*T*roops were on the move. At night, long black snakes of men marched through the empty streets. By day, grey columns of weary ghosts in straw sandals tramped through the yellow dust. Standing on the side of the road, Manying watched an officer on an ambling, fat white horse leading his men. Newspaper headlines had been proclaiming one victory after another in Burma: *Chinese Army Saves British, Little Jap Devils on the Run!* But the rumours were of the burning of Mandalay and of defeat and disarray. The last line of men marched past, umbrellas stuck in their backs. Manying crossed the road, walked in front of the sentries and the concrete machine gun emplacement, and went into the Ministry of Defence.

As usual, the door to the stuffy lieutenant's office was propped open with a piece of folded cardboard, but the habitual air of nonchalant boredom—or was it quiet efficiency, Manying was never quite sure which—had been replaced by fluster and flap. The lieutenant, sweating in shirtsleeves, was listening intently to someone on the telephone and quickly filling a page of paper with long spidery characters. Behind his desk, the typist worked the arms of a giant Chinese typewriter, double time. No sooner had the lieutenant put the telephone down than it rang again.

"Yes. Understood. Will do." He slammed the receiver down. Pausing for breath and wiping his brow, he caught sight of Manying.

"What's up?"

"Can't say, Madam." The lieutenant's face was grey with fatigue and a there was a shadow of stubble on his chin making him look like an adolescent boy.

"Please," she begged, "Please."

"The Jap devils are making a run on Lashio and the Burma Road."

"And the Thirty-eight?"

"They were given the order for re-deployment from Burma yesterday. Buddha, help them. I really don't know anymore. Please don't ask. I'm sorry."

The sergeant came in from the corridor, a red thermos flask painted with pink roses under his arm. "Hello Madam," he said brightly. "There's a letter for you at last! Lucky lady!"

The late April sunshine was already threatening with summer menace. Emerging from the Ministry of Defence, the harsh glare hurt Manying's eyes. She squinted again at the grubby, crumpled letter in her hand. It was postmarked 'Shantou', 27th December 1941. Addressed to Manying and Bear, it had been sent via a church friend to Ping Ping in Weizhou who had forwarded it to the lieutenant at the Ministry of Defence, as Bear had told her to. The return address was that of Aunt Feng and Young Uncle Chen.

Manying's legs felt wobbly and a haze came over her eyes. She managed to walk round the corner to a small teashop that was open to the street and sat down in the shade on a rickety stool at a folding table. Sipping on the silver water with a few leaves floating in it that passed for tea, she began to feel better. She ordered a bowl of noodles, more to justify her position in the shop than from hunger, and turned her attention to the letter. The battered envelope cracked and tore like a dry autumn leaf as she opened it. There was one page written by Aunt Feng.

Dearest Niece,

I hope that this letter finds you in good health and that you and your husband are blessed with as much good fortune as is possible in such times.

I find that I can no longer postpone telling of the calamity that has befallen us. If I have tarried too long, I beg you to forgive me. It was only because I feared to interrupt the period of special joy to which every new wife is entitled. It is with a heavy heart that at last I take up my pen.

It is my sad duty to inform you that your father and Pastor Wesley have been killed by the Japanese.

Soldiers came to the house two days after Pearl Harbour to take Pastor Wesley to Shantou to interview him. Your father refused to let him go with them. What could they possibly want with a senile old man who was no threat to anyone? But the Japanese would not listen, insisting that as an American who spoke Chinese he had to be interrogated. Crying out that Pastor Wesley was his own father and that they should take him instead, your dear father put himself between Pastor Wesley and the Japanese. A scuffle ensued, shots were fired and your father and Pastor Wesley were both shot and wounded. Uncle Chen and some friends did what they could for them and carried them to the hospital but it was already too late.

My dear niece, our hearts weep with you. Our

community has lost two great men. It was Pastor Wesley who first brought me to Jesus, but I can make no sense of why the Lord should take the lives of our two most beloved ministers in such a way.

Niece, you must not worry about your mother. She has come to live with us and although not in good health, asks me to tell you that her one remaining comfort is that you are alive and well. She hopes to hear good news from you before too long. We are managing well enough. I know it is difficult, but your primary duty is to your husband and his family. At this time your health is the most important thing. You must not think about returning to Gok Sek, for although in our sadness we all miss you, we are fine.

My dearest niece, do not weep too long. Trust in the Lord, for he will give you the strength to shoulder your grief with courage.

Free from their labours, thy rest in the arms of the Lord.

God be with you and bless you always.

Aunt Feng

PS My youngest son is doing well in the army and always asks after you in his letters.

With a scraping of chairs on the stone floor, the last lunchtime customers left the tea shop. Outside and to the right of Manying, children were making patterns with sticks on the ground, their voices like tweeting birds. Manying stared at Aunt Feng's elegant, black characters running in neat lines from the top right to the bottom left of the page. She wrote in the classical style of a bygone age. Compared with the daily bombardments of government news proclamations and slogans that no one believed, the simple truth of Aunt Feng's soft, stylised characters was strangely direct, yet Manying could not cry.

She sat for a long time staring at the splatterings of soup that she had dribbled onto the greasy wooden table. Ignoring her, the shopowner and his wife pulled some empty tables together, and lying upon them, settled down for their afternoon siesta. From the upstairs windows of the houses opposite came the drowsy voice of a woman humming a lullaby to a child.

The children in the street were collecting ants from the warm nooks and crannies in the steps and paving stones and placing them in a stockade that they had made out of twigs on the pavement. The game was to place obstacles in the way of the creatures and goad them to climb over stones by poking them with sticks. Best of all was to drop the ants one by one into a pool of water in the top of a jar. The children watched in fascination as the ants floated on their backs, their legs circling helplessly in the air. Pulling the half-drowned ants out of the water, the laughing children once again forced the groping, fumbling creatures over obstacles. Those that could not or would not move were "executed" with the stab of a stick. Those that tried to escape, dragging out futile damp circles on the cobbles were quickly "recaptured" and thrown back into the water. Manying felt no anger, no pain, only emptiness.

The city buildings blazed white in the afternoon heat. Manying did not know where she was going and did not care. Lady pedestrians floated past her like foam on water, their umbrellas and parasols up to protect their prized complexions. She was vaguely aware of feeling hot and of a peculiar burning sensation on her cheeks. Wandering around the streets she saw for the first time another city, a place of destruction, suffering and death. The main streets branched off into rubble. Many of the shops were mere stucco facades opening onto the fronts of houses behind, broken down walls or a courtyard with the base of a blackened chimney at its centre. In the alleys, no one cared when the toilet leaked into the street, the faeces oozing out across the yellow mud. Prostitutes, their legs covered by the welts of flea bites, stood smoking at the bottom of narrow stairwells. An old man, his face so thin you could almost see his bones, slept on an old door in the shade, and everywhere there were the bright eyes and devious hands of the gangs of orphans that lived and slept together under the steps by the river.

In the late afternoon, the moon appeared. It was far too early and hung ridiculously amongst the fluffy, white clouds in the blue sky. In the banking quarter of the city uniformed chauffeurs in sleek black cars waited in front of the banks and offices. Manying watched as fluttering lines of red triangles were slowly raised from the flag poles of the tallest buildings: the warning of an air raid. A stream of men in western suits emerged from swinging doors and hurried down the street, or climbed into cars or hailed rickshaws. A woman in a black and orange flowered cheongsam with little orange butterflies on her open-toed sandals stood in the door of a bank, summoning her car with an imperious movement of her hand.

Returning to the Street of Seven Stars, Manying stood unnoticed at the entrance to an alley. One after another, shutters banged down and crowds of shouting, pushing people flooded down the street to the ferry. Rickshaw men cursed, cars honked their horns and a frantic mother holding four suitcases screamed the name of her lost child. Why all the panic, Manying thought? What was there to be afraid of?

With nightfall came peace. In the alleys, gleeful rats scrabbled in the refuse, while in the cavernous air raid shelters beneath the city's steps the populace held its breath. Invigorated by the darkness the red and purple blotted moon enjoyed its chase with the clouds, illuminating the buildings like fairy palaces in one instant, and then plunging them into darkness at the next. On the corner of each street in the shadows of the gun emplacements and sentry boxes, white eyes and glinting bayonets followed Manying's progress. But no challenge was issued.

The wail of sirens heralded the imminent arrival of Japanese planes. They came, tiny silver stars out of the east: bombs falling, glistening in the moonlight. The distant booms were getting closer and closer, and in the short silences people were heard screaming. The planes were overhead, rolling out the thunder of death. The ground shook beneath Manying's feet but she heard nothing. She walked calmly on, an angel in the eye of a storm.

In an alley, houses were ablaze. Fire engines rushed to rescue the more prestigious buildings; the houses in the alley were, for the moment, left unattended: the flames a rage of leaping dragons, writhing snakes and dancing lions. Mesmerised by the scorching vision, Manying moved closer, her lips cracking like dry wood, her throat burning. Thirsty, thirsty, so thirsty. Suddenly the flames morphed into a terrifying face with a gaping, black mouth and eyes. It roared mockingly toward her, a primeval vision remembered in childhood nightmares. She first hesitated, then turned and ran.

Zheng stood in the compound of the Ministry of Defence chewing on an unlit cigarette, as the planes roared overhead, the notes of their engines mistuned so they ground against each other in a hellish cacophony as all around the boom of anti- aircraft fire continued. Never flinching, Zheng stared into the distance at the halo of a false red dawn. He never went to the shelter during air raids, not since the time he had been buried by debris from a shell in the battle for Shanghai. He preferred to see where the enemy was coming from and face it head on. Behind their sandbags, the sentries were used to Zheng's eccentric behaviour during air raids and put it down to the fact that he worked with the American General Stilwell and his team and had thus inevitably acquired crazy foreign habits.

"Halt or I'll shoot!" one of the sentries shouted, cocking the muzzle of his rifle over the top of the sandbags. A figure had emerged out of the darkness, a woman in a cheongsam, walking steadily toward the main entrance to the compound.

"Halt or I'll shoot!" The sentry's voice rose in pitch.

The moon raced out from behind a cloud, bathing the compound in white light. Zheng saw that the woman was walking unsteadily, staggering to the left, but she held her face up, gazing rapturously at the façade of the building. In that instant he knew.

"Hold your fire!" he barked to the sentry. Running forward, Zheng was unable to reach Manying before she collapsed in the dust in the gateway.

Zheng sat helplessly by Manying's bed in the hospital. Her temperature was a hundred and four degrees and she tossed and turned with the delirium of the fever. She had been like this ever since she had walked into the compound; she did not seem to know him. He had taken her straight to the house of an American doctor, who suspected pneumonia and said that the next few hours would be critical.

Leaning forward Zheng took a damp cloth and wiped the sweat from Manying's face.

"Don't leave me! Please don't leave me! I'm coming too." Manying muttered in Chaozhou dialect. "All alone...all alone."

"Come on, Manying. Don't give up now!" He gritted his teeth. "You must live. You *will* live."

Presuming that her husband's family would be worried, Zheng had sent a message to the address on Manying's identity papers. He knew from his mother's letters that

Manying was married and that her father and Pastor Wesley had been killed. He was, however, surprised when a woman introducing herself as Mrs Yao turned up at the hospital saying that Manying was billeted with them. He liked her straight away. She was a woman in her late thirties whose beauty had obviously been worn down by the cares of wartime living, but in her carefully mended cheongsam and highly polished, old shoes she maintained the old dignities and proprieties. Her concern for Manying was evident and she wanted to have her home just as soon as the doctor said she was well enough, adding that she thought of her as her little sister and would nurse her herself. It was from Mei Ren that Zheng learned that Manying's husband was a major with the Thirty-eight in Burma.

Eating a bowl of cold rice with some pieces of pickled vegetable on top that he had charmed the nurse to fetch for him, Zheng tried to put Manying's marriage out of his mind. What in heaven's name was the man thinking of when he married her? He was a soldier, for God's sake. Manying deserved better than an army life. The duty now fell on him to look out for her while her husband was away. He owed it to Manye, his best friend and sworn blood brother.

Fishing up the last bits of pickled cabbage to give flavour to the last mouthfuls of rice, Zheng remembered the night when, at the Military School, he and Manye were out on exercise in Guangdong province: a group of young officers sitting and lying around in a circle, their muscles warm and satisfied with a day of rigorous exercise, a hot meal and a few cups of rice wine.

"And was her pubic hair blond, like the hair on her head?" one of the officers had asked Manye, who was boasting his experience with a French woman in Guangzhou. Manye threw back his head and laughed to the stars.

"She told me her sister in Paris had written to her

asking a similar question about me; about us...do we Chinese have pubic hair?" Giggles and exclamations!

"Well, was it?"

"Was it what?"

"Blond?"

"Yep, as soft and white as a feather pillow." Manye raised his cup to his interrogator. "Bottoms up!" He gulped the wine and, sighing, inverted his cup to show that he had finished.

"Make the most of it boys...things will not be like this forever. The Jap devils are getting too big for their boots in Manchuria, and it will not be long before we must do our duty." Murmurs of assent went around the campfire; another round was served and cups raised.

"To saving the nation!"

"To us, the best of our generation! We who will chase the imperialist dogs out of China once and for all!"

One by one the officers lay down to sleep, a ring of sleepy black heads like children in a dormitory around the dying fire. Manye and Zheng, the Shantou Brothers, sat smoking, puffing their bravado into the thick night air. Zheng laid back on the bare ground to stare at the ghostly pantheon of stars.

"Almost as beautiful as Gok Sek...almost. Do you remember how as boys we were blood brothers?" He did not need to look at his friend to know that he was nodding.

"So the time has come..." Manye stubbed out the red embers of his cigarette in the dust.

Leaving the smell of cooking and snores behind, the two men walked some distance away from the camp until they found a suitable spot, a patch of clear ground, at the edge of a bamboo grove. Scrabbling around, they cobbled together an altar out of mud and stones—their makeshift temple. Zheng struck a match. It flared briefly in the windless night, just long enough for them to light two cigarettes. The familiar acrid smell of brotherhood tickled their nostrils and they sighed in the hot night air. Buttoning and smoothing down their sweaty shirts they stood opposite each other, holding the cigarettes vertically with two hands in the way of incense sticks.

We, Manye and Zheng, the Chaozhou brothers, sons of the Yellow Emperor, sons of China, hereby swear by Almighty Heaven that henceforth we are blood brothers. The honour of my brother is my own, the family of my brother is my own, and the salvation of the nation is our duty. Never forsaking each other, forever, as heaven is our witness, we swear.

Solemnly they bowed to each other eight times and pacing forward in step, stuck the cigarettes between the stones and mud on top of the altar. In the silence the last of the smoke wended its way to the impassive heaven, the ranks of bamboo stood stiffly at attention, and the blood brothers exchanged gifts; Zheng gave Manye a fountain pen his father had bought him on leaving for Whampoa Military Academy and Manye presented Zheng with his black revolver with a wooden handle.

*B*y early afternoon the doctor pronounced that the worst was over. Although Manying had still not regained consciousness her temperature was falling steadily, and Zheng allowed himself to slumber in his chair. His mind wandered from the little girl with bloodied knees, climbing rocks in a blue, cotton dress, to the chaos and defeat of the Burma campaign: the desperate crackling of telephone lines and incessant clunk of typewriters at the office, English and Chinese alternating in his head like a radio dial not tuned properly, the constant stream of orders changed from one day to the next; the Americans complaining that the Chinese had no will to fight and the red-faced Generalissimo, scalding himself with tea, the tiny porcelain cup smashing on the marble floor as he screeched furiously to tell General Stillwell that he would not sacrifice Chinese lives for British imperial interests. And the poor bastards fighting in the jungle: how the hell were they going to get to Mandalay and back over the Irrawaddy River to safety? What a fiasco!

22

*M*anying was out of hospital within seventy-two hours but her recovery was not quick. Sitting on the front step of the house, propped up by cushions, she watched the children playing air raid drills in the courtyard. A fly approached, buzzed, and landed on her knee. She let it rest, watching its wings quiver in the sunlight.

Odd words and casual sense emerged out of the murmuring in the sitting room behind.

"She doesn't say much. Doesn't go into town anymore," Mei Ren confided to Zheng, thinking Manying could not hear them.

"Not herself at all. Do you think a little trip out might help? I have a friend on the south bank of the river. Fresh air. It would do her good."

"What a good idea! Tea is ready, Manying! Come and have a cup with us!"

Rising and turning into the shadows, Manying saw Mei Ren patting Zheng on the forearm. "Manying is very lucky to have you: a big brother who can look out for her." Zheng winced and looked towards the windows at the far side of the room, and beyond, to the cliffs and the drop to the river.

Manying and Zheng took the paddle ferry across the river early one Sunday in mid-May. The steady old engine chugged reassuringly and the large black wheels threw out fountains of white foam in their wake. Like an animal emerging from hibernation, Manying blinked at the pine-clad hills opposite, watching as the wind ruffled the treetops, and the sunshine trailed shadows like long, black veils over the expanse of opal green.

A car was waiting for them on the other side driven by an earnest looking young man in shirtsleeves whom Zheng introduced as "my eminent friend Mr Liu", although he looked no more than a boy. They passed newly painted houses, their courtyards full of spring flowers. The car began the climb the steep hill. The road was new, and the marks in the rock left by pick axes were clearly visible. Manying wound the window down and breathed in the fresh, cool smell of the pine trees. Rounding a hairpin bend, the car suddenly pulled over to a passing place. Mr Liu gave something to Zheng who was sitting next to him in the passenger seat. Zheng nodded, got out of the car and climbed in the back with Manying, two long thin pieces of black cloth in his hand.

"We have to put these blindfolds on Manying. Mr Liu is a famous curator and he is taking us to see some very precious things that have been saved from the Japanese in Beijing and brought here for safety; things that belonged to the Emperors. Only the Generalissimo himself and a few trusted people know where these treasures are kept." Manying watched in disbelief as Zheng tied the blind fold around his own eyes. After a few seconds she was amazed to find herself following suit. Again, the car started its climb, and unable to see where they were going Manying slid awkwardly on the leather seat as it rounded a bend. Zheng put his arm across the back ledge behind her head.

It was something easy, natural, in the way it had been since she had opened her eyes to find him sitting by her bedside in the hospital.

"You are not kidnapping me, are you? My father warned me of such things!" she joked nervously. The men laughed. But she did not object when Zheng covered her hand with his.

It seemed an age before they reached their destination. Still blindfolded they climbed out of the car. There was a fresh breeze and birds were singing. They were led by hand along an unmade road for about half a minute and then up some concrete steps. An iron door clanged closed behind, and they were walking somewhere cold and dark.

"Now you can take off your blindfolds."

They were in a small cave with electric cables and lighting strung over the concave roof. The place was laid out like an office with desks in the centre and filing cabinets around the walls. There were two tunnels leading out of it, one with the iron door through which they had already passed under which daylight was creeping in, and the other leading into darkness. At the entrance to both tunnels men in civilian clothes stood with large guns across their chests. Fussing busily with a pile of papers on a desk Mr Liu ignored them as if they were no more than pieces of furniture. Taking two large torches from the top of a filing cabinet he gave one to the nearest guard and kept one for himself. He turned to address Manying.

"You understand that you must not tell anyone about what you are about to see." His brow wrinkled with responsibility, making him seem much older than he had first appeared. "These precious things used to belong to the Emperors; now they belong to the nation. We have brought them all the way from Beijing for safety here. Secrecy is of the utmost importance. Do you understand?" Manying nodded. "Good, for there are others who are not so understanding, and any indiscretion could have serious consequences for us all." At that, he turned and scuttled like a mole into the dark tunnel.

Zheng and Manying followed with the guard behind, the light of the torches flashing along the rock walls. Ahead of them a rushing, roaring sound, perhaps of a waterfall, got louder and louder with every step. Manying reached for Zheng's hand and was glad to find it waiting calmly for her. After a minute or so they emerged into another much larger cave, less well lit than the first and filled with boxes. It reverberated with the sound of a motor.

"For God's sake, turn the damn thing off!" Mr Liu shouted to the guard. Manying saw that it was a generator. As the motor ceased the lights faded out and they were left in the ghostly gloom of torchlight.

"Lights and air conditioning," Mr Liu announced. "These caves are pretty dry; all the same I like to run the air conditioning a couple of hours a day. Just to keep my babies well. This way!" Eagerly he removed the lids of crates and boxes at the side of the room. Gradually their eyes adjusted, and one by one the wonders emerged from hidden straw nests in the bottoms of boxes; a jade vase in the shape of a fish, a yellow enamel teapot with pink and blue chrysanthemums, the carved figure of a laughing Lohan Buddha washing his back, the black and gold helmet of an Emperor, its rubies, pearls and sapphires glinting in the darkness. "Qing Dynasty, Kang Xi, Qing Dynasty, Qian Long." Reverently, Mr Liu recited the period and reigns for each piece. "Here, look at this..."

Manying looked down at a tiny gold-painted lacquer box in the shape of a chicken lying in the palm of her hand.

"Open it."

Very carefully she took off the top, revealing an ivory dragon boat inside. She held her breath and stared at the intricacy of the carving: the dragon's spiky tail, the tiny perfectly formed balconies, canopies and balustrades of the boat.

"And this..." Mr Liu moved quickly, like an excited child. Opening a larger crate he heaved out a bronze ewer supported on the backs of four little male figures. "Much earlier, of course. Warring States Period. Used for washing hands in an ancient ritual. Very precious."

"Amazing!" Zheng reached out and stroked it with the tip of his index finger. His thin, almost feminine hands described elegant caresses around the square body of the ewer.

"This is the point of everything. When I wonder why we are living the nightmare of the destruction of our civilisation, I think of these ancient things that have been entrusted to us. The future is dark, but there is a future, and we are the inheritors of the past. If we wait patiently and survive, one day we will emerge into the light and our civilisation will be born anew."

For a long time no one said anything, and Manying found that she was crying.

After the visit was over, Mr Liu said that he had a few things to finish and suggested that a guard take them to a scenic spot where they could eat the lunches they had brought. He would pick them up later and take them back to the ferry. They were blindfolded again, and after a drive lasting what Manying judged to be about fifteen minutes, along very bumpy roads, they found themselves in a clearing in the pine trees high above the river, the city of Chongqing laid out like a model on the opposite bank.

"Mr Liu will pick you up again in about two hours. Here's a rug to sit on. Be good and don't wander off and get lost!" The hitherto taciturn guard with his shaved head suddenly became friendly. Accompanied by the big machine gun sitting upright in the front passenger seat he waved cheerfully as he backed the car out of the clearing.

They walked to a grassy spot on the edge of the cliff and sat down among the carpet of daisies. Below them the river twisted upon its course until it was lost to the eye in the infinity of a purple haze. High above, an eagle rode the graceful currents, sweeping effortlessly from one side of the gorge to the other, below it the small sampans, and beneath green camouflage on the opposite bank, the grey metal of a gunboat.

"Do you still make daisy chains?" Zheng teased as he unbuckled his gun belt and removed the jacket of his uniform, laying them neatly by his side

"Not anymore. I prefer to leave the flowers where I find them." Manying ruffled the tops of the happy daisies affectionately with the flat of her hand.

They ate the food that Mei Ren and the maid had prepared for them: hard boiled eggs, mantou bread and pickle, corn, and grapes. For the first time in weeks food tasted good to Manying, and she ate with relish.

"I am sorry," she said, biting through the soft yellow centre of an egg. "I have been so foolish. I've let everyone down: you, Mei Ren, my husband."

"Don't talk such rubbish. You've been ill, that's all. But now you are getting better." Zheng's reply sounded sharp in a way he had not intended.

"It's so beautiful," she said after a while. "Everything in the cave...all this!" She moved her hand slowly over the landscape below.

"This is China, our China," Zheng whispered. "This is the landscape that has inspired our poets and artists. The Japanese can drop as many bombs as they like, but we will never be destroyed."

When they had finished eating, Zheng lay back on the ground with his hands under his head. His shirt tight over his torso, Manying could still make out the long lines of the body of a boy in the frame of the man. Thick curls of black hair escaped from the neck of his shirt where he had undone his top buttons. Manying had never seen a Chinese man with so much chest hair. He did not look like a soldier, she thought. He was neither robust like Bear, nor carefree as her brother had been. He ought perhaps to have been a scholar, or an official. Lifting his hand to shade his eyes from the sun, Zheng sighed heavily, as if at last able to put down a heavy load.

"What's the matter?" Manying asked.

"Nothing." He sighed again. "It's just that sometimes I think that working as Liaison Officer for the Americans will be the death of me."

"How so? You are an ideal choice. There can't be many people in the army who speak such good English as you."

"The whole thing is such a joke! An American in charge of Chinese forces! Who ever heard of such a thing?" He sounded surprised at himself, as if such thoughts, long repressed and now forming themselves into words, were falling over each other to tumble out of his mouth before he could stop them. "You know, when General Stilwell first arrived, the Generalissimo gave him the title *Commander of the Chinese Armies in Burma*, but General Du also holds the same title. It is all for show. Chinese generals in Burma won't obey Stilwell's orders without first clearing it with the Generalissimo, so we have chaos and defeat. The two sides want different things, and I end up being piggy in the middle. The Americans are right. We must modernise our armies. How can we defeat the Japanese with diseased, malnourished conscripts and boys? But the Generalissimo has different ideas. He is terrified of creating a modern, efficient fighting force in case it is used against him, and when he does have modern forces such as the Fifth or your husband's Thirty-eighth, he won't use them in the offensive for fear of loosing them, and with them his political power. And so he hoards everything; American loans, tanks, guns, planes, ammunition—all to use against the Communists. It is the Japanese who are the real enemies, not the Communists. But he can't see it."

"Hush, hush." Manying was horrified and instinctively looked around to see if anyone was listening. But there were only fluttering white butterflies and the birds in the pine trees. "You must be careful what you say."

"Yes, yes! You are right. But sometimes, despite myself, I think that it is slipping through our fingers, and there is nothing any of us can do about it."

"Losing what?"

"This!" Slowly he dragged his hand, palm uplifted, across the horizon. "Our China, the China of our ancestors, and with it a sense of who we truly are. Ai ya! This bloody job! I dread the day when I have to make a choice."

Having spoken his piece to an old friend in his native dialect, Zheng seemed able to relax, the coiled muscles of his body unwinding in a series of twitches and gasps.

Manying listened as his breathing slowed into a gentle, slumbering snore. Her own eyes began to close as she sat; she could not remember feeling so at peace since she had left Gok Sek.

Opening her eyes, she saw Zheng's pistol lying in its holster at his side, and leaning over, she pulled it towards her. It was heavier than she had expected and the leather was soft and shiny under her hand. Slowly she unbuckled the holster and drew out the gun. It was warm from his body, and from the sun. She stroked the polished wooden butt and ran her finger up and down the matt black muzzle. So simple, so elegant; it was beautiful, almost a piece of jewellery. It was hard to believe that it could kill a person. Turning it over in her hand she saw that it had her brother's English name, Michael Wen, engraved on the butt. Brusquely she lifted the gun and with both hands pointed it right at the heart of the expanse of sky. What if she pulled the trigger? One shot...that's all it would take...the beautiful idyllic day shattering around her like a blue glass vase, the sharp, tiny pieces scattering all over the grassy green carpet, for someone, later, much later, years later, to sweep away.

Slowly she lowered the gun and, slipping it back into the holster, returned the belt to Zheng's side. The movement disturbed his sleep and he awoke, rubbing his eyes like a child. They sat in silence listening to the breeze rustling through the tops of pine trees behind them.

At length, Manying said, "Tell me about my brother. I want to know."

Zheng's face folded with pain, as if she had knifed him in the back. "Manying, ask me anything, but not that."

"Please, you are the only one who can tell me what happened. Isn't it always better to know the truth?"

Zheng hesitated, looking at her long and hard with his big eyes.

"I wish I could tell you that his death had made a difference, that he had died a hero. But it was not like that." He looked at her again, but she did not flinch from the intensity of his gaze.

"It was hopeless. They were blasting us constantly and our own artillery could only fire at night. We were losing thousands of men every hour. There was a big push to drive the Japanese back to the river. We were fighting from house to house and all the time they were bombarding us from the river. The last I saw of Manye he was urging his men forward and then the shell got him. I was buried for several hours myself before they dug me out. After dark, I went back to look for him but there was nothing left. Just a gaping hole in the ground." Zheng dropped his face forward into his hands, his shoulders shaking.

23

On the twentieth of May 1942 the American General Stilwell, accompanied by one hundred and fourteen sick, emaciated soldiers and civilians, walked out of the Burmese jungle and reached safety in Imphal in India. There had been no word from the Chinese troops. On the twenty-fourth of May, Stilwell flew to Delhi to give a press conference at which he asserted, "We got a hell of a beating. We were run out of Burma and it is humiliating as hell." The Chinese press in Chongqing did not report the general's statement in full, but there were many, including Zheng, who knew the truth. The following day, 25th of May, Zheng heard the news that remnants of the Thirty-eighth, led by General Sun Li Ren, had also begun arriving in Imphal. The survivors of the Burma campaign were duly proclaimed heroes by the Chinese and allied press.

Zheng made great efforts on Manying's behalf to find out about Bear, but it was not until nearly three weeks later that he was finally able to tell her that her husband was alive. In July Manying received a letter from Bear. Its triumphant tone was not what she was expecting.

My Dear Wife

Here I am in the capital of British India! Can you believe it? Our division was invited to represent China at the League of Nations Day review of the troops, and I was one of the lucky men selected to attend!

I am indeed blessed in many ways, not just because I had the honour to represent our nation at the parade today, but also because I am alive and in good health when so many of our brothers are dead or sick in hospital. I got off lighter than many, my main ailment now being sores from leeches, but they are healing well. General Sun himself told me that I must have been a lion in my past life, and I told him that in that case all the men in the Thirty-eighth were lions in their past lives! To which he replied that we were indeed a sorry band of mangy lions! But the food here is good and we are all regaining weight, so you must not worry.

My dear wife, the thought of you safe and well in Chongqing is my strength and solace. Indeed, I think that my survival must in part be due to your prayers. I will not say more for my heart overflows with tears at the loss of so many brave heroes. When you say your prayers tonight, you must remember them and also remember to say a big thank you to your God on my behalf for keeping me safe!

I wish you could have been at the parade ground in New Delhi to see us march! You would have been so proud to see the Chinese flag fluttering alongside those of all the other great nations! We were so smart in our battle dress with our helmets and leggings—all just so! The parade was led by an English bagpipe band! Have you ever heard such an incredible sound? The British Viceroy of India and a whole host of other generals reviewed the troops, and it is generally said that we Chinese were the smartest and best-presented troops on parade!

My dear wife, I miss you and hope that you are going on well. It seems that we will be staying here in India for a while to rest and rebuild our forces. We will be working with the Americans and will make our HQ at a place called Ramgarh. You can send letters via the Ministry to me there, although you must promise me not to depend too much on regular deliveries. I miss you and look forward to receiving news from you soon.

Your husband.
Bear.

14th June 1942

New Delhi, India

Manying read and re-read the letter a hundred times. She tried to imagine the reality behind her husband's carefully guarded words. What had really happened to him in Burma? But when she thought of the jungle, all that came to mind were ridiculous pictures from a story book in the mission school: a laughing monkey hanging by one arm from the branch of a palm tree eating a banana and a naughty elephant spraying muddy water over himself with his long trunk.

24

*O*blivious to the war, the seasons ran their course. The magnolia tree in Mei Ren's courtyard shed its leaves, blossomed and shed its leaves again. With a symphony of low grunts and squawks, illustrated by blushes, the voice of her elder son began to break. For her part Manying learned that a childless army wife must above all keep busy, so she worked as a teacher in the mornings at a local primary school. In the afternoons she helped Mei Ren's boys with their homework, and twice a week she met Zheng for a simple meal in one of the cheap cafes in town. On special occasions such as Chinese New Year, or when Zheng was promoted to lieutenant colonel, Zheng came up to the Yao's, or they all went to a restaurant to celebrate.

The Yao boys, their eyes popping out of their heads at the variety of dishes set before them, ate ravenously as their father expounded on one of his favourite gripes, the loss of traditional standards otherwise known as the decline of Chinese civilisation into barbarity. All the while Mei Ren would keep Zheng's bowl filled with food and, choosing her moment, playfully ask just when the lieutenant colonel was planning to get married.

"You know what they say! Thirty years old and now a man!"

"Not you too, Mrs Yao! You sound just like my mother." Zheng would fix Mei Ren with his laughing eyes and she would pout and shake her head in a mock display of dissatisfaction at his answer.

No one ever questioned the relationship between Manying and Zheng. It was a matter of honour between brothers in arms—every one knew that—and that it was Zheng's duty to look after his best friend's sister.

Manying and Zheng always sat on opposite sides of the table, meticulously avoiding all physical contact. But on the occasions when the laoban of a café mistook them for man and wife, they did not put him right.

Lying in bed at night Manying would place her pillow by her side and, snuggling into it, think of Bear. But she could not remember what he looked like; the soldier staring out of the photograph she kept under her pillow had become a stranger. Sometimes she took out old newspaper cuttings from the 1942 Burma campaign. Her favourite was a photograph of helmeted Generals Stilwell and Sun Li Ren in a trench. It was as if the picture could come to life, and as in a miraculous movie, Bear would walk out of the jungle undergrowth towards her. Once, in desperation, she had taken out an old Chinese-style gown that he had left with her when he had been deployed. Laying it out on the bed, she thrust her face deep into the soft, blue silk hoping that its familiar smell would spark her memories. But she had kept the gown so carefully that all traces of her husband were obliterated by the musty smell of mothballs. Sometimes insistent dreams brought solace in the form of a heavy, all-enveloping shadow of warm, pulsing pleasure. But when she opened her eyes it was Zheng's naked body that she held in her arms. Disgusted, she begged God for forgiveness and, hiding her face in her pillow, waited for fickle sleep to return. Nothing in her upbringing had prepared her for the nightly ravages of such contradictory emotions. As dawn broke, she thought of confiding in Mei Ren, but there were some things that could never be spoken, even between women. She vowed not to see Zheng until next month...until after Christmas...until after Chinese New Year. But the force driving the weekly cycle of suppers would have its way.

By the winter of 1943, the reconstituted Thirty-eighth Division was back fighting in Burma. Manying had not heard from Bear since the late summer. It was Christmas in Chongqing. On the Street of the Seven Stars the decorations in the shop windows made a brave display of silver and gold in the cold winter darkness, but the daylight revealed them as a bedraggled collection of creased and torn paper chains, grey, cotton wool snow and cracked baubles that had been recycled just once too often.

On Christmas Eve Manying arrived at the Pearl of the East, a well known restaurant where Zheng had told her to meet him. Its walls were undamaged by bombs, and with red carpets on the floor it was a completely different class of establishment from the rickety street cafes they were used to. On the wall was a large framed photograph of the original restaurant in Shanghai, but its pre-war pretensions had not quite survived the long trip from the east coast and it was a seedy imitation of its former self. Why would Zheng ask her to such an expensive restaurant? Manying suspected that something was wrong. Amazingly, despite the difficult times, the restaurant was doing a good trade; all the tables were filled with groups of army officers and officials. There were few women and there was no sign of Zheng.

"Can I help you, Madam?" A diminutive, shiny-faced manager in a grubby black suit and tie approached her.

"I am here to meet Lieutenant Colonel Chen."

"Ah, yes." The man nodded in a knowing way. "This way, please."

He led her up a narrow staircase at the back of the

restaurant that emerged into a corridor running the length
of the building. The carpet did not extend to the upstairs
and the bare boards were sticky underfoot from spilled
food. On either side of the corridor were small private
dining rooms separated from each other by flimsy wooden
walls. Raucous, male laughter came from the far end of the
corridor. Losing interest in Manying the manager pointed
to the third room on the left hand side. There she saw
Zheng leaning on the doorframe smoking a cigarette. He
greeted her with a big smile.

"Zheng, what's going on? Who else is coming?"
Manying could not contain herself.

"No one, just us! I just felt like celebrating Christmas,
that's all! It's full downstairs, so the manager put us up
here." He shrugged his shoulders.

"But it's so expensive."

"Not really. Anyway, the way things are, there is not
much point keeping money in the bank." Again he
shrugged his shoulders and helped her to remove her coat,
hanging it on the wooden hat stand in the far corner of the
room.

The musty room was not what Manying had been
expecting. The white wallpaper embossed with pink
flowers had swollen with damp and was quietly peeling off
the walls. Long fingers of green mould snaked around the
crevices and corners. A single dusty lightbulb without a
shade hung above the centre of the table. On the wall a
framed picture of plums on a branch was covered with
yellow and brown patches.

The meal was a simple one; a Shanghai meatball
speciality called Lion's Head Stew, steamed fish,
vegetables, Little Dragon Pork Dumplings and the
indulgence of warm Shaoxing wine into which they
dropped dried cherries to sweeten it. They talked quietly in
Chaozhou dialect, the privacy of which it afforded them
heightened by the intimacy of having a room all to
themselves. It was a long time since they had been alone in

such a way.

At length the food was consumed, except four Little Dragon meatballs left for Manying to take home for Mei Ren's boys. The wine bottle was empty and Zheng raised his glass to Manying for the final silent toast. Sitting back in his chair he lit a cigarette and drummed his long delicate fingers on the table cloth that stretched out between them like a snowy continent.

"Manying, I am leaving Chongqing. I have decided to take a post with the Chinese Expeditionary Force in Yunnan Province."

Manying's face was that of a drowning person, who having being rescued, was now being thrown back into the water. She stared at the bottom of the picture on the wall. A tiny brown bird picked at two purple plums, rotting on the ground.

"The American Chief of Staff there, Colonel Dorn, is keen to have another Chinese liaison officer like me on his staff, and my old boss, Colonel Zeng, Head of Chinese Administration at the Yunnan Training Centre, has fixed my transfer."

Zheng pressed on.

"I've got to get away from Chongqing, can't you see? The constant back stabbing, order and counter order. The Generalissimo is a great man, but he clearly has no intention of reforming the army, and without reform we will never defeat the Japanese. I have to get away from here before I get myself into trouble."

Manying did not look at him but nodded her head. "I'll miss you."

"For God's sake, Little Lamb, we can't go on like this. I'm going mad." Zheng thumped his fists on the table, his face dark with anger. "Being with you but not being able to have you...it's torture. I would take you home with me right now, kiss you between your legs and fuck you until you are mine, all mine." She took a sharp breath and felt the colour drain from her face.

"How dare you! How dare you... talk to me like that?" She rose to leave. Still, Zheng was not satisfied.

"Would to God you had never married him!"

"What was I supposed to do, live life as a nun? You never asked me. You could have asked me that night on Gok Sek. You could have..."

"How could I? I'm a soldier, and soldiers get killed. It could have been me in Shanghai, not your brother, and what if you were pregnant? Then what? Do you love him?"

"He is a good man."

"But do you love him?" Again Zheng thumped the table with his fist, so hard that the crockery jumped and the wine flask fell over. They both watched as it rolled off the table, and they heard it smash as it hit the wooden floor.

"I love you both," Manying answered calmly, looking him in the eye.

"Then you must choose."

"If I must choose," she whispered, "it is my duty to choose my husband."

Rhiannon Jenkins Tsang

HONG KONG

25
OCTOBER 1949

*F*or Heaven's sake, Miss! Get on with it! Bloody fish will have died of old age by the time you make up your mind. I'm going to charge you a gawpers' rate!" Ling Ling peered suspiciously at the fish in the fishmongers' buckets. A devout Buddhist, she never liked making the choice about which of them should live or die

"My sister-in-law will choose...Manying!" She tugged at Manying's sleeve. "She's a Christian...Manying!"

But Manying was shading her eyes, watching a stray plane grinding its way over the buildings of Central towards the airport at Kai Tak. Planes always approached over the harbour, not the island; something was not quite right.

It was many months since Zheng had put her on what turned out to have been the last train out of Nanjing before the Communist takeover, and still no news of her husband had arrived. That morning she would have preferred to stay at home sewing, but ever-the-tyrant Ling Ling had it all organised.

"Fresh air will do you good! Here's your cardigan!"

Ling Ling poked Manying in the ribs to get her way, and Manying forced herself to concentrate on the job in hand. The fish meandered around the buckets. There was not much in it.

"That one!" She chose one that was perhaps a little shinier than its comrades. With a huff and a puff the fishmonger plunged his arm elbow deep into the water. Perhaps sensing the end, the fish was reinvigorated, flicking silver fans of water droplets.

"Hurry up!" Ling Ling turned her face away. "Don't let it cast its beady eyes on me! It might recognise me in the next life." The mallet fell, the knife scythed. Guts spilled pink and grey, and Ling Ling dropped three coins into the fishmonger's blood stained palm.

It was nearly lunch time before they got home, to find a stranger in the sitting room.

"Where on earth have you been?" Bear the Elder appeared to be trying to chop mango, boil rice and brew tea all at the same time for a guest and was making a poor job of it. "Wife, there's nothing to eat in the house. It's a disgrace!"

"No matter. I'm not hungry." The voice of the guest was barely audible, as if coming from a distant place. His eye fell upon Manying. He seemed surprised and looked her frankly up and down. The baby on her back began to cry. Slowly the stranger stood up, wobbling slightly. Manying looked back without recognition. It was Ling Ling who cried out with joy.

"You're home! Oh Little Brother you are home!"

Bear was a man of dignity. After the defeat at the Battle of Huai Hai he had been on the road for many weeks and had no intention of arriving at his elder brother's house as a prodigal vagabond. He had been first to the Red Cross at the Tung Wah Hospital where he had washed, eaten, slept and obtained second hand clothes. The first thing he had asked his brother on arrival was to borrow a few pennies to pay the barber at the bottom of the street.

Nevertheless his efforts were in vain. The man who once had taken such pride in his physical training and his uniform wore a shrunken pair of Royal Navy trousers and a poorly matched, ill-fitting grey jacket. His face too was thin, and surplus skin sagged in sallow folds around his jaw. The hair that the barber had cut so tenderly and so quickly was now grey with a large bald patch.

In honour of his younger brother's return, and despite his wife's protests that the newcomer was tired, Bear the Elder insisted that a special dinner be prepared. Ling Ling and Manying spent the whole afternoon bumping bottoms and elbows in the tiny kitchen, chopping, marinating and generally preparing. At six o'clock, simpering, bowing neighbours began to arrive. Ever gracious, Bear held his head high and accepted the toasts and good wishes with a smile and a nod, but ate and said little. Later, when guests insisted that he hold his son, the baby kicked and screamed for his mother.

That night Ling Ling and Bear the Elder gave up their marital bed for the re- united couple. Sitting on the edge of the bed Manying fussed endlessly with her fractious son. Who was this man she called husband? Had she ever really known him? During most of their marriage he had been away fighting; first in Burma and then after the end of the war when they had moved back to the Capital of Nanjing he had been promoted to lieutenant general and been busy with army politics and anti-communist campaigns. Their son had been conceived during his last leave and he had never even seen him, until today. When the time came to climb into bed, she could not look him in the eye. They said a curt good-night before turning away to sleep back to back, as travellers ill met in a distant inn on a frontier road.

*T*he following day the family listened to the radio as Mao Ze Dong proclaimed the People's Republic of China from Tiananmen Square in Beijing.

"Well that's that!" Bear the Elder slapped his thighs and stood up to light a cigarette. "Could be worse. At least the country is united again, and free of the imperialists."

But Manying's husband banged his fist on the table, hissing through gritted teeth, "Big Brother, you don't understand the Communists. I have been fighting those bandits for the last ten years. I know them. I tell you, it will be a bloody disaster." He tapped his forehead with his finger. "There will not be an end to our nation's suffering. Millions will continue to die."

Bear passed his days sitting in the wicker chair in the tiny living room and would tell no one what had happened to him or to his men. Like some errant Buddha floating on clouds of cigarette smoke, he observed the scenes of domestic life playing out around him. Sometimes he would make it downstairs to the shop where once more he would simply sit and smoke and watch his brother grinding lenses. It went on like this for months, and people began to whisper, "Shame, such a shame." At best Bear would engage himself in a little calligraphy, painting over and over again fragments from an old poem.

Bones from the battles are trampled to dust
that flies into the eyes of men on the march

Brown clouds suddenly turn to black
As the ghosts of battle form weeping ranks.

But he could never be persuaded to complete the piece.

Seeing Bear sitting there day after day as the family toiled away at the business of keeping food on the table, Manying wanted to slap him, to boot him up the backside. Hadn't they all eaten bitterness, enough for a hundred lifetimes? Why was he any different? Once, in an attempt to galvanise him into action, Manying suggested that she went to the Tung Wah Hospital to try and get entry permits for Taiwan so Bear could join the Nationalist forces there. Bear stood up and paced the room, turning grey with anger.

"I'm not going to Taiwan to fight for that...that...idiot Chiang Kaishek. The man has no understanding of military affairs. I have spent my whole life engaged in glorified butchery. And for what? For what?" It was then that the family saw for the first time the fits of trembling that would come on at times of stress and that would blight the rest of Bear's life. Often they would start with a headache and a small twitch at the corner of his mouth and end up with him taking cover under a table, arms around himself as his body shivered and shook. They would finish with sweating and exhaustion.

Bear's health did begin to improve, around the time of Chinese New Year of 1950. But it was not due to the festivities, but because his son decided it was time to learn to walk. Despite the baby's initial reaction to the return of the stranger, he had soon grown used to the presence of the man they called Baba or Daddy. By day he would peek through the bars of his wooden cot in the corner of the sitting room, watching the fizz and flare of the match lighting yet another cigarette, and the idle flap-flapping of one rattan slipper back and forth against the bare sole of the other's foot. The second rattan slipper lay abandoned on the floor. Gradually the father became the sun in his son's world. An ever-present fixture at the centre of the room, he was never busy, tired or bad tempered like his mother. He provided that constancy which all children require.

Bear was, for a while, unaware of his importance to the squalling, smelly object that people insisted had something to do with him, and so pre-occupied Manying, who spent her days shovelling food into one end of it and cleaning it up at the other.

Thus it came as a great surprise when a little boy graduated from the cot to the floor, and one day Bear felt the soft warm pressure of tiny hands on his knee and saw a little bright-eyed cherub with a face like his own, standing up and grinning up at him. For the first time on his own initiative he took the child onto his lap. The child reached out to touch his mouth, poke his eyes and explore his top pocket where the cigarette packet was lodged, and in that moment Bear became a father.

"We're going for a walk." Manying and Ling Ling watched in amazement as he scooped up his son and appropriated a tweed flatcap of his brother's from the coat stand by the door, and for the child a school cap belonging to his cousin. Before the two women could collect themselves Bear had sailed out of the door, his son in the grey felt cap that was much too big for him, grinning happily over his shoulder.

26

*T*he walks soon became a regular part of the morning routine.

"Hang gai gai—go for a walk!" The child would pull at Bear's trouser leg as he shaved to hurry him up. Sometimes they would just amble around the neighbourhood where old ladies would fuss about whether the child had too many clothes on or too few and, with clucking disapproval, firmly tug the child's shirt down on the occasions it came out of his trousers to reveal his navel, through which it was believed people caught cold. Often father and son would take the tram to Victoria Park where the child ran along the pathways between the trees stopping every ten paces or so to crane his head forward to listen, enraptured, to the birdsong.

It was not long before Bear began to see faces on his morning walks. He had been a good officer. He never forgot names or faces, and now he encountered familiar ones at every turn; a cook from his old regiment making dumplings at a street stall, an adjutant from Nanjing days driving a tram, and a fat corporal who had once been a telegraph operator at the Ministry of Defence, dressed in a chauffeur's uniform at the wheel of a Rolls Royce that belonged to some Hong Kong big shot. One day at the playground in Victoria Park, an English lady in a red and white polka dot dress who was sitting in the shade fanning herself and supervising her two maids, who in turn supervised her three blue-eyed children, was amazed to see a gardener snap to attention and salute a disreputable looking Chinese man who was playing with his son on the slide. If she had taken the trouble to learn even basic Chinese, she might have understood that the gardener had simply said, "Colonel Xiong, good morning, sir!"

The man was Sergeant Ding, who had gone all the way through the Burma campaign at Colonel Bear's side. Despite shrapnel wounds to his thigh, he had continued to carry other wounded men on stretchers through the jungle to India. As the senior surving non-commissioned officer he had been made colour sergeant and drilled the men for the League of Nations victory parade in New Delhi in 1942, an event that Bear had so carefully selected as something appropriate to write about in a letter to his young wife.

A lifetime of discipline and training is not so easily lost, and Bear found himself returning the salute of a stocky gardener in a blue uniform standing in the middle of a flowerbed. Formalities over, the gardener hesitated a second or two before stepping awkwardly forward, half-bowing now in the manner of a peasant to his master.

"Remember me, sir?"

"Colour Sergeant Ding! No, no, don't bow to me like that. How's that leg of yours?" Now it was Bear's turn to hesitate, for he was not sure about the appropriate form of greeting in such circumstances even though it was his instinct to embrace the man. Once again it was the child that saved the day. With a milk-toothed grin and chubby outstretched palm he drove away, for a while at least, the hungry demons that gnaw and worry at the spirits of weary men.

"This your boy?" The sergeant squatted on his heels at the bottom of the slide and offered a gnarled forefinger to the child.

"My first born."

"Hello, Little Brother! What's your name?"

"We mostly just call him Tsai Tsai—Little One."

The sergeant laughed, and with him the child, who by now was quite at ease with the raggle-taggle assortment of mangy old men he encountered when out with his father.

"Again! Again!" The child pointed to the top of the slide, and so they played a game where Bear released the giggling boy from the red-painted top of the slide to be caught by the colour sergeant as he shot off the shiny bottom.

"You work here?" Bear gestured to the dappled expanse of dust and flowers that somehow counted as a park, and immediately regretted the question.

"Yes... yes... I like being outside, sir. Better that way. Actually, I went for a job yesterday at *The Cathay Hotel* in Kowloon; head doorman, good money. But, well..." He grinned widely, displaying to full effect a horrific range of yellow fangs, black cavities and gold teeth. Guess they want them young and beautiful, up front and all, sir!" In silence they played another round of sliding and catching the child. "You're not going to Taiwan, sir, a gentleman like you?" Now it was the colour sergeant's turn to wish he had kept his mouth shut. Bear frowned and said nothing. "Well, anyway, there are lots of us here in Hong Kong." The colour sergeant reeled off a positive roll call of names, ranks and present occupations. "A whole bloody army in waiting, sir! That's the way I look at it. The Old Man in Heaven has put us here for a reason and one day, one way or another, we will all go back. If not us, then our sons will re-take our country for us!"

Bear nodded. The child began to cry. Shamed, the former general made his excuses, for it was nearly lunchtime. The colour sergeant handed the boy back to his father. "That job, sir, at *The Cathay*... They want some one better than the likes of me. If you went this afternoon...ask for a Mister Ge-ma-ren, the gwailo manager. He speaks good Cantonese." He watched as Bear slowly heaved the boy onto his shoulders. "I always remember what you used to say to us in the jungle, sir. 'Sons of the Yellow Emperor, never give up! Sons of the Yellow Emperor shall live ten thousand years!'"

*B*ear marched into the office of Sandy Cameron, General Manager of the most famous hotel in the Crown Colony of Hong Kong, just before teatime one February afternoon. Dressed in a lightweight grey woollen suit of his brother's that was too big, he felt small standing at attention in front of Cameron's desk, his trilby hat dangling awkwardly at his right side.

"My name's Xiong, sir. I've come about the doorman's job," he said in English.

"Chief Doorman's job," Cameron corrected him and swapped his accounts ledger for the tea tray left by the secretary who had shown Bear into the office. "What experience and qualifications do you have?" Bear hesitated. He was accustomed to commanding respect on the basis of his field experience. He had never been to a job interview in his life.

"I was in the Chinese army, sir."

Cameron nodded and fished out a packet of cigarettes from his shirt pocket. Bear was grateful for his discretion, for the man clearly knew better than to solicit the exact rank from an officer of the defeated Nationalist Army.

"During the anti-Japanese war I was with General Sun Li Ren and the American General Stilwell in Burma, sir." Bear volunteered further information. "I like the Americans. They are a strong race, one that believes in itself. They're very organised, sir. If they decide they want to build an ice cream factory on the moon, then they will make it happen!" Cameron smiled, offered Bear a cigarette which he declined, and invited him to sit down.

"Ah, Burma!" He loosened his tie and inhaled deeply on his cigarette. "During the war I was interned by the Japanese at Stanley Camp." He gestured with his thumb over his shoulder through the window in the direction of the blue and green of the harbour and Hong Kong Island. "I did not have a pleasant stay." Bear smiled a half smile. "You're not planning on going to Taiwan, Mr Xiong?"

"I am Cantonese, sir. I have family here in Hong Kong. I have been away fighting all my adult life. It's time to retire from the army and spend time with my wife and son."

"Yes, war is one thing, Mr Xiong, but civil war is quite another thing all together." Again Cameron offered Bear a cigarette. This time he accepted it and lit it with Cameron's lighter. The two men puffed in silence and the room filled with easy clouds of smoke.

"I just can't get good staff these days," Cameron went on. "Take my bell boys; they turn up for work with shirts unironed and mud on their boots. One of them even arrived for his shift by the front door the other week. Said that it was his right! What is the world coming to, I ask you?"

Ever since his arrival in Hong Kong, Bear had often felt as if he were watching life through a telescope. The sensation came on him now with a shiver as he watched the portly grey-haired gwailo dunk a teaspoon into a jug of condensed milk and, like a child, slowly dribble it in circles into a cup of Indian tea. He saw that the fingernails on the man's right hand were black and stunted in the way they re-grow after having been pulled out under torture, and that the index finger had been cut off below the knuckle. With the gentle clink of silver on porcelain, Cameron stirred the black liquid until it became coffee brown. Without asking, he handed Bear a cup.

"Silly really... We've got fresh milk in the hotel of course, but I like it better this way... Bloody war! People have lost their standards; don't know what's up and what's down anymore. I tell you, the days of the British Empire are numbered. The twentieth century is the socialist century. Don't get me wrong, a bit of revolution is not a bad thing, good for the progress of mankind and all that. But a hotel is no place for revolutions. A hotel needs order and discipline. A hotel, Mr Xiong, is like the army. And hotels need good officers, like you, to keep the troops in order."

"I tell you, my boys, Hong Kong is a city of bitterness..."

Ling Ling sniggered as she rinsed a dinner bowl, and handed it to Manying to dry.

"Here he goes again...silly old husband of mine!" She whispered the next line of Bear the Elder's habitual after dinner talk to his young sons. "If you want to survive, what must you do?"

"Work hard, Baba!" The little boys banged their elbows on the table in time to the words, and looked eagerly toward their father in anticipation of his attention at the end of the day.

Suppressing a giggle, Manying put her finger to her lips, as the two women peeped through the door from the kitchen into the living room.

Bear the Elder was sitting at the table with his two young sons and Manying's husband, enjoying a drink and a cigarette.

"Do you think my money fell down from heaven? Do you?

"No, Baba!"

"Why do we live comfortably here, instead of in cardboard boxes on the street? Because I work hard for every penny, that's why! And tonight," he raised his cup of rice wine to Bear, "we celebrate your uncle's new job." Bear's face was flushed with alcohol, as if stung by a swarm of bees. He grinned indulgently and downed another shot of wine. Bear the Elder refilled his younger brother's cup.

"Enough!" Manying was relieved to see her husband put his palm over his cup. He was not really a drinker. Bear the Elder refilled his own cup, and pushed back his stool to stretch his legs.

"Look and learn from your uncle's example, boys! People look down on newcomers. Bumpkins who themselves are one generation out of the fields, sit in teahouses, poking at left over bits of pork bun and tittle-tattle about dirty refugees with no manners and unintelligible Chinese. But what is this called, my sons?"

"Snobbery, Baba!" the little boys chirped, enjoying their roll in this play.

"Snobbery! Exactly! New people means new business, new opportunities. How come I have managed to open two more shops in Kowloon?"

"Thousands of myopic eyes, Baba!"

"Exactly! Myopic eyes need glasses, food to eat and places to live. That is called doing business, my sons!" He tapped the middle of his forehead with the flat of the thumb of his cigarette-holding hand, and puffed a cloud of smoke towards the light bulb hanging in the middle of the ceiling. "You need to be quick. Spot the opportunity before the next man, or someone will eat you up. Grrrr!" With a roar he dived across the table toward the boys like a tiger. "Be off with you now! Away to bed!"

Sighing, he rubbed his stomach in a large circular motion to ease his digestion.

"Talking about places to live..." He looked at Bear. "Did I tell you an opportunity came up? A gift horse, you might say! I have just bought a place on the hillside above San Kei Bay to the east of the island, you know. Not your average jerry- built shack, but a proper stone house. A cottage, you might say. Now you are employed, I could offer you and your old wife the downstairs for a good price? I have already let the upper story to some cousins, or you could have had that too, if you had wanted it. What do you think?"

Manying did not wait for Bear to respond. As quick as a fishwife, dishcloth in hand, she barged into the living room.

"Done, Big Brother!" She looked daggers at Bear. "No arguments. Get on and settle a price."

The deal was made, and the evening concluded with Bear nagging his elder brother until he got out his almanac and charts to calculate an auspicious day for the move.

Spectacles perched on the end of his nose, a rather drunk Bear the Elder hunched at the table, and with much puffing and groaning, pretended to make heavy weather of the work in the manner of a school boy reluctant to do his lessons. Bear laughed and told Manying and Ling Ling that when they were boys he himself had taken no interest in learning the arts of the almanac from his father, and had complained in just such a way when forced to study them with their old man.

"You used to strut up and down the room like you had seen soldiers strut, and protest that you were a perfectly rational boy; with Mr Science and Mr Democracy, China should have no need of such mumbo-jumbo." Bear the Elder scraped back his stool, puffed out his chest and stomped up and down the room. Both brothers laughed and threw pretend punches. Somehow they ended up scuffling together like boys round the living room in mock combat, and Manying felt a pang that she remembered might be happiness.

The day that Bear the Elder had identified for Manying and Bear also turned out to be auspicious for other people to move, and for weddings. Dressed in their best clothes, it was approaching lunchtime by the time the family had everything packed and were ready to make the journey by tram. All along their route were scattered wedding parties, groups of red-faced young men, dishevelled after a night on the town, and morning-fresh old dragon ladies in silk cheongsam dresses organising nonchalant looking brides, some in traditional red, some in Western white, who looked each other up and down, assessing the quality and cost of the other's outfit and whether it was borrowed or bought. Amongst them all, impatient men and women lugged precious bits of corrugated iron, or pushed or pulled precariously balanced assortments of furniture on an ingenious assortment of homemade wheelbarrows and trailers.

The Xiong family got off the tram at the terminus, and bearing their bundles and suitcases began the long climb up the hill to the house. Between the rough assortments of dwellings that had grown up to house the refugees, they sweated their way up hundreds of crudely laid cement steps that had been put down in haste in an effort to postpone, or at least mitigate, the effects of inevitable landslides. The dwellings were of all styles and standards; some made entirely of cardboard, wood and corrugated iron, others of brick and stone. Mostly they were tiny single storey places with low wooden doors that looked as if they had been built for children to live in. Higher up the hill were the better brick houses, some pretentious with half-finished verandas, front yards and a few geraniums in pots, and everywhere lines of washing and old red banner couplets and characters for Prosperity that had been pasted upside down on the front doors last Chinese New Year. Ahead of them in a house that flew the flag of the Republic of China from a bamboo flagpole, a child squalled repeatedly in the midday heat. Bear's son, whom Manying was carrying, joined in sympathy.

Bear could see that Manying was counting the steps under her breath; a habit she said she had acquired in the hilly city of Chongqing: five hundred and fifty-nine, five hundred and sixty... God bless her! She had been a general's wife living in a choice neighbourhood in the city of Nanjing with a cook and a maid, and now she was making the best of this.

Lying safely in the nook between two hills to the north, with a view for miles over the harbour and into the New Territories, the house that Bear the Elder had built conformed to many of the classical ideas about feng shui.

"Such a site is bound to bring many sons and grandchildren." Proudly he handed the key to Manying. The house, or cottage, as they called it, did in fact turn out to be a palace compared to most of the other properties, and Manying was clearly pleased with it. There was a sitting room, a kitchen with running water with a tiled drainage area for washing and two small bedrooms. The front of the house had a paved yard with a fence and an iron gate. On that particular day it was packed with crowds of strangers that were Xiong family maternal relatives moving in upstairs. In the middle of the yard they had set up a trestle table with incense and offerings to the gods; fruit, flowers, rice, tea and dried noodles. An old lady with bound feet smoked a cigarette and fed a brazier with wodges of paper money as offering to the gods. The smoke and ash wafted across the yard dirtying people's clothes and making every one's eyes smart.

"Wei, wei, Cousin, did the gas canister come?" Bear the Elder called out to a skinny man who was cradling three carved figures of gods for the house in his arms. The man gestured with his chin over the head of the Goddess of Mercy to the corner of the yard where there was indeed a gas canister.

Ling Ling took charge as was her way, calling out to a couple of lads to hurry up and bring the canister inside, where it was soon installed, left a bit, right a bit, just right, under a gas ring so the cooking could begin. Before long another trestle table in Bear and Manying's living room was groaning with all manner of dishes: pork and vegetables, a steamed fish, noodles, rice and a soup. Manying and Ling Ling had had words about the new house. As a Christian, Manying had refused to have an altar erected to the kitchen god.

"But a house is not a home without a kitchen god. Whose lips will you sweeten with honey at New Year, and who will report to the Old Father in Heaven on your behalf at that time? Better to have one, just to be sure," Ling Ling had cajoled.

But Manying was not to be persuaded, and grumbling something about feudal superstition Bear would not overrule her. Lips pursed, Ling Ling had evidently decided that if Manying and Bear would not do things the proper way, then she at least could ensure a good feast for all the friends and relatives, for the sake of the family and her nephew at least.

And indeed they did come, crowds of cousins, aunts and uncles. They ate, drank tea and rice wine, re-arranged the few pieces of furniture to safeguard the feng shui, and advised on the safest way to hang the electric wires that snaked precariously across the ceiling. And then it was time for Bear's family to visit the relatives upstairs, and the entire process was repeated in reverse. As dusk fell with raucous jokes and ill-remembered verses of patriotic songs, the party finally dispersed into the night. Bear and Manying faced each other as strangers across the snoring body of their sleeping child, grubby and unwashed at the end of a day of wild play with his new neighbours.

27

*B*ear knew he was not a clever man, but understood that he had a way with people. Born after the abolition of the traditional civil service examinations in 1905 and before the Republican Revolution of 1911, his father, a middle income landlord, was never entirely convinced that the new ways were here to stay. To hedge his bets he had had his two sons educated with a mixture of traditional and modern schooling. Schooled at home in the classics until he was eleven, Bear was then sent off to join his brother at the Jesuit School in Guangzhou. Bear the Younger was an average student, good at mathematics and interested in engineering, railways, steamships and bridge building but a disappointment to the Jesuit Brothers in the department of the soul. He argued quite dispassionately in the way they themselves had taught him, that it was impossible that Jesus was the Son of God, and that he was merely a teacher and philosopher who at best could be thought of as laying out a way for the people to follow if they wished to know God and escape the wheels of suffering.

The plan had been for Bear to study engineering in France. To please his parents, and much against his better judgement, Bear had agreed to an arranged marriage before he left. She was a gentle girl who knew no life outside the house and acquiesced in her fate without protest. She was soon pregnant and Bear delayed his departure by a few months in order to hold his son in his arms, for he was sure it would be a boy. Her labour was long. For three days he sat in the courtyard eating melon seeds, spitting out the shells onto a table, and listening to her screaming, moaning and wailing. The jovial midwife, his mother and his father all emerged from time to time to pat him on the back and assure him that suffering was part of the process and that such a child would be strong. Suddenly the screaming stopped. Scattering the melon shells to the floor with the flat of his hand and ignoring the protests of his mother, he barged his way over the threshold and into her room. He found his wife lying, legs splayed like a pig, in a pool of blood on their marriage bed.

"Cover her up! For God's sake, she's my wife."

"I'm sorry. I'm so sorry." It was all his wife could say.

She died seven hours later in his arms, on the day before her sixteenth birthday. It was only then that Bear thought to ask about the baby, a boy, stillborn, who had been smuggled out of the room in a bucket.

In his rage Bear declared himself the perfectly rational man. Bleeding to death at the hands of peasant midwives, what sin from a past life could warrant such a fate? In her last days of torture no God, no Buddha, no Jesus had been there to take away her pain. Science and democracy were the way to defeat the Imperialists and build a strong modern China. It was the only way.

But his chance, too, was gone. The effects of the worldwide depression were being felt, even in rural China, and when the price of cash crops suddenly plummeted, the Xiong family's reception hall was filled with grovelling tenants, their weeping wives and starving children. Bear's father, a benevolent man, reduced and in some cases waived rents, which meant he could no longer support his son in his ambition to study in France. When one day Bear bumped into a friend in the street in Guangzhou who had a spare application form for the Central Military Academy, he filled it in and cycled immediately to Whampoa to drop it off twenty minutes before the deadline. Thus Bear became a new kind of hero, a soldier.

*B*ear was the only passenger getting off the tram at North Point that day. Unusually, he had left work a little early to avoid the crowds. The conductor rang the bell and the tram clanked and accelerated down the tracks. Bear turned crisply on his heel as if trying to stop it dragging him behind to some distant place. Sauntering into the covered walkway in front of some shops he leaned against a shady pillar. The white concrete was rough but cool on his back and he fumbled for cigarettes in his shirt pocket. Tobacco and matches were constant companions, and today they seemed his only friends. The bittersweet perfume of phosphorus flame mingled with tobacco and he inhaled deeply, holding the smoke in his lungs before blowing it out long and slowly through his nose, and throwing the spent match into the gutter.

For a fleeting moment this perfectly rational man wondered what he might have done to condemn himself to a life such as this; exiled to the barbarian fringes of the Chinese empire, working for the Imperialists for a meagre wage, although his lot was better than many, he knew. He could not rightly remember what he had dreamed of as a young man, but it was not this. That particular day a senior aide to the Generalissimo, a former Colonel Liu had come to the hotel in civilian clothes so as not to antagonise the British authorities. He had arrived in a convoy of three taxis with the familiar door slamming, brief case flapping, entourage of aides, and a powdered young woman in high-heeled red shoes and a white dress with huge petticoats that whispered like a willow tree in the breeze when she walked and was too young to be his wife. Of course the man had not recognised Bear, who had greeted him in the lobby. And Bear realised with a pang that he had become a mere frog living at the bottom of the well. Where once he had lived under the great expanse of the heaven of the Republic, there was now but a sliver of daylight.

*I*t all came back to him; the day he gone with Colonel Liu to inspect a group of Chinese conscripts that had been flown over the hump to India to augment the Chinese forces after the Burma debacle.

"Stinking, filthy place, India. God it's hot!" Colonel Liu climbed out of his staff car onto the runway. Bear saluted.

"This lot are to join your men, Major Xiong. Want to show General Sun what we can do! Get them trained as soon as possible, won't you?" Liu was tall and broad-shouldered. From Beijing, his Mandarin was too precise, and he swaggered with his hips forward in a way that seemed effeminate to Bear compared to the American soldiers.

The conscripts had been unloaded from a cargo plane and corralled in an airport hangar. They were urine, sweat-soaked green mire, lost under a grey mist of cigarette smoke. Bear bit down on his front lip and tried to make a head count. He saw their eyes; empty, past staring, their uniforms hanging off them like ragged seaweed. His sergeant proffered a clipboard in his direction

"Well, you better sign for the bastards, Major." Colonel Liu took the clipboard and handed it to him. "Three hundred Sons of the Yellow Emperor! Precious cargo indeed!"

Again Bear bit down hard to quell the anger rising inside him. Did the colonel really expect him to make modern soldiers out of starving, illiterate peasants? Already the colonel was waving to his driver to pull over to the door of the hangar and pick him up. Bear saluted and felt sick.

A voice came from the depths of the hangar: "Hospital

for this one. Query asthma? No. No. No. Fetch a stretcher." It was a firm but calm voice speaking English. Then he saw her moving with other American nurses amongst the hunkered men. Blond hair tied up in a ponytail, her captain's pips picked out by timid shafts of sunlight from the front of the hangar. The men gawped at her as if she were an angel descending from heaven. She looked up, saw Bear and stepped carefully around the bodies to make her way over to him.

"Major Xiong." She pronounced his name with a heavy '*shh*ing' sound.

"These men are not fit to fight. All of them are dehydrated and ninety-five percent of them malnourished, not to mention..."

He could not look her in the eye. She smiled a perfect American smile and handed him her clipboard.

"First off, I need all these Chinese names and numbers translated. I cannot feed them and treat them if I do not know who they are."

Her name was Cathy, from Illinois, and Bear had watched in amazement as she set about organising rotas and schedules for feeding the men and treating their festering sores. She never gave up hope, even on the sickest. On the second day after the men's arrival fresh supplies arrived. She was at his side in the yard helping to unload.

"Let me help you, Captain! Great! Medical supplies. I need this gear in the hospital." She banged the crate with the flat of her hand and put her right hand on her hip. Bear thought that while Chinese women spoke with their eyes, American women talked with smiles.

She was taller than him by half a foot, so he took most of the weight of the crate and was glad to do so. Together they manoeuvred it through the doors, down the corridor and into her office.

"Phew!" She dusted her hands, brushing back the stray hairs that had stuck to her forehead. The front and sleeves of her shirt had pulled up and he saw the white flesh of the tops of her breasts and arms, untouched by the Indian sun.

"I'll help you unpack." She did not object.

"Bandages; 10 packs. Syringes; 10 packs. Saline. Morphine." She read out the names on the boxes, patiently waiting until he ticked them off on her list, for he read English slower than Chinese.

"Don't you want to keep some back?" he asked as the nurses came to put everything away.

"Why?" She looked puzzled.

"You know...in case you run out?"

"Heavens no! If I run out, then I will just order more. Want a cigarette, Major?"

In that moment Bear had understood that America was a bottomless rice bowl. If only the Generalissimo would bite the bullet and throw everything against the Japanese, instead of hoarding supplies and equipment from the Americans, there would be more planes, tanks and ammunition than they could ever imagine.

$Bear$ stubbed out his cigarette with his toe, walked to the end of the row of shops, turned right and began the long climb up the steps to Manying and home. After a while he paused to catch his breath, concentrating on the juicy smell of suppers frying in cheap oil rather than the competing aromas of poor drains. Unlike most local residents and all their children, he never counted the steps, for his mother had once told him that steps represented the days of people's lives. Judging however from the line of women's laundry ahead of him, he knew that he was about three quarters of the way up to the house.

No point dwelling on the past. He did at least have Manying and the boy, and a warm feeling flooded his tired limbs at the thought of them. Poor Manying! It broke his heart to see her down on her knees like a peasant, mopping the floor, cooking meals and hauling the child and the shopping up the seven hundred steps that the neighbourhood children told him took you from the very bottom to the top. She deserved better than this, but he could not afford maids. What's more, they had not made love since his arrival in Hong Kong, and it troubled him. At first, he had been too exhausted to be interested, and then when the urges did return they were unpredictable and he had been afraid of disappointing her. No point dwelling on the past! Tonight, Bear decided, would be the night. Under the circumstances he deemed it wise to turn off the main path and not court bad luck by walking under the washing line with women's underwear that hung limply in the still night air.

28

Manying had not had a good day. She had left her son at home while she went to do the day's shopping. She could no longer carry him up and down the steps and it took him the whole day to walk up and down, examining every stone and insect and poking sticks into drains. By eight-thirty the mid-August heat was already pressing down on the maggot earth with all the vehemence of a personal vendetta, and traders at the market went about their daily business with lips curled and teeth bared like wild cats and dogs; everywhere they were demanding higher than normal prices. Manying haggled for over ten minutes with her usual fishmonger over the price of a piece of halibut, and when she finally gave up and took her business to another stall he followed her, telling the other vendor just what he thought of her, so she ended up paying the increased price in the end. With gritted teeth she turned for home. Cannibals, the lot of them! They were ready to tear the flesh off others for a quarter of a dollar. At home she found her toddler son happily shipwrecked between upturned wicker chairs in the middle of a pile of his parents' carefully ironed clothes that he had pulled from their drawers.

"Wei Wei, Mama! Gone!" He laughed pulling her best blouse over his head in the expectation that she would play peep-ho with him. But Manying was not in the mood. By the time she had tidied up, put away the vegetables and cooked noodles it was past one o'clock. Now the child was tired but, lying beside her on the bed, would not take his afternoon nap, pulling instead at his mother's hair, poking her eyes and making tiger noises. He wore her out during the rest of the afternoon, pulling Manying's sewing off the table and making it impossible to finish the shirt she was making for her husband. When Bear got home Manying was trying to chop vegetables with the child pulling at her trouser legs.

Bear took the boy out for a walk around the neighbourhood returning some ten minutes later with him fast asleep on his shoulder. He put him down on the bed.

"You shouldn't let him get so tired," he said curtly to Manying.

Husband and wife ate in silence. Manying looked across the table at the hunched old man with a nose like a wart that slurped his soup and spat fish bones out onto the table.

Later, when the child had been washed and fed and was once again asleep, Bear sat smoking, watching Manying in the kitchen washing dishes. He sidled into the kitchen carrying the ash tray and stubbed out his cigarette before emptying the tray into the bin.

"Let me help you." But his voice was gruff as he grabbed her arm.

Manying froze. She felt his hands squeezing her breasts as he tried to snuggle into her neck.

"I don't need any help."

"Come on, Manying. It's been so long." His breath was hot and stale and the day's growth of stubble grazed her cheeks.

"No! No!" She pushed him hard in the chest.

"What do you mean, no?" Bear tried to grab her again. She grabbed the meat cleaver from the drainer behind her.

"No means no!" she hissed. She waved the cleaver over her head, ready to strike. "I can't, that's all."

"Damn you! You're my wife. It's your duty..." Bear searched for the correct phrase. "It's my right!" The ridiculous word of worthless constitutions and loudspeaker political propaganda hit her like a slap in the face. She might have answered back: What about my right to watch my son play at his grandfather's knee, to see him climb mango trees with his uncle, to give birth with my mother and sister at my side and eat home cooking during my confinement? What about my right to live in peace, marry my childhood sweetheart and be free of guilt and loss? Instead I have a life not lived, the wrong life, this life.

But instead of speaking her mind, she raised the cleaver higher overhead.

"Leave me alone!" She hacked viciously at the air in her husband's direction. Amazed at this outburst from his gentle, undemanding wife, Bear raised his hands in surrender. She knew then that he knew; the measure of a love that had caused such an outburst, a love that did not belong to him. He stepped back and she fled past him into the night.

*S*till carrying the meat cleaver she ran blindly up the dirt track behind the house. Even the brightest stars were faint in the heat that night and all was still in the eye of the summer, autumn not yet in sight. Gradually, Manying's eyes became accustomed to the dark world of shadows. She passed the clearing where old people gathered for morning qi gong exercises, and set off on a narrow path that ran up the mountain. The children often found bones up here, arriving triumphantly in their kitchens with their trophies, a human skull, a scapula or a femur. It was said that there were several mass graves of victims of the

Japanese during the occupation on the mountain, and that the tortured spirits roamed at night. But Manying was not afraid. Indeed, the thought of such companions was a comfort.

She left the path, walking along one of the hundreds of dry water gullies that criss-crossed the mountain to carry away the typhoon rains. It made a good track and was blocked only occasionally by brambles bearing fruit yet to ripen, which she hacked away with the cleaver, letting the thorns bloody her hands. She was content to follow secret alleys with no desire to know where they led.

At length she emerged into a clearing on the top of another mountain further along the island. It was a place families came for picnics, and lovers for privacy, but tonight it was deserted.

*B*ear found her in the early hours of the morning. She was sitting surrounded by fireflies, in the centre of the clearing with the meat cleaver resting on her lap. The whisper of the rising morning breeze caressed the loose stands of her hair. Gently he took the cleaver from her and hurled it down the mountainside. She did not resist. Lifting their son from the sling on his back and laying him still sleeping on the ground, he sat down beside her. The bands of crickets had long since ended their chatter and most of the neon lights in Wanchai and Kowloon had been turned off, leaving only street lights and the beacons from the airport marking the runway. Man and woman sat in silence, staring at the black crouching dragon hills of Kowloon, and beyond them, China.

It was Manying who spoke first, in a whisper.

"Husband...I..."

"Hush..." He put his hand over her mouth just as she had once done with her baby son. He pressed harder as she tried to go on.

I shall not struggle, she thought, but it was over in an instant, and he released her.

"Let bygones be bygones, Manying. It has been a long war, too long, I know. We must look to the future, otherwise we shall all go mad." He put his arm around her shoulder and pulled her to him.

She was overcome by his smell; sweat and stale tobacco, and it reminded her of their wedding night, all those years ago.

A great silence echoed to the vaults of the temple sky, and the fireflies, knowing no boundaries, returned through the grey veil of dawn to the world beyond that has no name.

29

*A*iya! Success and status are as air and water to men. If they are deprived of them, they must create at least the illusion of them or perish." Ling Ling would raise her eyes to heaven and busy herself making tea each time Manying told her she was pregnant. In less than ten years she had given birth to four children, not counting one stillborn child, one who did not survive the first month, and umpteen miscarriages. She got used to the endless moods and discomforts of pregnancy, and by the end of the decade felt that her body had purposes that were other than her own.

Manying's second child, a son named Peter, was a demanding, skinny baby who expected much of life and squalled with rage whenever things did not go his way. Her third child was a daughter, who later took the English name Selina after the character for moon, which formed part of her Chinese name. A podgy baby who looked like a laughing Buddha, she grew into a pretty girl, and Bear predicated that her face would be her fortune.

It was shortly after the birth of Selina that the first letter from China arrived. It was from Manying's school friend Ping Ping and had been smuggled out via a relative of Bear The Elder's in Guangzhou. Written on poor quality paper in socialist red ink, it was the first communication she had received from her friend since the end of the anti-Japanese war.

Dear Comrade Manying, the letter began. Ping's firm, bold characters, clearly those of a primary teacher, were almost indistinguishable from Manying's own. They had been taught by the same teacher as children. But the fact that Ping Ping had taken the risk to send a letter out of the country at all told Manying that things were far from well.

> *You must forgive me for not having written sooner. We must all make sacrifices for the new People's Republic of China, and even the best old friendships are of secondary importance to the work of the revolution.*

> *I trust that this letter finds you well and in good health. The health of my husband declined after the liberation and the death of his younger brother. He was a stubborn man and found it difficult to make the sacrifices required to build a socialist China. He died in an accident in 1951.*

> *I keep myself busy and am working hard for the Three Selfs Movement to free the Chinese Church from foreign control.*

> *My sons are such big strong boys—quite the model workers! I hope that one day you will be able to meet them.*

> *Long Live the People's Republic of China! Long live Chairman Mao!*

> *Ping Ping*

This was a letter from a woman who throughout the anti- Japanese and civil wars had written long detailed letters bursting with the latest gossip, like the time she had told Manying about the time that the new French priest had been so frightened by the bark of the family's dog that he fled all the way down the back alley, gown hoisted over his fat knees. In his haste he had dropped his berretta and had never dared to come back to fetch it.

In the evening after supper, Manying showed the letter to Bear.

"So the bastards got Ping Ping's husband too—Nationalist connections—accused him of being a counter revolutionary most likely. Old Wong was always so naive." He took off his glasses, folded the letter and said no more.

That night Manying could not sleep. "Husband, what would have happened to us if we had stayed?"

Bear merely grunted from his side of the bed. Eventually he said, "One thing is sure, they'd have shot me years ago."

Years passed, sometimes as days, other times as decades, and Manying started going to church again. Practice brought a practical wisdom, and she and Bear would marvel at the growing children, the crazy assortment of faces and personalities that emerged unbidden from their nights of precious comfort.

Early one evening in the spring of 1958, Manying sat at the table with her three children. Peter was sewing painstakingly around the edges of two white towels to make sacks while the eldest, Jack, was helping Selina to wrap rice, noodles, chicken stock cubes and tea in brown paper. Heavily pregnant once more, Manying jumped as the child kicked under her ribs. Poor baby! With all the mouths to feed money was tight, and despite her husband's joy at the sight of her swollen belly, as far as she was concerned, the child was not welcome. She was doing her best to ignore its presence. Placing her hand on her stomach to sooth it, she adjusted the position of the cushion in the small of her back and read another letter that had been smuggled out of China, this time via the church, and that the local pastor's wife had delivered to her that morning. Like the previous letter, she knew that this one too had been written out of desperation. For despite the rhetoric of glorious socialist utopia, the policy of the Great Leap Forward had led to famine and mass starvation in China.

This time the letter was from Zheng. She was surprised to find that her hand trembled as it held the paper. How strange after all these years to think that she was touching what he had touched.

As with Ping Ping's letters, its stilted brevity spoke volumes. Comrade Wen, he was sorry that he had not written earlier but hoped to find her in good health. His mother and father had died shortly after the liberation. He was well and happy under the leadership of the Great Helmsman and working hard for the revolution. Their new baby was well although his wife had been rather slow in recovering from the birth, but they were sure that now the baby was in the nursery and now that they were all eating in the communal kitchen with the other comrades from their work unit, she would soon regain her strength. Hoping that Manying would be able to find the time to write to them, the letter gave the address of the Nanjing City Hospital.

"Finished!" Triumphantly Peter held up the finished product; his sack made out of towels. Laughing, he draped it over Selina's head. As she protested it fell back like a hood.

"Enough!" Sharply, Manying snatched the sack away.

The children were startled by her tone of voice. Usually their mother was the biggest child of all: the one who laughed longest and loudest at family tomfoolery. But Manying was not going to tell them that the towel on Selina's head resembled a white mourning hat worn at funerals. That would have been a temptation to fate.

Sending the children to get ready for bed, Manying smoothed the towel sack flat on the table. Taking a cheap indelible pen, carefully she wrote Zheng's address on the front and back of the bag. One by one she put the little packages of food into the bag. It had been Bear's idea to buy cheap towels and use them to make a bag, which could be unpacked and used by the recipient. Sighing, she put the last packet of tea into the bag. As an afterthought she fetched a small packet of red dates from the kitchen that she had been using to make into soup for herself; dates were women's food and she understood all too well the debilitation of childbirth. These and the other precious treasures had been saved out of her meagre housekeeping over months. Still, they seemed a paltry offering.

Manying went into the bedroom to settle the children, and returning to the sitting room heard Bear's voice in the yard. Recently, there had been rumours of riots between the Communists and Nationalist supporters in Kowloon, as had happened two years ago when over fifty people had been killed, including the wife of the Swiss Consul who had burned to death in her car at the hands of the mob. Bear had sent a message with a boy at five o'clock to say that something unexpected had come up and that he would not be back until late.

The front door opened, and a man stepped over the threshold followed by Bear. A lot taller than Bear, he removed his hat and blinked nervously through round-rimmed spectacles in the harsh light of the naked light bulb. Despite the mild weather, the stranger wore a woollen coat that had probably once been expensive. He carried an old suitcase and there was mud on his boots. His bedroll was slung over Bear's shoulder.

The stranger's face was thin but retained traces of the fuller openness of youth. Manying found it difficult to determine his age, although he certainly was not young. It was, however, instantly obvious to her that he was not a military man; he was a different breed altogether, and she was on her guard.

"Welcome! Welcome!" Bear said to the stranger in Shanghai dialect, gesturing for him to sit down. "My wife." Manying just nodded her head.

"I am sorry to burst into your home unannounced at this late hour. Your husband says that you have a room to let?" The stranger had switched back to Cantonese, but it was the heavily accented Cantonese of a person from Shanghai. Characterised by a gentle lisping and a hotch-potch of words that were bastardised versions of both dialects, it was not easy to understand and sounded peculiarly feminine. Despite herself, Manying found that she was smiling. She looked to Bear for guidance. He stared back at her, his face desperately old and tired, his eyes made big as if to say, don't let me down on this one. Letting a room was something that they had toyed with a few months previously but had done nothing about.

"Mrs Xiong, I have agreed with your husband to pay weekly for the first month and then monthly thereafter—lodging only—I will eat outside"

Hearing the disturbance, Jack and Peter appeared sleepy-eyed at the bedroom door. The points of their knees and elbows sticking out of their pyjamas, they looked like ragamuffins, and Manying was embarrassed. Hurrying them back to bed she desperately tried to think how to relocate the children from the second of the two small bedrooms to make the most of the rental opportunity. They would have to put a bunk bed in the back of the living room, and a curtain, and...

"Mrs Xiong, I am sorry to turn up like this. My previous landlord had an unexpected visit from his brother and his family, so I had to move in a hurry. I am very grateful to you and your husband for offering me a room at such short notice. I can sleep on the floor tonight. We can sort the details out in the morning." Curtly, Manying nodded as the stranger handed over the first week's rent to

Bear. Such a lot of money, and he hadn't even seen the room he was paying for. A desperate man, perhaps?

30

*I*n time the family got used to having their lodger, Mr Li, around, although Manying saw little of him. He rose early and returned late and she preferred to keep her distance. Sometimes working men from the docks or factories would turn up at the house bearing small gifts of cigarettes, tea or rice wine and asking shiftily in poor Cantonese for Mr Li. When they greeted him they would bow their heads and clasp their hands with respect, and on occasion even cry.

At first the children were shy of Mr Li: the tall man who lived in what used to be their bedroom so that they had to sleep in bunk beds behind the curtains in the living room. But like small animals, investigating something new, over time they became more familiar, until they would loiter around the front of the house waiting to catch him when he returned from work or on weekends. Their favourite game was to tease him about his Cantonese. Eyes crinkled with fun, Mr Li played along in the manner of a country bumpkin, pretending not to understand anything at all and agreeing to the most ridiculous of their requests. As Mr Li stood on one leg, holding his breath, with one arm stretched up in the air with his hat on it, like a hat stand, the children threw themselves flat on their backs while holding their stomachs with laughter, and even Manying had to smile.

Bear, too, told Manying he had not immediately taken to Mr Li the day he had first turned up at the hotel trying to sell Japanese industrial washing machines. For him people from Shanghai were not reliable and were always trying to pull a fast one. This lanky man whose head and shoulders stooped forward as if others were beneath him, would be no different. But Mr Li had timed his visit well. The local laundries had raised the price per pound of washing some time ago, and Mr Cameron was on the look out for alternatives. So Bear had given Li an audience and the man's figures had been persuasive. Ever with an eye to logistics, Bear had followed up with a visit to Uncle Li's small warehouse by the docks where he had assured himself that Li did indeed have a supply chain and could provide spare parts. The deal had been concluded in the presence of Cameron at a dim sum restaurant on Nathan Road. Mr Li was prepared to push the boat out on such occasions, but he had not reckoned on the appetite of the old gwailo for whom the memory of the years of semi-starvation in Stanley prison were more powerful than any compulsion to good manners. The gwailo ate slowly, ruminating each mouthful like an old cow. All the while, his beady eyes lusted across the spread of dishes, the pork spare ribs, rice dumplings with peanuts, sticky sausage rice; which would it be? His chopsticks worked overtime to supply his desire. He left the negotiating to Bear, intervening with a nod and a grunt at crucial times as he polished off the remains of every dish so that Mr Li had to order more or lose face. At last, when the figures had been trimmed to everyone's satisfaction and a service agreement drawn up, Cameron had eaten his fill.

"Poor little pork bun!" He wiped it around the plate

that had once contained spare ribs to soak up the gravy and popped the bun into his mouth. Leaning back in his chair he laid down his chopsticks and patted his stomach. "Very satisfactory. Very satisfactory indeed!"

The following week the machines were delivered as agreed and Mr Li came in blue workman's overalls with a boy of sixteen or so to install them. Bear was there to supervise the work, but, discussing water pressure with Mr Li, he could not resist the temptation to participate and soon found himself crawling along a ventilation shaft to check the location of pipes and electric wires. Sleeves rolled up, the day was spent organising, banging, drilling and fixing. Hands on stuff, it was what Bear was good at and it reminded him of happy days as a young officer with the regiment. At the end of the day, like a gaggle of geese, the hotel maids in white shirts and black trousers clucked their way down to the laundry for the demonstration. The bellies of the machines were loaded with sheets and towels and they roared and tumbled to life with the appetite of great hungry dragons.

"Ai ya, too big, too noisy, water not hot enough. Call that clean?" Nothing was right for the women, and Bear and Li retired to the yard. Men of the world both, they knew full well that complaint was the highest form of gratitude.

They sat in companionable silence, relishing the American beer and cigarettes that Cameron signed off for them at the hotel bar. Their old worlds had crumbled to dust and they had been left with nothing. But the sweat and bitterness of small and desperate endeavours such as the business of second-hand washing machines gave new purpose, and that was enough.

Of course Mr Li gave Bear an envelope for facilitating the deal. Cameron had figured on this too, and nothing more needed to be said between the three men. Li adhered to the terms of the contract and turned up to service the machines at regular intervals, and when he got into a fight with some Communists who were sticking up posters and agitating in the block where he lived in Kowloon, it was natural that Bear should offer to rent him a room, high on the hill on Hong Kong Island, away from the trouble.

Despite her misgivings even Manying had to admit as time went by that the rent money went a long way to improving their standard of living. After their fourth child was born in the summer of 1958 she had already saved enough money to go to the *Wah Fung* department store in North Point and have a silk cheongsam made. It was of beautiful dark green silk with black flowers on it and despite herself, it reminded her of the pine forests around Chongqing. She wore it on Sundays to the little Baptist church at the bottom of the hill and knew she looked good in it.

The new baby, a girl, was quite the "dolly" of the family, hence her nickname. Serious and patient, she was the opposite of her unruly brothers and Manying could not remember her crying even at birth. She grew into a self-contained child, whose idea of heaven was to escape the mayhem of family life and bury her head in a book. When Manying looked at the small black and white photograph of her father in a Chinese gown that she had brought from Nanjing, the child was the spitting image of her grandfather.

Manying's relief at the birth of a healthy fourth child was marred by a slow but steady decline in Bear's health. He was able to keep himself together at work, but was good for nothing in the evenings. His trembling fits were becoming more frequent and for no obvious reason he would start to shake and take refuge under the kitchen table. The children were used to their father's behaviour. When the worst of a fit had passed, Jack and Peter would calmly help him to bed, cover him with the quilt and fetch him a cup of rice wine.

One evening in the summer of 1960 Bear did not

return home for supper. Manying despatched the boys to look for him. By nine o'clock there was still no sign of him. Manying was preparing to leave the children in the care of her eldest and go to the hotel herself, when the door opened and Mr Li, his arm around Bear's waist, brought him into the sitting room. Manying's first thought was that they were drunk. But one look at her husband's quivering face, dripping with sweat, told her otherwise.

"I found him sitting in a corner, by the church." Mr Li was panting with the effort of supporting Bear. "He was spitting blood and shaking." Manying thought only the family knew about Bear's health but said nothing.

"It's OK. No big deal. Fetch some wine. Been working too hard, that's all." Bear collapsed in the chair.

Manying brought the bottle and two cups. Slowly the alcohol returned the colour to Bear's pasty cheeks and the trembling in his hands relaxed into a spasmodic twitching.

"Need to slow down, old chap." Mr Li raised his cup to drink with Bear.

"Go to bed, Old Wife! Leave us men to chew the cud." Manying was not convinced. Her eyes met Mr Li's. He nodded reassuringly.

"Make sure you lock up," she said and shuffled reluctantly into the kitchen to wash.

The doors were open to make the most of what breeze there was on that stifling night. In the darkness Manying lay on the far side of the bed listening to the whirring crickets and the men's conversation.

"It was the Battle of Huai Hai that did it for me." Bear's voice was expressionless. "At least there was a point in killing Little Devil Japs, and with American backing and training we were the best the Chinese army had ever seen, and we knew it. But civil war...Chinese killing Chinese...brother against brother..." A chair creaked; the bottle clinked against the cups. Another long silence. Bear's voice laboured through the viscous darkness.

"By December of 1948 we were surrounded by thirty

three communist divisions led by General Liu Bo-cheng. Our men fought well, but under heavy shelling, with food supplies exhausted and temperatures below zero, I can't say I was surprised when, in the end, divisions began to defect to the Communists."

"At the end of the first week of December I was summoned away from the front line to the Divisional HQ. Things were chaotic. On the way, I passed troops in retreat, and when I arrived the place was in an uproar—clearly being prepared for evacuation."

General Chen in Command of the Corps, and a General Tang who introduced himself as the personal envoy of Chiang Kai Shek, were waiting to see me. I will always remember entering that room; there was still a large brazier burning and they wore their uniforms without coats. I'd become so used to seeing men on the front line in layers of padding against the cold that I'd forgotten how smart a soldier could look in uniform!"

"General Chen got straight to the point. That's when I knew things were bad—none of the usual beating around the bush, which is the curse on Chinese efficiency. They needed a good man for a vital mission. The loyalty of General Xiong was well known within and therefore they wanted to offer me the job. The survival of us all depended on it, and so on and so on."

"And you accepted?" Uncle Li's voice was soothing and soft in the blackness. Bear chuckled.

"I thanked the general for the honour. Of course, if it were just a matter of myself...but we had been under heavy shelling for days and my men were exhausted, and I could not ask more of them... Then General Tang put in his oar; gun holster and shoes all pristine with fresh polish, it made me sick.

"'General Xiong, I bear message from Generalissimo Chiang Kai Shek for you, one of the illustrious graduates of our famous Central Military Academy,'" Bear mocked, speaking in the pompous tone of official edicts and radio propaganda. "'The Generalissimo hopes very much that you will do him the honour of agreeing to command this difficult mission, *for the honour of the Academy*,'"Bear cackled. "'For the honour of the Academy and all my brother officers!' How could I not accept? After all, it was for the honour of the Military Academy! What a joke!

"After I had accepted the command, the blood drained out of General Chen's face. It was the same earth-shattering look of defeat that I had seen in the eyes of the Japanese colonel whose surrender I had accepted in 1945. Then he turned fatherly, asking me to sit near the brazier and have something to eat. But when the time came for me to leave he could no longer look me in the eye, and I knew that he had just signed the death warrant for my division. But General Tang? He called to his aide to hurry up and get his car, grabbed his briefcase and rushed out the door even before buttoning of his coat.

"Remember the Battle of Taerzhuang? God willing, we will have another such victory."

"Our task? To make a strategic stand in the town of Datudui so that the rest of the army could break out and live to fight another day. We were to hold until further orders and then make our own retreat as best we could."

"The sacrificial lamb?"

"You might say so. The three regiments in my division took positions around Datudui. Their morale remained good. We had been crack divisions trained by the Americans. My friend Young Wong from Burma days was in command of one regiment. We watched as the exhausted, raggle-taggle bits of the 12th Army retreated past our lines. They left what ammunition and supplies they could spare—sometimes a pat on the back or a curse or two by way of encouragement. But it was not long before we were on our own and the communists turned their big guns on our positions.

"By the 14th of December I had lost at least half the men in the division and we were running out of ammunition." Bear spoke slowly and calmly, determined to put the record straight. "In my last communication with HQ I asked how long we would be required to hold. The answer came back that the breakout was going well, and they just needed another forty-eight hours.

"The shelling on the 14th of December was particularly remorseless; it went on all day, without let up. I got stuck at some forward position in the town and couldn't get back. During that afternoon a shell wounded my friend Young Wong: shrapnel in the chest. He died in my arms."

Manying heard the striking of a match in the silence and imagined that Mr Li had given Bear a cigarette. It was a long time before Bear continued.

"Around dusk on the night of the 14th of December the shelling suddenly stopped. It was eerie. At first I thought I had gone deaf with all the noise and it was just that I couldn't hear it any longer. I banged my ears with my hands like this, as if I had been swimming, to get rid of the water. There was no sound of birds, no wind. Slowly, as my ears adjusted and I heard the moans of the wounded and the shouts of the medics and the surviving troops quietly numbering off. For fun the survivors of one platoon a little way off were using English numbers as some of them had done in training with the Americans. The foreign words were as out of place as the black stumps of trees abandoned in the snow of no man's land.

"As the smoke cleared across no man's land, a very strange thing happened. Someone was walking toward us from the communist lines. When he got within range my men started to shoot, but I ordered them to hold their fire; he was carrying a white flag.

"'Maybe the communists are going to surrender to us after all,' someone said, and we all laughed. As the figure approached we thought he was just a boy. But he was strong and made quick progress towards my precise position, almost as if he knew just where to find me.

"The boy turned out to be a man: a very short man

with a round face and tobacco stained teeth, dressed in the green, padded uniform of the People's Liberation Army. He offered us all cigarettes, and when I shook my head he laughed, 'No matter. Russian cigarettes are an acquired taste away!'

"He addressed me as Comrade General and introduced himself as Comrade Deng Xiaoping , Political Commissar. He came quickly to the point, like an American. That impressed me.

"'General Liu Bo-cheng and I have seen how bravely you and your men have fought over the last few days. We congratulate you.' At first I wanted to laugh. The man was an earnest dwarf, with the most ridiculous squeaky Sichuan accent, like a film running too fast.

"'General Liu and I admire you all for your courage. We know that you are good men and are holding these positions so that your fellow comrades in the Twelfth Army can escape. I come to tell you now that their breakout has failed. Many of your comrades in the Twelfth Army have already come over to us. The People's Liberation Army, your army, is winning this battle, and before long we are going to take China. Why waste your lives? We're all Chinese. We're brothers. Let's put a stop to the madness. Today, let us spill no more blood! Join us! Together we can build a new China!'

"At this point I interrupted. 'Comrade Deng, I agree with you that it is madness for Chinese to kill Chinese. Today I have lost one of my own dearest brothers, and many good men besides. But we are soldiers of the Republic of China. We know our duty. My men will escort you back to the front line.'

"The little man sighed, the breath from his mouth rising to the heavens like the smoke from burning incense. 'The loss of comrade brothers is always very painful. I myself lost many dear comrades on the Long March.' Suddenly his expression changed. No longer a chubby faced boy but a veteran campaigner who at last had victory in his sights, he screeched at me. 'Comrade General, you have it within your power to prevent the slaughter of more innocent men. I will give you two hours to consider my offer. After that we will resume shelling and I guarantee, come tomorrow, you will all be dead. The hour of our victory is nigh! You have two hours.'

"After the comrade had left, I met with my surviving senior officers and presented them with the choice: believe what the little man said about the failure of the breakout; surrender and join the communists or hold and thereby give our people their extra forty-eight hours. To a man, the officers voted to hold their positions.

"'In that case, gentlemen,' I said, 'let's concentrate our men in key positions and retrieve all the spare ammunition from the dead and seriously wounded. It only remains for me to say that it has been a privilege to command the best of Sons of the Yellow Emperor. Good luck.'"

Bear sounded exhausted; his speech monotonous and slightly slurred, like a medium relaying to mere mortals a communication from a terrible supernatural world. The effort of recall and narration was draining the life out of him. He took a deep breath.

"We decided to hold out. The comrade was true to his word and gave us the two hours, after which the shelling recommenced. It went on all night and late into the following day when the communists began to advance on our positions.

"After that I can't remember so well what happened. Later, I reckoned that I must have been knocked out by the blast or debris from a shell. I remember lying under a pile of dead bodies. They were still warm. I thought at first that I was in bed, wrapped in a thick quilt in the old family courtyard house where I grew up. When I eventually came to my senses it was after dawn. I must have been unconscious for about ten hours. Lying there I heard a little bird greeting the dawn, flower lace tweeting, far, far above. It was the sound of heaven. But there were no voices. Crawling out from beneath bodies, I looked at my watch. It had stopped at 23:54.

"I scrabbled through the ruins, in and out of the foxholes, calling familiar names, turning bodies over, looking for survivors. Mostly I found just bits of bodies; an arm, a hand, a leg, a piece of a face. I started to try to sort them and put them to rest with their owners. But it was difficult to find the owners—blown to bits and scattered to the four winds. I was angry, slighted, like a diligent child given a puzzle that was way beyond my ability. I thought that I ought to be able to complete the task— it was just that I was too stupid. I kept trying until I was too exhausted to continue. That was when I understood...my men were dead. I thought that maybe I too was dead, that I had been condemned to roam the world as a ghost as a penance for my crimes.

"It was not long before they caught me. They were kind, the communist bandits. They had fires burning in the camps and gave me hot rice. I was corralled with a bunch of men, some of them my own. But none of them betrayed my identity. It was not long before I realised the communists were pulling out senior officers for interrogation. I had not removed my uniform and still wore my general's stripes in full glory on my shoulder. When my time came a young captain who told me he had once been a farmer in Anhui province interviewed me. He offered me a cigarette and tea. Tea! I had not tasted it in months.

"He barked questions at me about my army commands, my family, and my connections. His accent was difficult to understand. Sometimes I had to guess what he was saying and anyway I did not have the energy to lie. What was the point? I was a petty general in a defeated army. I would be shot.

"'A man such as you would have much to contribute to the new China. We need men of experience,' the young captain began once more, yawned and looked at his watch.

It was nearly time for dinner.

"'No,' I said. 'I am spent. I have seen too many men die in vain.' The captain sighed and puffed on his cigarette.

"'What is your rank, comrade...lieutenant general?' He squinted at the muddied pips on my shoulders. I did not correct him.

"'What will you do if I let you go, Comrade?'

"I was surprised. 'Go home...go home to my family.'

"'How do I know you will not come back and fight us another day?' There was a long silence.

"'Look at us!' I snorted, jerking my thumb over my shoulder at the huddles of abandoned, leaderless men. 'Don't make me laugh!'

"He hesitated, looked me up and down one last time, then took up his pen, pulled a sheet of paper from a box on the table and painstakingly filled in a form. He wrote like a child, hunched down, his pen grasped in his fist, breathing heavily as he laid down each stroke. His literacy was hard won, and I admired him for that. At last he stood up, his chair scraping on the floor as if the painful lesson could not have ended too soon. Deftly he spat into the bucket to his left and shoved the piece of paper at me. He was out the door calling to his orderly for rice before I had time to realise what it was all about. I had a travel pass in my hand.

"And so do we need a capital here? Providence spared me and I became a ghost. At first I made for Nanjing. Despite my pass I kept off the main roads, ate what I could find and travelled alone. But there were many ghosts wandering the countryside, and it was impossible to avoid them completely. They were dressed in rags, their eyes huge and sunken in their emaciated heads, mouths hanging open, their faces fixed in the grimace of death. They whispered to me that Nanjing had fallen. So I turned south for Hong Kong. As I walked I remembered General Sun Li Ren's words before we left for Burma. 'We can only fight a victorious war not a losing war...If you are killed and I alone am left, I too will die at your side. It is the most glorious thing to die in battle for the survival of the nation.'"

"You and I are both living ghosts." Uncle Li's voice was hoarse. There was the sound of another match being struck, wine cups clinking together and a long pause. In the shadows, Manying let her forehead rest against the bedroom doorframe. "I had to leave Shanghai in a hurry. There were certain compromises I made in the past...I thought it would just be for a while, until things settled down again...I too have not left things as I might have liked."

31

*I*n September 1960, Manying and Bear's eldest son, Jack, moved out of the family house. With Bear's health in decline and the addition of little Dolly to the family, they could no longer afford to keep him in school. Mr Li got him a job as a delivery boy at a bakery in the Central district and he went to live with some cousins so that he could be nearer to his place of work.

Standing at the front door holding Dolly's hand, Manying watched him leave, accompanied by his father. She felt guilty. Her ancestors had been Imperial Degree Holders. Her father had been an educated man and even she was well-educated for a woman of her generation. In her heart of hearts she knew that her eldest son had drawn the short straw. The child that she had carried with her out of China in the spring of 1949 had simply been born in the wrong place at the wrong time.

There he was, already much taller than his father; he looked such a man as he shouldered his bedrole and strode off down the hill to start his own life.

*I*n the late autumn of 1960, eleven years since Bear had arrived as a beggar in Hong Kong, he was taken seriously ill with stomach pains and bleeding. The doctor diagnosed stomach cancer and gave him three months to live. By Christmas he was dead.

The last months of Bear's life were lost to pain, but in the final days morphine was prescribed. The drug stretched out his furrowed brow, and made him young again.

The family was at his bedside when he died. He lifted his hands from the sheet, playing with the air.

"The fireflies...so beautiful...all around me. I am with the fireflies."

*T*he funeral was organised by Bear the Elder. Mr Cameron was the only gwailo to attend, standing next to a small army of mangy old men who had soldiered or worked with Bear, and had given up half a day's pay to be there. Colour Sergeant Ding, now the head gardener at Victoria Park and the proud owner of a complete new set of modern false teeth, ordered the men into tidy lines to salute the coffin.

Wearing white mourning gowns and tall peaked hats, Manying and the children received the condolences of friends and neighbours. Manying felt nothing during the rituals; the barometer of her emotions was at its lowest. She stood stiff and tall, and shed no tears even as the children wept for their father.

Alone in bed for the first time in ten years she was racked from head to foot by terrible pain. Sitting up, she expected that the sheets would be drenched in blood but was surprised to find that they were not. She stuffed her face into her pillow so that the children would not hear her cries. Dolly slept peacefully by her side, her arms flung back above her head. Occasionally her left leg twitched in her sleep just as it had in the womb, catching painfully under Manying's ribs. Manying knocked her head against the stone of the outside wall.

"Husband, husband, why did you have to leave me? God forgive me!"

The following morning, facing madness or routine, routine proved the stronger and she was up as usual to cook breakfast for the children. People from the church called throughout the day with offers of food and help and Manying was grateful, but when Peter and Selina returned home from school hungry and tired at lunchtime, she was filled with rage. How could Bear have left her on her own with small children?

During the calm of his last days, Bear had smiled at her and stroked the back of her hand. "The children will look after you, Little Lamb. We are indeed blessed."

Manying banged the pots as she washed up in the kitchen. Born to be a gentleman in another age, there were some things Bear had never understood. How could he have been so stubborn?

Family life changed after Bear's death. Money was extremely tight and Manying was short tempered and had no energy for games. They survived on Mr Li's rent and what she could earn as a seamstress. Some days she felt like a soldier in a snowstorm, surrounded by mountain peaks in the propaganda pictures of the communist's Long March. There was no choice but to battle on. Her shoulders ached with the heavy load, and with her body braced against the wind she was unable to look to the left or to the right. Sensing the crisis, the children grew prematurely into adults, taking responsibility for each other and their mother, and recycling without complaint the red envelope money they received at Chinese New Year so that their mother had some to give to other children.

The biggest change in their routine was that Mr Li started to eat with the family. After Bear had become too ill to work, Mr Li had proposed paying more rent to Manying. At first she had refused since he was offering to pay way over the odds and it was embarrassing for her to accept, but eventually a compromise was reached whereby Mr Li would pay more rent but take his breakfast and evening meals with the family. But life had taught Manying to be wary of strangers and she kept her distance. It was the children who were closest to Mr Li; indeed it was they who suggested that he might teach their mother to cook Shanghai food. During Bear's last days, when Manying was at the hospital, it was Mr Li who had cooked the evening meals for the children. He was a good cook and could produce all the Shanghai delicacies. The children thought that Mr Li's Shanghai food was simply the best!

The first cooking lesson was scheduled for late one Saturday afternoon after Mr Li had come back from work on the tram. At first Manying was angry, but when the children dragged her into the kitchen where Mr Li, who had already bought all the ingredients, was wearing shorts and plastic slippers as he chopped vegetables, she had to laugh. He handed her the chopper.

"Let's see if a Li and a Wen can make a Wizard Chu Ge Liang!"

The wok sizzled and deep, rich smells of good food filled the air. Manying relaxed. Mr Li too was enjoying himself. He clearly took great pleasure in good food, and when Manying asked him where he had learned to cook, he shrugged his shoulders.

"Living as a bachelor in Hong Kong...needs must!"

An hour or so later the children returned in a state of great excitement. They had been playing beside the road where they had seen a car accident. A British policeman had arrived on the scene and asked them in English what they had seen.

"And what did you tell him?" asked Mr. Li.

"I told him in English, 'One car come. One car come. Bang, bang. One man sleeping. One man ai ya, ai ya!" As Peter spoke, he performed the actions to illustrate his words; a man slumped forward over the steering wheel, the other man stamping his feet with rage. Manying laughed so much she thought she would never stop.

That night they feasted on Mr Li's Shanghai delicacies and some of Manying's Chaozhou dishes. The only incident to mar the occasion was that Mr Li burned his hand while serving food from the wok. He swore loudly but let Manying hold his wound under the tap. There was a large red blister across the back of his hand. Over the following weeks it healed, but left a permanent white scar.

The following Sunday, Manying put on her green cheongsam and took Dolly down the dirt road to the Baptist Church in North Point. The day was still cool and the church was full of people in their Sunday best. For the first time since Bear had died, Manying found that she was enjoying the atmosphere and smiled as people greeted her. The pastor talked in deep, steady tones about the joy of living in Jesus. His voice echoed from the microphone around the white walls of the new church, and Manying found new meaning in his words.

After the service some girls came to play with Dolly. Delighted to be part of the big girls' gang, Dolly ran off to the back of the church with them. But then the pastor's wife emerged from the cover of the congregation, making straight for Manying. She was a lot younger than her husband and the sort of thin woman who would have benefited from being a little plumper. Manying had judged her to be a gossip and a busybody, and preferred not to be too friendly.

"Mrs Xiong! How nice to see you! Can I have a word?" Manying was manoeuvred onto the steps of the church. After the dim cool church, the midday sun was overpowering. Further brief platitudes were exchanged, and then smiling charmingly, the pastor's wife came to the point.

"Mrs Xiong, I feel it is my duty to say something—as your friend, you understand. People are starting to gossip about your lodger." Manying blinked in the blinding sunlight. The artillery from the pastor's wife fired on. "He can't do you or your family any good. It's not just your reputation, you understand." The pastor's wife positioned her mouth closer to Manying's ear for targeted mortar fire. "What do you really know about him? People are saying all sorts of things! How come his business with the Japanese is so good? Think about it!" She withdrew her head and fired for the kill from her eyes. "They even say he has got a mistress on the Kowloon side; a woman from Shanghai, from before the war. I think you really should get rid of him. Your husband was a good man. You need to be careful about whom you choose to associate with—for your own sake and that of your children. I am saying this because I am your friend and I don't want to see you in trouble."

Furious, Manying strode up the hill back to the house. Who did that woman think she was? In her blue suit and pearls and little white gloves and hat, did she think she was the Big Boss English Queen of the Territory?

"Ah Ma, what's the matter?" Not much got past Dolly.

"Nothing."

But the child frowned, unconvinced.

The thoughts in Manying's head beat time with her marching feet. How could people be so hypocritical? Weren't they all refugees with a past? War was war. Some were Nationalist, some Communist, and some past caring. Everyone knew that it was safer to live in the present and not ask questions. How could the pastor's wife call herself a Christian? Oh yes, people had helped at first after Bear's death with visits and kind words. The headmaster of the boys' school was paying Peter to pick up his newspaper for him every day and deliver it to him in his office. Manying knew that the headmaster was perfectly capable of fetching his own newspaper on the way to work, but that it was a way for him to put a little money into the family. But there was no one who had been so kind and helpful with money as Mr Li. God knows where she and her family would have been without him. Begging more alms from her brother-in-law, or selling herself to American sailors on the streets of Wanchai? One thing she was sure of, however: she would never find another tenant that was willing to pay such a generous rent for a tiny room and expect no favours.

After lunch, the children draped themselves over chairs and on their beds reading books and comics. It was too hot to move. Towards late afternoon, as the day cooled, they became livelier and went out into the streets to play, leaving Manying with Mr Li.

A gentle breeze blew in through the open front door wafting the beaded curtain and revealing chinks of harbour blue. Mr Li went to his room and returned with a large bag of provisions and two big white towels. He looked apologetic.

"Do you want me to sew the towels to send a food parcel?" Manying asked.

"If it's not too much trouble. Cooking, I can do; sewing is another matter!"

Manying took the towels to the sewing machine in the corner of the room and quickly whirred around the sides. When she had finished she held the bag as Mr Li loaded the provisions.

"How bad do you think things are over there?" She gestured in the general direction of the New Territories and the border with China.

"Difficult to know for sure, but bad enough." He took the bag back from Manying and passed it back and forth from hand to hand to weigh it up. She waited for him to say more, but he did not and she never asked.

*F*ate procrastinated and Manying became immune to the gossip. So the years bound ever tighter her life and that of her children to "Uncle Li." In the late sixties his business really took off. There was a huge demand for second hand textile machinery in the Territory. Uncle Li made regular business trips to Japan, and when Japanese clients visited Hong Kong he brought them up to the house in his new Austin to have a meal and meet "his family."

These meals were riotous occasions with the Japanese bearing gifts and making a huge fuss of the children. Peter in particular enjoyed the visits of the Japanese and kept their cups filled to the brim with rice wine. Uncle Li said that he was a natural businessman and promised to take him into the business when he left school.

In 1967, Selina enrolled in a secretarial training course. She might have chosen a better time because the chaos of the Chinese Cultural Revolution was spilling over the border into Hong Kong and the Maoists were on the streets. Sometimes the college was closed because of the riots between Maoists and the police. At other times there was no water or public transport because the unions had called workers in essential services out on strike. Selina got used to walking all the way into Central to college, picking her way around the burnt-out cars and debris from a bombed out bank or shop. But she and her friends were young. To them the disturbances were exciting and they would try to outdo each other with stories of how they got to school that day. When the communists set up a loud speaker on the roof of a building near to the college, she spent a day typing in time with the rhythm of the propaganda slogans, until the following day when the British set up a more powerful speaker on top of the opposite building, which broadcast Beijing Opera. On that day she told her mother, at last she had achieved her target of sixty words a minute!

But to Uncle Li and Manying and those who had known war and revolution, the situation was serious. During the worst of the indiscriminate bombing campaigns Uncle Li and his staff slept in his warehouse with an illegal policeman's revolver at his side. Worried about Uncle Li and desperate for news of Zheng, Manying scrutinised whatever newspapers came to hand, including the communist ones which talked in gloriously inarticulate long sentences about the success of Chairman Mao's Great Proletarian Cultural Revolution. In China, schools and colleges were being shut down and people were being called upon to fight the "four olds" in society; old customs, old habits, old culture and old thinking. Teachers, doctors, intellectuals and anyone who had had any links with the Nationalists were all targets for persecution. The Hong Kong rumour machine went into overdrive. Still Manying could not fully comprehend what people said until Uncle Li told her that every day they were fishing bodies out of the harbour with their hands tied behind their backs that had washed down the Pearl River from Guangzhou.

By the end of the year the worst of the troubles in Hong Kong were over and at Chinese New Year in 1968, Uncle Li took the family for a daytrip into the New Territories. He had done this every year since he had bought a car and it had become a much anticipated annual outing. For Manying it was a chance to escape the overcrowded city and enjoy the green scenery and fresh air.

They left after breakfast and drove to the beach at Castle Peak for a picnic. Even Selina forgot that she was now a lady and took off her high heels and stockings to join the boys and her little sister at the water's edge. It was not a warm day but the children did not care. They whooped at the cold and chased each other up and down the beach. But sitting in the car, Manying could not enjoy herself. She had not been sleeping well. She put it down to the disturbances of last year but the bad dreams would not go away. Always it was Zheng, beaten and bleeding in a wooden shack, calling out for her and their imaginary garden with its fountains and peacocks. She pulled her cardigan tighter over her new blue silk cheongsam and watched Uncle Li making his way back up the beach towards her. He was waving and laughing, shirt neck open, hair blown by the wind. When he got to the road he dusted the sand off his feet, put on his shoes and socks, and climbed into the driver's seat next to Manying.

"Oh to be young again!" Sighing, he put his arm around the back of her seat, just as Zheng had done in Chongqing all those years ago.

For a while they watched the children running back and forth against the backdrop of blue sea, then Uncle Li took Manying's hands in his and, smiling gently, pried apart the fists that unconsciously she had been holding clenched on her lap.

"Manying. I want to ask you to marry me," he said simply.

Her jaw dropped.

"Manying, you have given me a family, a new life."

"I can't," she said.

He frowned, confused. "Why? Is it Bear? He would have wanted you to be happy."

"No. No. Not Bear. I just can't, that's all. Don't ask me why." Tears welled in her eyes. Angry at her weakness, she tried to blink them back.

Lips pursed, Mr Li got out of the car, walked back down to the beach and lit a cigarette. The puffs of grey smoke mimicked the steely clouds overhead. When he had finished he put out the stub with his shoe and ambled back to the car, his hands behind his back. Leaning on the open window next to Manying, he attempted a smile.

"Don't worry about the communists. The worst is over now. The British will hold the line. No doubt about that. Everything will be fine. I promise"

In truth, that was what everyone was saying and what everyone wanted to believe, but the disturbances of the previous year had reminded Manying of the fragility of the frontier between the safety and relative prosperity of British Hong Kong and the Dark Age terror of what was going on beyond.

32
FEBRUARY 1972

Manying and Mr Li watched the television they had bought to see the moon landing, as President Nixon met Chairman Mao, surrounded by books and spittoons in his untidy study in Beijing. Mr Li had said nothing when Taiwan lost its seat at the United Nations to the People's Republic of China, but was furious that Mao should lose the Chinese nation such face by entertaining the American president in such a shoddy manner.

A month later Manying received a letter from Nanjing: the first in over ten years. *Dear Comrade Auntie*, the letter began. The writer, Zheng's son, used the form of address for an aunt on the paternal side of the family, but hedged his bets with the addition of Comrade. His sparse spiky characters were in the simplified form taught in schools after the revolution. They looked crude and half finished to Manying, and were difficult to read.

> *It is my painful duty to carry out one of my father's last wishes and write to thank you for all the help you*

have offered our family over the years. When I was little my father often told me stories about the aunty who lived in Hong Kong. Do you still have peacocks and a fountain with gold fish in your beautiful garden?

The road to true socialism is not always easy and all comrades have had to make sacrifices. The support of overseas friends is important as we work together for a better future. We thank you.

My father died on Christmas Day in 1967, during the Cultural Revolution. It was difficult and we miss him very much.

My sister and I are well. I got married last year and my wife is expecting a baby in the summer. My mother's health has not been good since the death of my father. We hope the birth of a grandchild will do her good.

My mother also wishes me to pass on her sincere thanks for all your kindness. Although she never met you, she knows that you are a good person, a true comrade. She asks you to remember the words of my father's favourite character, Guan Yu in the Romance of the Three Kingdoms.

'Neither riches nor honours can corrupt me, nor pressure bow me.'

Wishing you and your family good health and long life,

Chen Wei Mao.

Zheng's son had enclosed a black and white box camera photograph with the letter: a family of four standing in a brick lane, an old lady, her hair tied in a bun wearing a white shirt and black trousers, a pretty young woman, her hair in pigtails, a tall earnest man in his late twenties or early thirties with a pudding bowl hair cut and a skinny old man in a baggy Mao suit and heavy black rimmed spectacles. Manying stared at him. He would have been unrecognisable had it not been for his huge eyes. They had lost their sparkle, but they were the same eyes that had once coveted and disrobed her, the same eyes in which she had chosen to bathe and ultimately drown, all those years ago.

There was no one in whom Manying could confide. She put the letter and photograph in the box under her bed with Ping Ping's letters and some family photographs. Zheng had been killed by the Red Guards—that much was obvious—but she could not cry. And yet it was a relief to know the truth.

A month later it was Manying's birthday. During the preceding weeks she had been aware that there was something odd going on in her family. At Chinese New Year her children and Mr Li had whispered to each other behind closed doors, and even Dolly had a secretive air of importance about her as she helped Manying to make New Year's dumplings. For the life of her Manying could not figure out what was going on.

In recent, more prosperous years, Uncle Li had taken to marking Manying's birthday by hosting a family supper in a local restaurant. That year, however, he announced that he would be taking Manying out for the day, but when pressed he would not say where. The evening before the appointed day her eldest son Jack telephoned to tell his mother to be sure to wear her best cheongsam; the new pink and blue one.

They set off in the cool of the early morning. More than middle aged, less than old, they were a pallid couple in conservative Sunday best.

"So where are you taking me?" As they crossed the

harbour on the ferry Manying ruthlessly tidied away the heap of memories that might tumble out of the cupboard at the back of her mind, of a similar expedition with Zheng in Chongqing, all those years ago. She was surprised that on this occasion it was so easy to forget the past.

Mr Li refused to say where they were going. He drove along the coast and past the new housing blocks that were being built by the government to house people as the post-war shantytown areas were redeveloped. Uncle Li turned inland and drove up a hill and into the underground parking of one such building. It was part of a complex, and the unfinished buildings behind were still supported by bamboo scaffolding. They took the lift to a sales office overlooking the communal garden between the buildings, where Mr Li was greeted by the salesman, who was obviously expecting them.

Grabbing keys from his desk, the salesman accompanied them back into the shiny lift and up to the fourteenth floor. One arm dramatically outstretched like a television showman, he opened the door to a flat and ushered Manying inside. With pristine white walls and a view over the hills behind, it too was almost a celluloid dream. Patiently, the salesman showed her around; the balcony, the bathroom with its bath and shower, a tiny kitchen, a living room and three separate bedrooms. In every room light switches were neatly plastered into the freshly painted walls.

"Madam, please try." Manying clicked the light switch on and off. She thought about her little house on the hill, precariously lit with wires trailing across the ceiling from room to room.

The salesman made his exit, deftly dropping the key into Mr. Li's hand. Manying walked from room to room, expertly measuring the space by eye.

"Do you like it?" Uncle Li took out a packet of cigarettes and put them away again.

"It's very beautiful." Manying pulled back the sliding

doors and went out onto the balcony.

"If you like it, we can buy it. You can grow your flowers out here." He pulled out a huge wodge of notes from his breast pocket and proffered the money in Manying's direction.

"It's enough for the deposit. If you want it, we can buy it today."

Manying was speechless. After several attempts she croaked, "I like it very much."

"You won't be able to stay where you are forever anyway." In his excitement Mr Li spoke quickly, his Shanghai accent reasserting itself. "Within a year or so the government will send the bulldozers to redevelop the area, and you would be rehoused in government flats. I don't want that. This is a private flat—much bigger, much better, a good investment for the future." By way of afterthought: "And the harbour tunnel will be open by the end of the year, so I can even drive to the office!" Manying smiled and ran her hands over the smooth white walls. It all made sense but it was as if a great ball were stuck in her throat that stopped her from speaking.

"So that is settled then," Mr Li said, and Manying nodded. He smiled and once more took out his cigarette packet and lighter. He put a cigarette in his mouth and fiddled with the lighter but did not light it. "Manying, there is one more thing. I would like to ask you once more if you will do me the honour...marry me." Manying's hand dropped to her side from the wall. Uncle Li clicked the cigarette lighter on and off. "Last time...perhaps it was too soon. Maybe things are different now?" He took the unlit cigarette from his mouth, and put in back in the packet. "I bought this for you on my last visit to Japan. I hope you like it." Fumbling in his jacket pocket he pulled out a small purple box and handed it to her.

Manying opened it to find a huge diamond solitaire ring. Taking her finger, Mr Li carefully put on the ring and held her hand up to the light to examine the effect. Tiny rainbows reflected onto the backs of their clasped hands. Fascinated, each turned the hand of the other: scuffed finger tips, dish-water wrinkled palms, nicotine stained, horny nails, brown liver spots and thick blue lazy veins, softly, caressing back and forth, playing with the glorious spectrum of purples, blues, pinks and yellows.

At last, Mr Li lit his cigarette and inhaled deeply.

"The most important thing is that when we are married the flat belongs to both of us. If anything happens to me, you are my legal wife and no one can take it away from you."

Thus the deposit was paid and the marriage agreed. It was so easy, so comfortable, and clearly now the right thing to do. They ate a dim sum lunch in one of the tiny local restaurants that had just opened to serve the new estate. As she sipped tea and picked the little meaty morsels from the bamboo steamers set in front of them, Manying could not take her eyes from Mr Li's kind face. He ate ravenously, finishing up her portion when she was full and grinning at her as he chewed. Laughing shyly, she looked at the ring on her finger.

"Aiya! Just like young girl who is about to get married! What a lucky man I am!" For the first time in years Manying began to enjoy in herself that understated confidence that is afforded a woman blessed with security and status.

After lunch they decided to drive up to Tai Mo Mountain. On the way Uncle Li placed Manying's hand under his on the gear stick and Manying, who had never learned to drive, felt how the stick moved around the imaginary H shape. They wound the windows down and let the wind blow in their hair.

"Delicious. Can't you just taste the spring?" Uncle Li smacked his lips as if eating the air.

The car slowed down as they rounded a bend and they saw a small squad of Ghurkha troops with their British officer, who had been training somewhere in the mountains, taking a rest in the shade by the side of the road. Without knowing why, Manying waved. Holding their water bottles and grinning, they waved back.

"My children knew about the flat all along, didn't they? But did they know you were going to ask me to marry you?"

"I never quite spelled it out, but I think they probably guessed."

Manying shrugged.

"They will all be happy. My eldest already calls you The Great Saviour of the Family." Then it was Uncle Li who did not know what to say.

On the way down the north side of the mountain, he stopped the car and they got out to enjoy the view. On the plain, the distant military airfield and barracks were like matchbox models beneath the huge, green mountains.

"How strange it is that Hong Kong is so small, yet with its city, mountains and rivers you could almost believe it was the whole world."

Uncle Li laughed. "How much easier it would be if we could live like the ancient sage Lao Ze, content with our lot, with no desire or need to know what is going on in the neighbouring valley."

Later, as it drew towards dusk, Manying said, "Sometimes I think that Old Heaven deliberately gives some people all the bitterness to eat, so that others can be free of suffering. It is so unfair."

The birds stopped singing. The sun disappeared behind the mountains. Manying shivered in the darkness: scrabbling out of the recesses of her mind, old itches, and new doubts. Better not to ask. Instead, she turned to Uncle Li and buried her head in his chest.

SHANGHAI

33

Dolly stared at the strange old woman who was her mother. She had thought she knew her, but events of recent months had shown that her Wen Manying's life was in fact a mystery to them all; a labyrinth of secret criss-crossed lanes of light and shade with an uncomfortable history. The old woman sat bolt upright, eyes closed, in the business class airline seat that Dolly had insisted on and that Manying had refused to recline. Her mother's face was framed by the smart blue and red antimacassar in the airline's colours. Her thinning black hair, still with only a hint of grey, was pulled back with a neat black velvet hair band. Her face was soft and fallen, her dimples brown and sunken, like a pear kept too long into autumn.

In the neighbouring seats, businessmen with tiny, platinum-coloured spectacles and blue cotton shirts sipped their digestifs, rustled newspapers or tapped out high-peaked graphic projections on laptops. Dolly was uncomfortable. Her mother did not belong on this flight to Shanghai. What good would she be able to do? Against her better judgement, Dolly had agreed to it. She almost wanted to apologise to the businessmen for their intrusion, for her mistake, and was disgusted with herself at the thought.

When she thought of her mother, she smelled stale cooking oil and saw her in the tiny kitchen in Hong Kong, washing up or throwing food into the wok. The former was a meticulous routine that had remained unchanged since Dolly had been a little girl. First the bowls and chopsticks were washed with soap and piled on the side, waiting for a rinse. The clean bowls were then neatly stacked on a wooden drainer, and finally, taking a fistful of upright chopsticks, like the pencil monitor at school, Mother stuffed them into an old jar to dry.

Until a month ago it had never occurred to Dolly that her mother had a past, a life before the family. She was just Mother, a lady in black trousers and a flowery polyester blouse who on New Year and on birthdays dressed up in a silk cheongsam and three-inch heels—much to the annoyance of her daughters who were terrified she might trip and break a hip. Nowadays, in Vancouver, she snoozed on the black leather settee in front of the Hong Kong television soap operas as her children and grandchildren lived their lives around her.

This China trip was madness, the whole situation insane. Dolly pulled the flight blanket out of its plastic bag and swaddled herself in it. She opened the screw-topped, plastic bottle of Remy Martin, poured it into the glass and sipped gingerly in anticipation of the desired effect. How had the twisted threads of fate brought them all to this?

*H*er mother had emigrated to Canada with Dolly's two brothers Jack and Peter and their families after the Tiananmen Massacre. Dolly had been visiting from Australia that summer of 1989 and they had watched the events in Beijing unfold on the television in her mother's Kowloon flat. The night the tanks had rolled into Tiananmen Square, someone in the opposite flat had played the Li Sao on a Chinese zither, the melancholic sound echoing around and around the space between the tower blocks. She had learned the words of Qu Yuan's poem as a child:

Truly, ways of these times...are willful and loose,
who now is able...to avoid being changed?

She remembered the panic and uncertainty in Hong Kong that followed that night, the mad scramble for foreign passports and bolt holes. What happened in Beijing could happen on the streets of Hong Kong after the handover that was coming. Dolly and her sister Selina were safe in that she was a Professor of Economics in New South Wales, and Selina's family all held British passports. Nevertheless, Selina shipped all her husband's family's valuable antiques to their flat in London, just to be on the safe side. Mother, for her part, had been most insistent that the boys and their families should leave Hong Kong.

But the handover had not been the Armageddon that people had feared, and in recent years people had begun to trickle back to Hong Kong. Her mother had begged Peter not to expand the machine business that he had inherited from Uncle Li in Shanghai. Dolly remembered the rows.

"I want to invest in the motherland," Peter had told his mother. "It's opening up. There is money to be made. Big money!"

"Motherland? Dog's fart!" Mother had spat back at him. "I tell you the Motherland will not thank you. She will drag you down and maul you, beating you to a pulp on the ground, and when she is done, she will feed you to the dogs. I have lost enough of my family and friends to the Motherland, and I will not lose anymore!" But Peter had not heeded his mother's words.

How could he have been so stubborn and so foolish? Dolly had never had much time for her scatterbrained brother whose logic and moneymaking schemes twisted around like the noodles that he slurped so hurriedly from the end of his chopsticks.

When news of Peter's arrest while on a business trip to Shanghai had first reached the family, they could not believe it. Even when they realised that it was true they kept the news from their mother for as long as possible. It was, after all, a mistake, and would soon be sorted out. It was only when weeks turned into months, and after Dolly had been out to visit her brother and actually seen him in prison with her own eyes, that they were confident enough of the reality to tell Mother.

Mother had accepted the news with calm resignation, almost as if she had been expecting it. They were doing everything to get Peter released, Dolly confidently told her. Amnesty International had taken up his case, and his name was on the Canadian government's Human Rights Watch List.

But a year passed, and when Peter was finally brought to trial and was sentenced to thirteen years in prison for espionage and tax evasion, they were appalled. A few weeks later a copy of the court papers arrived at the house along with a bill for Peter's medical expenses. In desperation the family went public with the news of Peter's arrest, and articles were published in the North American and Hong Kong press.

*D*olly finished her brandy with a slug anticipating the warm flush spreading up her neck and face and looked again at her sleeping mother. She knew her mother was disappointed that she had never married. Mother had told her as much and said that she was too choosy. Maybe she was. She preferred the explanation that Chinese men do not like wives with Doctorates who are more highly educated than them. There had once been a foreigner, but he was married, and even though he had immigrated to Australia, somehow she had never been quite able to overcome the great cultural obstacle that Chinese should marry Chinese. If she were honest with herself, the truth was that she did not want to become like her mother, a slave to the family and dependent on the largesse of men. Mother, of course, had had little choice, but her generation had options and she had chosen to put financial independence and career first.

On the television screen on the back of the seat in front, a blonde, gamin actress flapped her hands at a chocolate cake, and daubed her husband in gooey icing in a kitchen comedy. Dolly thought about Peter in his cell in Beijing. It was unlikely he would survive thirteen years, and even if he did it would leave him an old man. She sighed. The last year had been a nightmare. As the scholar in the family, the main burden had fallen on her, although Selina had been doing her part with the Hong Kong media. There had been endless petitions, articles, and lobby meetings with diplomats in pinstriped suits that took notes and sympathised in the manner of old-fashioned family doctors.

"There are similar cases, if it's any consolation. Some American academics were released just last week. It's just a matter of time."

And now, to cap it all, were the revelations Mother had made last month. Why had she never been interested in the history of her own family, Dolly wondered? It was not that she had not had questions, but rather that she had left them unasked. Perhaps she was afraid of the answers.

Mother's bombshell, coming the day after they had received Peter's court papers and medical bills, had amazed them all. No one in the family had had any idea. It was a fine spring day and Dolly had been visiting Vancouver via Ottawa for Easter. Her sister-in-law Mercy's garden gushed with fountains of magnolia. Snow-clad fingers of cherry blossom beckoned like the arms of elegant ladies in long evening gloves. Daffodils gently nodded their heads in the long border framing the green lawn. Here and there voluptuous tulips flaunted red satin gowns.

But the gentle spring breeze did not reach inside the hermetically sealed house. Looking from the kitchen window, Dolly had the impression that she was watching a silent film. With her husband Peter away on business, Mercy had spent long periods alone with their children, Joseph and Eva, in Vancouver. She had never really settled in her new country, and since his arrest, the paranoia to which all new immigrants are susceptible had taken hold. She'd had iron bars fitted at all the windows and now kept them shut, even on the finest of days.

Mother took off her spectacles and put the court report on the kitchen table; a thick pile of papers, acres of neat black characters amongst the jolly red and green flowers printed on the plastic tablecloth.

"Uncle Li had another family in Shanghai. This has something to do with it. I am sure of it." Silent shadows flashed in from the garden. The neighbours were coming out onto their deck with its blue and green, checkered awning. Dolly, Joseph and Mercy struggled to comprehend what Mother had just said.

"What do you mean another family?" Joseph was the first to respond.

"He has a wife and a daughter in Shanghai. I only found out after his death." Mother hesitated and took a deep breath. "First there were the letters."

"What letters?" Now it was Dolly's turn to interrupt.

"Letters from a lawyer...and then I had a visits from them."

"Them?"

"Lawyers...and once Uncle Li's grandson came to see me in the old flat in Kowloon, after his father had died." Silence. The Canadian neighbours mimed laughing faces as they fired up the big gas barbecue, its silver hood glistening like a squat rocket in the sun.

"They said I was not Uncle Li's legal wife: just a concubine, and therefore I had no claim to his property. All assets belonged to his true family in Shanghai. I told them that my son now ran the business, and that the profits were a result of his hard work. They said that by the time of the handover in 1997, I wouldn't be able to count on the protection of the 'Blood Stinking Imperialists' and that Chinese law would prevail in Hong Kong. They'd get me, one way or the other. Anyone above the rank of general was automatically indicted by the communists as a war criminal in 1949, you know."

"But Uncle Li wasn't a soldier. He was a businessman."

"Your father was a general. They said they could seize our assets that way too."

"Why on earth didn't you say something?" Dolly shouted in exasperation. Mother could be so stubborn. Joseph put his hand on her arm.

"Let Grandma finish!"

"Some things should not be passed onto the next generation. After Tiananmen Square in 1989, when the time came to immigrate, I never let Uncle Li's family have our new address. I thought that would be the end of the matter." Mother's face was expressionless. The tousled, red-haired, neighbour's children ran back and forth under the garden sprinkler.

"I still have the family's address in Shanghai. Uncle Li's grandson works as Secretary to the Chairman of the Association of Shanghai Textile Companies. It is time for me to go to China myself, to sort things out."

They protested that she was too old for such a long journey, but the more they argued, the more determined she became. She straightened out the court papers and medical bills with three gentle knocks against the table and slipped them back into their brown envelope

"My life is nothing compared to that of my son. I was born in China, and if I die there, don't bother to bring my body back to Canada." She looked at her children, challenging them with her brown eyes, twinkling with new post-cataract plastic lenses. "What would you have me do? Wait until they send me the bill for the bullet?" Dolly stared at a cluster of tulips at the end of the garden; their petals had fallen open revealing gaping black centres.

Dolly's head buzzed with the noise of the aircraft. The celluloid people on the screen in front of her flitted like butterflies in the cabin's half-light. Dolly was an academic. She prided herself on dealing with matters in a logical and rational way. She had taken legal advice, which was that under Chinese law, by the time Uncle Li had married Mother, his original marriage would have been null and void due to the separation of twenty years.

"You wouldn't believe the skeletons coming out the cupboard in the run-up to the handover," the English-educated lawyer in his teak panelled office overlooking Hong Kong harbour had said as he leaned back in his big leather chair.

"Messy business! But don't worry. None of it would ever stand up in a Hong Kong court." Dolly had been reassured but not entirely convinced.

And what of the phone call Mother had insisted she made to the son of an old friend, Mei Ren, who worked in the US State Department. Amazingly, he had promised to get Peter's name on America's list of political prisoners. So Mother had connections! Whatever next?

Placing the pillow on her left shoulder, Dolly tried to find a comfortable position. Little things were starting to make sense. Why the name on Uncle Li's tombstone in the cemetery in Kowloon was different from the one he had used in Hong Kong. Why Uncle Li never talked about the past, and the food parcels that as a little girl she had helped Mother pack...they were always left without an address for Uncle Li to take to the office to post.

Dolly did not like Shanghai. On the long taxi ride from the airport to their hotel on Yenan Road she decided that. It was a Legoland of architectural styles, cobbled together by an over-enthusiastic child: here a pink stucco Las Vegas palace, there a baby blue tower topped with a crystal peak, lifted from 1980s boom time in Tokyo or Taipei. These, the new highrise Temples of Ten Thousand years, jostled for prestige and space along the main roads. Between them, Dolly caught glimpses of the old, what the Chinese called "Imperialist Shanghai" and now could not tear down fast enough; red-bricked, grey-tiled houses, their once grand balconies adorned with the ever present washing.

Dolly had never felt at ease in China. Her first visit to "the Motherland" from Hong Kong as a student in the late 1970s had not been what she had expected. Despite her Chinese face, her dress, mannerisms and clumsy Mandarin, all marked her out as "not one of us." If this was China, then she was not Chinese, but a Hong Kong girl. Twenty years later, she was still surprised by the extent of her own alienation, even revulsion.

They checked into the Hotel Equatorial. Feeling stubborn she spoke quickly in English to the receptionists. The room was a standard twin on the twenty-first floor. The air conditioning roared away at maximum. The two women shivered. Goose pimples appeared on Dolly's bare arms. She unpacked and programmed the wardrobe safe. Mother set about boiling water and making tea in the self-boil thermos, quite at home as if she were in Mercy's kitchen in Vancouver. To Dolly's surprise, Mother showed none of the emotions of homecoming. Perhaps it was because in ambitious, sanitised, twenty-first century Shanghai, there was little for her to recognise. Her China had been lost fifty years ago. Perhaps it was just as well, Dolly thought.

Dolly made some phone calls, one to the Canadian Consulate General, another to the Association of Shanghai Textile Companies where she left a message with an unhelpful secretary for Mr Zhang Han, Uncle Li's grandson. She had written to him before their departure requesting a meeting, and he had faxed back that she should telephone on their arrival.

They took an early supper in the Shanghai Lou Restaurant, which was around the corner from the hotel and above a karaoke bar catering to the once detested Japanese. It was early but busy, and it was only a Wednesday night. Shanghai yuppies, their hair streaked purple and blond in imitation of the latest Hong Kong pop stars, and sporting the latest designer fakes, had money to spend. Dolly and her mother were given a table on the balcony behind the wrought iron railings that ran around the four corners of the restaurant in colonial style. The young waitress soon came to take their order.

"What do you have that isn't sweet? Shanghai food is always too sweet." Dolly knew she was being rude but could not help herself. The waitress was taken aback. In the end they settled on spicy mapo tofu, roast belly of pork Shanghai style, steamed vegetables and river crab.

The shiny red pork was indeed too sweet. Watching her mother sucking with relish on the fatty bits, Dolly wondered what other secrets were hidden behind the craggy facades of old age. After a while she said, "You said that Uncle Li had a factory in Shanghai, before..."

Mother nodded, continuing to eat. "Two cotton factories. Business was good, but of course he had to leave in 1949. Lost them both to the communists." Mother fished a small river crab from the main platter and began to dissect it. Her finger joints, brown and knobbed with arthritis, were remarkably nimble with chopsticks.

"He had to; you see...war is good business. Even little Japanese soldiers need underwear!" Mother sniggered and pushed a chopstick into the crab's leg to extract the meat, as if she were not aware of the significance of what she had said.

"Underwear for the Japanese?" Dolly was incredulous, appalled. It meant that the man who had brought her up, fed and clothed her, paid for her education, the only father she had really known, was a Japanese collaborator. Mother nodded.

"Don't look so surprised!" Mother spoke sharply. "At that time no one could afford to be too clean. The main thing was to survive. One way or another, all of us of that generation have blood on our hands. We are all guilty. Your Uncle Li was not a bad man. He used his Japanese connections to save the lives of many people, tipping them off before the Japanese secret police came. You could say that his connections saved our lives too. How else do you think he set up business from scratch again in Hong Kong after the war?"

Dolly stared at the bits of soggy white cabbage and dismembered crabs' limbs discarded in the middle of the table. She felt sick.

34

*F*or three days Dolly played a frustrating game of telephone tag with Zhang Han's secretary.

"Mr Zhang is in Suzhou. Yes, Mr Zhang received your message. Madame must understand that Mr Zhang is a busy man." Dolly could barely contain her anger. Either Mother was right, and the Zhang family had something to do with her brother's detention, or they had come all this way on the whim of a deluded old lady. She wanted to get everything arranged so that she could go to see Peter in prison by the following Tuesday at the latest.

Dolly visited the Canadian Consulate General in Shanghai, where once again the diplomats were politely unhelpful and asked to be kept informed of developments in Peter's case. The rest of the time she spent in bookshops on Fuzhou Road. Mother, on the other hand, was unperturbed, happily spending her days sitting in the hotel coffee shop or watching television in the room.

"Don't worry, Little Dolly. I am the bait. It is just a question of waiting for the fish to bite."

On Friday afternoon the phone call came. Mr Zhang would like to meet them for dinner that night. He would pick them up at the hotel at 6:30 pm. At last!

Uncle Li's grandson was a handsome man in his mid to late thirties. Despite the summer heat he wore an English-style tweed jacket over a pink polo shirt. He was accompanied by his wife who had aspirations to be glamorous but in a low cut, purple cotton dress and four-inch white court shoes did not quite achieve the desired effect.

"Aunt! Cousin! We are indeed honoured to have you here in China. Welcome!" Shoulders back, hips forward, his belt adorned with mobile phones and beepers, Zhang Han greeted them with a polished handshake and ushered them authoritatively into a taxi. He took them to a large Taiwanese restaurant with minimalist chrome and pine decor. At the table two others were waiting for them, Uncle Li's daughter and her husband, both now in their sixties.

The restaurant was clearly a new experience for the old people who fidgeted uneasily with their napkins. Zhang Han, however, was no stranger to the restaurant staff. Within a minute of taking their seats, the fat young Taiwanese patron was fussing at his side.

"Nice to see you again... And how is the Chairman?"

"Busy, as always. We are expecting a major delegation from the European Union next week." Dolly had done her research. The "Chairman" was Zhang Han's boss, head of the Association of Shanghai Textile Companies, who just happened to be a son of a senior government minister. Zhang Han clearly enjoyed basking in the great man's reflected glory. He set about orchestrating the meal with a series of terse orders and nods. A click of his fingers and three bottles of Qingdao beer appeared.

"Tonight is my treat. It is my duty," he announced proudly in English. Then in Mandarin, "Aunt, you really must try the special Japanese beef soup." The waitress scuttled off to fetch it. "Mother, the teriyaki prawns are excellent." He turned his plastic smile on Dolly. She felt she was acting in a carefully staged black comedy. Zhang Han and his father were supposed to be responsible for all the trouble; now here they were sitting down to a jolly family meal. Excusing herself, she went off to help herself at the salad bar.

When she returned to the table a seafood platter piled high with lobster, crab, prawns, oysters and whelks had arrived.

"Welcome! Honoured Family from afar! Aunty! Good health and long life!" Zhang Han raised his beer glass to Mother who responded with a smile. The two old ladies and young Mrs Zhang gorged themselves on the lobsters, the juices dripping from their mouths. Zhang Han sat back in his chair. Surveying the scene with satisfaction he lit a cigarette and blew the smoke towards the ceiling.

"Cousin, you are not eating!" He hoisted the leg of a lobster onto Dolly's plate. She did not touch it, picking at the cherry tomatoes in her salad instead.

Uncle Li's daughter, Fang Meiting, now an old lady with a fuzzy grey perm, bit the pink whiskery head off a pink prawn and spat it into her bowl. In contrast to her daughter-in-law, whose thin face was smeared like a geisha with white powder and red lipstick, the old lady had a fresh, scrubbed complexion that had probably only known soap and water. Dolly imagined that when she was young she had been the kind of socialist virgin that inspired the artists who made the airbrushed posters of model women workers driving tractors and shovelling coal into blast furnaces.

Young Mrs Zhang tried very hard to be charming, peeling prawns and putting them on Dolly and her Mother's plates. They must think China very backward... What are restaurants like in Canada? She was disappointed when Dolly replied that nowadays they were pretty much the same as in Shanghai. All the while, the father, old Mr Zhang, chewed rhythmically on spare ribs, splitting the bones with his teeth and sucking out the marrow. He kept his eyes down on the bowl of rice his son had ordered for him and said nothing: distant, remote, as if he had some kind of amnesia.

Desserts arrived: slices of watermelon, and an assortment of biscuits and pink and yellow Western-style cakes topped with angelica. The evening looked as if it would pass without a mention of the matter at hand. Finishing a chocolate-coated shortbread, Dolly could contain herself no longer.

"Mr Zhang." She could not bring herself to call him cousin. "About my brother..."

"Ah, yes...a sad predicament indeed. Such a young man! Such a shame!" A shake of the head, a well timed pause; he could have been a seasoned politician embarking on a favourite speech. "Unfortunately, many overseas Chinese come to China with unrealistic expectations. Regrettably, sometimes they get themselves into trouble." He was still smiling.

"What do you mean?" Dolly snapped.

"Exactly what I said. They come here expecting to mint money, throw their weight around, treat us like country bumpkins and think we should kowtow and be grateful." Dolly's face flushed purple. Another perfectly timed pause from Zhang Han, just long enough for the rack to tighten another notch.

"Of course, dear cousin, your brother was not that sort of man. I myself had the honour of meeting him on several occasions. Unfortunately, he never really understood the way things were done here. That was his problem."

"How dare you?" Dolly exploded. Zhang Han lifted the flat of his hand like a traffic policeman and continued unabashed.

"Cousin, cousin! Families should not quarrel. These things take time, but there might be a way for me to help." Faintly raising the corner of an eyebrow, he summoned the waiter. "We can discuss business tomorrow. I will pick you up at the hotel at one-thirty."

"Give me the bill!" Dolly ordered the waiter.

"The bill, Madam, has already been paid." Dolly was speechless with rage. She glared at Zhang Han who smiled back, white teeth bared like a gruesome waxwork. The old Zhangs went on eating, scraping up the last sad pieces of broccoli and picking over the fish bones.

Back at the hotel, Mother took a bath. Dolly stormed around the room, arms folded across her chest. Business! How dare he talk about Peter as business? Zhang Han was behind the whole thing. She was sure of it. The old people were just peasants invited to high table. They didn't have connections. She opened the minibar. The cold air wrapped itself around her legs. Bending down she took out a small bottle of brandy and a packet of peanuts. It was so obvious: all Zhang Han had to do was pull a few of his big party strings, convince people that his Hong Kong relatives were loaded and, come the handover in 1997, they would all be in for a cut. Easy! But ridiculous! For Christ's sake, it was not as if her family were millionaires! But that was not, as Mother herself had said, the point.

"They think we have a lot of money. That's all that matters. Dolly, you must be more patient, for your brother's sake."

The following morning, in her old university t-shirt and saggy, grey, jogging pants, Dolly pumped a state of the art exercise bike in the hotel gym. The flywheel spun noiselessly in front of her; the green LCD flickered through eight kilometres. She had wanted to swim but the pool was the size of a bird bath and she would have had to turn every five strokes. She looked around the tiny gym with its low ceiling and soft lighting. A skinny young Chinese woman in a pink leotard and matching tights, with a towel draped around her neck, was perched elegantly on the cycle next to her. Sullenly, cool behind the music from her personal stereo, she cycled sedately. It would be no good to sweat, for that would spoil the makeup and the image. Who kept her, Dolly wondered? A Hong Kong businessman with a nice harbour view apartment in the Mid-levels with a son and daughter at university in America? Perhaps her sister was a friend of his wife...

Dolly gritted her teeth. She must not give in to it; this velvet mirage of modernity, the soft white towels with a hotel logo, the beguiling, deep navy of the swimming pool, the soothing lull of air conditioning interrupted only by the whispers of the obliging staff and the muffled ping of the lift from the cream-curtained lobby.

The butterfly cocoon was tightening around her, stifling her. Panting, she got off the bike. Oh my brother, my brother!

*T*rue to his word Zhang Han arrived at the hotel at one-thirty. This time he came alone, without the flowery language and expansive handshakes. He helped Mother into the taxi, leaving Dolly to her own devices on the side away from the curb. The blue and gold liveried doorman tried to help her, but she gestured him away.

Zhang Han spoke quickly to the driver in Shanghai dialect. Dolly looked at Mother and saw her make a small nod. He had given the old family address in the former French concession. They drove along the famous tree-lined Huai Hai Road, the old Avenue Joffre. Fashionable once again, Saturday afternoon shoppers thronged in and out of the flagship foreign stores and the Xiang Yang Market offering designer knock-offs. Above the glitzy coffee shops, amongst the signs and advertising hoarding, were rusting Parisian-style wrought iron railings and traditional Chinese stone door lintels.

The taxi driver turned onto another street. Before the revolution this had been an expensive residential area. An old man with his trousers rolled up above his knees cycled stubbornly in front of them. The driver honked his horn. At the second honk the old man gave way. They passed large, red brick houses behind high walls or iron fences. Many of them had been converted into government offices. Standard black characters announcing this or that bureau ran vertically down the signs on the gateways and walls. The car pulled into the driveway of a house, which, judging by the washing hanging from the front porch and balconies, was still used for residential purposes and divided between several families.

It was the hottest part of the day. The molten light evaporated the colour from the facade of the house and surrounding trees, leaving the scene like an aged black and white photograph left too long on a sunny mantle piece. Outside the car, all was still. Slowly they climbed out. The mind-numbing din of crickets was their only welcome. Dolly tugged at her trousers where they had stuck to the back of her legs. The house reminded her of the dilapidated mansions used in American ghost films. The once carefully tended lawn where fair-haired children had played with their maids in crisp white blouses and black trousers had been abandoned to dust and rubbish bins. At the bottom of the garden a gangling skeletal rose bush, still faithful perhaps to its colonial mistress, offered a bouquet of pallid pink roses. No one had bothered to repair the front steps that pushed out into the garden in a once graceful oval. Mother tottered on a piece of loose brick. Dolly grabbed her arm just in time. A lizard, surprised while basking in the sun, scuttled into the shade of the door.

In the grand entrance hall, where once there would have been elegant mosaic tiles or plush carpets, there was now an undulating sea of hard concrete marked with small arcs, where at the time of laying, it had been smoothed down with a piece of wood. It was pleasantly cool through the soles of Dolly's sandals. The wide, wooden staircase had no banisters, and the walls were bare brick and plaster, their panels lost long ago, probably to some winter fuel shortage. In place of chandeliers the hall was garlanded with washing, like limp flags in a temple at the end of a festival.

In the corner by the stairwell, behind a small desk, an old woman in a white overall slept; her head bowed and her left hand around a white enamel cup. Hearing their footsteps, she slowly opened her eyes then closed them again. A door creaked upstairs; there were footsteps on the landing. Dark brown eyes peered down through the washing.

"This way!" Zhang Han strode across the hall to a double doorway. Dolly, with Mother on her arm, followed. A waft of stale urine greeted them as they passed the stairwell.

Before Zhang Han could reach the double doors, the left hand one opened. Zhang's father slopped into the hallway in his blue plastic slippers. He wore shorts and a vest, his goose-like flesh hanging in pathetic, skinny folds under his armpits and around his knees. He grunted in acknowledgement of his son, looked straight through Dolly and her mother, spat in the direction of the stairwell, and shuffled across the hall to the open front door.

They entered a room that had clearly been the main drawing room of the house and would have had a view onto the main lawn if the windows and shutters had not been closed. Most of the paint had long since flaked off, exposing bare cracked wood. Miraculously, the stucco around the central light had survived the ravages of the Cultural Revolution, its grey leaves curling protectively around the naked light bulb. The room was divided in half by a large blue curtain suspended from a bamboo pole. The half of the room they were in was set up as the living room and kitchen. The air was stale and still and it was difficult to breathe.

"You're here!" Zhang Han's mother Fang Meiting got up from one of three arm chairs. "You've just missed your dad."

"We saw him. Is she here?" Zhang Han replied quickly

in Shanghai dialect.

Fang Meiting nodded and gestured to the two armchairs for them to sit.

"I'll make some tea." Dolly started to protest that it was not necessary, but was silenced by a look of thunder from her mother.

Dolly watched Fang Meiting shuffle over to the square sink, two gas rings and an old fashioned thermos with its cork stopper that counted as the kitchen. My God! They had been camping out in this semi-permanent, post apocalyptic state for fifty years. Had the entire house at one time belonged to Uncle Li? Had the family been reduced to this one room after the revolution?

"It won't be forever!" They would have been stoical at first. They would not, could not, have resisted the revolutionary tide. "There are people living in straw huts who need accommodation. It is our duty! All comrades must work together." And they had stood by as furniture and possessions were allocated amongst newcomers. As the years passed, more and more of their possessions had been lost to the ravages of time: a pink cashmere twin set, no longer acceptable attire in the age of blue and black Mao suits, eaten by moths as it lay wrapped in its tissue paper in a bottom drawer; photographs, paintings and porcelain destroyed in the Four Olds Campaign of the Cultural Revolution. And so they had learned to bend and twist, to distort themselves like great, gnarled trees on a savage coastline, constantly raked by salty winds.

Fang Meiting brought the thermos back and put it on the stained fold-up table between the armchairs. She poured out the tea and methodically set about cutting a mango. Her dignity lay in the ordering of her meagre possessions and in her failure to see the squalor.

"Mother, it's hot!" Even Zhang Han could not stand the heat and wiped the beads of sweat of his forehead with a carefully ironed handkerchief. Fang Meiting nodded, and going to the window nearest the curtain, reached up to turn on the air conditioning. It was the only concession to modernity in the whole room. With a great shuddering and clanking it whirred into action. A white cat squealed and jumped onto the floor. It slipped on a red and black rag mat as it landed, its claws desperately scrabbling on the bare floor. Righting itself, it squealed an affronted protest and fled under the curtain to safety.

Gradually the air conditioning settled into a regular whirr offering a reassuring thump on the off beat every half minute or so. Fang Meiting put the little lids on top of the yellow mugs and offered them to Dolly and Mother. Zhang Han sucked on a piece of mango, the juice running down his chin and hands. No one said anything. They waited.

35

A long, red fingernailed hand reached around the opening in the curtains. There was a rustling, as if some great diva were preparing to make her stage entrance. The curtain twitched slightly. With a tinkle of jade bracelets, a figure pushed through. A beauty, with vermilion lips, in a crimson and gold silk jacket and skirt. A princess! Except that the princess was an old crone: shrunken, bald and hump-backed—a grotesque skeleton in an ornate red wedding gown.

"So, you have come at last!" She paused for effect. Her voice, though quavering, retained the high-pitched, singsong of a woman who remembered all too well the vitality of her youth. Speechless, they stared at the twisted apparition of rotten beauty.

"Grandma?" Zhang Han choked on his mango.

"Don't you remember me, Manying?"

Dolly saw the blood drain from her mother's face.

"Thought I was dead, didn't you? Oh no! I wouldn't let you escape that easily!" The old crone spoke in a Chinese dialect that Dolly struggled to understand.

"Jie Jie? Sister?" Mother whispered.

The old crone's voice rose to an agitated squeak. "I was always an outcast. You and your family destroyed me, twice over."

"What...what... do you mean?" Mother stuttered with shock and the unfamiliar language, which Dolly now recognised as Chaozhou dialect.

"What do I mean? You come here and still you do not know!" The old crone too struggled with the dialect that had remained dormant for over half a century. She mixed Chaozhou with Shanghai dialect and Mandarin. "Your family murdered my grandfather and you stole my husband!" In her agitation the old crone could not maintain the affectations of youth. Her squealing became even more agitated as she struggled to breathe and speak at the same time. Fang Meiting got up to go to her mother's aid but the old crone gestured her away. "No! The truth will out!" She gasped for breath and Dolly thought she was going to topple over. Instead she straightened her jacket, her wrists moving in graceful arcs, like a young actress.

"Chinese New Year, 1937. Do you remember?"

Mother nodded cupping her hands on her lap to stop them trembling.

"Teddy and I went to see the old fortune teller with the black crow that sat on the quay in Shantou. It was a great joke! He would tell us that we would have long life and happiness. For a long time he just stared at my face. He looked so sad and I began to be afraid. At last he told me that the lines of my fate were particularly complicated, that it was difficult to untangle them, but that the past was clear. I was an orphan. My own family had become rich in the shipping trade, but my grandfather was a great trader who always wore a white suit. He had got on the wrong side of a Chaozhou Mandarin and was executed in Guangzhou for murder. After that the fortunes of my family had declined until my parents chose immigration over starvation. I was orphaned—right there on the quay at Shantou. It was then I knew the old fortune teller was speaking the truth.

"'Heaven makes its own designs,' he said. 'The man who found you that day abandoned on the quay was the son of the Mandarin who destroyed your father.'"

Nobody moved. Dolly, Zhang Han and Fang Meiting struggled to make sense of the mix of dialects. Mother, however, understood everything.

"But my parents loved you as if you were their own child. We all did: me, my brother...especially him. You two were always the best of friends. Don't you remember?" The old crone brushed away Mother's protests with a wave of her hand. This was her swan song. She had waited for years to sing it, and she was going to finish.

Communism had not been kind to her, the wife of a bourgeois factory owner who was well known for his business with the Imperialists. The Communist Party and her neighbours took no account of the fact that he had abandoned her with her daughter in order to save his own skin. When they denounced her, former servants forgot to mention that their former master was a hard working, average businessman who had been a good employer, giving them all time off at New Year and paying for them to see the doctor if they got sick. On the contrary, they took great pleasure in remembering that their mistress, like Madame Chiang Kai Shek, would wear only silk, visited the hairdresser once a week to have her hair curled, and gambled at mah-jong. Lai Di had been, however, what the Party might call a success. A survivor, she had been quick to adapt, willingly writing self-criticisms, spouting the latest slogans and waving Mao's Little Red Book as enthusiastically as the next person. For years she had continued to love her husband, worrying about him and holding the memory of his caresses and many kind words tenderly in her mind. In those last crazy hours before the communists had entered Shanghai, it had been a matter of life and death for him. She knew he would have come for her and their daughter if it had been possible. All that mattered was that he was safe and one day would come back for her. But the years went by. In 1952, she got tuberculosis from the hospital where she worked as a nurse. She nearly died, and the disease left her shrunken and deformed. In the years of famine and semi-starvation, during the worst of which she boiled grass to eat, she came to wonder how it was that her husband had been able to withdraw all the money from the bank before he left Shanghai, yet had no time to fetch his wife and daughter. She began to fill the long, barren years of communist cold and hunger with imagining what might have been; a big house in Hong Kong, servants, a whole juicy chicken to eat every day. One day a relative of her husband with a cousin in Hong Kong told her that her husband was keeping a mistress there. She was tortured by the images of that other faceless woman who was not forced to wear blue and grey Mao suits every day, but dressed in bright dresses, sported lipstick and washed with lavender soap, and who was enjoying what was hers. It is said that there is no poison like a woman's heart, but anger made her strong. During the Cultural Revolution when she was tied for long hours with her hands behind her back in the "aeroplane position" before being released to clean the communal toilets because of her bourgeois background, and when others like her were unable to stand such humiliations and were taking their own lives, it was the knowledge that one day she would have her revenge that kept her going. She would go to Hong Kong and find that women and throw her bastard babies to their death from the balcony, watching their heads crack open like ripe watermelons on the concrete far below. What would it be like, jumping after them, flying absolutely free into the painless embrace of death? After Chairman Mao's death, when life began to settle down again, she began to take her grandson on long walks in the springtime. The child had long since learned to curb his natural curiosity and never asked questions or volunteer personal information. Nevertheless, swearing him to secrecy, she began to whisper tales of the grandfather in Hong Kong and the inheritance that was rightfully his. His soft warm hand resting in his grandmother's, his eyes seemed swallowed by his forehead as he squinted up at her against the sun. And the child, who had never left the flat grey plain and endless rice paddies around Shanghai, began to see pink and golden mountains in the clouds.

Lai Di had waited a lifetime for this day, and now she was going to enjoy it.

"How dare you, Manying! Come here and talk to me of love! You who stole my husband! Yes! The man you knew as Li was my husband. You, who always thought yourself better than me! You were nothing but his concubine! His whore!" With the stylised movement of a Beijing opera singer reaching the climax of a song she turned her heavy head and lifted her chin. "You must have been happy when I drowned. Good riddance to bad rubbish! But lepers found me, washed up downstream. They nursed me, and when I recovered I went to Fuzhou and then on to Shanghai to find Teddy.

"I spent my last pennies on lipstick and went round to all the bars and hotels where the Americans used to go. I nearly gave up hope of ever finding him, but one night, in the street after a dance, I saw him coming out with another man. They were dressed in dinner jackets and black ties and laughing!

"'Teddy! Teddy! It's me!'

"'Some one knows you.' His friend pointed at me, with his white gloved hand.

"Teddy looked me straight in the eye. He knew who I was.

"'She must be mistaken.' He thrust some dollars into my hand and rushed across the pavement to his car.

'Unfinished business. Don't tell Nancy!' he said to his friend.

"The chauffeur pushed me away.

"'Be a good girl! Don't create a scene.' The door slammed the car door and I never saw Teddy again.

"A few months later I met my husband in a coffee house on Nanjing Road where I was working as a waitress. He was kind to me and we were married in 1939."

With a flourish the old crone pulled a piece of paper from the sleeve of her jacket and thrust it in Mother's direction. It was a photograph of a beautiful, young Lai Di in the red wedding dress she was wearing that day, with a handsome young man with Uncle Li's kind face. Dolly handed the picture to Mother who thrust a fist into her mouth to smother her groans.

"My God! My God!"

A small smile appeared on the old crone's face, revealing black gaps where her lower front teeth had been. In the heat, the lipstick was beginning to bleed into the white powder around her mouth.

"He always did like a pretty face!" Lai Di's words came quickly now, incoherently, as she hurried to finish before her time ran out. "But I didn't know it was you who was his Hong Kong whore until my grandson visited you and took this." Coughing, she leaned forward and put another piece of paper on the table: a small, square, black and white photograph taken of Manying in the old flat in Kowloon. She sat awkwardly on the settee, deliberately looking away from the camera. The old crone tottered on her feet. Just in time Dolly vacated her chair and pushed her into it. Her frail body shrunk inside the still frame of heavy silk brocade.

"The money is mine!" she screeched. "You lived in luxury while we, his real family, starved."

"You had the money." Mother's face was red with anger, her lips and chin trembling. "After my husband died, I saw his bank accounts. He sent you money every month for twenty-five years. Do you think it was easy for us in Hong Kong? Do you think we did not eat bitterness too? The parcels were food out of the mouths of my own children."

"Food parcels!" The old crone was still gasping for breath." Your family destroyed my grandfather, my father, my husband and me! Now you will destroy my children and grandchildren. I will not let you!" Her chest heaved. "I am his wife. I will have my inheritance. If you will not give it to us, we will fight and we will win. Now it is your turn to suffer. You will never see your son again." There will be a reckoning day and we will reclaim what is ours."

*L*ips pursed and pale, Mother sat in the taxi. It was not until they got back to the hotel that Dolly realised she was shivering.

Her mother stood helpless in the middle of the room, like a child who had just come out of the bath and was unable to dry itself. Dolly wrapped her in a blanket and helped her into bed. She refused to lie down so Dolly propped her up on pillows and sat with an arm around her. She had never cuddled her mother and was shocked to feel how thin she was beneath her cotton shirt.

"Why didn't you tell me?" Dolly tried not to sound angry.

"I didn't know."

"What do you mean, you did not know? It is impossible. I mean the whole thing is completely crazy!" She could not contain herself now.

Mother could not stop shaking her head from side to side.

"After 1949, we all stopped asking questions. We had to survive. It was the only way. I knew that there was a family left behind in China. It was the same for many people. Our old world was lost so suddenly, almost overnight. Lots of people got caught on the wrong side. At least I did not know she was my step sister! The same thing might have happened to me. If I had not left Nanjing in 1949....Oh, God, forgive us all!"

Dolly ordered supper from room service, but her mother would not eat. With threats of calling a doctor, she cajoled her into eating some noodles and slowly the colour returned to her face. But an hour later she vomited. Dolly supported her as she sat on the bath, her head over the toilet. When she had finished Dolly saw that she was weeping. She had never credited her mother with profound emotions and never seen her cry.

"My happiness was always borrowed at others' expense. I knew it when I married him. But I chose to ignore it."

Dolly looked at her mother, lying in the bed in her brushed-cotton pyjamas with teddy bears on the chest that her eldest granddaughter had given her last Christmas. She did not settle down until after midnight, rambling on about her lost sister and asking Dolly to pay the money and bring her son home. Even now Dolly was not sure that she was really asleep.

She went over to the window and drew back the curtain slightly. Their room overlooked the former Kadoorie residence, a sprawling, floodlit mansion in an oasis of empty lawn. To her left, at the road junction, the silent headlight beams criss-crossed under the shadowy, pedestrian walkway.

What now? Getting out a paper and pen, she sat at the little round table to minute the afternoon's meeting: who had said what to whom, for the lawyers. Better to have everything down in black and white. Of course the old crone was mad—of that there was no doubt. Fifty years of communism had left these people with no traditional standards. Everything was about money. They were all crazy. Dolly had no intention of paying them a penny. Zhang Han was a Party man and doing well enough. He could afford to keep his parents and grandmother. Most likely, the old people simply did not want to move out of the home they had known all their lives. Heaven knows!

Zhang Han probably had a plush new apartment over in Pudong or Xintiandi.

Dolly went over to the bed to check on her mother. She was snoring heavily. She picked up the half-finished cup of brandy from the bedside table, which Dolly had given her to help her sleep, and downed it herself in one gulp. Returning to the table by the window she tried to concentrate on her notes: the garbled conversation of the two old ladies, step sisters, now enemies, the half-understood sounds, distorted by dialect and time. She tried to tune out the static, to form clear, black words on the virgin page. But the characters would not come. A Western trained scholar, it was years since she had attempted to write Chinese. Once again she was a terrified primary schoolgirl in Hong Kong taking a test for homophone characters, staring blankly at the picture of the Queen of England in a diaphanous blue ball gown on the white classroom wall. In desperation she tried to make the notes in English, but the words, the thoughts, refused to be translated.

She put down her pen. This was not a proper history. She wanted to tie up the loose ends, form neat conclusions as she did in her academic articles. But she could not. Where was she to begin to tell the story of fifty years of festering bitterness, paranoia and distrust?

EPILOGUE

SHANTOU
SEPTEMBER 2005

The blue screen of my laptop flickers in front of me. It is appropriate that the story comes to an end here in Shantou, in the darkness of my hotel room. I can see the neon lights of the modern city through the veil of net curtains. Now and again, far below, in defiance of the new car horn regulations, the sound of a wayward klaxon spirals up to my bird box on the twentieth floor.

It is nearly a year since Grandma passed away. She outlived her adopted sister, Lai Di, by six months. We buried her last Christmas in a snow covered cemetery cradled by mountains, high above Vancouver. She had chosen the spot herself, on a south facing slope, next to a small holly bush. She is one of the last of the generation of Chinese that remembers life in the old China, and I hope that she rests peacefully.

Grandma's health deteriorated after the visit to Shanghai. She lost interest in going out for dim sum lunches and even in buying roast duck in the supermarket. She snoozed through the daily diet of Cantonese soap operas. Her carefully tended roses in my mother's garden wilted and died.

My father Peter was released in the autumn of 2004, just when we had begun to give up hope. It seems that the influence of the son of Grandma's old friend Mei Ren, who had an influential position in the US State Department, had had something to do with it, although my father maintains that it was not that simple. In a bizarre episode after his release, and before he left Beijing, the former Chinese Ambassador to Washington, now retired, took him out for dinner and apologised for "mistakes and misunderstandings."

Whatever the truth of the matter, we were glad to have him home. If you have ever wondered what someone looks like after release from a Chinese prison, the answer is thin, grey and disorientated, like a modern day Rip Van Winkle. We coped by joking that the weight loss had done his health good, but the modern world moves on quickly and it has taken him a while to adjust to the speed of change in the use of the Internet and mobile phones. Last time I visited Mom and Dad in Vancouver, Dad assured me that he was "shaken but not stirred" by the whole experience.

Nevertheless, he has sold the business and retired to Vancouver where he now divides his time between charity work for a local hospital and working as a photographer, taking pictures at local Chinese weddings, photography being his longtime hobby. Needless to say, he is not very happy about my working back in Hong Kong. But the money is double what I could ever earn in Canada. Every day I discover an old school friend who has returned to work in Hong Kong, China. With foreign passports safe in our back pockets, houses in North America or Australia, and our children at school at Harvard or Yale, Oxford or Cambridge, Princeton or MIT, we find it easy to be generous about reform in China!

I should perhaps tell you that I never intended to write

this story, but in the end I did so. It began on Christmas Eve, 1999, in the run up to the Millennium.

"Grandma," I said, unable to bear the sight of the sleepy, old lady slumped in the corner of Mom's sofa. "How about a drive up to Queen Elizabeth Park?" I expected her to decline the offer, but lifting her chin from her chest she smiled and said yes.

"Joseph, you go with her: just the two of you," Mom whispered to me as she gave me the keys to her SUV. "You always were her favourite grandchild!"

We drove around the park, stopping here and there to enjoy the view. At the café I suggested a cup of tea. Again, to my surprise, Grandma said yes.

The café was empty. The people of Vancouver had, it seemed, other things to do at eleven o'clock on the morning of Christmas Eve. We took the best table next to the window, the pine trees, their branches lightly sprinkled with snow, our silent companions. The park rolled out in grey, misty tiers below us, the lawns covered with a deeper quilt of snow. Grandma ordered tea and a chocolate muffin. She had a sweet tooth and my mom always tried to control her cake intake because of some mild form of diabetes. But it was Christmas, and anyway, at her age, what was the point? I sipped my cappuccino. Giggling like a little girl, Grandma pulled the muffin apart with her fingers as if opening a tiny present. She offered me half. She had adapted to life in the West. She would never have used her fingers to eat anything in Hong Kong. She laughed at me when I asked the waitress for a fork.

The sun came out from behind a cloud, glistening on the snow and reaching its long, golden fingers across our wooden table. Bathed in its precious warmth, we stared in awe at the majestic, snow-capped mountains on the other side of the bay. I don't know why, but suddenly I said, "Grandma, tell me about when you were a little girl!"

She stopped eating her muffin.

"When I was a little girl?" Her eyes lit up and she

sighed. "When I was a little girl, I grew up in the most beautiful place you have ever seen—you cannot imagine—the most beautiful island in the world."

And so with a simple question this book began; there in the chalet café, listening to the last echoes of silent wilderness, Grandma wanted to talk. Perhaps it was easier for her to confide in me, one who has never tasted such bitterness, and easier too for me to write than for the older members of the family. With our phones, music and Calvin Klein's, people of our generation are defined as consumers, not Nationalists or Communists. The café was closed for Christmas Day, but we came back the day after that and then every day for a week: just the two of us. Aunt Selina and her husband were staying with Mom for the Millennium, and if truth be told, it was a relief for rest of the family to go for yam cha lunches and escape for a while the worry about my father, unhindered by the tired, old lady.

On our second visit to the café Grandma stuck her fork into a piece of apple pie. "I didn't tell it right the other day. I remembered some things in the night. It was a long time ago." Her head cocked shyly to one side, she talked as she ate. After a while I asked her if she minded if I recorded our conversations, and the addition of the little tape recorder in its black case to our party seemed to help. She was no longer talking to her grandson, but to a stranger who passed no judgements.

Gradually over the following week as her memory came to life, she went over bits of her tale again, embroidering the details, amending, clarifying and explaining. Practical, pragmatic, she was the grandma who had changed our nappies, held our hands above our heads as we learned to walk, and painted bright purple antiseptic on our playground cuts and bruises. When the tears did come, she brushed them away with the back of her hand and stared towards the distant mountains, their peaks draped in mist, until she was ready to continue.

As I listened, the idea came to me to write her stories down, a kind of golden family history, so my children and grandchildren would not forget our Chinese roots. In the evenings I played the tapes, took notes and began my research. But when I finally came to write, to knock the stories into shape, I realised that like Aunt Dolly, I too was trying to sanitise, to present the facts in orthodox columns as I had been trained to do as an accountant, to justify the way things worked out for the next generation. After many false starts, I decided that I must write the story the way I had received it.

Unlike others who have embarked on similar quests, I have not had the luxury of inheriting a chest of family papers. Grandma had only an A4 box file with the few photographs and letters she brought out from Nanjing in 1949, letters written to her in Hong Kong, and small box camera photographs of my father and uncles and aunts on the beach with Uncle Li. Grandma's generation was one that had had to look to the future.

The story has not turned out to be the kind of history extolling the virtues of our ancestors that I intended to write. For those readers who expected something different, I apologise. The past is indeed elusive. During the course of my writing I have come to imagine it as a jade pendant, a cold, lifeless piece of green stone buried at the bottom of an old jewellery box. Once hoisted out of its hideaway and strung on a piece of red string or gold chain and placed around the neck, it takes on the character of the wearer, swirling clouds flecked with red on one person, a gentle, translucent landscape when handed on to another.

I have been in Shantou four days now, auditing a local shoe factory for one of our big Malaysian clients. I volunteered for the job, hoping to use the opportunity to visit the places where Grandma grew up.

At first I was disappointed. My requests to the factory manager, a Malaysian Chinese called Ng, for a pre-dinner tour of the old colonial centre of the city were met with blank looks and evasion. When finally we did visit the area, on the way to a karaoke bar, I understood why. The old buildings had been flattened to make way for new offices and department stores.

"Backward. Very backward." The taxi driver, speaking in heavily accented Mandarin for my benefit, gestured with his thumb to entire sections of streets, left like bomb sites awaiting their renaissance. "New is better."

Today, Saturday, or more properly, yesterday, for it is now after midnight as I write, I managed to free myself from the clutches of my over-zealous hosts and spent the morning wandering at leisure around the city. The mélange of seedy dilapidation with the aggressive glitz of progress reminded me of the Hong Kong of my childhood, before we moved to Vancouver.

Bedraggled and deflated by the late summer heat, I wandered around looking for somewhere to eat lunch.

"Dog Meat! Very sweet! Very tasty." A street vendor in a grubby white hat and coat called out to me from behind his little white cart that had been cobbled together out of an old box and a pair of bicycle wheels. I waved him aside trying not to look at the pathetic creatures in the cage on the pavement next to the gas cylinder: three mangy brown dogs and a fluffy white cat with huge eyes that was tiny enough to sit in the palm of your hand like a bird. I hurried off in the direction of the neon and glass fronted "Fortune Noodle Shop" further down the street.

Very much in her own time, the young lady laoban brought my food. I had swapped my work attire for some shorts, t-shirt, sandals and a baseball cap and was obviously not local. Face fixed in what she supposed was the expression of sullen sophistication, beloved by overseas Chinese pop stars, the lady laoban tried to play it cool, but her curiosity got the best of her.

"Hong Kong person?" she asked in heavily accented Cantonese, slamming the bowl of noodles and a local speciality, a spinach and egg omelette, in front of me. I nodded knowing that if I said I was Canadian it might complicate things. She said something else in dialect, which I interpreted to mean, 'Eat more; you are too thin.' I was glad when she left me alone to watch the nubile teenage singer, in shorts and yellow sun top, miming her routine on the karaoke screen in the corner of the bar. The subtitles for the chorus came round again.

I'm just a little Doll.
Don't know much 'bout anything
Except I love you.

I felt old. I ate the noodles and dipped the pieces of omelette in the leftover soup to wash off the grease.

*I*n the afternoon I hired a local taxi driver and told him that I wanted to visit a church on the island of Gok Sek. He seemed to understand, and after much haggling about the price, we set off. We sped over the new bridge connecting the mainland with the island. The effects of food and heat weighed on my eyelids. A small, carved Guan Shi Yin Buddha bounced up against a photograph of Mao Ze Dong, underneath the driver's rear view mirror. The scenery flashed by like a movie on fast forward: a brilliant mosaic of blues, white and greens, the undulating sea beneath acres of clear sky; ahead of us, the island, its rocky outcroppings of burnished gold. Here at last was Grandma's island of Gok Sek!

On the island we drove along the wide, coastal road, past a series of navy installations: the frigates and warships, smart and business-like, in the sunshine

"The church?" I asked urgently pointing up the hill.

"I know, I know. Mister, put camera away!" The taxi driver gestured to the long lens Olympus in my lap. "Military area. Very sensitive." As he spoke three jet planes roared in formation in front of our windscreen.

"Defend against Taiwan." He poked his index finger aggressively towards the roof of the car.

"Okay, okay." Knowing all too well that these were forces I should not mess with, I pushed my camera into my rucksack at my feet.

The driver took me first to a new Buddhist temple on the waterfront. With huge airy courtyards and shiny gold statues, it had been built by contributions from overseas Chinese. It nestled with its back to the rocky, green mountains and looked out over the bay to Shantou. I had to admit it was beautiful. I bought a can of lemonade, sat under a small tree laden with gourds, and realised how long it was since my last real holiday. The sun seeped deep into the muscles of my bare legs and soothed my shoulders, knotted from late nights at the word processor. The smell of salt on my lips, the seagulls squawking overhead, the breeze in my hair and the sensations tingling through my veins were a soporific drug.

The taxi turned inland and began a long winding ascent. As I suspected, the driver did not really know where the church was. We stopped at a small lake where a group of old men had gathered to pass the time of day in the dark green shade of the trees. The frogs croaked, the crickets sang, the locals pointed up the hill. The road got narrower and the trees, with their thick, waxy leaves, cut out the worst of the sun's glare. The higher we drove, the more agitated the driver became. At last we reached a small village with grey brick, pre-revolutionary houses. I told the driver to wait and got out to explore.

I walked along the deserted, sun-dappled, street. My plastic soled sandals made no sound on the concrete. The lazy birds twittered intermittently to each other through the heat of the afternoon. Now and again domestic sounds escaped from the houses behind their walls, and down in the little valley to my right, the clatter of dishes, the thump of an axe on wood, the bark of a dog.

The church was there, just as Grandma had described

it, at the end of the lane, secluded behind high walls in its own compound. With its bizarre Greek portico and three-tiered Chinese-style roof, it is a magnificent tribute to the vision of missionaries like Pastor Wesley. I pressed my face against the iron gate. It was not locked. It creaked on its hinges as I entered.

An old lady appeared from the caretaker's house to the right of the church and shouted something. I tried to explain, but she replied in dialect. I took out paper and pencil and wrote that my grandmother had grown up here. Her face lit up.

"Not many foreign visitors these days." Feeling more confident at the sight of the written word, she managed to dredge up a few words of Mandarin.

"Sir, see church?" She took a bunch of keys from her trouser pocket and opened the front doors. There I was in Pastor Wesley's church. My great grandfather's church!

The hymnbooks were neatly stacked upon a little white bookshelf next to the entrance, just where Grace, Blind Singing Girl, might have left them. The rows of empty wooden pews waited to be filled. That pew, by the door on the right, just catching the golden light from the stained glass window, perhaps that was where Grandmother and Lai Di had sat as little girls. And the pulpit, now adored with a microphone—there my great grandfather had preached the passionate sermon that had caused the break between him and Pastor Wesley. In the silence, I listened for the voices that had become so familiar to me over the past year, but the church remained empty, cool, white and still.

"The balcony." The old lady pointed upwards. "Built during Cultural Revolution for political meetings." She raised an eyebrow and giggled, handing me a leaflet about the current congregation at the church. It had blurred colour pictures of a rural clinic and a savings bank, smiling children at Sunday school, and serious young men in white shirts sitting behind desks, studying on the one-year theological programme. The little seed planted by Pastor Wesley all those years ago had survived nearly half a century of drought. It was a miracle.

I admonished myself. I should have got in touch with the present pastor before I arrived. The people at the Shantou Church in Hong Kong had been very helpful during the course of my research. It was through them that I had been able to trace Pastor Wesley. I asked the old lady if the current pastor lived nearby. She nodded then shook her head. "Gone Guangzhou. Meeting. Mister, drink tea, leave message."

I sat in the tiled office on the ground floor of the caretaker's house and watched the old lady going through the old ritual, familiar to me since my earliest days. Patience tea, pungent, invigorating, endowed with medicinal powers and beloved of the Chaoshan people! Surely they must be born with a gene for tea making. It is perhaps the one local tradition that had survived in our family. The Chaoshan dialect was already lost by the time of my father's generation.

The old lady tipped hot water into the tiny teapot and threw away the first brew. She waited, just a moment, and poured the steaming nectar until it overflowed the tiny tea cups. The sharp smell, the bitter taste, two sips or one gulp; just a mouthful, and the cup is empty. The clink of clay pots as the tea cups are rinsed and refilled. The old lady handed me a note pad and pencil and I left a message for the pastor. I was sorry to have missed him...my great grandfather.... my grandmother... I would be honoured if he would permit me to get in touch next time I was in Shantou. Scrawled on the thin white paper the words were impossibly banal. I signed my name and left my business card. For good measure, the old lady stapled it to the top of the page

On the way out I stopped to admire her roses.

"They are past their best." Gently, she lifted a dropping white flower with the tip of her index finger. She reminded me of Grandma.

I found my driver sitting on a bench outside the compound smoking a cigarette and told him to drive me to the top of the island. Grandma's childhood playground is now a scenic park. The sandy, mountain tracks are a tarmac road with metal crash barriers and pristine signposts. At the gate to the park we paid our money and were handed a route map. Each scenic point was marked with a little triangle and name: Cape of Good Hope, Deer and Crow Cave. The car crawled slowly up the hill. We stopped at the first viewpoint with its green tiled, concrete pagoda. A family was just packing up the remains of a picnic and setting off toward the road. A red-faced, grubby-kneed little boy, his face still stained with the remains of an ice cream consumed earlier in the day, started to cry. Young lovers pressed side by side inside the pagoda. Ahead of them, the modern port and the high rise city of Shantou hummed and pulsed through the haze. A ship loaded with green and red containers slid imperceptibly out of its berth.

We drove on, higher and higher. At each scenic point people were leaving. The autumn sun was quickly losing its strength and a cool sea breeze was beginning to bite. Ahead of us, on top of a rocky outcrop, was a tiny pagoda marked on the map as Mountain Peak. I asked the driver to stop. He looked doubtful and pointed to his watch.

"Six o'clock—my wife waiting—not afternoon now—evening more expensive."

We re-negotiated. I left him in the car smugly calling his wife on his mobile phone, and began the climb to Mountain Peak.

Unlike the other vistapoints, there were no concrete steps, nor easy paths to follow. I scrabbled up the narrow track. The loose stones slipped and crunched as I walked. My feet were covered in yellow dust and I panted with the effort. At last I was at the top. It was deserted, except for a crushed coke can. The island fell away to the silent blue sea: to my left, the city; to my right, the vast ocean. I stood in the centre of the little pagoda and lifted my face to soak up the last rays of sunshine. The sun began to glow orange and slipped slowly towards the horizon. Picking up the coke can and putting it in my rucksack, I sat down to wait for the fireflies.

NOTE ON ROMANIZATION, PLACE NAMES AND FAMILY NAMES

Although some readers might be more familiar with place names written in their traditional forms, I have chosen, for the sake of consistency, to render all names in the pinyin Romanisation which is generally used today, unless the usage seems artificial.

Canton for Guangzhou

Swatow for Shantou

Peking for Beijing: capital of the People's Republic of China from 1949 to the present day.

Chungking for Chongqing: the wartime capital of the Republic of China 1938 to 1945.

Nanking for Nanjing: capital of the Republic of China 1946-1949 and for periods prior to the Second World War.

Chinese family names can cause confusion for Western readers. During the course of writing this book, I have tried to be sensitive to this issue and have simplified names as far as possible without losing authenticity.

Chinese surnames precede given names so that, for example, Wen Huaming would be called Huaming rather than Wen in a conversation. Given names are usually made up of two characters or sounds, although one or three is not unknown.

Chinese women retain their maiden names on marriage but they may also be known by the courtesy title of Mrs. For example, on marriage to Mr Xiong, Wen Manying (nee Wen) might be known as Mrs Xiong.

The Chinese language has very specific words for different relatives. The family hierarchies are clear in the language and one knows immediately by the title whether the person is a maternal or paternal relative and junior or senior to the speaker; for example, *gege* for elder brother and *didi* for younger brother. Chinese people often address each other by reference to their position in the family; for example Elder Brother, Little Sister, Maternal Aunt (*Aiyi*) or Paternal Aunt (*Gugu*) rather than by using given names. Furthermore, nicknames following the Chinese year of someone's birth or a part of the character in a name are often used, rather than formal given names or family titles; for example Little Lamb, Bear or Young Uncle Chen.

I have usually kept people's names in pinyin, unless nickname or dialect usage gives good reason to do otherwise.

LIST OF KEY CHARACTERS

Wen Manying: Daughter of Wen Huaming and Jade. Sister of **Wen Michael Manye**. Marries a man with the surname Bear, the Chinese for which is Xiong. She was therefore known as Mrs Xiong after her marriage.

Lai Di/Deborah: Orphan taken in by Manying's father and mother.

Bear or Mr Xiong: Officer in the Nationalist Army. Married Manying.

Bear the Elder: Manying's brother in law. Optician in Hong Kong.

Ling Ling: Manying's sister in law. Married to Bear the Elder.

Jack: Eldest son of Manying and Bear.

Peter: Second son of Manying and Bear. Married to **Mercy**. Two children, **Joseph** and **Eva**.

Selina: Eldest daughter of Manying and Bear.

Dolly: Second daughter of Manying and Bear.

Wen En: Manying's paternal grandfather. Two sons, **Wen Huaguang** and **Wen Huaming** (Manying's father).

Wen Huaguang: Manying's Uncle married to **Feng. Feng** later marries their former servant **Young Uncle Chen**.

Zheng: Youngest son of **Young Uncle Chen** and **Feng**. Best friend of Manying's brother **Manye**.

Pastor Wesley Hutton: American Pastor of Baptist Church on the island of Gok Sek opposite the port of Shantou. Married **Grace**, who was also known as Blind Singing Girl or Singing Girl.

Uncle Li: Businessman from Shanghai and Manying and Bear's lodger.

Zhang Han: Uncle Li's grandson.

Fang Meiting: Uncle Li's daughter. Her surname is different from that of her father because Uncle Li changed his name after arriving in Hong Kong.

BRIEF HISTORICAL TIMELINE

1894 Start of the First Sino-Japanese War.

1905 Abolition of the traditional Civil Service examinations.

1911 Republican Revolution.

1912 Founding of the Republic of China.

1937 Start of the war of resistance against Japan. Chinese capital moves from Nanjing to Wuhan (briefly) and then Chongqing.

1945 Victory over the Japanese. Chinese capital moves back to Nanjing

1946-1949 Chinese civil war between the Nationalists and Communists.

1949 Communist victory. Founding of The People's Republic of China. Chinese capital moves to Beijing.

1958 The Great Leap Forward. Famine and mass starvation.

1966 Beginning of the Cultural Revolution.

1967 Riots in Hong Kong

1976 Death of Mao Zedong

1997 Handover of Hong Kong to The People's Republic of China.

ACKNOWLEDGEMENTS

So many people have helped and encouraged me during the process of writing this book. I am very grateful to you all. You know who you are! In particular however, I must thank my husband, Steve, my son, William, and my father, Edgar Jenkins, who continued to encourage and support me when I was beginning to doubt myself. To my friend, Graham Hutchings, who kindly took the time to diligently read the manuscript and provide much needed critical feedback, I owe a big thank you. Much of this book was drafted when my son was small and the work could not have been done without the loving care of Dolar Dave, who helped look after William, enabling me to steal a few hours in which to write. David Ross and Kelly Huddleston at *Open Books* have worked patiently and kindly to put my work into print. Always at the end of Skype, smiling and explaining, I thank them for their generous vote of confidence in my writing. Lastly but, most importantly, I must thank my mother-in-law, Chan Kwok Wing, whose anecdotes provided the spark for this story.

19906807R00192

Made in the USA
Charleston, SC
17 June 2013